THE BODLEY HEAD

FORD MADOX FORD

VOLUME III

PARADE'S END: PART ONE

SOME DO NOT . . .

with an introduction by
GRAHAM GREENE

THE BODLEY HEAD
LONDON

SOME DO NOT... *was first published in 1924*

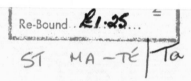
All rights reserved
Printed and bound in Great Britain for
The Bodley Head Ltd
10 Earlham Street, London WC2
by William Clowes and Sons Ltd, Beccles
Set in Linotype Plantin
First published in this edition 1963

INTRODUCTION

It seems likely that, when time has ceased its dreary work of erosion, Ford Madox Ford will be remembered as the author of three great novels, a little scarred, stained here and there and chipped perhaps, but how massive and resistant compared with most of the work of his successors. *The Fifth Queen* trilogy and *The Good Soldier* have already been published in the first volumes of The Bodley Head Ford, and there remains *Parade's End*, the title Ford himself gave to what is often known, after the name of the principal character, as the Tietjens tetralogy—the terrifying story of a good man tortured, pursued, driven into revolt, and ruined as far as the world is concerned by the clever devices of a jealous and lying wife.

Ford always wanted to see his nov printed as one book, but he wanted to see it as a trilogy, consisting only of *Some Do Not...*, *No More Parades* and *A Man Could Stand Up*—the final book, *Last Post*, was an afterthought which he had not intended to write and which later he regretted having written. In a letter dealing with the possibility of an omnibus edition, which is quoted by Mr John A. Meixner in his critical study, *Ford Madox Ford's Novels*, Ford wrote: 'I strongly wish to omit *Last Post* from the edition. I do not like the book and have never liked it and always intended to end up with *A Man Could Stand Up*.' It can be said therefore that in this edition, for the first time, we have Ford's own version of *Parade's End*.

I think it could be argued that *Last Post* was more than a mistake—it was a disaster, a disaster which has delayed a full critical appreciation of *Parade's End*. The sentimentality which sometimes lurks in the shadow of Christopher Tietjens, the last Tory (Ford sometimes seems to be writing about 'the last English gentleman'), emerged there unashamed. Everything was cleared up—all the

5

valuable ambiguities concerning the parenthood of Christopher's son (the suggestion chosen by his wife Sylvia to
torture him), his father's possible suicide, his father's possible relationship to Valentine, Christopher's mistress—all,
all are brought into the idyllic sunshine of Christopher's
successful escape into the life of a Kentish small-holder.
Even Sylvia—surely the most possessed evil character in
the modern novel—groped in *Last Post* towards goodness,
granted Christopher his divorce, took back—however
grudgingly—her lies. It is as though Lady Macbeth
dropped her dagger beside the sleeping Duncan.

This is a better book, a thousand times, which ends in
the confusion of Armistice Night 1918—the two lovers
united, it is true, but with no absolute certainties about
the past so deformed by Sylvia's lies (if they are lies) or
about the future with that witch-wife still awaiting them
there. Those of us who, even though we were children,
remember Armistice Day (so different from that sober,
reflective V.E. day of 1945) remember it as a day out of
time—an explosion without a future. It was the Armistice
only which counted, it was the Armistice too for the poor
tortured lovers: perhaps there would never be a peace. . . .

They were prancing. The whole world round them
was yelling and prancing round. They were the centre
of unending roaring circles. The man with the eyeglass had stuck a half-crown in his other eye. He was
well-meaning. A brother. She had a brother with the
V.C. All in the family.

Tietjens was stretching out his two hands from the
waist. It was incomprehensible. His right hand was
behind her back, his left in her right hand. She was
frightened. She was amazed. Did you ever! He was
swaying slowly. The elephant! They were dancing!
Aranjuez was hanging on to the tall woman like a kid
on a telegraph pole. The officer who had said he had
picked up a little bit of fluff . . . well, he had! He had
run out and fetched it. It wore white cotton gloves and

a flowered hat. It said: "Ow! Now!"... There was a
fellow with a most beautiful voice. He led: better
than a gramophone. Better ...

    Les petites marionettes, font! font! font ...

    On an elephant. A dear, meal-sack elephant. She
was setting out on ...

This is the end of *A Man Could Stand Up*, and this—
not the carefully arranged happy *finale* of *Last Post*—was
the true conclusion of a story of unhappy marriage, of
Sylvia's tortuous intrigues which had begun, before the
so-called Great War had closed in, in a little resort among
the pine-woods of Lobscheid. 'They were sitting playing
bridge in the large, shadowy dining-hall of the hotel:
Mrs Satterthwaite, Father Consett, Mr Bayliss. A young
blond sub-lieutenant of great obsequiousness who was there
for a last chance for his right lung and his career, and the
bearded Kur-doctor cut in.' Sylvia had not yet entered
'like a picture of Our Lady by Fra Angelico,' but I have
always been reminded of another wicked setting, in a poem
written at much about the same time:

> In depraved May, dogwood and chestnut,
>   flowering judas,
> To be eaten, to be divided, to be drunk
> Among whispers; by Mr Silvero
> With caressing hands, at Limoges
> Who walked all night in the next room;
>
> By Hakagawa, bowing among the Titians;
> By Madame de Tornquist, in the dark room
> Shifting the candles; Fräulein von Kulp
> Who turned in the hall, one hand on the door.

This is not a war-book in the ordinary sense of the
term; it was produced by the experiences of 1914–18,
but while a novel like *All Quiet on the Western Front*
confined its horror to the physical, to the terrors of the
trenches, so that it is even possible to think of such physical
terrors as an escape for some characters from the burden

of thought and mental pain, Ford turned the screw. Here there was no escape from the private life. Sylvia pursued her husband even to the headquarters of his regiment. Unlikely? Read in *The Memoirs of Lord Chandos* how, just out of the heavily shelled Ginchy valley, he and his friend were greeted by the disquieting telegrams from home. I remember a week-end reunion in the dug-outs of Dien-Bien-Phu, as the troops waited day by day for the assault. The private life cannot be escaped and death does not come when it is most required.

GRAHAM GREENE

SOME DO NOT...

SOME DO NOT

PART ONE

I

THE two young men—they were of the English public official class—sat in the perfectly appointed railway carriage. The leather straps to the windows were of virgin newness; the mirrors beneath the new luggage racks immaculate as if they had reflected very little; the bulging upholstery in its luxuriant, regulated curves was scarlet and yellow in an intricate, minute dragon pattern, the design of a geometrician in Cologne. The compartment smelt faintly, hygienically of admirable varnish; the train ran as smoothly—Tietjens remembered thinking—as British gilt-edged securities. It travelled fast; yet had it swayed or jolted over the rail joints, except at the curve before Tonbridge or over the points at Ashford where these eccentricities are expected and allowed for, Macmaster, Tietjens felt certain, would have written to the company. Perhaps he would even have written to *The Times*.

Their class administered the world, not merely the newly created Imperial Department of Statistics under Sir Reginald Ingleby. If they saw policemen misbehave, railway porters lack civility, an insufficiency of street lamps, defects in public services or in foreign countries, they saw to it, either with nonchalant Balliol voices or with letters to *The Times*, asking in regretful indignation: 'Has the British This or That come to *this*?' Or they wrote, in the serious reviews of which so many still survived, articles taking under their care, manners, the Arts, diplomacy, inter-Imperial trade, or the personal reputations of deceased statesmen and men of letters.

Macmaster, that is to say, would do all that: of himself
Tietjens was not so certain. There sat Macmaster; smallish;
Whig; with a trimmed, pointed black beard, such as a
smallish man might wear to enhance his already germinated
distinction; black hair of a stubborn fibre, drilled down
with hard metal brushes; a sharp nose; strong, level teeth;
a white, butterfly collar of the smoothness of porcelain; a
tie confined by a gold ring, steel-blue speckled with black
—to match his eyes, as Tietjens knew.

Tietjens, on the other hand, could not remember what
coloured tie he had on. He had taken a cab from the office
to their rooms, had got himself into a loose, tailored coat
and trousers, and a soft shirt, had packed, quickly, but still
methodically, a great number of things in an immense two-
handled kit-bag, which you could throw into a guard's van
if need be. He disliked letting that 'man' touch his things;
he had disliked letting his wife's maid pack for him. He
even disliked letting porters carry his kit-bag. He was a
Tory—and as he disliked changing his clothes, there he sat,
on the journey, already in large, brown, hugely welted and
nailed golf boots, leaning forward on the edge of the
cushion, his legs apart, on each knee an immense white
hand—and thinking vaguely.

Macmaster, on the other hand, was leaning back, reading
some small, unbound printed sheets, rather stiff, frowning
a little. Tietjens knew that this was, for Macmaster, an impressive moment. He was correcting the proofs of his first
book.

To this affair, as Tietjens knew, there attached themselves many fine shades. If, for instance, you had asked
Macmaster whether he were a writer, he would have
replied with the merest suggestion of a deprecatory shrug.

'No, dear lady!' for of course no man would ask the
question of anyone so obviously a man of the world. And
he would continue with a smile: 'Nothing so fine! A mere
trifler at odd moments. A critic, perhaps. Yes! A little of a
critic.'

Nevertheless Macmaster moved in drawing-rooms that,

with long curtains, blue china plates, large-patterned wall-papers and large, quiet mirrors, sheltered the long-haired of the Arts. And, as near as possible to the dear ladies who gave the At Homes, Macmaster could keep up the talk—a little magisterially. He liked to be listened to with respect when he spoke of Botticelli, Rossetti, and those early Italian artists whom he called 'The Primitives.' Tietjens had seen him there. And he didn't disapprove.

For, if they weren't, these gatherings, Society, they formed a stage on the long and careful road to a career in a first-class Government office. And, utterly careless as Tietjens imagined himself of careers or offices, he was, if sardonically, quite sympathetic towards his friend's ambitiousnesses. It was an odd friendship, but the oddnesses of friendships are a frequent guarantee of their lasting texture.

The youngest son of a Yorkshire country gentleman, Tietjens himself was entitled to the best—the best that first-class public offices and first-class people could afford. He was without ambition, but these things would come to him as they do in England. So he could afford to be negligent of his attire, of the company he kept, of the opinions he uttered. He had a little private income under his mother's settlement; a little income from the Imperial Department of Statistics; he had married a woman of means, and he was, in the Tory manner, sufficiently a master of flouts and jeers to be listened to when he spoke. He was twenty-six; but, very big, in a fair, untidy, Yorkshire way, he carried more weight than his age warranted. His chief, Sir Reginald Ingleby, when Tietjens chose to talk of public tendencies which influenced statistics, would listen with attention. Sometimes Sir Reginald would say: 'You're a perfect encyclopaedia of exact material knowledge, Tietjens,' and Tietjens thought that that was his due, and he would accept the tribute in silence.

At a word from Sir Reginald, Macmaster, on the other hand, would murmur: 'You're very good, Sir Reginald!' and Tietjens thought that perfectly proper.

Macmaster was a little the senior in the service, as he was probably a little the senior in age. For, as to his room-mate's years, or as to his exact origins, there was a certain blank in Tietjens' knowledge. Macmaster was obviously Scotch by birth, and you accepted him as what was called a son of the manse. No doubt he was really the son of a grocer in Cupar or a railway porter in Edinburgh. It does not matter with the Scotch, and as he was very properly reticent as to his ancestry, having accepted him, you didn't, even mentally, make enquiries.

Tietjens always had accepted Macmaster—at Clifton, at Cambridge, in Chancery Lane and in their rooms at Gray's Inn. So for Macmaster he had a very deep affection—even a gratitude. And Macmaster might be considered as returning these feelings. Certainly he had always done his best to be of service to Tietjens. Already at the Treasury and attached as private secretary to Sir Reginald Ingleby, whilst Tietjens was still at Cambridge, Macmaster had brought to the notice of Sir Reginald Tietjens' many great natural gifts, and Sir Reginald, being on the look-out for young men for his ewe lamb, his newly founded depart-ment, had very readily accepted Tietjens as his third in command. On the other hand, it had been Tietjens' father who had recommended Macmaster to the notice of Sir Thomas Block at the Treasury itself. And, indeed, the Tietjens family had provided a little money—that was Tietjens' mother really—to get Macmaster through Cam-bridge and install him in Town. He had repaid the small sum—paying it partly by finding room in his chambers for Tietjens when in turn he came to Town.

With a Scots young man such a position had been per-fectly possible. Tietjens had been able to go to his fair, ample, saintly mother in her morning-room and say:

'Look here, mother, that fellow Macmaster! He'll need a little money to get through the University,' and his mother would answer:

'Yes, my dear. How much?'

With an English young man of the lower orders that

would have left a sense of class obligation. With Macmaster it just didn't.

During Tietjens' late trouble—for four months before Tietjens' wife had left him to go abroad with another man—Macmaster had filled a place that no other man could have filled. For the basis of Christopher Tietjens' emotional existence was a complete taciturnity—at any rate as to his emotions. As Tietjens saw the world, you didn't 'talk.' Perhaps you didn't even think about how you felt.

And, indeed, his wife's flight had left him almost completely without emotions that he could realize, and he had not spoken more than twenty words at most about the event. Those had been mostly to his father, who, very tall, very largely built, silver-haired and erect, had drifted, as it were, into Macmaster's drawing-room in Gray's Inn, and after five minutes of silence had said:

'You will divorce?'

Christopher had answered:

'No! No one but a blackguard would ever submit a woman to the ordeal of divorce.'

Mr Tietjens had suggested that, and after an interval had asked:

'You will permit her to divorce you?'

He had answered:

'If she wishes it. There's the child to be considered.'

Mr Tietjens said:

'You will get her settlement transferred to the child?'

Christopher answered:

'If it can be done without friction.'

Mr Tietjens had commented only:

'Ah!' Some minutes later he had said:

'Your mother's very well.' Then: 'That motor-plough *didn't* answer,' and then: 'I shall be dining at the club.'

Christopher said:

'May I bring Macmaster in, sir? You said you would put him up.'

Mr Tietjens answered:

'Yes, do. Old General ffolliot will be there. He'll second him. He'd better make his acquaintance.' He had gone away.

Tietjens considered that his relationship with his father was an almost perfect one. They were like two men in the club—the *only* club; thinking so alike that there was no need to talk. His father had spent a great deal of time abroad before succeeding to the estate. When, over the moors, he went into the industrial town that he owned, he drove always in a coach-and-four. Tobacco smoke had never been known inside Groby Hall: Mr Tietjens had twelve pipes filled every morning by his head gardener and placed in rose bushes down the drive. These he smoked during the day. He farmed a good deal of his own land; had sat for Holdernesse from 1876 to 1881, and had not presented himself for election after the redistribution of seats; he was patron of eleven livings; rode to hounds every now and then, and shot fairly regularly. He had three other sons and two daughters, and was now sixty-one.

To his sister Effie, on the day after his wife's elopement, Christopher had said over the telephone:

'Will you take Tommie for an indefinite period? Marchant will come with him. She offers to take charge of your two youngest as well, so you'll save a maid, and I'll pay their board and a bit over.'

The voice of his sister—from Yorkshire— had answered:

'Certainly, Christopher.' She was the wife of a vicar, near Groby, and she had several children.

To Macmaster Tietjens had said:

'Sylvia has left me with that fellow Perowne.'

Macmaster had answered only: 'Ah!'

Tietjens had continued:

'I'm letting the house and warehousing the furniture. Tommie is going to my sister Effie. Marchant is going with him.'

Macmaster had said:

'Then you'll be wanting your old rooms.' Macmaster

occupied a very large storey of the Gray's Inn buildings. After Tietjens had left him on his marriage he had continued to enjoy solitude, except that his man had moved down from the attic to the bedroom formerly occupied by Tietjens.

Tietjens said:

'I'll come in to-morrow night if I may. That will give Ferens time to get back into his attic.'

That morning, at breakfast, four months having passed, Tietjens had received a letter from his wife. She asked, without any contrition at all, to be taken back. She was fed-up with Perowne and Brittany.

Tietjens looked up at Macmaster. Macmaster was already half out of his chair, looking at him with enlarged, steel-blue eyes, his beard quivering. By the time Tietjens spoke Macmaster had his hand on the neck of the cut-glass brandy decanter in the brown wood tantalus.

Tietjens said:

'Sylvia asks me to take her back.'

Macmaster said:

'Have a little of this!'

Tietjens was about to say: 'No,' automatically. He changed that to:

'Yes. Perhaps. A liqueur glass.'

He noticed that the lip of the decanter agitated, tinkling on the glass. Macmaster must be trembling.

Macmaster, with his back still turned, said:

'Shall you take her back?'

Tietjens answered:

'I imagine so.' The brandy warmed his chest in its descent. Macmaster said:

'Better have another.'

Tietjens answered:

'Yes. Thanks.'

Macmaster went on with his breakfast and his letters. So did Tietjens. Ferens came in, removed the bacon plates and set on the table a silver water-heated dish that con-

tained poached eggs and haddock. A long time afterwards
Tietjens said:

'Yes, in principle I'm determined to. But I shall take
three days to think out the details.'

He seemed to have no feelings about the matter. Certain
insolent phrases in Sylvia's letter hung in his mind. He
preferred a letter like that. The brandy made no difference
to his mentality, but it seemed to keep him from shivering.

Macmaster said:

'Suppose we go down to Rye by the 11.40. We could
get a round after tea now the days are long. I want to call
on a parson near there. He has helped me with my book.'

Tietjens said:

'Did your poet know parsons? But of course he did.
Duchemin is the name, isn't it?

Macmaster said:

'We could call about two-thirty. That will be all right in
the country. We stay till four with a cab outside. We can be
on the first tee at five. If we like the course we'll stay next
day: then Tuesday at Hythe and Wednesday at Sandwich.
Or we could stay at Rye all your three days.'

'It will probably suit me better to keep moving,' Tietjens
said. 'There are those British Columbia figures of yours. If
we took a cab now I could finish them for you in an hour
and twelve minutes. Then British North Africa can go
to the printers. It's only 8.30 now.'

Macmaster said, with some concern:

'Oh, but you *couldn't*: I can make our going all right
with Sir Reginald.'

Tietjens said:

'Oh yes, I can. Ingleby will be pleased if you tell him
they're finished. I'll have them ready for you to give him
when he comes at ten.'

Macmaster said:

'What an extraordinary fellow you are, Chrissie. Almost
a genius!'

'Oh,' Tietjens answered: 'I was looking at your papers
yesterday after you'd left and I've got most of the totals in

my head. I was thinking about them before I went to sleep.
I think you make a mistake in over-estimating the pull of
Klondyke this year on the population. The passes are
open, but relatively no one is going through. I'll add a
note to that effect.'

In the cab he said:

'I'm sorry to bother you with my beastly affairs. But
how will it affect you and the office?'

'The office,' Macmaster said, 'not at all. It is supposed
that Sylvia is nursing Mrs Satterthwaite abroad. As for
me, I wish . . .'—he closed his small, strong teeth—'I wish
you would drag the woman through the mud. By God I
do! Why should she mangle you for the rest of your life?
She's done enough!'

Tietjens gazed out over the flap of the cab.

That explained a question. Some days before, a young
man, a friend of his wife's rather than of his own, had
approached him in the club and had said that he hoped
Mrs Satterthwaite—his wife's mother—was better. He
said now:

'I see. Mrs Satterthwaite has probably gone abroad to
cover up Sylvia's retreat. She's a sensible woman, if a bitch.'

The hansom ran through nearly empty streets, it being
very early for the public official quarters. The hoofs of the
horse clattered precipitately. Tietjens preferred a hansom,
horses being made for gentlefolk. He had known nothing
of how his fellows had viewed his affairs. It was breaking
up a great, numb inertia to enquire.

During the last few months he had employed himself in
tabulating from memory the errors in the *Encyclopaedia
Britannica,* of which a new edition had lately appeared. He
had even written an article for a dull monthly on the subject. It had been so caustic as to miss its mark, rather. He
despised people who used works of reference; but the
point of view had been so unfamiliar that his article had
galled no one's withers, except possibly Macmaster's.
Actually it had pleased Sir Reginald Ingleby, who had
been glad to think that he had under him a young man

with a memory so tenacious and so encyclopaedic a knowledge. . . .

That had been a congenial occupation, like a long drowse. Now he had to make enquiries. He said:

'And my breaking up the establishment at twenty-nine? How's that viewed? I'm not going to have a house again.'

'It's considered,' Macmaster answered, 'that Lowndes Street did not agree with Mrs Satterthwaite. That accounted for her illness. Drains wrong. I may say that Sir Reginald entirely—expressly—approves. He does not think that young married men in Government offices should keep up expensive establishments in the S.W. district.'

Tietjens said:

'Damn him.' He added: 'He's probably right though.' He then said: 'Thanks. That's all I want to know. A certain discredit has always attached to cuckolds. Very properly. A man ought to be able to keep his wife.'

Macmaster exclaimed anxiously:

'No! No! Chrissie.'

Tietjens continued:

'And a first-class public office is very like a public school. It might very well object to having a man whose wife had bolted amongst its members. I remember Clifton hated it when the Governors decided to admit the first Jew and the first nigger.'

Macmaster said:

'I wish you wouldn't go on.'

'There was a fellow,' Tietjens continued, 'whose land was next to ours. Conder his name was. His wife was habitually unfaithful to him. She used to retire with some fellow for three months out of every year. Conder never moved a finger. But we felt Groby and the neighbourhood were unsafe. It was awkward introducing him—not to mention her—in your drawing-room. All sorts of awkward-nesses. Everyone knew the younger children weren't Conder's. A fellow married the youngest daughter and took over the hounds. And not a soul called on her. It wasn't rational or just. But that's why society distrusts the cuckold, really. It never knows when it mayn't be driven into something irrational and unjust.'

'But you *aren't*,' Macmaster said with real anguish, 'going to let Sylvia behave like that.'

'I don't know,' Tietjens said. 'How am I to stop it? Mind you, I think Conder was quite right. Such calamities are the will of God. A gentleman accepts them. If the woman won't divorce, he *must* accept them, and it gets talked about. You seem to have made it all right this time. You and, I suppose, Mrs Satterthwaite between you. But you won't be always there. Or I might come across another woman.'

Macmaster said:

'Ah!' and after a moment:

'What then?'

Tietjens said:

'God knows... There's that poor little beggar to be considered. Marchant says he's beginning to talk broad Yorkshire already.'

Macmaster said:

'If it wasn't for that.... That would be a solution.'

Tietjens said: 'Ah!'

When he paid the cabman, in front of a grey cement portal with a gabled arch, reaching up, he said:

'You've been giving the mare less liquorice in her mash. I told you she'd go better.'

The cabman, with a scarlet, varnished face, a shiny hat, a drab box-cloth coat and a gardenia in his buttonhole, said:

'Ah! Trust you to remember, sir.'

In the train, from beneath his pile of polished dressing and despatch cases—Tietjens had thrown his immense kit-bag with his own hands into the guard's van—Macmaster looked across at his friend. It was, for him, a great day. Across his face were the proof-sheets of his first, small, delicate-looking volume.... A small page, the type black and still odorous! He had the agreeable smell of the

printer's ink in his nostrils; the fresh paper was still a
little damp. In his white, rather spatulate, always slightly
cold fingers was the pressure of the small, flat, gold pencil
he had purchased especially for these corrections. He had
found none to make.

He had expected a wallowing of pleasure—almost the
only sensuous pleasure he had allowed himself for many
months. Keeping up the appearances of an English gentleman on an exiguous income was no mean task. But to
wallow in your own phrases, to be rejoiced by the savour
of your own shrewd pawkiness, to feel your rhythm
balanced and yet sober—that is a pleasure beyond most,
and an inexpensive one at that. He had had it from mere
'articles'—on the philosophies and domestic lives of such
great figures as Carlyle and Mill, or on the expansion of
inter-colonial trade. This was a book.

He relied upon it to consolidate his position. In the
office they were mostly 'born,' and not vastly sympathetic.
There was a sprinkling, too—it was beginning to be a
large one—of young men who had obtained their entry by
merit or by sheer industry. These watched promotions
jealously, discerning nepotic increases of increment and
clamouring amongst themselves at favouritisms.

To these he had been able to turn a cold shoulder. His
intimacy with Tietjens permitted him to be rather on the
'born' side of the institution, his agreeableness—he knew
he was agreeable and useful!—to Sir Reginald Ingleby
protecting him in the main from unpleasantness. His
'articles' had given him a certain right to an austerity of
demeanour; his book he trusted to let him adopt an almost
judicial attitude. He would then be *the* Mr Macmaster, the
critic, the authority. And the first-class departments are
not averse to having distinguished men as ornaments
to their company; at any rate the promotions of the distinguished are not objected to. So Macmaster saw—almost
physically—Sir Reginald Ingleby perceiving the *empresse-
ment* with which his valued subordinate was treated in the
drawing-rooms of Mrs Leamington, Mrs Cressy, the Hon.

Mrs de Limoux; Sir Reginald would perceive that, for he
was not a reader himself of much else than Government
publications, and he would feel fairly safe in making easy
the path of his critically gifted and austere young helper.
The son of a very poor shipping clerk in an obscure Scotch
harbour town, Macmaster had very early decided on the
career that he would make. As between the heroes of Mr
Smiles, an author enormously popular in Macmaster's boy-
hood, and the more distinctly intellectual achievements
open to the very poor Scot, Macmaster had had no difficulty in choosing. A pit lad *may* rise to be a mine owner;
a hard, gifted, unsleeping Scots youth, pursuing unobtru-
sively and unobjectionably a course of study and of public
usefulness, *will* certainly achieve distinction, security, and
the quiet admiration of those around him. It was the
difference between the *may* and the *will,* and Macmaster
had had no difficulty in making his choice. He saw himself by now almost certain of a career that should give
him at fifty a knighthood, and long before that a competence, a drawing-room of his own and a lady who should
contribute to his unobtrusive fame, she moving about, in
that room, amongst the best of the intellects of the day,
gracious, devoted, a tribute at once to his discernment
and his achievements. Without some disaster he was sure
of himself. Disasters come to men through drink, bankruptcy, and women. Against the first two he knew himself
immune, though his expenses had a tendency to outrun
his income, and he was always a little in debt to Tietjens.
Tietjens fortunately had means. As to the third, he was
not so certain. His life had necessarily been starved of
women and, arrived at a stage when the female element
might, even with due respect to caution, be considered as
a legitimate feature of his life, he had to fear a rashness of
choice due to that very starvation. The type of woman he
needed he knew to exactitude: tall, graceful, dark, loose-
gowned, passionate yet circumspect, oval-featured, de-
liberate, gracious to everyone around her. He could almost
hear the very rustle of her garments.

And yet . . . He had had passages when a sort of blind unreason had attracted him almost to speechlessness towards girls of the most giggling, behind-the-counter order, big-bosomed, scarlet-cheeked. It was only Tietjens who had saved him from the most questionable entanglements.

'Hang it,' Tietjens would say, 'don't get messing round that trollop. All you could do with her would be to set her up in a tobacco shop, and she would be tearing your beard out inside the quarter. Let alone you can't afford it.'

And Macmaster, who would have sentimentalized the plump girl to the tune of *Highland Mary*, would for a day damn Tietjens up and down for a coarse brute. But at the moment he thanked God for Tietjens. There he sat, near to thirty, without an entanglement, a blemish on his health, or a worry with regard to any woman.

With deep affection and concern he looked across at his brilliant junior, who hadn't saved himself. Tietjens had fallen into the most barefaced snare, into the cruellest snare, of the worst woman that could be imagined.

And Macmaster suddenly realized that he wasn't wallowing, as he had imagined that he would, in the sensuous current of his prose. He had begun spiritedly with the first neat square of a paragraph. . . . Certainly his publishers had done well by him in the matter of print:

> 'Whether we consider him as the imaginer of mysterious, sensuous and exact plastic beauty; as the manipulator of sonorous, rolling and full-mouthed lines; of words as full of colour as were his canvases; or whether we regard him as the deep philosopher, elucidating and drawing his illumination from the arcana of a mystic hardly greater than himself, to Gabriel Charles Dante Rossetti, the subject of this little monograph, must be accorded the name of one who has profoundly influenced the outward aspects, the human contacts, and all those things that go to make up the life of our higher civilization as we live it to-day. . . .'

Macmaster realized that he had only got thus far with
his prose, and had got thus far without any of the relish
that he had expected, and that then he had turned to the
middle paragraph of page three—after the end of his
exordium. His eyes wandered desultorily along the
line:

'The subject of these pages was born in the western
central district of the metropolis in the year . . .'

The words conveyed nothing to him at all. He understood that that was because he hadn't got over that morning. He had looked up from his coffee-cup—over the rim—
and had taken in a blue-grey sheet of notepaper in Tietjens'
fingers, shaking, inscribed in the large, broad-nibbed writing of that detestable harridan. And Tietjens had been
staring—staring with the intentness of a maddened horse—
at his, Macmaster's, face! And grey! Shapeless! The nose
like a pallid triangle on a bladder of lard! That was
Tietjens' face. . . .

He could still feel the blow, physical, in the pit of his
stomach! He had thought Tietjens was going mad; that he
was mad. It had passed. Tietjens had assumed the mask of
his indolent, insolent self. At the office, but later, he had
delivered an extraordinarily forceful—and quite rude—
lecture to Sir Reginald on his reasons for differing from
the official figures of population movement in the western
territories. Sir Reginald had been much impressed. The
figures were wanted for a speech of the Colonial Minister
—or an answer to a question—and Sir Reginald had
promised to put Tietjens' views before the great man.
That was the sort of thing to do a young fellow good—
because it got kudos for the office. They had to work on
figures provided by the Colonial Government, and if they
could correct those fellows by sheer brain work—that
scored.

But there sat Tietjens, in his grey tweeds, his legs
apart, lumpish, clumsy, his tallowy, intelligent-looking
hands drooping inert between his legs, his eyes gazing

at a coloured photograph of the port of Boulogne beside
the mirror beneath the luggage rack. Blond, high-coloured,
vacant apparently, you couldn't tell what in the world he
was thinking of. The mathematical theory of waves, very
likely, or slips in someone's article on Arminianism. For
absurd as it seemed, Macmaster knew that he knew next
to nothing of his friend's feelings. As to them, practically
no confidences had passed between them. Just two:

On the night before his starting for his wedding in
Paris Tietjens had said to him:

'Vinny, old fellow, it's a back door way out of it. She's
bitched *me*.'

And once, rather lately, he had said:

'Damn it! I don't even know if the child's my own!'

This last confidence had shocked Macmaster so irreme-
diably—the child had been a seven months' child, rather
ailing, and Tietjens' clumsy tenderness towards it had been
so marked that, even without this nightmare, Macmaster
had been affected by the sight of them together—that
confidence then had pained Macmaster so frightfully, it
was so appalling, that Macmaster had regarded it almost
as an insult. It was the sort of confidence a man didn't
make to his equal, but only to solicitors, doctors, or the
clergy who are not quite men. Or, at any rate, such confidences are not made between men without appeals for
sympathy, and Tietjens had made no appeal for sympathy
He had just added sardonically:

'She gives me the benefit of the agreeable doubt. And
she's as good as said as much to Marchant'—Marchant had
been Tietjens' old nurse.

Suddenly—and as if in a sort of unconscious losing of
his head—Macmaster remarked:

'You can't say the man wasn't a poet!'

The remark had been, as it were, torn from him, because he had observed, in the strong light of the compartment, that half of Tietjens' forelock and a roundish patch
behind it was silvery white. That might have been going

on for weeks: you live beside a man and notice his changes very little. Yorkshire men of fresh colour and blondish hair often go speckled with white very young; Tietjens had had a white hair or two at the age of fourteen, very noticeable in the sunlight when he had taken his cap off to bowl.

But Macmaster's mind, taking appalled charge, had felt assured that Tietjens had gone white with the shock of his wife's letter: in four hours! That meant that terrible things must be going on within him; his thoughts, at all costs, must be distracted. The mental process in Macmaster had been quite unconscious. He would not, advisedly, have introduced the painter-poet as a topic.

Tietjens said:

'I haven't said anything at all that I can remember.' The obstinacy of his hard race awakened in Macmaster:

' "Since",' he quoted,

> ' "when we stand side by side
>   Only hands may meet,
> Better half this weary world
>   Lay between us, sweet!
> Better far tho' hearts may break
>   Bid farewell for aye!
> Lest thy sad eyes, meeting mine,
>   Tempt my soul away!" '

'You can't,' he continued, 'say that that isn't poetry! Great poetry.'

'I can't say,' Tietjens answered contemptuously. 'I don't read poetry except Byron. But it's a filthy picture. . . .'

Macmaster said uncertainly:

'I don't know that I know the picture. Is it in Chicago?'

'It isn't painted!' Tietjens said. 'But it's there!' He continued with sudden fury:

'Damn it. What's the sense of all these attempts to justify fornication? England's mad about it. Well, you've got your John Stuart Mills and your George Eliots for the high-class thing. Leave the furniture out! Or leave me out at least. I tell you it revolts me to think of that obese, oily man who never took a bath, in a grease-spotted dressing-gown and the underclothes he's slept in, standing beside a five-shilling model with crimped hair, or some Mrs. W. Three Stars, gazing into a mirror that reflects their fetid selves and gilt sunfish and drop chandeliers and plates sickening with cold bacon fat and gurgling about passion.'

Macmaster had gone chalk white, his short beard bristling:

'You daren't ... you daren't talk like that,' he stuttered.

'I *dare!*' Tietjens answered; 'but I oughtn't to ... to you! I admit that. But you oughtn't, almost as much, to talk about that stuff to me, either. It's an insult to my intelligence.'

'Certainly,' Macmaster said stiffly, 'the moment was not opportune.'

'I don't understand what you mean,' Tietjens answered. 'The moment can never be opportune. Let's agree that making a career is a dirty business—for me as for you! But decent augurs grin behind their masks. They never preach to each other.'

'You're getting esoteric,' Macmaster said faintly.

'I'll underline,' Tietjens went on. 'I quite understand that the favour of Mrs Cressy and Mrs de Limoux is essential to you! They have the ear of that old don Ingleby.'

Macmaster said:

'Damn!'

'I quite agree,' Tietjens continued, 'I quite approve. It's the game as it has always been played. It's the tradition, so it's right. It's been sanctioned since the days of the *Précieuses Ridicules.*'

'You've a way of putting things,' Macmaster said.

'I haven't,' Tietjens answered. 'It's just because I haven't that what I *do* say sticks out in the minds of fellows like you who are always fiddling about after literary expression. But what I do say is this: I stand for monogamy.'

Macmaster uttered a '*You!*' of amazement.

Tietjens answered with a negligent '*I!*' He continued:

'I stand for monogamy and chastity. And for no talking about it. Of course, if a man who's a man wants to have a woman, he has her. And again, no talking about it. He'd no doubt be in the end better, and better off, if he didn't. Just as it would probably be better for him if he didn't have the second glass of whisky and soda. . . .'

'You call that monogamy and chastity!' Macmaster interjected.

'I do,' Tietjens answered, 'and it probably is, at any rate it's clean. What is loathsome is all your fumbling in placketholes and polysyllabic Justification by Love. You stand for lachrymose polygamy. That's all right if you can get your club to change its rules.'

'You're out of my depth,' Macmaster said. 'And being very disagreeable. You appear to be justifying promiscuity. I don't like it.'

'I'm probably being disagreeable," Tietjens said. 'Jeremiahs usually are. But there ought to be a twenty years' close time for discussions of sham sexual morality. Your Paolo and Francesca—and Dante's—went, very properly to Hell, and no bones about it. You don't get Dante justifying them. But your fellow whines about creeping into Heaven.'

'He *doesn't*!' Macmaster exclaimed. Tietjens continued with equanimity:

'Now your novelist who writes a book to justify his every tenth or fifth seduction of a commonplace young woman in the name of the rights of shop boys . . .'

'I'll admit,' Macmaster coincided, 'that Briggs is going too far. I told him only last Thursday at Mrs Limoux's . . .'

'I'm not talking of anyone in particular,' Tietjens said. 'I don't read novels. I'm supposing a case. And it's a cleaner case than that of your Pre-Raphaelite horrors! No! I don't read novels, but I follow tendencies. And if a fellow chooses to justify his seductions of uninteresting and viewy young females along the lines of freedom and the rights

of man, it's relatively respectable. It would be better just
to boast about his conquests in a straightforward and
exultant way. But . . .'

'You carry joking too far sometimes,' Macmaster said.
'I've warned you about it.'

'I'm as solemn as an owl!' Tietjens rejoined. 'The lower
classes are becoming vocal. Why shouldn't they? They're
the only people in this country who are sound in wind and
limb. They'll save the country if the country's to be
saved.'

'And you call yourself a Tory!' Macmaster said.

'The lower classes,' Tietjens continued equably, 'such of
them as get through the secondary schools, want irregular
and very transitory unions. During holidays they go together on personally conducted tours to Switzerland and
such places. Wet afternoons they pass in their tiled bath-
rooms, slapping each other hilariously on the back and
splashing white enamel paint about.'

'You say you don't read novels,' Macmaster said, 'but I
recognize the quotation.'

'I don't *read* novels,' Tietjens answered. 'I know what's
in 'em. There has been nothing worth *reading* written in
England since the eighteenth century except by a
woman. . . . But it's natural for your enamel splashers to
want to see themselves in a bright and variegated literature.
Why shouldn't they? It's a healthy, human desire, and now
that printing and paper are cheap they get it satisfied. It's
healthy, I tell you. Infinitely healthier than . . .' He paused.

'Than what?' Macmaster asked.

'I'm thinking,' Tietjens said, 'thinking how not to be too
rude.'

'You want to be rude,' Macmaster said bitterly, 'to
people who lead the contemplative . . . the circumspect
life.'

'It's precisely that,' Tietjens said. He quoted.

> ' "She walks, the lady of my delight,
>   A shepherdess of sheep;

She is so circumspect and right:
She has her thoughts to keep." '

Macmaster said:
'Confound you, Chrissie. You know everything.'

'Well, yes,' Tietjens said musingly, 'I think I should want to be rude to her. I don't say I should be. Certainly I shouldn't if she were good looking. Or if she were your soul's affinity. You can rely on that.'

Macmaster had a sudden vision of Tietjens' large and clumsy form walking beside the lady of his, Macmaster's, delight, when ultimately she was found—walking along the top of a cliff amongst tall grass and poppies and making himself extremely agreeable with talk of Tasso and Cimabue. All the same, Macmaster imagined, the lady wouldn't like Tietjens. Women didn't, as a rule. His looks and his silences alarmed them. Or they hated him. . . . Or they liked him very much indeed. And Macmaster said conciliatorily:

'Yes, I think I could rely on that!' He added: 'All the same I don't wonder that . . .'

He had been about to say:

'I don't wonder that Sylvia calls you immoral.' For Tietjens' wife alleged that Tietjens was detestable. He bored her, she said, by his silences; when he did speak she hated him for the immorality of his views. . . . But he did not finish his sentence, and Tietjens went on:

'All the same, when the war comes it will be these little snobs who will save England, because they've the courage to know what they want and to say so.'

Macmaster said loftily:

'You're extraordinarily old-fashioned at times, Chrissie. You ought to know as well as I do that a war is impossible —at any rate with this country in it. Simply because . . .' He hesitated and then emboldened himself: '*We*—the circumspect—yes, the circumspect classes, will pilot the nation through the tight places.'

'War, my good fellow,' Tietjens said—the train was

slowing down preparatorily to running into Ashford—'is inevitable, and with this country plumb centre in the middle of it. Simply because you fellows are such damn hypocrites. There's not a country in the world that trusts us. We're always, as it were, committing adultery—like your fellow!—with the name of Heaven on our lips.' He was jibing again at the subject of Macmaster's monograph.

'He never!' Macmaster said in almost a stutter. 'He never whined about Heaven.'

'He did,' Tietjens said. 'The beastly poem you quoted ends:

"Better far though hearts may break,
    Since we dare not love,
Part till we once more may meet
    In a Heaven above." '

And Macmaster, who had been dreading that shot—for he never knew how much or how little of any given poem his friend would have by heart—Macmaster collapsed, as it were, into fussily getting down his dressing-cases and clubs from the rack, a task he usually left to a porter. Tietjens who, however much a train might be running into a station he was bound for, sat like a rock until it was dead-still, said:

'Yes, a war is inevitable. Firstly, there's you fellows who can't be trusted. And then there's the multitude who mean to have bathrooms and white enamel. Millions of them; all over the world. Not merely here. And there aren't enough bathrooms and white enamel in the world to go round. It's like you polygamists with women. There aren't enough women in the world to go round to satisfy your insatiable appetites. And there aren't enough men in the world to give each woman one. And most women want several. So you have divorce cases. I suppose you won't say that because you're so circumspect and right there shall be no more divorce? Well, war is as inevitable as divorce. . . .'

Macmaster had his head out of the carriage window and was calling for a porter.

On the platform a number of women in lovely sable cloaks, with purple or red jewel cases, with diaphanous silky scarves flying from motor hoods, were drifting towards the branch train for Rye, under the shepherding of erect, burdened footmen. Two of them nodded to Tietjens.

Macmaster considered that he was perfectly right to be tidy in his dress; you never knew whom you mightn't meet on a railway journey. This confirmed him as against Tietjens, who preferred to look like a navvy.

A tall, white-haired, white-moustached, red-cheeked fellow limped after Tietjens, who was getting his immense bag out of the guard's van. He clapped the young man on the shoulder and said:

'Hullo! How's your mother-in-law? Lady Claude wants to know. She says come up and pick a bone to-night if you're going to Rye.' He had extraordinarily blue, innocent eyes.

Tietjens said:

'Hullo, General,' and added: 'I believe she's much better. Quite restored. This is Macmaster. I think I shall be going over to bring my wife back in a day or two. They're both at Lobscheid . . . a German spa.'

The General said:

'Quite right. It isn't good for a young man to be alone. Kiss Sylvia's finger-tips for me. She's the real thing, you lucky beggar.' He added, a little anxiously: 'What about a foursome to-morrow? Paul Sandbach is down. He's as crooked as me. We can't do a full round at singles.'

'It's your own fault,' Tietjens said. 'You ought to have gone to my bone-setter. Settle it with Macmaster, will you?' He jumped into the twilight of the guard's van.

The General looked at Macmaster, a quick penetrating scrutiny:

'You're *the* Macmaster,' he said. 'You would be if you're with Chrissie.'

A high voice called:

'General! General!'

'I want a word with you,' the General said, 'about the figures in that article you wrote about Pondoland. Figures are all right. But we shall lose the beastly country if . . . But we'll talk about it after dinner to-night. You'll come up to Lady Claudine's. . . .'

Macmaster congratulated himself again on his appearance. It was all very well for Tietjens to look like a sweep; he was of these people. He, Macmaster, wasn't. He had, if anything, to be an authority, and authorities wear gold tie-rings and broadcloth. General Lord Edward Campion had a son, a permanent head of the Treasury department that regulated increases of salaries and promotions in all the public offices. Tietjens only caught the Rye train by running alongside it, pitching his enormous kit-bag through the carriage window and swinging on the footboard. Macmaster reflected that if he had done that half the station would have been yelling, 'Stand away there.'

As it was Tietjens a stationmaster was galloping after him to open the carriage door and grinningly to part:

'Well caught, sir!' for it was a cricketing county.

'Truly,' Macmaster quoted to himself.

> ' "The gods to each ascribe a differing lot:
> Some enter at the portal. Some do not!" '

II

Mrs Satterthwaite with her French maid, her priest, and her disreputable young man, Mr Bayliss, were at Lobscheid, an unknown and little-frequented air resort amongst the pinewoods of the Taunus. Mrs Satterthwaite was ultrafashionable and consummately indifferent—she only really lost her temper if at her table and under her nose you consumed her famous Black Hamburg grapes without

taking their skin and all. Father Consett was out to have
an uproarious good time during his three weeks' holiday
from the slums of Liverpool; Mr Bayliss, thin like a
skeleton in tight blue serge, golden haired and pink, was so
nearly dead of tuberculosis, was so dead penniless, and of
tastes so costly that he was ready to keep stone quiet, drink
six pints of milk a day and behave himself. On the face of
it, he was there to write the letters of Mrs Satterthwaite,
but the lady never let him enter her private rooms for fear
of infection. He had to content himself with nursing a
growing adoration for Father Consett. This priest, with
an enormous mouth, high cheek bones, untidy black hair,
a broad face that never looked too clean and waving hands
that always looked too dirty, never kept still for a moment,
and had a brogue such as is seldom heard outside old-
fashioned English novels of Irish life. He had a perpetual
laugh, like the noise made by a steam round-about. He
was, in short, a saint, and Mr Bayliss knew it, though he
didn't know how. Ultimately, and with the financial assis-
tance of Mrs Satterthwaite, Mr Bayliss became almoner to
Father Consett, adopted the rule of St. Vincent de Paul
and wrote some very admirable, if decorative, devotional
verse.

They proved thus a very happy, innocent party. For
Mrs Satterthwaite interested herself—it was the only
interest she had—in handsome, thin and horribly disreputable young men. She would wait for them, or send her
car to wait for them, at the gaol gates. She would bring
their usually admirable wardrobes up to date and give
them enough money to have a good time. When contrary
to all expectations—but it happened more often than not!—
they turned out well, she was lazily pleased. Sometimes
she sent them away to a gay spot with a priest who needed
a holiday; sometimes she had them down to her place in
the west of England.

So they were a pleasant company and all very happy.
Lobscheid contained one empty hotel with large verandahs
and several square farmhouses, white with grey beams,

painted in the gables with bouquets of blue and yellow flowers or with scarlet huntsmen shooting at purple stags. They were like gay cardboard boxes set down in fields of long grass; then the pinewoods commenced and ran, solemn, brown and geometric for miles up and down hill. The peasant girls wore black velvet waistcoats, white bodices, innumerable petticoats and absurd parti-coloured headdresses of the shape and size of halfpenny buns. They walked about in rows of four to six abreast, with a slow step, protruding white-stockinged feet in dancing pumps, their headdresses nodding solemnly; young men in blue blouses, knee-breeches and, on Sundays, in three-cornered hats, followed behind singing part-songs.

The French maid—whom Mrs Satterthwaite had borrowed from the Duchesse de Carbon Château-Herault in exchange for her own maid—was at first inclined to find the place *maussade*. But getting up a tremendous love affair with a fine, tall, blond young fellow, who included a gun, a gold-mounted hunting knife as long as his arm, a light, grey-green uniform, with gilt badges and buttons, she was reconciled to her lot. When the young Förster tried to shoot her—'*et pour cause*,' as she said—she was ravished and Mrs Satterthwaite lazily amused.

They were sitting playing bridge in the large, shadowy dining-hall of the hotel: Mrs Satterthwaite, Father Consett, Mr Bayliss. A young blond sub-lieutenant of great obsequiousness who was there as a last chance for his right lung and his career, and the bearded Kur-doctor cut in. Father Consett, breathing heavily and looking frequently at his watch, played very fast, exclaiming: 'Hurry up now; it's nearly twelve. Hurry up wid ye.' Mr Bayliss being dummy, the Father exclaimed: 'Three no trumps; I've to make. Get me a whisky and soda quick, and don't drown it as ye did the last.' He played his hand with extreme rapidity, threw down his last three cards, exclaimed: 'Ach! Botheranouns an' all; I'm two down and I've revoked on the top av it,' swallowed down his whisky and soda, looked at his watch and exclaimed: 'Done it to the minute! Here, doctor, take my hand and finish the rubber.' He was to take the mass next day for the local priest, and mass must be said fasting from midnight, and without cards played. Bridge was his only passion; a fortnight every year was what, in his worn-out life, he got of it. On his holiday he rose at ten. At eleven it was: 'A four for the Father.' From two to four they walked in the forest. At five it was: 'A four for the Father.' At nine it was: 'Father, aren't you coming to your bridge?' And Father Consett grinned all over his face and said: 'It's good ye are to a poor ould soggart. It will be paid back to you in Heaven.'

The other four played on solemnly. The Father sat him-self down behind Mrs Satterthwaite, his chin in the nape of her neck. At excruciating moments he gripped her shoulders, exclaimed: 'Play the *queen*, woman!' and breathed hard down her back. Mrs Satterthwaite would play the two of diamonds, and the Father, throwing him-self back, would groan. She said over her shoulder:

'I want to talk to you to-night, Father,' took the last trick of the rubber, collected 17 marks 50 from the doctor and 8 marks from the unter-leutnant. The doctor exclaimed:

'You gan't dake that immense sum from us and then ko off. Now we shall pe ropped py Herr Payliss at gutt-throat.'

She drifted, all shadowy black silk, across the shadows of the dining-hall, dropping her winnings into her black satin vanity bag and attended by the priest. Outside the door, beneath the antlers of a royal stag, in an atmosphere of paraffin lamps and varnished pitch-pine, she said:

'Come up to my sitting-room. The prodigal's returned. Sylvia's here.'

The Father said:

'I thought I saw her out of the corner of my eye in the bus after dinner. She'll be going back to her husband. It's a poor world.'

'She's a wicked devil!' Mrs Satterthwaite said.

'I've known her myself since she was nine,' Father Consett said, 'and it's little I've seen in her to hold up to the commendation of my flock.' He added: 'But maybe I'm made unjust by the shock of it.'

They climbed the stairs slowly.

Mrs Satterthwaite sat herself on the edge of a cane chair. She said:

'Well!'

She wore a black hat like a cart-wheel and her dresses appeared always to consist of a great many squares of silk that might have been thrown on to her. Since she considered that her complexion, which was matt white, had gone slightly violet from twenty years of make-up, when she was not made-up—as she never was at Lobscheid—she wore bits of puce-coloured satin ribbon stuck here and there, partly to counteract the violet of her complexion, partly to show she was not in mourning. She was very tall and extremely emaciated; her dark eyes that had beneath them dark brown thumb-marks were very tired or very indifferent by turns.

Father Consett walked backwards and forwards, his hands behind his back, his head bent, over the not too well-polished floor. There were two candles, lit but dim, in imitation pewter *nouvel art* candlesticks, rather dingy; a sofa of cheap mahogany with red plush cushions and rests, a table covered with a cheap carpet, and an American roll-top desk that had thrown into it a great many papers in scrolls or flat. Mrs Satterthwaite was extremely indifferent to her surroundings, but she insisted on having a piece of furniture for her papers. She liked also to have a profusion of hot-house, not garden, flowers, but as there were none of these at Lobscheid she did without them. She insisted also, as a rule, on a comfortable chaise longue which she rarely, if ever, used; but the German Empire of those days did not contain a comfortable chair, so she did without it, lying down on her bed when she was really tired. The walls of the large room were completely covered with pictures of animals in death agonies: capercailzies giving up the ghost with gouts of scarlet blood on the snow; deer dying with their heads back and eyes glazing, gouts of red blood on their necks; foxes dying with scarlet blood on green grass. These pictures were frame to frame, representing sport, the hotel having been a former Grand Ducal hunting-box, freshened to suit the taste of the day with varnished pitch-pine, bath-rooms, verandahs, and excessively modern but noisy lavatory arrangements which had been put in for the delight of possible English guests.

Mrs Satterthwaite sat on the edge of her chair; she had always the air of being just about to go out somewhere or of having just come in and being on the point of going to take her things off. She said:

'There's been a telegram waiting for her all the afternoon. I knew she was coming.'

Father Consett said:

'I saw it in the rack myself. I misdoubted it.' He added: 'Oh dear, oh dear! After all we've talked about it; now it's come.'

Mrs Satterthwaite said:

'I've been a wicked woman myself as these things are measured; but . . .'

Father Consett said:

'Ye have! It's no doubt from you she gets it, for your husband was a good man. But one wicked woman is enough for my contemplation at a time. I'm no St Anthony. . . . The young man says he will take her back?'

'On conditions,' Mrs Satterthwaite said. 'He is coming here to have an interview.'

The priest said:

'Heaven knows, Mrs Satterthwaite, there are times when to a poor priest the rule of the Church as regards marriage seems bitter hard and he almost doubts her inscrutable wisdom. He doesn't mind you. But at times I wish that that young man would take what advantage—it's all there is!—that he can of being a Protestant and divorce Sylvia. For I tell you there are bitter things to see amongst my flock over there . . .' He made a vague gesture towards the infinite. . . . 'And bitter things I've seen, for the heart of man is a wicked place. But never a bitterer than this young man's lot.'

'As you say,' Mrs Satterthwaite said, 'my husband was a good man. I hated him, but that was as much my fault as his. More! And the only reason I don't wish Christopher to divorce Sylvia is that it would bring disgrace on my husband's name. At the same time, Father . . .'

The priest said:

'I've heard near enough.'

'There's this to be said for Sylvia,' Mrs Satterthwaite went on. 'There are times when a woman hates a man—as Sylvia hates her husband. . . . I tell you I've walked behind a man's back and nearly screamed because of the desire to put my nails into the veins of his neck. It was a fascination. And it's worse with Sylvia. It's a natural antipathy.'

'Woman!' Father Consett fulminated, 'I've no patience wid ye! If the woman, as the Church directs, would have children by her husband and live decent, she would have no such feelings. It's unnatural living and unnatural practices that cause these complexes. Don't think I'm an ignoramus, priest if I am.'

Mrs Satterthwaite said:

'But Sylvia's had a child.'

Father Consett swung round like a man that has been shot at.

'Whose?' he asked, and he pointed a dirty finger at his interlocutress. 'It was that blackguard Drake's, wasn't it? I've long suspected that.'

'It was probably Drake's,' Mrs Satterthwaite said.

'Then,' the priest said, 'in the face of the pains of the hereafter how could you let that decent lad in the hotness of his sin . . . ?'

'Indeed,' Mrs Satterthwaite said, 'I shiver sometimes when I think of it. Don't believe that I had anything to do with trepanning him. But I couldn't hinder it. Sylvia's my daughter, and dog doesn't eat dog.'

'There are times when it should,' Father Consett said contemptuously.

'You don't seriously,' Mrs Satterthwaite said, 'say that I, a mother, if an indifferent one, with my daughter appearing in trouble, as the kitchenmaids say, by a married man —that I should step in and stop a marriage that was a Godsend. . . .'

'Don't,' the priest said, 'introduce the sacred name into an affair of Piccadilly bad girls. . . .' He stopped. 'Heaven help me,' he said again, 'don't ask me to answer the question of what you should or shouldn't have done. You know I loved your husband like a brother, and you know I've loved you and Sylvia ever since she was tiny. And I thank God that I am not your spiritual adviser, but only your friend in God. For if I had to answer your question I could answer it only in one way.' He broke off to ask: 'Where is that woman?'

Mrs Satterthwaite called:

'Sylvia! Sylvia! Come here!'

A door in the shadows opened and light shone from another room behind a tall figure leaning one hand on the handle of the door. A very deep voice said:

'I can't understand, mother, why you live in rooms like a sergeants' mess.' And Sylvia Tietjens wavered into the room. She added: 'I suppose it doesn't matter. I'm bored.'

Father Consett groaned:

'Heaven help us, she's like a picture of Our Lady by Fra Angelico.'

Immensely tall, slight and slow in her movements, Sylvia Tietjens wore her reddish, very fair hair in great bandeaux right down over her ears. Her very oval, regular face had an expression of virginal lack of interest such as used to be worn by fashionable Paris courtesans a decade before that time. Sylvia Tietjens considered that, being privileged to go everywhere where one went and to have all men at her feet, she had no need to change her expression or to infuse into it the greater animation that marked the more common beauties of the early twentieth century. She moved slowly from the door and sat languidly on the sofa against the wall.

2*

'There you are, Father,' she said. 'I'll not ask you to shake hands with me. You probably wouldn't.'

'As I am a priest,' Father Consett answered. 'I could not refuse. But I'd rather not.'

'This,' Sylvia repeated, 'appears to be a boring place.'

'You won't say so to-morrow,' the priest said. 'There's two young fellows. . . . And a sort of policeman to trepan away from your mother's maid!'

'That,' Sylvia answered, 'is meant to be bitter. But it doesn't hurt. I am done with men.' She added suddenly: 'Mother, didn't you one day, while you were still young, say that you had done with men? Firmly! And mean it?'

Mrs Satterthwaite said:

'I did,'

'And did you keep to it?' Sylvia asked.

Mrs Satterthwaite said:

'I did.'

'And shall I, do you imagine?'

Mrs Satterthwaite said:

'I imagine you will.'

Sylvia said:

'Oh dear!'

The priest said:

'I'd be willing to see your husband's telegram. It makes a difference to see the words on paper.'

Sylvia rose effortlessly.

'I don't see why you shouldn't,' she said. 'It will give you no pleasure.' She drifted towards the door.

'If it would give me pleasure,' the priest said, 'you would not show it me.'

'I would not,' she said.

A silhouette in the doorway, she halted, drooping, and looked over her shoulder.

'Both you and mother,' she said, 'sit there scheming to make life bearable for the Ox. I call my husband the Ox. He's repulsive: like a swollen animal. Well . . . you can't do it.' The lighted doorway was vacant. Father Consett sighed.

'I told you this was an evil place,' he said. 'In the deep forests. She'd not have such evil thoughts in another place.'

Mrs Satterthwaite said:

'I'd rather you didn't say that, Father. Sylvia would have evil thoughts in any place.'

'Sometimes,' the priest said, 'at night I think I hear the claws of evil things scratching on the shutters. This was the last place in Europe to be Christianised. Perhaps it wasn't ever even Christianised and they're here yet.'

Mrs Satterthwaite said:

'It's all very well to talk like that in the day-time. It makes the place seem romantic. But it must be near one at night. And things are bad enough as it is.'

'They are,' Father Consett said. 'The devil's at work.'

Sylvia drifted back into the room with a telegram of several sheets. Father Consett held it close to one of the candles to read, for he was short-sighted.

'All men are repulsive,' Sylvia said; 'don't you think so, mother?'

Mrs Satterthwaite said:

'I do not. Only a heartless woman would say so.'

'Mrs Vanderdecken,' Sylvia went on, 'says all men are repulsive and it's woman's disgusting task to live beside them.'

'You've been seeing that foul creature?' Mrs Satterthwaite said. 'She's a Russian agent. And worse!'

'She was at Gosingeaux all the time we were,' Sylvia said. 'You needn't groan. She won't split on us. She's the soul of honour.'

'It wasn't because of that I groaned, if I did,' Mrs Satterthwaite answered.

The priest, from over his telegram, exclaimed:

'Mrs Vanderdecken! God forbid.'

Sylvia's face, as she sat on the sofa, expressed languid and incredulous amusement.

'What do you know of her?' she asked the Father.

'I know what you know,' he answered, 'and that's enough.'

'Father Consett,' Sylvia said to her mother, 'has been renewing his social circle.'

'It's not,' Father Consett said, 'amongst the dregs of the people that you must live if you don't want to hear of the dregs of society.'

Sylvia stood up. She said:

'You'll keep your tongue off my best friends if you want me to stop and be lectured. But for Mrs. Vanderdecken I should not be here, returned to the fold!'

Father Consett exclaimed:

'Don't say it, child. I'd rather, heaven help me, you had gone on living in open sin.'

Sylvia sat down again, her hands listlessly in her lap.

'Have it your own way,' she said, and the Father returned to the fourth sheet of the telegram.

'What does this mean?' he asked. He had returned to the first sheet. 'This here: *"Accept resumption yoke"?*' he read, breathlessly.

'Sylvia,' Mrs Satterthwaite said, 'go and light the spirit lamp for some tea. We shall want it.'

'You'd think I was a district messenger boy,' Sylvia said as she rose. 'Why don't you keep your maid up? ... It's a way we had of referring to our ... union,' she explained to the Father.

'There was sympathy enough between you and him then,' he said, 'to have bywords for things. It was that I wanted to know. I understood the words.'

'They were pretty bitter bywords, as you call them,' Sylvia said. 'More like curses than kisses.'

'It was you that used them then,' Mrs Satterthwaite said. 'Christopher never said a bitter thing to you.'

An expression like a grin came slowly over Sylvia's face as she turned back to the priest.

'That's mother's tragedy,' she said. 'My husband's one of her best boys. She adores him. And he can't bear *her*.'

She drifted behind the wall of the next room and they heard her tinkling the tea-things as the Father read on again beside the candle. His immense shadow began at the centre and ran along the pitch-pine ceiling, down the wall and across the floor to join his splay feet in their clumsy boots.

'It's bad,' he muttered. He made a sound like 'Umble-umbleumble. . . . Worse than I feared . . . umbleumble . . . *"accept resumption yoke but on rigid conditions."* What's this: *esoecially*; it ought to be a "p," *"especially regards child reduce establishment ridiculous our position remake settlements in child's sole interests flat not house entertaining minimum am prepared resign office settle Yorkshire but imagine this not suit you child remain sister Effie open visits both wire if this rough outline provisionally acceptable in that case will express draft general position Monday for you and mother reflect upon follow self Tuesday arrive Thursday Lobscheid go Wiesbaden fortnight on social task discussion Thursday limited solely, comma emphasized comma to affairs."* '

'That means,' Mrs Satterthwaite said, 'that he doesn't mean to reproach her. *Emphasized* applies to the word *solely*. . . .'

'Why d'you take it. . . .' Father Consett asked, 'did he spend an immense lot of money on this telegram? Did he imagine you were in such trepidation . . .?' He broke off. Walking slowly, her long arms extended to carry the tea-tray, over which her wonderfully moving face had a rapt expression of indescribable mystery, Sylvia was coming through the door.

'Oh, child,' the Father exclaimed, 'whether it's St Martha or that Mary that made the bitter choice, not one of them ever looked more virtuous than you. Why aren't ye born to be a good man's help-meet?'

A little tinkle sounded from the tea-tray and three pieces of sugar fell on to the floor. Mrs Tietjens hissed with vexation.

'I *knew* that damned thing would slide off the teacups,' she said. She dropped the tray from an inch or so of height on to the carpeted table. 'I'd made it a matter of

luck between myself and myself,' she said. Then she faced
the priest.

'I'll tell you,' she said, 'why he sent the telegram. It's
because of that dull display of the English gentleman that
I detested. He gives himself the solemn airs of the Foreign
Minister, but he's only a youngest son at the best. That is
why I loathe him.'

Mrs Satterthwaite said:

'That isn't the reason why he sent the telegram.'

Her daughter had a gesture of amused, lazy tolerance.

'Of course it isn't,' she said. 'He sent it out of consideration: the lordly, full-dress consideration that drives me
distracted. As he would say: "He'd imagine I'd find it
convenient to have ample time for reflection." It's like
being addressed as if one were a monument and by a herald
according to protocol. And partly because he's the soul of
truth like a stiff Dutch doll. He wouldn't write a letter
because he couldn't without beginning it "Dear Sylvia"
and ending it "Yours sincerely" or "truly" or "affec-
tionately." . . . He's that sort of precise imbecile. I tell you
he's so formal he can't do without all the conventions there
are and so truthful he can't use half of them.'

'Then,' Father Consett said, 'if ye know him so well,
Sylvia Satterthwaite, how is it ye can't get on with him
better? They say: *Tout savoir c'est tout pardonner*.'

'It isn't,' Sylvia said. 'To know everything about a
person is to be bored . . . bored . . . bored!'

'And how are you going to answer this telegram of his?'
the Father asked. 'Or have ye answered it already?'

'I shall wait until Monday night to keep him as bothered
as I can to know whether he's to start on Tuesday. He
fusses like a hen over his packings and the exact hours of
his movements. On Monday I shall telegraph: "Righto"
and nothing else.'

'And why,' the Father asked, 'will ye telegraph him a
vulgar word that you never use, for your language is the
one thing about you that isn't vulgar?'

Sylvia said:

'Thanks!' She curled her legs up under her on the sofa and laid her head back against the wall so that her Gothic arch of a chinbone pointed at the ceiling. She admired her own neck, which was very long and white.

'I know!' Father Consett said. 'You're a beautiful woman. Some men would say it was a lucky fellow that lived with you. I don't ignore the fact in my cogitation. He'd imagine all sorts of delights to lurk in the shadow of your beautiful hair. And they wouldn't.'

Sylvia brought her gaze down from the ceiling and fixed her brown eyes for a moment on the priest, speculatively.

'It's a great handicap we suffer from,' he said.

'I don't know why I selected that word,' Sylvia said, 'it's one word, so it costs only fifty pfennigs. I couldn't hope really to give a jerk to his pompous self-sufficiency.'

'It's great handicaps we priests suffer from,' the Father repeated. 'However much a priest may be a man of the world—and he has to be to fight the world . . .'

Mrs Satterthwaite said:

'Have a cup of tea, Father, while it's just right. I believe Sylvia is the only person in Germany who knows how to make tea.'

'There's always behind him the Roman collar and the silk bib, and you don't believe in him,' Father Consett went on, 'yet he knows ten—a thousand times!—more of human nature than ever you can.'

'I don't see,' Sylvia said placably, 'how you can learn in your slums anything about the nature of Eunice Vanderdecken, or Elizabeth B. or Queenie James, or any of my set.' She was on her feet pouring cream into the Father's tea. 'I'll admit for the moment that you aren't giving me pi-jaw.'

'I'm glad,' the priest said, 'that ye remember enough of yer schooldays to use the old term.'

Sylvia wavered backwards to her sofa and sank down again.

'There you are,' she said, 'you can't really get away

from preachments. Me for the pyore young girl is always at the back of it.'

'It isn't,' the Father said. 'I'm not one to cry for the moon.'

'You don't want me to be a pure young girl,' Sylvia asked with lazy incredulity.

'I do not!' the Father said, 'but I'd wish that at times ye'd remember you once were.'

'I don't believe I ever was,' Sylvia said, 'if the nuns had known I'd have been expelled from the Holy Child.'

'You would not,' the Father said. 'Do stop your boasting. The nuns have too much sense. . . . Anyhow, it isn't a pure young girl I'd have you or behaving like a Protestant deaconess for the craven fear of hell. I'd have ye be a physically healthy, decently honest-with-yourself young devil of a married woman. It's them that are the plague and the salvation of the world.'

'You admire mother?' Mrs. Tietjens asked suddenly. She added in parenthesis: 'You see you can't get away from salvation.'

'I mean keeping bread and butter in their husbands' stomachs,' the priest said. 'Of course I admire your mother.'

Mrs Satterthwaite moved a hand slightly.

'You're at any rate in league with her against me,' Sylvia said. She asked with more interest: 'Then would you have me model myself on her and do good works to escape hell fire? She wears a hair shirt in Lent.'

Mrs Satterthwaite started from her doze on the edge of her chair. She had been trusting the Father's wit to give her daughter's insolence a run for its money, and she imagined that if the priest hit hard enough he might, at least, make Sylvia think a little about some of her ways.

'Hang it, no, Sylvia,' she exclaimed more suddenly. 'I may not be much, but I'm a sportsman. I'm afraid of hell-fire; horribly, I'll admit. But I don't bargain with the Almighty. I hope He'll let me through; but I'd go on trying to pick men out of the dirt—I suppose that's what you and Father Consett mean—if I were as certain of going to hell as I am of going to bed to-night. So that's that!'

' "And lo! Ben Adhem's name led all the rest!" ' Sylvia jeered softly. 'All the same I bet you wouldn't bother to reclaim men if you could not find the young, good-looking, interestingly vicious sort.'

'I wouldn't,' Mrs Satterthwaite said. 'If they didn't interest me, why should I?'

Sylvia looked at Father Consett.

'If you're going to trounce me any more,' she said, 'get a move on. It's late, I've been travelling for thirty-six hours.'

'I will,' Father Consett said. 'It's a good maxim that if you swat flies enough some of them stick to the wall. I'm only trying to make a little mark on your common sense. Don't you see what you're going to?'

'What?' Sylvia said indifferently. 'Hell?'

'No,' the Father said, 'I'm talking of this life. Your confessor must talk to you about the next. But I'll not tell you what you're going to. I've changed my mind. I'll tell your mother after you're gone.'

'Tell me,' Sylvia said.

'I'll not,' Father Consett answered. 'Go to the fortune-tellers at the Earl's Court exhibition; they'll tell ye all about the fair woman you're to beware of.'

'There's some of them said to be rather good,' Sylvia said. 'Di Wilson's told me about one. She said she was going to have a baby. . . . You don't mean that, Father? For I swear I never will. . . .'

'I daresay not,' the priest said. 'But let's talk about men.'

'There's nothing you can tell me I don't know,' Sylvia said.

'I daresay not,' the priest answered. 'But let's rehearse what you do know. Now suppose you could elope with a new man every week and no questions asked? Or how often would you want to?'

Sylvia said:

'Just a moment, Father,' and she addressed Mrs Satterthwaite: 'I suppose I shall have to put myself to bed.'

'You will,' Mrs Satterthwaite said. 'I'll not have any
maid kept up after ten in a holiday resort. What's she to
do in a place like this? Except listen for the bogies it's full
of?'

'Always considerate!' Mrs Tietjens gibed. 'And perhaps
it's just as well. I'd probably beat that Marie of yours'
arms to pieces with a hair-brush if she came near me.' She
added: 'You were talking about men, Father. . . .' And
then began with sudden animation to her mother:

'I've changed my mind about that telegram. The first
thing to-morrow I shall wire: *"Agreed entirely but arrange
bring Hullo Central with you."* '

She addressed the priest again.

'I call my maid Hullo Central because she's got a tinny
voice like a telephone. I say: "Hullo Central"—when she
answers "Yes, modd'm," you'd swear it was the Exchange
speaking. . . . But you were telling me about men.'

'I was reminding you!' the Father said. 'But I needn't
go on. You've caught the drift of my remarks. That is why
you are pretending not to listen.'

'I assure you, no,' Mrs Tietjens said. 'It is simply that if
a thing comes into my head I have to say it. . . . You were
saying that if one went away with a different man for
every week-end . . .'

'You've shortened the period already,' the priest said. 'I
gave a full week to every man.'

'But, of course, one would have to have a home,' Sylvia
said, 'an address. One would have to fill one's mid-week
engagements. Really it comes to it that one has to have a
husband and a place to store one's maid in. Hullo Central's
been on board-wages all the time. But I don't believe she
likes it. . . . Let's agree that if I had a different man every
week I'd be bored with the arrangement. That's what
you're getting at, isn't it?'

'You'd find,' the priest said, 'that it whittled down until
the only divvy moment was when you stood waiting in the

booking-office for the young man to take the tickets. . . .
And then gradually that wouldn't be divvy any more. . . .
And you'd yawn and long to go back to your husband.'

'Look here,' Mrs Tietjens said, 'you're abusing the
secrets of the confessional. That's exactly what Tottie
Charles said. She tried it for three months while Freddie
Charles was in Madeira. It's *exactly* what she said down to
the yawn and the booking-office. *And* the "divvy." It's only
Tottie Charles who uses it every two words. Most of us
prefer ripping! It *is* more sensible.'

'Of course I haven't been abusing the secrets of the confessional,' Father Consett said mildly.

'Of course you haven't,' Sylvia said with affection.
'You're a good old stick and no end of a mimic, and you
know us all to the bottom of our hearts.'

'Not all that much,' the priest said, 'there's probably a
good deal of good at the bottom of your hearts.'

Sylvia said:

'Thanks.' She asked suddenly: 'Look here. *Was* it what
you saw of us—the future mothers of England, you know,
and all—at Miss Lampeter's—that made you take to the
slums? Out of disgust and despair?'

'Oh, let's not make melodrama out of it,' the priest
answered. 'Let's say I wanted a change. I couldn't see that
I was doing any good.'

'You did us all the good there was done,' Sylvia said.
'What with Miss Lampeter always drugged to the world,
and all the French mistresses as wicked as hell.'

'I've heard you say all this before,' Mrs Satterthwaite
said. 'But it was supposed to be the best finishing school in
England. I know it cost enough!'

'Well, say it was we who were a rotten lot,' Sylvia concluded; and then to the Father: 'We *were* a lot of rotters,
weren't we?'

The priest answered:

'I don't know. I don't suppose you were—or are—any
worse than your mother or grandmother, or the patri-
cianesses of Rome or the worshippers of Ashtaroth. It

seems we have to have a governing class and governing classes are subject to special temptations.'

'Who's Ashtaroth?' Sylvia asked. 'Astarte?' and then: 'Now, Father, after your experiences would you say the factory girls of Liverpool, or any other slum, are any better women than us that you used to look after?'

'Astarte Syriaca,' the Father said, 'was a very powerful devil. There's some that hold she's not dead yet. I don't know that I do myself.'

'Well, I've done with her,' Sylvia said.

The Father nodded:

'You've had dealings with Mrs Profumo?' he asked. 'And that loathsome fellow. . . . What's his name?'

'Does it shock you?' Sylvia asked. 'I'll admit it was a bit thick. . . . But I've done with it. I prefer to pin my faith to Mrs Vanderdecken. And, of course, Freud.'

The priest nodded his head and said:

'Of course! Of course. . . .'

But Mrs Satterthwaite exclaimed, with sudden energy:

'Sylvia Tietjens, I don't care what you do or what you read, but if you ever speak another word to that woman, you never do to me!'

Sylvia stretched herself on her sofa. She opened her brown eyes wide and let the lids slowly drop again.

'I've said once,' she said, 'that I don't like to hear my friends miscalled. Eunice Vanderdecken is a bitterly mis-judged woman. She's a real good pal.'

'She's a Russian spy,' Mrs Satterthwaite said.

'Russian grandmother,' Sylvia answered. 'And if she is, who cares? She's welcome for me. . . . Listen now, you two. I said to myself when I came in: "I daresay I've given them both a rotten time." I know you're both more nuts on me than I deserve. And I said I'd sit and listen to all the pi-jaw you wanted to give me if I sat till dawn. And I will. As a return. But I'd rather you let my friends alone.'

Both the elder people were silent. There came from the shuttered windows of the dark room a low, scratching rustle.

'You hear!' the priest said to Mrs Satterthwaite.

'It's the branches,' Mrs Satterthwaite answered.

The Father answered: 'There's no tree within ten yards! Try bats as an explanation.'

'I've said I wish you wouldn't, once,' Mrs Satterthwaite shivered. Sylvia said:

'I don't know what you two are talking about. It sounds like superstition. Mother's rotten with it.'

'I don't say that it's devils trying to get in,' the Father said. 'But it's just as well to remember that devils *are* always trying to get in. And there are especial spots. These deep forests are noted among others.' He suddenly turned his back and pointed at the shadowy wall. 'Who,' he asked, 'but a savage possessed by a devil could have conceived of *that* as a decoration?' He was pointing to a life-sized, coarsely daubed picture of a wild boar dying, its throat cut, and gouts of scarlet blood. Other agonies of animals went away into all the shadows.

'*Sport!*' he hissed. 'It's devilry!'

'That's perhaps true,' Sylvia said. Mrs Satterthwaite was crossing herself with great rapidity. The silence remained.

Sylvia said:

'Then if you're both done talking I'll say what I have to say. To begin with . . .' She stopped and sat rather erect, listening to the rustling from the shutters.

'To begin with,' she began again with impetus, 'you spared me the catalogue of the defects of age; I know them. One grows skinny—my sort—the complexion fades, the teeth stick out. And then there is the boredom. I know it; one is bored . . . bored . . . bored! You can't tell me anything I don't know about that. I'm thirty. I know what to expect. You'd like to have told me, Father, only you were afraid of taking away from your famous man of the world effect—you'd like to have told me that one can insure against the boredom and the long, skinny teeth by love of husband and child. The home stunt! I believe it!

I do quite believe it. Only I hate my husband . . . and I hate
. . . I hate my child.'

She paused, waiting for exclamations of dismay or dis-
approbation from the priest. These did not come.

'Think,' she said, 'of all the ruin that child has meant
for me; the pain in bearing him and the fear of death.'

'Of course,' the priest said, 'child-bearing is for women
a very terrible thing.'

'I can't say,' Mrs Tietjens went on, 'that this has been a
very decent conversation. You get a girl . . . fresh from
open sin, and make her talk about it. Of course you're a
priest and mother's mother; we're *en famille*. But Sister
Mary of the Cross at the convent had a maxim: "Wear
velvet gloves in family life." We seem to be going at it with
gloves off.'

Father Consett still didn't say anything.

'You're trying, of course, to draw me,' Sylvia said. 'I can
see that with half an eye. . . . Very well then, you shall. . . .'
She drew a breath.

'You want to know why I hate my husband. I'll tell you;
it's because of his simple, sheer immorality. I don't mean
his actions; his views! Every speech he utters about everything makes me—I swear it makes me—in spite of myself,
want to stick a knife into him, and I can't prove he's wrong,
not ever, about the simplest thing. But I can pain him.
And I will. . . . He sits about in chairs that fit his back,
clumsy, like a rock, not moving for hours. . . . And I can
make him wince. Oh, without showing it. . . . He's what
you call loyal . . . oh, loyal. . . . There's an absurd little chit
of a fellow . . . oh, Macmaster . . . and his mother . . . whom
he persists in a silly mystical way in calling a saint . . . a
Protestant saint! . . . And his old nurse, who looks after the
child . . . and the child itself. . . . I tell you I've only got to
raise an eyelid . . . yes, cock an eyelid up a little when anyone of them is mentioned . . . and it hurts him dreadfully.
His eyes roll in a sort of mute anguish. . . . Of course he
doesn't say anything. He's an English country gentleman.'

Father Consett said:

'This immorality you talk about in your husband. . . . I've never noticed it. I saw a good deal of him when I stayed with you for the week before your child was born. I talked with him a great deal. Except in the matter of the two communions—and even in these I don't know that we differed so much—I found him perfectly sound.'

'Sound.' Mrs Satterthwaite said with sudden emphasis; 'of course he's sound. It isn't even the word. He's the best ever. There was your father, for a good man . . . and him. That's an end of it.'

'Ah,' Sylvia said, 'you don't know. . . . Look here. Try and be just. Suppose I'm looking at *The Times* at break-fast and say, not having spoken to him for a week: "It's wonderful what the doctors are doing. Have you seen the latest?" And at once he'll be on his high-horse—he knows everything!—and he'll prove . . . *prove* . . . that all un-healthy children must be lethal-chambered or the world will go to pieces. And it's like being hypnotised; you can't think of what to answer him. Or he'll reduce you to speech-less rage by proving that murderers ought not to be executed. And then I'll ask, casually, if children ought to be lethal-chambered for being constipated. Because Mar-chant—that's the nurse—is always whining that the child's bowels aren't regular and the dreadful diseases that leads to. Of course *that* hurts him. For he's perfectly soppy about that child, though he half knows it isn't his own. . . . But that's what I mean by immorality. He'll profess that murderers ought to be preserved in order to breed from because they're bold fellows, and innocent little children executed because they're sick. . . . And he'll almost make you believe it, though you're on the point of retching at the ideas.'

'You wouldn't now,' Father Consett began, and almost coaxingly, 'think of going into retreat for a month or two.'

'I wouldn't,' Sylvia said. 'How could I?'

'There's a convent of female Premonstratensians near Birkenhead, many ladies go there,' the Father went on. 'They cook very well, and you can have your own furniture and your own maid if ye don't like nuns to wait on you.'

'It can't be done,' Sylvia said, 'you can see for yourself. It would make people smell a rat at once. Christopher wouldn't hear of it. . . .'

'No, I'm afraid it can't be done, Father,' Mrs Satterthwaite interrupted finally. 'I've hidden here for four months to cover Sylvia's tracks. I've got Wateman's to look after. My new land steward's coming in next week.'

'Still,' the Father urged, with a sort of tremulous eagerness, 'if only for a month. . . . If only for a fortnight. . . . So many Catholic ladies do it. . . . Ye might think of it.'

'I see what you're aiming at,' Sylvia said with sudden anger; 'you're revolted at the idea of my going straight from one man's arms to another.'

'I'd be better pleased if there could be an interval,' the Father said. 'It's what's called bad form.'

Sylvia became electrically rigid on her sofa.

'Bad form!' she exclaimed. 'You accuse me of bad form.'

The Father slightly bowed his head like a man facing a wind.

'I do,' he said. 'It's disgraceful. It's unnatural. I'd travel a bit at least.'

She placed her hand on her long throat.

'I know what you mean,' she said,' 'you want to spare Christopher . . . the humiliation. The . . . the nausea. No doubt he'll feel nauseated. I've reckoned on that. It will give me a little of my own back.'

The Father said:

'That's enough, woman. I'll hear no more.'

Sylvia said:

'You will then. Listen here. . . . I've always got this to look forward to: I'll settle down by that man's side. I'll be as virtuous as any woman. I've made up my mind to it and I'll be it. And I'll be bored stiff for the rest of my life. Except for one thing. I can torment that man. And I'll do it. Do you understand how I'll do it? There are many ways. But if the worst comes to the worst I can always

drive him silly . . . by corrupting the child!' She was panting a little, and round her brown eyes the whites showed.
'I'll get even with him. I can. I know how, you see. And
with you, through him, for tormenting me. I've come all
the way from Brittany without stopping. I haven't slept.
. . . But I can . . .'

Father Consett put his hand beneath the tail of his
coat.

'Sylvia Tietjens,' he said, 'in my pistol pocket I've a
little bottle of holy water which I carry for such occasions.
What if I was to throw two drops of it over you and cry:
Exorcizo te Ashtaroth in nomine? . . .

She erected her body above her skirts on the sofa, stiffened like a snake's neck above its coils. Her face was quite
pallid, her eyes staring out.

'You . . . you *daren't*,' she said. 'To me . . . an outrage!'
Her feet slid slowly to the floor; she measured the distance
to the doorway with her eyes. 'You *daren't*,' she said
again; 'I'd denounce you to the Bishop. . . .'

'It's little the Bishop would help you with them burning into your skin,' the priest said. 'Go away, I bid you, and
say a Hail Mary or two. Ye need them. Ye'll not talk of
corrupting a little child before me again.'

'I won't,' Sylvia said. 'I shouldn't have . . .'

Her black figure showed in silhouette against the open
doorway.

When the door was closed upon them, Mrs Satterthwaite
said:

'Was it necessary to threaten her with that? You know
best, of course. It seems rather strong to me.'

'It's a hair from the dog that's bit her,' the priest said.
'She's a silly girl. She's been playing at black masses along
with that Mrs Profumo and the fellow whose name I
can't remember. You could tell that. They cut the throat
of a white kid and splash its blood about. . . . That was at
the back of her mind. . . . It's not very serious. A parcel of
silly, idle girls. It's not much more than palmistry or

fortune-telling to them if one has to weigh it, for all its ugliness, as a sin. As far as their volition goes, and it's volition that's the essence of prayer, black or white. . . . But it was at the back of her mind, and she won't forget to-night.'

'Of course, that's your affair, Father,' Mrs Satterthwaite said lazily. 'You hit her pretty hard. I don't suppose she's ever been hit so hard. What was it you wouldn't tell her?'

'Only,' the priest said, 'I wouldn't tell her because the thought's best not put in her head. . . . But her hell on earth will come when her husband goes running, blind, head down, mad after another woman.'

Mrs Satterthwaite looked at nothing; then she nodded.

'Yes,' she said; 'I hadn't thought of it. . . . But will he? He *is* a very sound fellow, isn't he?'

'What's to stop it?' the priest asked. '*What* in the world but the grace of our blessed Lord, which he hasn't got and doesn't ask for? And then . . . He's a young man, full-blooded, and they won't be living . . . *maritalement*. Not if I know him. And then. . . . *Then* she'll tear the house down. The world will echo with her wrongs.'

'Do you mean to say,' Mrs Satterthwaite said, 'that Sylvia would do anything vulgar?'

'Doesn't every woman who's had a man to torture for years when she loses him?' the priest asked. 'The more she's made an occupation of torturing him, the less right she thinks she has to lose him.'

Mrs Satterthwaite looked gloomily into the dusk.

'That poor devil. . . .' she said. 'Will he get any peace anywhere? . . . What's the matter, Father?'

The Father said:

'I've just remembered she gave me tea and cream and I drank it. Now I can't take mass for Father Reinhardt. I'll have to go and knock up his curate, who lives away in the forest.'

At the door, holding the candle, he said:

'I'd have you not get up to-day nor yet to-morrow, if ye can stand it. Have a headache and let Sylvia nurse you. . . .

You'll have to tell how she nursed you when you get back
to London. And I'd rather ye didn't lie more out and out
than ye need, if it's to please me. . . . Besides, if ye watch
Sylvia nursing you, you might hit on a characteristic touch
to make it seem more truthful. . . . How her sleeves
brushed the medicine bottles and irritated you, maybe . . .
or—*you'll* know! If we can save scandal to the congrega-
tion, we may as well.'

He ran downstairs.

III

At the slight creaking made by Macmaster in pushing open
his door, Tietjens started violently. He was sitting in a
smoking-jacket, playing patience engrossedly in a sort of
garret bedroom. It had a sloping roof outlined by black
oak beams, which cut into squares the cream-coloured
patent distemper of the walls. The room contained also a
four-post bedstead, a corner cupboard in black oak, and
many rush mats on a polished oak floor of very irregular
planking. Tietjens, who hated these disinterred and waxed
relics of the past, sat in the centre of the room at a flimsy
card-table beneath a white-shaded electric light of a brilliance that, in these surroundings, appeared unreasonable.
This was one of those restored old groups of cottages that
it was at that date the fashion to convert into hostelries. To
it Macmaster, who was in search of the inspiration of the
past, had preferred to come. Tietjens, not desiring to interfere with his friend's culture, had accepted the quarters,
though he would have preferred to go to a comfortable
modern hotel as being less affected and cheaper. Accustomed to what he called the grown-oldness of a morose,
rambling Yorkshire manor house, he disliked being among
collected and rather pitiful bits which, he said, made him
feel ridiculous, as if he were trying to behave seriously at
a fancy-dress ball. Macmaster, on the other hand, with
gratification and a serious air, would run his finger tips

along the bevellings of a darkened piece of furniture, and would declare it 'genuine Chippendale' or 'Jacobean oak,' as the case might be. And he seemed to gain an added seriousness and weight of manner with each piece of ancient furniture that down the years he thus touched. But Tietjens would declare that you could tell the beastly thing was a fake by just cocking an eye at it and, if the matter happened to fall under the test of professional dealers in old furniture, Tietjens was the more often in the right of it, and Macmaster, sighing slightly, would prepare to proceed still further along the difficult road to connoisseurship. Eventually, by conscientious study, he got so far as at times to be called in by Somerset House to value great properties for probate—an occupation at once distinguished and highly profitable.

Tietjens swore with the extreme vehemence of a man who has been made, but who much dislikes being seen, to start.

Macmaster—in evening dress he looked extremely miniature!—said:

'I'm sorry, old man, I know how much you dislike being interrupted. But the General is in a terrible temper.'

Tietjens rose stiffly, lurched over to an eighteenth-century rosewood folding washstand, took from its top a glass of flat whisky and soda, and gulped down a large quantity. He looked about uncertainly, perceived a note-book on a 'Chippendale' bureau, made a short calculation in pencil and looked at his friend momentarily.

Macmaster said again:

'I'm sorry, old man. I must have interrupted one of your immense calculations.'

Tietjens said:

'You haven't. I was only thinking. I'm just as glad you've come. What did you say?'

Macmaster repeated:

'I said, the General is in a terrible temper. It's just as well you didn't come up to dinner.'

Tietjens said:

'He isn't . . . He isn't in a temper. He's as pleased as punch at not having to have these women up before him.'

Macmaster said:

'He says he's got the police scouring the whole county for them, and that you'd better leave by the first train to-morrow.'

Tietjens said:

'I won't. I can't. I've got to wait here for a wire from Sylvia.'

Macmaster groaned:

'Oh dear! oh dear!' Then he said hopefully: 'But we could have it forwarded to Hythe.'

Tietjens said with some vehemence:

'I tell you I won't leave here. I tell you I've settled it with the police and that swine of a Cabinet Minister. I've mended the leg of the canary of the wife of the police-constable. Sit down and be reasonable. The police don't touch people like us.'

Macmaster said:

'I don't believe you realise the public feeling there is . . .'

'Of course I do, amongst people like Sandbach,' Tietjens said. 'Sit down I tell you. . . . Have some whisky. . . .' He filled himself out another long tumbler, and, holding it, dropped into a too low-seated, reddish wicker armchair that had cretonne fixings. Beneath his weight the chair sagged a good deal and his dress-shirt bulged up to his chin.

Macmaster said:

'What's the matter with you?' Tietjens' eyes were blood-shot.

'I tell you,' Tietjens said, 'I'm waiting for a wire from Sylvia.'

Macmaster said:

'Oh!' And then: 'It can't come to-night, it's getting on for one.'

'It can,' Tietjens said, 'I've fixed it up with the post-master—all the way up to Town! It probably won't come

because Sylvia won't send it until the last moment, to
bother me. None the less, I'm waiting for a wire from
Sylvia and this is what I look like.'

Macmaster said:

'That woman's the cruellest beast . . .'

'You might,' Tietjens interrupted, 'remember that
you're talking about my wife.'

'I don't see,' Macmaster said, 'how one can talk about
Sylvia without . . .'

'The line is a perfectly simple one to draw,' Tietjens
said. 'You can relate a lady's actions if you know them
and are asked to. You mustn't comment. In this case you
don't know the lady's actions even, so you may as well hold
your tongue.' He sat looking straight in front of him.

Macmaster sighed from deep in his chest. He asked
himself if this was what sixteen hours' waiting had done
for his friend, what were all the remaining hours going to
do?

Tietjens said:

'I shall be fit to talk about Sylvia after two more
whiskies. . . . Let's settle your other perturbations first. . . .
The fair girl is called Wannop: Valentine Wannop.'

'That's the Professor's name,' Macmaster said.

'She's the late Professor Wannop's daughter,' Tietjens
said. 'She's also the daughter of the novelist.'

Macmaster interjected:

'But . . .'

'She supported herself for a year after the Professor's
death as a domestic servant,' Tietjens said. 'Now she's
housemaid for her mother, the novelist, in an inexpensive
cottage. I should imagine the two experiences would make
her desire to better the lot of her sex.'

Macmaster again interjected a 'But . . .'

'I got that information from the policeman whilst I was
putting his wife's canary's leg in splints.'

Macmaster said:

'The policeman you knocked down?' His eyes expressed

unreasoning surprise. He added: 'He knew Miss ... eh ...
Wannop then!'

'You would not expect much intelligence from the
police of Sussex,' Tietjens said. 'But you would be wrong.
P.C. Finn is clever enough to recognise the young lady
who for several years past has managed the constabulary's
wives' and children's annual tea and sports. He says Miss
Wannop holds the quarter-mile, half-mile, high jump, long
jump and putting the weight records for East Sussex. That
explains how she went over that dyke in such tidy style. ...
And precious glad the good, simple man was when I told
him he was to leave the girl alone. He didn't know, he said,
how he'd ever a had the face to serve the warrant on Miss
Wannop. The other girl—the one that squeaked—is a
stranger, a Londoner probably.'

Macmaster said:

'*You* told the policeman ...'

'I gave him,' Tietjens said, 'the Rt. Hon. Stephen Fenick
Waterhouse's compliments, and he'd be much obliged if
the P.C. would hand in a 'No Can Do' report in the
matter of those ladies every morning to his inspector. I
gave him also a brand new fi' pun note—from the Cabinet
Minister—and a couple of quid and the price of a new
pair of trousers from myself. So he's the happiest constable in Sussex. A very decent fellow; he told me how to
know a dog otter's spoor from a gravid bitch's. ... But
that wouldn't interest you.'

He began again:

'Don't look so inexpressibly foolish. I told you I'd been
dining with that swine. ... No, I oughtn't to call him a
swine after eating his dinner. Besides, he's a very decent
fellow. ...'

'You didn't tell me you'd been dining with Mr Waterhouse,' Macmaster said. 'I hope you remembered that, as
he's amongst other things the President of the Funded
Debt Commission he's the power of life and death over the
department and us.'

'You didn't think,' Tietjens answered, 'that you are the

only one to dine with the great ones of the earth! I wanted to talk to that fellow ... about those figures their cursed crowd make me fake. I meant to give him a bit of my mind.'

'You *didn't!*' Macmaster said with an expression of panic. 'Besides, they didn't ask you to fake the calculation. They only asked you to work it out on the basis of given figures.'

'Anyhow,' Tietjens said, 'I gave him a bit of my mind. I told him that, at threepence, it must run the country—and certainly himself as a politician!—to absolute ruin.'

Macmaster uttered a deep 'Good Lord!' and then: 'But won't you ever remember you're a Government servant? He could ...'

'Mr Waterhouse,' Tietjens said, 'asked me if I wouldn't consent to be transferred to his secretary's department. And when I said: "Go to hell!" he walked round the streets with me for two hours arguing.... I was working out the chances on a $4\frac{1}{2}d$. basis for him when you interrupted me. I've promised to let him have the figures when he goes up by the 1.30 on Monday.'

Macmaster said:

'You haven't.... But by Jove you're the only man in England that could do it.'

'That was what Mr Waterhouse said,' Tietjens commented. 'He said old Ingleby had told him so.'

'I do hope,' Macmaster said, 'that you answered him politely!'

'I told him,' Tietjens answered, 'that there were a dozen men who could do it as well as I, and I mentioned your name in particular.'

'But I *couldn't*,' Macmaster answered. 'Of course I could convert a $3d$. rate into $4\frac{1}{2}d$. But these are the actuarial variations; they're infinite. I couldn't touch them.'

Tietjens said negligently: 'I don't want my name mixed up in the unspeakable affair. When I give him the papers on Monday I shall tell him you did most of the work.'

Again Macmaster groaned.

Nor was this distress mere altruism. Immensely ambitious for his brilliant friend, Macmaster's ambition was one ingredient of his strong desire for security. At Cambridge he had been perfectly content with a moderate, quite respectable place on the list of mathematical postulants. He knew that that made him safe, and he had still more satisfaction in the thought that it would warrant him in never being brilliant in after life. But when Tietjens, two years after, had come out as a mere Second Wrangler, Macmaster had been bitterly and loudly disappointed. He knew perfectly well that Tietjens simply hadn't taken trouble; and, ten chances to one, it was on purpose that Tietjens hadn't taken trouble. For the matter of that, for Tietjens it wouldn't have been trouble.

And, indeed, to Macmaster's upbraidings, which Macmaster hadn't spared him, Tietjens had answered that he hadn't been able to think of going through the rest of his life with a beastly placard like Senior Wrangler hung round his neck.

But Macmaster had early made up his mind that life for him would be safest if he could go about, not very much observed but still an authority, in the midst of a body of men all labelled. He wanted to walk down Pall Mall on the arm, precisely, of a largely lettered Senior Wrangler; to return eastward on the arm of the youngest Lord Chancellor England had ever seen; to stroll down Whitehall in familiar converse with a world-famous novelist, saluting on the way a majority of My Lords Commissioners of the Treasury. And, after tea, for an hour at the club all these, in a little group, should treat him with the courtesy of men who respected him for his soundness. Then he would be safe.

And he had no doubt that Tietjens was the most brilliant man in England of that day, so that nothing caused him more anguish than the thought that Tietjens might not make a brilliant and rapid career towards some illustrious position in the public services. He would very willingly—he desired, indeed, nothing better—have seen Tietjens pass

over his own head! It did not seem to him a condemnation
of the public services that this appeared to be unlikely.

Yet Macmaster was still not without hope. He was quite
aware that there are other techniques of careers than that
which he had prescribed for himself. He could not imagine
himself, even in the most deferential way, correcting a
superior; yet he could see that, though Tietjens treated
almost every hierarch as if he were a born fool, no one very
much resented it. Of course Tietjens was a Tietjens of
Groby; but was that going to be enough to live on for
ever? Times were changing, and Macmaster imagined this
to be a democratic age.

But Tietjens went on, with both hands as it were, throwing away opportunity and committing outrage. . . .

That day Macmaster could only consider to be one of
disaster. He got up from his chair and filled himself another
drink; he felt himself to be distressed and to need it.
Slouching among his cretonnes, Tietjens was gazing in
front of him. He said:

'Here!' without looking at Macmaster, and held out his
long glass. Into it Macmaster poured whisky with a hesi-
tating hand. Tietjens said: 'Go on!'

Macmaster said:

'It's late; we're breakfasting at the Duchemins' at ten.'

Tietjens answered:

'Don't worry, sonny. We'll be there for your pretty
lady.' He added: 'Wait another quarter of an hour. I want
to talk to you.'

Macmaster sat down again and deliberately began to
review the day. It had begun with disaster, and in disaster
it had continued.

And, with something like a bitter irony, Macmaster remembered and brought up now for digestion the parting
words of General Campion to himself. The General had
limped with him to the hall door up at Mountby and,
standing patting him on the shoulder, tall, slightly bent and
very friendly, had said:

'Look here, Christopher Tietjens is a splendid fellow.

But he needs a good woman to look after him. Get him back to Sylvia as quick as you can. Had a little tiff, haven't they? Nothing serious? Chrissie hasn't been running after the skirts? No? I daresay a little. No? Well then . . .'

Macmaster had stood like a gate-post, so appalled. He had stuttered:

'No! No!'

'We've known them both so long,' the General went on. 'Lady Claudine in particular. And, believe me, Sylvia is a splendid girl. Straight as a die; the soul of loyalty to her friends. And fearless—she'd face the devil in his rage. You should have seen her out with the Belvoir! Of course you know her. . . . Well then!'

Macmaster had just managed to say that he knew Sylvia, of course.

'Well then . . .' the General had continued . . . 'you'll agree with me that if there *is* anything wrong between them he's to blame. And it will be resented. Very bitterly. He wouldn't set foot in this house again. But he says he's going out to her and Mrs Satterthwaite. . . .'

'I believe . . .' Macmaster had begun . . . 'I believe he is . . .'

'Well then!' the General had said: 'It's all right. . . . But Christopher Tietjens needs a good woman's backing. . . . He's a splendid fellow. There are few young fellows for whom I have more . . . I could almost say respect. . . . But he needs that. To ballast him.'

In the car, running down the hill from Mountby, Macmaster had exhausted himself in the effort to restrain his execrations of the General. He wanted to shout that he was a pig-headed old fool: a meddlesome ass. But he was in the car with the two secretaries of the Cabinet Minister: the Rt. Hon. Edward Fenwick Waterhouse, who, being himself an advanced Liberal down for a week-end of golf, preferred not to dine at the house of the Conservative member. At that date there was, in politics, a phase of bitter social feud between the parties: a condition that had not till lately been characteristic of English political life. The prohibition had not extended itself to the two younger men.

Macmaster was not unpleasurably aware that these two fellows treated him with a certain deference. They had seen Macmaster being talked to familiarly by General Lord Campion. Indeed, they and the car had been kept waiting whilst the General patted their fellow guest on the shoulder; held his upper arm and spoke in a low voice into his ear. . . .

But that was the only pleasure that Macmaster got out of it.

Yes, the day had begun disastrously with Sylvia's letter; it ended—if it was ended!—almost more disastrously with the General's eulogy of that woman. During the day he had nerved himself to having an immensely disagreeable scene with Tietjens. Tietjens *must* divorce the woman; it was necessary for the peace of mind of himself, of his friends, of his family; for the sake of his career; in the very name of decency!

In the meantime Tietjens had rather forced his hand. It had been a most disagreeable affair. They had arrived at Rye in time for lunch—at which Tietjens had consumed the best part of a bottle of Burgundy. During lunch Tietjens had given Macmaster Sylvia's letter to read, saying that, as he should later consult his friend, his friend had better be made acquainted with the document.

The letter had appeared extraordinary in its effrontery, for it said nothing. Beyond the bare statement, 'I am now ready to return to you,' it occupied itself simply with the fact that Mrs Tietjens wanted—could no longer get on without—the services of her maid, whom she called Hullo Central. If Tietjens wanted her, Mrs Tietjens, to return to him he was to see that Hullo Central was waiting on the doorstep for her, and so on. She added the detail that there was *no one else*, underlined, she could bear round her while she was retiring for the night. On reflection Macmaster could see that this was the best letter the woman could have written if she wanted to be taken back; for, had

she extended herself into either excuses or explanations, it
was ten chances to one Tietjens would have taken the line
that he couldn't go on living with a woman capable of such
a lapse in taste. But Macmaster had never thought of Sylvia
as wanting in *savoir faire*.

It had, none the less, hardened him in his determination
to urge his friend to divorce. He had intended to begin this
campaign in the fly, driving to pay his call on the Rev. Mr
Duchemin, who, in early life, had been a personal disciple
of Mr Ruskin and a patron and acquaintance of the poet-
painter, the subject of Macmaster's monograph. On this
drive Tietjens preferred not to come. He said that he would
loaf about the town and meet Macmaster at the golf club
towards four-thirty. He was not in the mood for making
new acquaintances. Macmaster, who knew the pressure
under which his friend must be suffering, thought this
reasonable enough, and drove off up Iden Hill by himself.

Few women had ever made so much impression on
Macmaster as Mrs Duchemin. He knew himself to be in a
mood to be impressed by almost any woman, but he considered that that was not enough to account for the very
strong influence she at once exercised over him. There had
been two young girls in the drawing-room when he had
been ushered in, but they had disappeared almost simul-
taneously, and although he had noticed them immediately
afterwards riding past the window on bicycles, he was
aware that he would not have recognized them again. From
her first words on rising to greet him: 'Not *the* Mr Macmaster!' he had had eyes for no one else.

It was obvious that the Rev. Mr Duchemin must be one
of those clergymen of considerable wealth and cultured
taste who not infrequently adorn the Church of England.
The rectory itself, a great, warm-looking manor house of
very old red brick, was abutted on to by one of the largest
tithe barns that Macmaster had ever seen; the church itself,
with a primitive roof of oak shingles, nestled in the corner
formed by the ends of rectory and tithe barn, and was by so

much the smallest of the three and so undecorated that but
for its little belfry it might have been a good cow-byre. All
three buildings stood on the very edge of the little row of
hills that looks down on the Romney Marsh; they were
sheltered from the north wind by a great symmetrical fan
of elms and from the south-west by a very tall hedge and
shrubbery, all of remarkable yews. It was, in short, an ideal
cure of souls for a wealthy clergyman of cultured tastes, for
there was not so much as a peasant's cottage within a mile
of it.

To Macmaster, in short, this was the ideal English home.
Of Mrs Duchemin's drawing-room itself, contrary to his
habit, for he was sensitive and observant in such things, he
could afterwards remember little except that it was perfectly sympathetic. Three long windows gave on to a
perfect lawn, on which, isolated and grouped, stood standard rose trees, symmetrical half globes of green foliage
picked out with flowers like bits of carved pink marble.
Beyond the lawn was a low stone wall; beyond that the
quiet expanse of the marsh shimmered in the sunlight.

The furniture of the room was, as to its woodwork,
brown, old, with the rich softnesses of much polishing with
beeswax. What pictures there were Macmaster recognized
at once as being by Simeon Solomon, one of the weaker
and more frail aesthetes—aureoled, palish heads of ladies
carrying lilies that were not very like lilies. They were in
the tradition—but not the best of the tradition. Macmaster
understood—and later Mrs Duchemin confirmed him in
the idea—that Mr Duchemin kept his more precious specimens of work in a sanctum, leaving to the relatively public
room, good-humouredly and with slight contempt, these
weaker specimens. That seemed to stamp Mr Duchemin
at once as being of the elect.

Mr Duchemin in person was, however, not present; and
there seemed to be a good deal of difficulty in arranging a
meeting between the two men. Mr Duchemin, his wife said,
was much occupied at the week-ends. She added, with a
faint and rather absent smile, the word, 'Naturally.' Mac-

master at once saw that it was natural for a clergyman to
be much occupied during the week-ends. With a little hesi-
tation Mrs Duchemin suggested that Mr Macmaster and
his friend might come to lunch on the next day—Saturday.
But Macmaster had made an engagement to play the foursome with General Campion—half the round from twelve
till one-thirty: half the round from three to half-past four.
And, as their then present arrangements stood, Macmaster
and Tietjens were to take the 6.30 train to Hythe; that
ruled out either tea or dinner next day.

With sufficient, but not too extravagant regret, Mrs
Duchemin raised her voice to say:

'Oh dear! Oh dear! But you must see my husband and
the pictures after you have come so far.'

A rather considerable volume of harsh sound was coming
through the end wall of the room—the barking of dogs,
apparently the hurried removal of pieces of furniture or perhaps of packing cases, guttural ejaculations. Mrs Duchemin
said, with her far-away air and deep voice:

'They are making a good deal of noise. Let us go into
the garden and look at my husband's roses, if you've a
moment more to give us.'

Macmaster quoted to himself:

' "I looked and saw your eyes in the shadow of your
hair...." '

There was no doubt that Mrs Duchemin's eyes, which
were of a dark, pebble blue, were actually in the shadow of
her blue-black, very regularly waved hair. The hair came
down on the square, low forehead. It was a phenomenon
that Macmaster had never before really seen, and, he congratulated himself, this was one more confirmation—if
confirmation were needed!—of the powers of observation
of the subject of his monograph!

Mrs Duchemin bore the sunlight! Her dark complexion
was clear; there was, over the cheekbones, a delicate suf-
fusion of light carmine. Her jawbone was singularly clear-
cut, to the pointed chin—like an alabaster, mediaeval
saint's.

She said:

'Of course you're Scotch. I'm from Auld Reekie myself.'

Macmaster would have known it. He said he was from the Port of Leith. He could not imagine hiding anything from Mrs Duchemin. Mrs Duchemin said with renewed insistence:

'Oh, but of *course* you must see my husband and the pictures. Let me see. . . . We must think. . . . Would breakfast now . . . ?'

Macmaster said that he and his friend were Government servants and up to rising early. He had a great desire to breakfast in that house. She said:

'At a quarter to ten, then, our car will be at the bottom of your street. It's a matter of ten minutes only, so you won't go hungry long!'

She said, gradually gaining animation, that of course Macmaster would bring his friend. He could tell Tietjens that he should meet a very charming girl. She stopped and added suddenly: 'Probably, at any rate.' She said the name which Macmaster caught as 'Wanstead.' And possibly another girl. And Mr Horsted, or something like it, her husband's junior curate. She said reflectively:

'Yes, we might try quite a party . . .' and added, 'quite noisy and gay. I hope your friend's talkative!' Macmaster said something about trouble.

'Oh, it can't be too much trouble,' she said. 'Besides it might do my husband good.' She went on: 'Mr Duchemin is apt to brood. It's perhaps too lonely here.' And added the rather astonishing words: 'After all.'

And, driving back in the fly, Macmaster said to himself that you couldn't call Mrs Duchemin ordinary, at least. Yet meeting her was like going into a room that you had long left and never ceased to love. It felt good. It was perhaps partly her Edinburgh-ness. Macmaster allowed himself to coin that word. There was in Edinburgh a society—he himself had never been privileged to move in it, but its annals are part of the literature of Scotland!—where the

ladies are all great ladies in tall drawing-rooms; circumspect yet shrewd: still yet with a sense of the comic: frugal
yet warmly hospitable. It was perhaps just Edinburgh-ness
that was wanting in the drawing-rooms of his friends in
London. Mrs Cressy, the Hon. Mrs Limoux and Mrs
Delawnay were all almost perfection in manner, in speech,
in composure. But, then they were not young, they weren't
Edinburgh—and they weren't strikingly elegant!

Mrs Duchemin was all three. Her assured, tranquil
manner she would retain to any age: it betokened the
enigmatic soul of her sex, but, physically, she couldn't be
more than thirty. That was unimportant, for she would
never want to do anything in which physical youth
counted. She would never, for instance, have occasion to
run: she would always just 'move'—floatingly! He tried
to remember the details of her dress.

It had certainly been dark blue—and certainly of silk:
that rather coarsely woven, exquisite material that has on
it folds as of a silvery shimmer with minute knots. But very
dark blue. And it contrived to be at once artistic—absolutely in the tradition! And yet well cut! Very large
sleeves, of course, but still with a certain fit. She had worn
an immense necklace of yellow polished amber: on the
dark blue! And Mrs Duchemin had said, over her husband's roses, that the blossoms always reminded her of
little mouldings of pink cloud come down for the cooling
of the earth. . . . A charming thought!

Suddenly he said to himself:

'What a mate for Tietjens!' And his mind added: 'Why
should she not become an Influence!'

A vista opened before him in time! He imagined
Tietjens, in some way proprietarily responsible for Mrs
Duchemin: quite *pour le bon*, tranquilly passionate and
accepted, *motif*; and 'immensely improved' by the association. And himself, in a year or two, bringing the at last
found Lady of his Delight to sit at the feet of Mrs
Duchemin—the Lady of his Delight whilst circumspect
would be also young and impressionable!—to learn the

3*

mysterious assuredness of manner, the gift of dressing, the knack of wearing amber and bending over standard roses—and the Edinburgh-ness!

Macmaster was thus not a little excited, and finding Tietjens at tea amid the green-stained furnishings and illustrated papers of the large, corrugated-iron golf-house, he could not help exclaiming:

'I've accepted the invitation to breakfast with the Duchemins to-morrow for us both. I hope you won't mind,' although Tietjens was sitting at a little table with General Campion and his brother-in-law, the Hon. Paul Sandbach, Conservative member for the division and husband of Lady Claudine. The General said pleasantly to Tietjens:

'Breakfast! With Duchemin! You go, my boy! You'll get the best breakfast you ever had in your life.'

He added to his brother-in-law: 'Not the eternal mock kedgeree Claudine gives us every morning.'

Sandbach grunted:

'It's not for want of trying to steal their cook. Claudine has a shy at it every time we come down here.'

The General said pleasantly to Macmaster—he spoke always pleasantly, with a half smile and a slight sibilance:

'My brother-in-law isn't serious, you understand. My sister wouldn't think of stealing a cook. Let alone from Duchemin. She'd be frightened to.'

Sandbach grunted:

'Who wouldn't?'

Both these gentlemen were very lame: Mr Sandbach from birth and the General as the result of a slight but neglected motor accident. He had practically only one vanity, the belief that he was qualified to act as his own chauffeur, and since he was both inexpert and very careless, he met with frequent accidents. Mr Sandbach had a dark, round, bull-dog face and a violent manner. He had twice been suspended from his Parliamentary duties for applying to the then Chancellor of the Exchequer the epithet 'lying attorney,' and he was at that moment still suspended.

Macmaster then became unpleasantly perturbed. With his sensitiveness he was perfectly aware of an unpleasant chill in the air. There was also a stiffness about Tietjens' eyes. He was looking straight before him; there was a silence too. Behind Tietjens' back were two men with bright green coats, red knitted waistcoats and florid faces. One was bald and blond, the other had black hair, remarkably oiled and shiny; both were forty-fivish. They were regarding the occupants of the Tietjens table with both their mouths slightly open. They were undisguisedly listening. In front of each were three empty sloe-gin glasses and one half-filled tumbler of brandy and soda. Macmaster understood why the General had explained that his sister had not tried to steal Mrs Duchemin's cook.

Tietjens said:

'Drink up your tea quickly and let's get started.' He was drawing from his pocket a number of telegraph forms which he began arranging. The General said:

'Don't burn your mouth. We can't start off before all . . . all these other gentlemen. We're too slow.'

'No, we're beastly well stuck,' Sandbach said.

Tietjens handed the telegraph forms to Macmaster.

'You'd better take a look at these,' he said. 'I mayn't see you again to-day after the match. You're dining up at Mountby. The General will run you up. Lady Claude will excuse me. I've got work to do.'

This was already matter for dismay for Macmaster. He was aware that Tietjens would have disliked dining up at Mountby with the Sandbachs, who would have a crowd, extremely smart but more than usually unintelligent. Tietjens called this crowd, indeed, the plague-spot of the party —meaning of Toryism. But Macmaster couldn't help thinking that a disagreeable dinner would be better for his friend than brooding in solitude in the black shadows of the huddled town. Then Tietjens said:

'I'm going to have a word with that swine!' He pointed his square chin rather rigidly before him, and looking past the two brandy drinkers, Macmaster saw one of those

faces that frequent caricature made familiar and yet
strange. Macmaster couldn't, at the moment, put a name to
it. It must be a politician, probably a Minister. But which?
His mind was already in a dreadful state. In the glimpse he
had caught of the telegraph form now in his hand, he had
perceived that it was addressed to Sylvia Tietjens and
began with the word 'agreed.' He said swiftly:

'Has that been sent or is it only a draft?'

Tietjens said:

'That fellow is the Rt. Hon. Stephen Fenwick Waterhouse. He's chairman of the Funded Debt Commission.
He's the swine who made us fake that return in the office.'

That moment was the worst Macmaster had ever known.
A worse came. Tietjens said:

'I'm going to have a word with him. That's why I'm not
dining at Mountby. It's a duty to the country.'

Macmaster's mind simply stopped. He was in a space,
all windows. There was sunlight outside. And clouds. Pink
and white. Woolly! Some ships. And two men: one dark
and oily, the other rather blotchy on a blond baldness.
They were talking, but their words made no impression on
Macmaster. The dark, oily man said that he was not going
to take Gertie to Budapest. Not half! He winked like a
nightmare. Beyond were two young men and a pre-
posterous face. . . . It was all so like a nightmare that the
Cabinet Minister's features were distorted for Macmaster.
Like an enormous mask of pantomime: shiny, with an immense nose and elongated, Chinese eyes.

Yet not unpleasant! Macmaster was a Whig by conviction, by nature, by temperament. He thought that
public servants should abstain from political activity.
Nevertheless, he couldn't be expected to think a Liberal
Cabinet Minister ugly. On the contrary, Mr Waterhouse
appeared to have a frank, humorous, kindly expression. He
listened deferentially to one of his secretaries, resting his
hand on the young man's shoulder, smiling a little, rather
sleepily. No doubt he was overworked. And then, letting
himself go in a side-shaking laugh. Putting on flesh!

What a pity! What a *pity*! Macmaster was reading a string of incomprehensible words in Tietjens' heavily scored writing. *Not entertain ... flat not house ... child remain at sister....* His eyes went backwards and forwards over the phrases. He could not connect the words without stops. The man with the oily hair said in a sickly voice that Gertie was hot stuff, but not the one for Budapest with all the Gitana girls you were telling me of! Why, he'd kept Gertie for five years now. More like the real thing! His friend's voice was like a result of indigestion. Tietjens, Sandbach and the General were stiff, like pokers.

What a pity! Macmaster thought.

He ought to have been sitting.... It would have been pleasant and right to be sitting with the pleasant Minister. In the ordinary course he, Macmaster, would have been. The best golfer in the place was usually set to play with distinguished visitors, and there was next to no one in the south of England who ordinarily could beat him. He had begun at four, playing with a miniature cleek and a found shilling ball over the municipal links. Going to the poor school every morning and back to dinner; and back to school and back to bed! Over the cold, rushy, sandy links, beside the grey sea. Both shoes full of sand. The found shilling ball had lasted him three years....

Macmaster exclaimed: 'Good God.' He had just gathered from the telegram that Tietjens meant to go to Germany on Tuesday. As if at Macmaster's ejaculation, Tietjens said:

'Yes. It *is* unbearable. If you don't stop those swine, General, I shall.'

The General sibilated low, between his teeth:

'Wait a minute.... Wait a minute.... Perhaps that other fellow will.'

The man with the black oily hair said:

'If Budapest's the place for the girls you say it is, old pal, with the Turkish baths and all, we'll paint the old town red all right next month,' and he winked at Tietjens. His friend, with his head down, seemed to make internal rumblings, looking apprehensively beneath his blotched forehead at the General.

'Not,' the other continued argumentatively, 'that I don't love my old woman. She's all right. And then there's Gertie. 'Ot stuff, but the real thing. But I say a man wants...' He ejaculated, 'Oh!'

The General, his hands in his pockets, very tall, thin, red-cheeked, his white hair combed forward in a fringe, sauntered towards the other table. It was not two yards, but it seemed a long saunter. He stood right over them, they looking up, open-eyed, like schoolboys at a balloon. He said:

'I'm glad you're enjoying our links, gentlemen.'

The bald man said: 'We are! We are! First-class. A treat!'

'But,' the General said, 'it isn't wise to discuss one's ... eh ... domestic circumstances ... at ... at mess, you know, or in a golf house. People might hear.'

The gentleman with the oily hair half rose and exclaimed:

'Oo, the ...' The other man mumbled: 'Shut up, Briggs.'

The General said:

'I'm the president of the club, you know. It's my duty to see that the *majority* of the club and its visitors are pleased. I hope you don't mind.'

The General came back to his seat. He was trembling with vexation.

'It makes one as beastly a bounder as themselves,' he said. 'But what the devil else was one to do?' The two city men had ambled hastily into the dressing-rooms; the dire silence fell. Macmaster realised that, for these Tories at least, this was really the end of the world. The last of England! He returned, with panic in his heart, to Tietjens' telegram. ... Tietjens was going to Germany on Tuesday. He offered to throw over the department. ... These were unthinkable things. You couldn't imagine them!

He began to read the telegram all over again. A shadow

fell upon the flimsy sheets. The Rt. Hon. Mr Waterhouse was between the head of the table and the windows.
He said:

'We're much obliged, General. It was impossible to hear
ourselves speak for those obscene fellows' smut. It's
fellows like that make our friends the suffragettes! That
warrants them. . . .' He added: 'Hullo! Sandbach! Enjoying your rest?'

The General said:

'I was hoping you'd take on the job of telling these
fellows off.'

Mr Sandbach, his bull-dog jaw sticking out, the short
black hair on his scalp appearing to rise, barked:

'Hullo, Waterslop! Enjoying your plunder?'

Mr Waterhouse, tall, slouching and untidy-haired, lifted
the flaps of his coat. It was so ragged that it appeared as if
straws stuck out of the elbows.

'All that the suffragettes have left of me,' he said laughingly. 'Isn't one of you fellows a genius called Tietjens?'
He was looking at Macmaster. The General said:

'Tietjens . . . Macmaster . . .' The Minister went on very
friendly:

'Oh, it's you? . . . I just wanted to take the opportunity
of thanking you.'

Tietjens said:

'Good God! What for?'

'*You* know!' the Minister said, 'we couldn't have got the
Bill before the House till next session without your figures.
. . .' He said slyly: 'Could we, Sandbach?' and added to
Tietjens: 'Ingleby told me. . . .'

Tietjens was chalk-white and stiffened. He stuttered:

'I can't take any credit. . . . I consider . . .'

Macmaster exclaimed:

'Tietjens . . . you . . .' he didn't know what he was going
to say.

'Oh, you're too modest,' Mr Waterhouse overwhelmed
Tietjens. 'We know whom we've to thank . . .' His eyes
drifted to Sandbach a little absently. Then his face lit up.

'Oh! Look here, Sandbach,' he said. . . . 'Come here, will you?' He walked a pace or two away, calling to one of his young men: 'Oh, Sanderson, give the bobbie a drink. A good stiff one.' Sandbach jerked himself awkwardly out of his chair and limped to the Minister.

Tietjens burst out:

'Me too modest! *Me*! . . . The swine . . . The unspeakable swine!'

The General said:

'What's it all about, Chrissie? You probably are too modest.'

Tietjens said:

'Damn it. It's a serious matter. It's driving me out of the unspeakable office I'm in.'

Macmaster said:

'No! No! You're wrong. It's a wrong view you take.' And with a good deal of real passion he began to explain to the General. It was an affair that had already given him a great deal of pain. The Government had asked the statistical department for figures illuminating a number of schedules that they desired to use in presenting their new Bill to the Commons. Mr Waterhouse was to present it.

Mr Waterhouse at the moment was slapping Mr Sandbach on the back, tossing the hair out of his eyes and laughing like an hysterical schoolgirl. He looked suddenly tired. A police constable, his buttons shining, appeared, drinking from a pewter-pot outside the glazed door. The two city men ran across the angle from the dressing-room to the same door, buttoning their clothes. The Minister said loudly:

'Make it guineas!'

It seemed to Macmaster painfully wrong that Tietjens should call anyone so genial and unaffected an unspeakable swine. It was unjust. He went on with his explanation to the General.

The Government had wanted a set of figures based on a calculation called B 7. Tietjens, who had been working on one called H 19—for his own instruction—had persuaded himself that H 19 was the lowest figure that was actuarially sound.

The General said pleasantly: 'All this is Greek to me.'

'Oh no, it needn't be,' Macmaster heard himself say. 'It amounts to this. Chrissie was asked by the Government— by Sir Reginald Ingleby—to work out what 3 × 3 comes to: it was that sort of thing in principle. He said that the only figure that would not ruin the country was nine times nine. . . .'

'The Government wanted to shovel money into the working man's pockets, in fact,' the General said. 'Money for nothing . . . or votes, I suppose.'

'But that isn't the point, sir,' Macmaster ventured to say. 'All that Chrissie was asked to do was to say what 3 × 3 was.'

'Well, he appears to have done it and earned no end of kudos,' the General said. 'That's all right. We've all, always, believed in Chrissie's ability. But he's a strong-tempered beggar.'

'He was extraordinarily rude to Sir Reginald over it,' Macmaster went on.

The General said:

'Oh dear! Oh dear!' He shook his head at Tietjens and assumed with care the blank, slightly disappointing air of the regular officer. 'I don't like to hear of rudeness to a superior. In *any* service.'

'I don't think,' Tietjens said with extreme mildness, 'that Macmaster is quite fair to me. Of course he's a right to his opinion as to what the discipline of a service demands. I certainly told Ingleby that I'd rather resign than do that beastly job. . . .'

'You shouldn't have,' the General said. 'What would become of the services if everyone did as you did?'

Sandbach came back laughing and dropped painfully into his low arm-chair.

'That fellow . . .' he began.

The General slightly raised his hand.

'A minute!' he said. 'I was about to tell Chrissie, here,

that if I am offered the job—of course it's an order really —of suppressing the Ulster Volunteers ... I'd rather cut my throat than do it. ...'

Sandbach said:

'Of course you would, old chap. They're our brothers. You'd see the beastly, lying Government damned first.'

'I was going to say that I should accept,' the General said, 'I shouldn't resign my commission.'

Sandbach said:

'Good *God*!'

Tietjens said:

'Well, I didn't.'

Sandbach exclaimed:

'General! You! After all Claudine and I have said. ...'

Tietjens interrupted:

'Excuse me, Sandbach. I'm receiving this reprimand for the moment. I wasn't, then, rude to Ingleby. If I'd expressed contempt for what he said or for himself, that would have been rude. I didn't. He wasn't in the least offended. He looked like a cockatoo, but he wasn't offended. And I let him over-persuade me. He was right, really. He pointed out that, if I didn't do the job, those swine would put on one of our little competition wallah head clerks and get all the schedules faked, as well as starting off with false premises!'

'That's the view I take,' the General said, 'if I don't take the Ulster job the Government will put on a fellow who'll burn all the farm-houses and rape all the women in the three counties. They've got him up their sleeve. He only asks for the Connaught Rangers to go through the north with. And you know what *that* means. All the same ...' He looked at Tietjens: 'One should not be rude to one's superiors.'

'I tell you I wasn't rude,' Tietjens exclaimed. 'Damn your nice, paternal old eyes. Get that into your mind!'

The General shook his head:

'You brilliant fellows!' he said. 'The country, or the army, or anything, could not be run by you. It takes stupid

fools like me and Sandbach, along with sound moderate
heads like our friend here.' He indicated Macmaster and,
rising, went on: 'Come along. You're playing me, Macmaster. They say you're hot stuff. Chrissie's no good. He
can take Sandbach on.'

He walked off with Macmaster towards the dressing-
room.

Sandbach, wriggling awkwardly out of his chair,
shouted:

'Save the country.... Damn it....' He stood on his
feet. 'I and Campion ... Look at what the country's come
to.... What with swine like these two in our club houses!
And policemen to go round the links with Ministers to
protect them from the wild women.... By God! I'd like
to have the flaying of the skin off some of their backs I
would. My God I would.'

He added:

'That fellow Waterslops is a bit of a sportsman. I
haven't been able to tell you about our bet, you've been
making such a noise.... Is your friend really plus one at
North Berwick? What are you like?'

'Macmaster is a good plus two anywhere when he's in
practice.'

Sandbach said:

'Good Lord.... A stout fellow....'

'As for me,' Tietjens said, 'I loathe the beastly game.'

'So do I,' Sandbach answered. 'We'll just lollop along
behind them.'

IV

They came out into the bright open where all the distances
under the tall sky showed with distinct prismatic outlines.
They made a little group of seven—for Tietjens would not
have a caddy—waiting on the flat, first teeing ground.
Macmaster walked up to Tietjens and said under his
voice:

'You've really *sent* that wire? . . .'

Tietjens said:

'It'll be in Germany by now!'

Mr Sandbach hobbled from one to the other explaining the terms of his wager with Mr Waterhouse. Mr Waterhouse had backed one of the young men playing with him to drive into and hit twice in the eighteen holes the two city men who would be playing ahead of them. As the Minister had taken rather short odds, Mr Sandbach considered him a good sport.

A long way down the first hole Mr Waterhouse and his two companions were approaching the first green. They had high sandhills to the right and, to their left, a road that was fringed with rushes and a narrow dyke. Ahead of the Cabinet Minister the two city men and their two caddies stood on the edge of the dyke or poked downwards into the rushes. Two girls appeared and disappeared on the tops of the sandhills. The policeman was strolling along the road, level with Mr Waterhouse. The General said:

'I think we could go now.'

Sandbach said:

'Waterslops will get a hit at them from the next tee. They're in the dyke.'

The General drove a straight, goodish ball. Just as Macmaster was in his swing Sandbach shouted:

'By God! He nearly did it. See that fellow jump!'

Macmaster looked round over his shoulder and hissed with vexation between his teeth:

'Don't you know that you don't shout while a man is driving? Or haven't you played golf?' He hurried fussily after his ball.

Sandbach said to Tietjens:

'Golly! That chap's got a temper!'

Tietjens said:

'Only over this game. You deserved what you got.'

Sandbach said:

'I did. . . . But I didn't spoil his shot. He's outdriven the General twenty yards.'

Tietjens said:

'It would have been sixty but for you.'

They loitered about on the tee waiting for the others to get their distance. Sandbach said:

'By Jove, your friend is on with his second. . . . You wouldn't believe it of such a *little* beggar!' He added: 'He's not much class, is he?'

Tietjens looked down his nose.

'Oh, about *our* class!' he said. 'He wouldn't take a bet about driving into the couple ahead.'

Sandbach hated Tietjens for being a Tietjens of Groby: Tietjens was enraged by the existence of Sandbach, who was the son of an ennobled mayor of Middlesbrough, seven miles or so from Groby. The feuds between the Cleveland landowners and the Cleveland plutocrats are very bitter. Sandbach said:

'Ah, I suppose he gets you out of scrapes with girls and the Treasury, and you take him about in return. It's a practical combination.'

'Like Pottle Mills and Stanton,' Tietjens said. The financial operations connected with the amalgamating of these two steelworks had earned Sandbach's father a good deal of odium in the Cleveland district. . . . Sandbach said:

'Look here, Tietjens. . . .' But he changed his mind and said:

'We'd better go now.' He drove off with an awkward action but not without skill. He certainly outplayed Tietjens.

Playing very slowly, for both were desultory and Sandbach very lame, they lost sight of the others behind some coastguard cottages and dunes before they had left the third tee. Because of his game leg Sandbach sliced a good deal. On this occasion he sliced right into the gardens of the cottages and went with his boy to look for his ball among potato-haulms, beyond a low wall. Tietjens patted his own ball lazily up the fairway and, dragging his bag behind him by the strap, he sauntered on.

Although Tietjens hated golf as he hated any occupation that was of a competitive nature, he could engross himself in the mathematics of trajectories when he accompanied Macmaster in one of his expeditions for practice. He accompanied Macmaster because he liked there to be one pursuit at which his friend undisputably excelled himself, for it was a bore always brow-beating the fellow. But he stipulated that they should visit three different and, if possible, unknown courses every week-end when they golfed. He interested himself then in the way the courses were laid out, acquiring thus an extraordinary connoisseurship in golf architecture, and he made abstruse calculations as to the flight of balls off sloped club-faces, as to the foot-poundals of energy exercised by one muscle or the other, and as to theories of spin. As often as not he palmed Macmaster off as a fair, average player on some other unfortunate fair, average stranger. Then he passed the afternoon in the club-house studying the pedigrees and forms of racehorses, for every club-house contained a copy of Ruff's Guide. In the spring he would hunt for and examine the nests of soft-billed birds, for he was interested in the domestic affairs of the cuckoo, though he hated natural history and field botany.

On this occasion he had just examined some notes of other mashie shots, had put the notebook back in his pocket, and had addressed his ball with a niblick that had an unusually roughened face and a head like a hatchet. Meticulously, when he had taken his grip he removed his little and third fingers from the leather of the shaft. He was thanking heaven that Sandbach seemed to be accounted for for ten minutes at least, for Sandbach was miserly over lost balls and, very slowly, he was raising his mashie to half cock for a sighting shot.

He was aware that someone, breathing a little heavily from small lungs, was standing close to him and watching him: he could indeed, beneath his cap-rim, perceive the tips of a pair of boy's white sand-shoes. It in no way perturbed him to be watched, since he was avid of no personal glory when making his shots. A voice said:

'I say . . .' He continued to look at his ball.

'Sorry to spoil your shot,' the voice said. 'But . . .'

Tietjens dropped his club altogether and straightened his back. A fair young woman with a fixed scowl was looking at him intently. She had a short skirt and was panting a little.

'I say,' she said, 'go and see they don't hurt Gertie. I've lost her . . .' She pointed back to the sandhills. 'There looked to be some beasts among them.'

She seemed a perfectly negligible girl except for the frown: her eyes blue, her hair no doubt fair under a white canvas hat. She had a striped cotton blouse, but her fawn tweed skirt was well hung.

Tietjens said:

'You've been demonstrating.'

She said:

'Of course we have, and of course you object on principle. But you won't let a girl be man-handled. Don't wait to tell me, I know it. . . .'

Noises existed. Sandbach, from beyond the low garden wall fifty yards away, was yelping, just like a dog: 'Hi! Hi! Hi! Hi!' and gesticulating. His little caddy, entangled in his golfbag, was trying to scramble over the wall. On top of a high sandhill stood the policeman: he waved his arms like a windmill and shouted. Beside him and behind, slowly rising, were the heads of the General, Macmaster and their two boys. Farther along, in completion, were appearing the figures of Mr Waterhouse, his two companions and *their* three boys. The Minister was waving his driver and shouting. They all shouted.

'A regular rat-hunt,' the girl said; she was counting. 'Eleven and two more caddies!' She exhibited satisfaction. 'I headed them all off except two beasts. They couldn't run. But neither can Gertie. . . .'

She said urgently:

'Come along! You aren't going to leave Gertie to those beasts! They're drunk. . . .'

Tietjens said:

'Cut away then. I'll look after Gertie.' He picked up his bag.

'No, I'll come with you,' the girl said.

Tietjens answered: 'Oh, you don't want to go to gaol. Clear out!'

She said:

'Nonsense. I've put up with worse than that. Nine months as a slavey. . . . Come *along*!'

Tietjens started to run—rather like a rhinoceros seeing purple. He had been violently spurred, for he had been pierced by a shrill, faint scream. The girl ran beside him.

'You . . . can . . . run!' she panted, 'put on a spurt.'

Screams protesting against physical violence were at that date rare things in England. Tietjens had never heard the like. It upset him frightfully, though he was aware only of an expanse of open country. The policeman, whose buttons made him noteworthy, was descending his conical sand-hill, diagonally, with caution. There is something grotesque about a town policeman, silvered helmet and all, in the open country. It was so clear and still in the air; Tietjens felt as if he were in a light museum looking at specimens. . . .

A little young woman, engrossed, like a hunted rat, came round the corner of a green mound. 'This is an assaulted female!' the mind of Tietjens said to him. She had a black skirt covered with sand, for she had just rolled down the sandhill; she had a striped grey and black silk blouse, one shoulder torn completely off, so that a white camisole showed. Over the shoulder of the sandhill came the two city men, flushed with triumph and panting; their red knitted waistcoats moved like bellows. The black-haired one, his eyes lurid and obscene, brandished aloft a fragment of black and grey stuff. He shouted hilariously:

'Strip the bitch naked! . . . Ugh . . . Strip the bitch stark naked!' and jumped down the little hill. He cannoned into Tietjens, who roared at the top of his voice:

'You infernal swine. I'll knock your head off if you move!'

Behind Tietjens' back the girl said:

'Come along, Gertie.... It's only to there...'

A voice panted in answer:

'I ... can't.... My heart...'

Tietjens kept his eye upon the city man. His jaw had fallen down, his eyes stared! It was as if the bottom of his assured world, where all men desire in their hearts to bash women, had fallen out. He panted:

'Ergle! Ergle!'

Another scream, a little farther than the last voices from behind his back, caused in Tietjens a feeling of intense weariness. What did beastly women want to scream for? He swung round, bag and all. The policeman, his face scarlet like a lobster just boiled, was lumbering unenthusiastically towards the two girls who were trotting towards the dyke. One of his hands, scarlet also, was extended. He was not a yard from Tietjens.

Tietjens was exhausted, beyond thinking or shouting. He slipped his clubs off his shoulder and, as if he were pitching his kit-bag into a luggage van, threw the whole lot between the policeman's running legs. The man, who had no impetus to speak of, pitched forward on to his hands and knees. His helmet over his eyes, he seemed to reflect for a moment; then he removed his helmet and with great deliberation rolled round and sat on the turf. His face was completely without emotion, long, sandy-moustached and rather shrewd. He mopped his brow with a carmine handkerchief that had white spots.

Tietjens walked up to him.

'Clumsy of me!' he said. 'I hope you're not hurt.' He drew from his breast pocket a curved silver flask. The policeman said nothing. His world, too, contained uncertainties, and he was profoundly glad to be able to sit still without discredit. He muttered:

'Shaken. A bit! Anybody would be!'

That let him out and he fell to examining with attention the bayonet catch of the flask top. Tietjens opened it for him. The two girls, advancing at a fatigued trot, were near the dyke side. The fair girl, as they trotted, was trying to adjust her companion's hat; attached by pins to the back of her hair it flapped on her shoulder.

All the rest of the posse were advancing at a very slow walk, in a converging semi-circle. Two little caddies were running, but Tietjens saw them check, hesitate and stop. And there floated to Tietjens' ears the words:

'Stop, you little devils. She'll knock your heads off.'

The Rt. Hon. Mr Waterhouse must have found an admirable voice trainer somewhere. The drab girl was balancing tremulously over a plank on the dyke; the other took it at a jump; up in the air—down on her feet; perfectly business-like. And, as soon as the other girl was off the plank, she was down on her knees before it, pulling it towards her, the other girl trotting away over the vast marsh field.

The girl dropped the plank on the grass. Then she looked up and faced the men and boys who stood in a row on the road. She called in a shrill, high voice, like a young cockerel's:

'Seventeen to two! The usual male odds! You'll *have* to go round by Camber railway bridge, and we'll be in Folkestone by then. We've got bicycles!' She was half going when she checked and, searching out Tietjens to address, exclaimed: 'I'm sorry I said that. Because some of you didn't want to catch us. But some of you *did*. And you *were* seventeen to two.' She addressed Mr Waterhouse:

'Why *don't* you give women the vote?' she said. 'You'll find it will interfere a good deal with your indispensable golf if you don't. Then what becomes of the nation's health?'

Mr Waterhouse said:

'If you'll come and discuss it quietly . . .'

She said:

'Oh, tell that to the marines,' and turned away, the men in a row watching her figure disappear into the distance of the flat land. Not one of them was inclined to risk that jump: there was nine foot of mud in the bottom of the dyke. It was quite true that, the plank being removed, to go after the women they would have had to go several miles round. It had been a well-thought-out raid. Mr Waterhouse said that girl was a ripping girl: the others found her just ordinary. Mr Sandbach, who had only lately ceased to shout: 'Hi!' wanted to know what they were going to do about catching the women, but Mr Waterhouse said: 'Oh, chuck it, Sandy,' and went off.

Mr Sandbach refused to continue his match with Tietjens. He said that Tietjens was the sort of fellow who was the ruin of England. He said he had a good mind to issue a warrant for the arrest of Tietjens—for obstructing the course of justice. Tietjens pointed out that Sandbach wasn't a borough magistrate and so couldn't. And Sandbach went off, dot and carry one, and began a furious row with the two city men who had retreated to a distance. He said they were the sort of men who were the ruin of England. They bleated like rams. . . .

Tietjens wandered slowly up the course, found his ball, made his shot with care and found that the ball deviated several feet less to the right of a straight line than he had expected. He tried the shot again, obtained the same result and tabulated his observations in his notebook. He sauntered slowly back towards the club-house. He was content.

He felt himself to be content for the first time in four months. His pulse beat calmly; the heat of the sun all over him appeared to be a beneficent flood. On the flanks of the older and larger sandhills he observed the minute herbage, mixed with little purple aromatic plants. To these the constant nibbling of sheep had imparted a protective tininess. He wandered, content, round the sandhills to the small, silted harbour mouth. After reflecting for some time on the wave-curves in the sloping mud of the water sides, he had a long conversation, mostly in signs, with a Finn who hung over the side of a tarred, stump-masted, battered vessel that had a gaping, splintered hole where the anchor should have hung. She came from Archangel; was of several hundred tons burthen, was knocked together anyhow, of soft wood, for about ninety pounds, and launched, sink or swim, in the timber trade. Beside her, taut, glistening with brasswork, was a new fishing boat, just built here for the Lowestoft fleet. Ascertaining her price from a man who was finishing her painting, Tietjens reckoned that you could have built three of the Archangel timber ships for the cost of that boat, and that the Archangel vessel would earn about twice as much per hour per ton....

It was in that way his mind worked when he was fit: it picked up little pieces of definite, workmanlike information. When it had enough it classified them: not for any purpose, but because to know things was agreeable and gave a feeling of strength, of having in reserve something that the other fellow would not suspect.... He passed a long, quiet, abstracted afternoon.

In the dressing-room he found the General, among lockers, old coats and stoneware washing-basins set in scrubbed wood. The General leaned back against a row of these things.

'You are the ruddy *limit*!' he exclaimed.

Tietjens said:

'Where's Macmaster?'

The General said he had sent Macmaster off with Sandbach in the two-seater. Macmaster had to dress before going up to Mountby. He added: 'The *ruddy* limit!' again.

'Because I knocked the bobbie over?' Tietjens asked. 'He liked it.'

The General said:

'Knocked the bobbie over ... I didn't see that.'

'He didn't want to catch the girls,' Tietjens said, 'you could see him—oh, yearning not to.'

'I don't want to know anything about that,' the General
said. 'I shall hear enough about it from Paul Sandbach.
Give the bobbie a quid and let's hear no more of it. I'm
a magistrate.'

'Then what have I done?' Tietjens said. 'I helped those
girls to get off. *You* didn't want to catch them; Waterhouse didn't, the policeman didn't. No one did except the
swine. Then what's the matter?'

'Damn it all!' the General said, 'don't you remember
that you're a young married man?'

With the respect for the General's superior age and
achievements, Tietjens stopped himself laughing.

'If you're really serious, sir,' he said, 'I always remember
it very carefully. I don't suppose you're suggesting that
I've ever shown want of respect for Sylvia.'

The General shook his head.

'I don't know,' he said. 'And, damn it all, I'm worried.
I'm ... Hang it all, I'm your father's oldest friend.' The
General looked indeed worn and saddened in the light of
the sand-drifted, ground-glass windows. He said: 'Was
that skirt a ... a friend of yours? Had you arranged it
with her?'

Tietjens said:

'Wouldn't it be better, sir, if you said what you had on
your mind? ...'

The old General blushed a little.

'I don't like to,' he said straightforwardly. 'You brilliant
fellow ... I only want, my dear boy, to hint that ...'

Tietjens said, a little more stiffly:

'I'd prefer you to get it out, sir.... I acknowledge your
right as my father's oldest friend.'

'Then,' the General burst out, 'who was the skirt you
were lolloping up Pall Mall with? On the last day they
Trooped the Colour?... I didn't see her myself.... Was it
this same one? Paul said she looked like a cook maid.'

Tietjens made himself a little more rigid.

'She was, as a matter of fact, a bookmaker's secretary,'
Tietjens said. 'I imagine I have the right to walk where I

like, with whom I like. And no one has the right to question it. . . . I don't mean you, sir. But no one else.'

The General said puzzledly:

'It's you *brilliant* fellows. . . . They all say you're brilliant. . . .'

Tietjens said:

'You might let your rooted distrust of intelligence . . . It's natural of course; but you might let it allow you to be just to me. I assure you there was nothing discreditable.'

The General interrupted:

'If you were a stupid young subaltern and told me you were showing your mother's new cook the way to the Piccadilly tube, I'd believe you. . . . But, then, no young subaltern would do such a damn, blasted, tomfool thing! Paul said you walked beside her like the king in his glory! Through the crush outside the Haymarket, of all places in the world!'

'I'm obliged to Sandbach for his commendation. . . .' Tietjens said. He thought for a moment. Then he said:

'I was trying to get that young woman. . . . I was taking her out to lunch from her office at the bottom of the Haymarket. . . . To get her off a friend's back. That is, of course, between ourselves.'

He said this with great reluctance because he didn't want to cast reflection on Macmaster's taste, for the young lady had been by no means one to be seen walking with a really circumspect public official. But he had said nothing to indicate Macmaster, and he had other friends.

The General choked.

'Upon my soul,' he said, 'what do you take me for?' He repeated the words as if he were amazed. 'If,' he said, 'my G.S.O. II—who's the stupidest ass I know—told me such a damn-fool lie as that I'd have him broke to-morrow.' He went on expostulatorily: 'Damn it all, it's the first duty of a soldier—it's the first duty of all Englishmen—to be able to tell a good lie in answer to a charge. But a lie like that . . .'

He broke off breathless, then he began again:

'Hang it all, I told that lie to my grandmother and my grandfather told it to *his* grandfather. And they call you brilliant!...' He paused and then asked reproachfully: 'Or do you think I'm in a state of senile decay?'

Tietjens said:

'I know you, sir, to be the smartest general of division in the British Army. I leave you to draw your own conclusions as to why I said what I did....' He had told the exact truth, but he was not sorry to be disbelieved.

The General said:

'Then I'll take it that you tell me a lie meaning me to know that it's a lie. That's quite proper. I take it you mean to keep the woman officially out of it. But look here, Chrissie'—his tone took a deeper seriousness—'if the woman that's come between you and Sylvia—that's broken up your home, damn it, for that's what it is!—is little Miss Wannop...'

'Her name was Julia Mandelstein,' Tietjens said.

The General said:

'Yes! Yes! Of course!... But if it *is* the little Wannop girl and it's not gone too far ... Put her back ... Put her back, as you used to be a good boy! It would be too hard on the mother....'

Tietjens said:

'General! I give you my word...'

The General said:

'I'm not asking any questions, my boy; I'm talking now. You've told me the story you want told and it's the story I'll tell for you! But that little piece is ... she used to be! ... as straight as a die. I daresay you know better than I. Of course when they get among the wild women there's no knowing what happens to them. They say they're all whores.... I beg your pardon, if you like the girl...'

'Is Miss Wannop,' Tietjens asked, 'the girl who demonstrates?'

'Sandbach said,' the General went on, 'that he couldn't see from where he was whether that girl was the same as the one in the Haymarket. But he thought it was . . . He was pretty certain.'

'As he's married your sister,' Tietjens said, 'one can't impugn his taste in women.'

'I say again, I'm not asking,' the General said. 'But I do say again too: put her back. Her father was a great friend of your father's: or your father was a great admirer of his. They say he was the most brilliant brain of the party.'

'Of course I know who Professor Wannop was,' Tietjens said. 'There's nothing you could tell me about him.'

'I daresay not,' the General said drily. 'Then you know that he didn't leave a farthing when he died and the rotten Liberal Government wouldn't put his wife and children on the Civil List because he'd sometimes written for a Tory paper. And you know that the mother has had a deuced hard row to hoe and has only just turned the corner. If she can be said to have turned it. I know Claudine takes them all the peaches she can cadge out of Paul's gardener.'

Tietjens was about to say that Mrs Wannop, the mother, had written the only novel worth reading since the eighteenth century. . . . But the General went on:

'Listen to me, my boy. . . . If you can't get on without women . . . I should have thought Sylvia was good enough. But I know what we men are. . . . I don't set up to be a saint. I heard a woman in the promenade of the Empire say once that it was the likes of them that saved the lives and figures of all the virtuous women of the country. And I daresay it's true. . . . But choose a girl that you can set up in a tobacco shop and do your courting in the back parlour. Not in the Haymarket. . . . Heaven knows if you can afford it. That's your affair. You appear to have been sold up. And from what Sylvia's let drop to Claudine . . .'

'I don't believe,' Tietjens said, 'that Sylvia's said anything to Lady Claudine . . . She's too straight.'

'I didn't say "said," ' the General exclaimed, 'I particularly said "let drop." And perhaps I oughtn't to have said as much as that, but you know what devils for ferreting out women are. And Claudine's worse than any woman I ever knew. . . .'

'And, of course, she's had Sandbach to help,' Tietjens said.

'Oh, that fellow's worse than any woman,' the General exclaimed.

'Then what does the whole indictment amount to?' Tietjens asked.

'Oh, hang it,' the General brought out, 'I'm not a beastly detective, I only want a plausible story to tell Claudine. Or not even plausible. An obvious lie as long as it shows you're not flying in the face of society—as walking up the Haymarket with the little Wannop when your wife's left you because of her would be.'

'What does it amount to?' Tietjens said patiently: 'What Sylvia "let drop"?'

'Only,' the General answered, 'that you are—that your views are—immoral. Of course they often puzzle me. And, of course, if you have views that aren't the same as other people's, and don't keep them to yourself, other people will suspect you of immorality. That's what put Paul Sandbach on your track! . . . and that you're extravagant. . . . Oh, hang it. . . . Eternal hansoms, and taxis and telegrams. . . . You know, my boy, times aren't what they were when your father and I married. We used to say you could do it on five hundred a year as a younger son. . . . And then this girl too. . . .' His voice took on a more agitated note of shyness—pain. . . . 'It probably hadn't occurred to you. . . . But, of course, Sylvia has an income of her own. . . . And, don't you see . . . if you outrun the constable and . . . In short, you're spending Sylvia's money on the other girl, and that's what people can't stand.' He added quickly: 'I'm bound to say that Mrs Satterthwaite backs you through thick and thin. Thick and thin! Claudine wrote to her. But you know what women are with a handsome son-in-law that's always polite to them. But I may tell you that but for your mother-in-law, Claudine would have cut you out of her visiting list months ago. And you'd have been cut out of some others too. . . .'

Tietjens said:

'Thanks. I think that's enough to go on with. . . . Give me a couple of minutes to reflect on what you've said. . . .'

'I'll wash my hands and change my coat,' the General said with intense relief.

At the end of two minutes Tietjens said:

'No; I don't see that there is anything I want to say.'

The General exclaimed with enthusiasm:

'That's my good lad! Open confession is next to reform. . . . And . . . and try to be more respectful to your superiors. . . . Damn it; they say you're brilliant. But I thank heaven I haven't got you in my command. . . . Though I believe you're a good lad. But you're the sort of fellow to set a whole division by the ears. . . . A regular . . . what's 'is name? A regular Dreyfus!'

'Did you think Dreyfus was guilty?' Tietjens asked.

'Hang it,' the General said, 'he was worse than guilty—the sort of fellow you couldn't believe in and yet couldn't prove anything against. The curse of the world. . . .'

Tietjens said:

'Ah.'

'Well, they are,' the General said: 'fellows like that *unsettle* society. You don't know where you are. You can't judge. They make you uncomfortable. . . . A brilliant fellow too! I believe he's a brigadier-general by now. . . .' He put his arm round Tietjens' shoulders.

'There, there, my dear boy,' he said, 'come and have a sloe gin. That's the real answer to all beastly problems.'

It was some time before Tietjens could get to think of his own problems. The fly that took them back went with the slow pomp of a procession over the winding marsh road in front of the absurdly picturesque red pyramid of the very old town. Tietjens had to listen to the General suggesting that it would be better if he didn't come to the golf-club till Monday. He would get Macmaster some good games. A good, sound fellow that Macmaster now. It was a pity Tietjens hadn't some of his soundness!

Two city men had approached the General on the course and had used some violent invectives against Tietjens: they had objected to being called ruddy swine to their faces: they were going to the police. The General said that he had told them himself, slowly and guiltily, that they *were* ruddy swine and that they would never get another ticket at that club after Monday. But till Monday, apparently, they had the right to be there and the club wouldn't want scenes. Sandbach, too, was infuriated about Tietjens.

Tietjens said that the fault lay with the times that permitted the introduction into gentlemen's company of such social swipes as Sandbach. One acted perfectly correctly, and then a dirty little beggar like that put dirty little constructions on it and ran about and bleated. He added that he knew Sandbach was the General's brother-in-law, but he couldn't help it. That was the truth. . . . The General said: 'I know, my boy: I know. . . .' But one had to take society as one found it. Claudine had to be provided for and Sandbach made a very good husband, careful, sober, and on the right side in politics. A bit of a rip; but they couldn't ask for everything! And Claudine was using all the influence she had with the other side—which was not a little, women were so wonderful!—to get him a diplomatic job in Turkey, so as to get him out of the way of Mrs Crundall! Mrs Crundall was the leading Anti-Suffragette of the little town. That was what made Sandbach so bitter against Tietjens. He told Tietjens so that Tietjens might understand.

Tietjens had hitherto flattered himself that he could examine a subject swiftly and put it away in his mind. To the General he hardly listened. The allegations against himself were beastly; but he could usually ignore allegations against himself, and he imagined that if he said no more about them he would himself hear no more. And, if there were, in clubs and places where men talk, unpleasant rumours as to himself he preferred it to be thought that he was the rip, not his wife the strumpet. That was normal, male vanity: the preference of the English gentleman! Had it been a matter of Sylvia spotless and himself as spotless as he was—for in all these things he knew himself to be spotless!—he would certainly have defended himself, at least, to the General. But he had acted practically in not defending himself more vigorously. For he imagined that, had he really tried, he could have made the General believe him. But he had behaved rightly! It was not mere vanity. There was the child up at his sister Effie's. It was better for a boy to have a rip of a father than a whore for mother!

The General was expatiating on the solidity of a squat castle, like a pile of draughts, away to the left, in the sun, on the flatness. He was saying that we didn't build like that nowadays.

Tietjens said:

'You're perfectly wrong, General. All the castles that Henry VIII built in 1543 along this coast are mere monuments of jerry-building. . . . *"In 1543 jactat castra Delis, Sandgatto, Reia, Hastingas Henricus Rex"* . . . That means he chucked them down. . . .'

The General laughed:

'You are an incorrigible fellow. . . . If ever there's any known, certain fact . . .'

'But go and *look* at the beastly things,' Tietjens said. 'You'll see they've got just a facing of Caen stone that the tide floated here, and the fillings-up are just rubble, any rubbish. . . . Look here! It's a known certain fact, isn't it, that your eighteen-pounders are better than the French seventy-fives. They tell us so in the House, on the hustings, in the papers: the public believes it. . . . But would you put one of your tiny pet things firing—what is it?—four shells a minute?—with the little bent pins in their tails to stop the recoil—against their seventy-fives with the compressed-air cylinders. . . .'

The General sat stiffly upon his cushion:

'That's different,' he said. 'How the devil do you get to know these things?'

'It isn't different,' Tietjens said, 'it's the same muddle-headed frame of mind that sees good building in Henry VIII as lets us into wars with hopelessly antiquated field guns and rottenly inferior ammunition. You'd fire any fellow on your staff who said we could stand up for a minute against the French.'

'Well, anyhow,' the General said, 'I thank heaven you're not on my staff, for you'd talk my hind leg off in a week. It's perfectly true that the public . . .'

But Tietjens was not listening. He was considering that it was natural for an unborn fellow like Sandbach to betray the solidarity that should exist between men. And it was natural for a childless woman like Lady Claudine Sandbach, with a notoriously, a flagrantly unfaithful husband, to believe in the unfaithfulness of the husbands of other women!

The General was saying:

'Who did you hear that stuff from about the French field gun?'

Tietjens said:

'From you. Three weeks ago!'

And all the other society women with unfaithful husbands. . . . They must do their best to down and out a man. They would cut him off their visiting lists! Let them. The barren harlots mated to faithless eunuchs. . . . Suddenly he thought that he didn't know for certain that he was the father of his child and he groaned.

'Well, what have I said wrong now?' the General asked. 'Surely you don't maintain that pheasants do eat man-golds. . . .'

Tietjen proved his reputation for sanity with:

'No! I was just groaning at the thought of the Chancellor! That's sound enough for you, isn't it?' But it gave him a nasty turn. He hadn't been able to pigeon-hole and padlock his disagreeable reflections. He had been as good as talking to himself. . . .

In the bow-window of another hostelry than his own he caught the eye of Mr Waterhouse, who was looking at the view over the marshes. The great man beckoned to him and he went in. Mr Waterhouse was aware that Tietjens—whom he assumed to be a man of sense—should get any pursuit of the two girls stopped off. He couldn't move in the matter himself, but a five pound note and possibly a police promotion or so might be handed round if no advertisement were given to the mad women on account of their raid of that afternoon.

It was not a very difficult matter: for where the great man was to be found in the club lounge, there, in the bar, the major, the town clerk, the local head of the police, the doctors and solicitors would be found drinking together. And after it was arranged the great man himself came into the bar, had a drink and pleased them all immensely by his affability. . . .

Tietjens himself, dining alone with the Minister to whom he wanted to talk about his Labour Finance Act, didn't find him a disagreeable fellow: not really foolish, not sly except in his humour, tired obviously, but livening up after a couple of whiskys, and certainly not as yet plutocratic; with tastes for apple-pie and cream of a fourteen-year-old boy. And, even as regards his famous Act, which was then shaking the country to its political foundations, once you accepted its fundamental unsuitedness to the temperament and needs of the English working-class, you could see that Mr Waterhouse didn't want to be dishonest. He accepted with gratitude several of Tietjens' emendations in the actuarial schedules. . . . And over their port they agreed on two fundamental legislative ideals: every working man to have a minimum of four hundred a year and every beastly manufacturer who wanted to pay less to be hung. That, it appeared, was the High Toryism of Tietjens as it was the extreme Radicalism of the extreme Left of the Left. . . .

And Tietjens, who hated no man, in face of this simple-minded and agreeable schoolboy type of fellow, fell to wondering why it was that humanity that was next to always

agreeable in its units was, as a mass, a phenomenon so
hideous. You look at a dozen men, each of them not by any
means detestable and not uninteresting: for each of them
would have technical details of their affairs to impart: you
formed them into a Government or a club, and at once,
with oppressions, inaccuracies, gossip, backbiting, lying,
corruption and vileness, you had the combination of wolf,
tiger, weasel, and louse-covered ape that was human
society. And he remembered the words of some Russian:
'Cats and monkeys. Monkeys and cats. All humanity is
there.'

Tietjens and Mr Waterhouse spent the rest of the evening together.

Whilst Tietjens was interviewing the policeman, the
Minister sat on the front steps of the cottage and smoked
cheap cigarettes, and when Tietjens went to bed, Mr
Waterhouse insisted on sending by him kindly messages
to Miss Wannop, asking her to come and discuss female
suffrage any afternoon she liked in his private room at the
House of Commons. Mr Waterhouse flatly refused to believe that Tietjens hadn't arranged the raid with Miss Wannop. He said it had been too neatly planned for any
woman, and he said Tietjens was a lucky fellow, for she
was a ripping girl.

Back in his room under the rafters, Tietjens fell, nevertheless, at once a prey to real agitation. For a long time he
pounded from wall to wall and, since he could not shake
off the train of thought, he got out at last his patience cards,
and devoted himself seriously to thinking out the conditions of his life with Sylvia. He wanted to stop scandal if he
could; he wanted them to live within his income, he wanted
to subtract that child from the influence of its mother.
These were all definite but difficult things. . . . Then one
half of his mind lost itself in the rearrangement of schedules, and on his brilliant table his hands set queens on
kings and checked their recurrences.

In that way the sudden entrance of Macmaster gave him
a really terrible physical shock. He nearly vomited: his

brain reeled and the room fell about. He drank a great
quantity of whisky in front of Macmaster's goggling eyes;
but even at that he couldn't talk, and he dropped into his
bed faintly aware of his friend's efforts to loosen his
clothes. He had, he knew, carried the suppression of
thought in his conscious mind so far that his unconscious
self had taken command and had, for the time, paralysed
both his body and his mind.

V

'It doesn't seem quite fair, Valentine,' Mrs Duchemin
said. She was rearranging in a glass bowl some minute
flowers that floated on water. They made there, on the
breakfast-table, a patch, as it were, of mosaic amongst
silver chafing dishes, silver epergnes piled with peaches in
pyramids and great silver rose-bowls filled with roses, that
drooped to the damask cloth, a congeries of silver large-
nesses made as if a fortification for the head of the table;
two huge silver urns, a great silver kettle on a tripod, and a
couple of silver vases filled with the extremely tall blue
spikes of delphiniums that, spreading out, made as if a fan.
The eighteenth-century room was very tall and long;
panelled in darkish wood. In the centre of each of four of
the panels, facing the light, hung pictures, a mellowed
orange in tone, representing mists and the cordage of ships
in mists at sunrise. On the bottom of each large gold frame
was a tablet bearing the ascription: 'J. M. W. Turner.'
The chairs, arranged along the long table that was set
for eight people, had the delicate, spidery, mahogany
backs of Chippendale; on the golden mahogany sideboard
that had behind it green silk curtains on a brass-rail were
displayed an immense, crumbed ham, more peaches on an
epergne, a large meat-pie with a varnished crust, another
epergne that supported the large pale globes of grapefruit;
a galantine, a cube of inlaid meats, encased in thick jelly.
'Oh, women have to back each other up in these days,'

Valentine Wannop said. 'I couldn't let you go through this alone after breakfasting with you every Saturday since I don't know when.'

'I do feel,' Mrs Duchemin said, 'immensely grateful to you for your moral support. I ought not, perhaps, to have risked this morning. But I've told Parry to keep him out till 10.15.'

'It's, at any rate, tremendously sporting of you,' the girl said. 'I think it was worth trying.'

Mrs Duchemin, wavering round the table, slightly changed the position of the delphiniums.

'I think they make a good screen,' Mrs Duchemin said.

'Oh, nobody will be able to see him,' the girl answered reassuringly. She added with a sudden resolution, 'Look here, Edie. Stop worrying about my mind. If you think that anything I hear at your table after nine months as an ash-cat at Ealing, with three men in the house, an invalid wife and a drunken cook, can corrupt my mind, you're simply mistaken. You can let your conscience be at rest, and let's say no more about it.'

Mrs Duchemin said, 'Oh, Valentine! How could your mother let you?'

'She didn't know,' the girl said. 'She was out of her mind for grief. She sat for most of the whole nine months with her hands folded before her in a board and lodging house at twenty-five shillings a week, and it took the five shillings a week that I earned to make up the money.' She added, 'Gilbert had to be kept at school of course. And in the holidays, too.'

'I don't understand!' Mrs Duchemin said. 'I simply don't understand.'

'Of course you wouldn't,' the girl answered. 'You're like the kindly people who subscribed at the sale to buy my father's library back and present it to my mother. That cost us five shillings a week for warehousing, and at Ealing they were always nagging at me for the state of my print dresses. . . .'

She broke off and said:

4*

'Let's not talk about it any more, if you don't mind. You have me in your house, so I suppose you've a right to references, as the mistresses call them. But you've been very good to me and never asked. Still, it's come up; do you know I told a man on the links yesterday that I'd been a slavey for nine months. I was trying to explain why I was a suffragette; and, as I was asking him a favour, I suppose I felt I needed to give *him* references too.'

Mrs Duchemin, beginning to advance towards the girl impulsively, exclaimed:

'You darling!'

Miss Wannop said:

'Wait a minute. I haven't finished. I want to say this: I never talk about that stage of my career because I'm ashamed of it. I'm ashamed because I think I did the wrong thing, not for any other reason. I did it on impulse and I stuck to it out of obstinacy. I mean it would probably have been more sensible to go round with the hat to benevolent people, for the keep of mother and to complete my education. But if we've inherited the Wannop ill-luck, we've inherited the Wannop pride. And I *couldn't* do it. Besides I was only seventeen, and I gave out we were going into the country after the sale. I'm not educated at all, as you know, or only half, because father, being a brilliant man, had ideas. And one of them was that I was to be an athlete, not a classical don at Cambridge, or I might have been, I believe. I don't know why he had that tic ... But I'd like you to understand two things. One I've said already: what I hear in this house won't ever shock or corrupt me; that it's said in Latin is neither here nor there. I understand Latin almost as well as English because father used to talk it to me and Gilbert as soon as we talked at all. . . . And, oh yes: I'm a suffragette because I've been a slavey. But I'd like you to understand that, though I was a slavey and am a suffragette—you're an old-fashioned woman and queer things are thought about these two things—then I'd like you to understand that in spite of it all I'm pure! Chaste, you know. . . . Perfectly virtuous.'

Mrs Duchemin said:

'Oh, Valentine! Did you wear a cap and apron? You! In a cap and apron.'

Miss Wannop replied:

'Yes! I wore a cap and apron and sniffled "M'm" to the mistress; and slept under the stairs, too. Because I woud not sleep with the beast of a cook.'

Mrs Duchemin now ran forward and, catching Miss Wannop by both hands, kissed her first on the left and then on the right cheek.

'Oh, Valentine,' she said, 'you're a heroine. And you only twenty-two! . . . Isn't that the motor coming?'

But it wasn't the motor coming and Miss Wannop said:

'Oh, no! I'm not a heroine. When I tried to speak to that Minister yesterday, I just couldn't. It was Gertie who went for him. As for me, I just hopped from one leg to the other and stuttered: "V . . . V . . . Votes for W . . . W . . . W . . . omen!" . . . If I'd been decently brave I shouldn't have been too shy to speak to a strange man. . . . For that was what it really came to.'

'But that surely,' Mrs Duchemin said—she continued to hold both the girl's hands—'makes you all the braver. . . . It's the person who does the thing he's afraid of who's the real hero, isn't it?'

'Oh, we used to argue that old thing over with father when we were ten. You can't tell. You've got to define the term brave. I was just abject. . . . I could harangue the whole crowd when I got them together. But speak to one man in cold blood I couldn't. . . . Of course I *did* speak to a fat golfing idiot with bulging eyes, to get him to save Gertie. But that was different.'

Mrs Duchemin moved both the girl's hands up and down in her own.

'As you know, Valentine,' she said, 'I'm an old-fashioned woman. I believe that woman's true place is at her husband's side. At the same time . . .'

Miss Wannop moved away.

'Now, don't, Edie, don't!' she said. 'If you believe that,

you're an anti. Don't run with the hare and hunt with the
hounds. It's your defect really. . . . I tell you I'm *not* a
heroine. I *dread* prison: I *hate* rows. I'm thankful to goodness that it's my duty to stop and housemaid-typewrite for
mother, so that I can't really *do* things. . . . Look at that
miserable, adenoidy little Gertie, hiding upstairs in our
garret. She was crying all last night—but that's just nerves.
Yet she's been in prison five times, stomach-pumped and
all. Not a moment of funk about her! . . . But as for me, a
girl as hard as a rock that prison wouldn't touch. . . . Why,
I'm all of a jump now. That's why I'm talking nonsense
like a pert schoolgirl. I just dread that every sound may
be the police coming for me.'

Mrs Duchemin stroked the girl's fair hair and tucked a
loose strand behind her ear.

'I wish you'd let me show you how to do your hair,' she
said. 'The right man might come along at any moment.'

'Oh, the right man!' Miss Wannop said. 'Thanks for
tactfully changing the subject. The right man for me, when
he comes along, will be a married man. That's the Wannop luck!'

Mrs Duchemin said, with deep concern:

'Don't talk like that. . . . Why should you regard yourself as being less lucky than other people? Surely
your mother's done well. She has a position; she makes
money. . . .'

'Ah, but mother isn't a Wannop,' the girl said, 'only by
marriage. The real Wannops . . . they've been executed,
and attaindered, and falsely accused and killed in carriage
accidents and married adventurers or died penniless like
father. Ever since the dawn of history. And then, mother's
got her mascot . . .'

'Oh, what's that?' Mrs Duchemin asked, almost with
animation, 'a relic . . .?'

'Don't you know mother's mascot?' the girl asked. 'She
tells everybody. . . . Don't you know the story of the man
with the champagne? How mother was sitting contemplating suicide in her bed-sitting-room and there came in a

man with a name like Tea-tray; she always calls him the
mascot and asks us to remember him as such in our
prayers.... He was a man who'd been at a German
university with father years before and loved him very
dearly; but had not kept touch with him. And he'd been
out of England for nine months when father died and
round about it. And he said: "Now, Mrs Wannop, what's
this?" And she told him. And he said, "What you want is
champagne!" And he sent the slavey out with a sovereign
for a bottle of Veuve Clicquot. And he broke the neck of the
bottle off against the mantelpiece because they were slow
in bringing an opener. And he stood over her while she
drank half the bottle out of her toothglass. And he took
her out to lunch...o...o...oh, it's cold!... And
lectured her... And got her a job to write leaders on a
paper he had shares in....'

Mrs Duchemin said:

'You're shivering!'

'I know I am,' the girl said. She went on very fast. 'And
of course, mother always *wrote* father's articles for him.
He found the ideas, but couldn't write, and she's a
splendid style.... And, since then, he—the mascot—Tea-
tray—has always turned up when she's been in tight places.
Then the paper blew her up and threatened to dismiss
her for inaccuracies! She's frightfully inaccurate. And he
wrote her out a table of things every leader-writer must
know, such as that "A. Ebor" is the Archbishop of York,
and that the Government is Liberal. And one day he
turned up and said: "Why don't you write a novel on
that story you told me?" And he lent her the money to
buy the cottage we're in now, to be quiet and write in
...Oh, I can't go on!'

Miss Wannop burst into tears.

'It's thinking of those beastly days,' she said. 'And that
beastly, *beastly* yesterday!' She ran the knuckles of both
her hands fiercely into her eyes, and determinedly eluded
Mrs Duchemin's handkerchief and embraces. She said
almost contemptuously:

'A nice, considerate person I am. And you with this ordeal hanging over you! Do you suppose I don't appreciate all your silent heroism of the home, while we're marching about with flags and shouting? But it's just to stop women like you being tortured, body and soul, week in, week out, that we ...'

Mrs Duchemin had sat down on a chair near one of the windows; she had her handkerchief hiding her face.

'Why women in your position don't take lovers ...' the girl said hotly. 'Or that women in your position do take lovers. ...'

Mrs Duchemin looked up; in spite of its tears her white face had an air of serious dignity:

'Oh, *no*, Valentine,' she said, using her deeper tones. 'There's something beautiful, there's something *thrilling* about chastity. I'm not narrow-minded. Censorious! I don't *condemn*! But to preserve in word, thought and action a lifelong fidelity. ... It's no mean achievement. ...'

'You mean like an egg and spoon race,' Miss Wannop said.

'It isn't,' Mrs Duchemin replied gently, 'the way I should have put it. Isn't the real symbol Atalanta, running fast and not turning aside for the golden apple? That always seemed to me the real truth hidden in the beautiful old legend. ...'

'I don't know,' Miss Wannop said, 'when I read what Ruskin says about it in the *Crown of Wild Olive*. Or no! It's the *Queen of the Air*. That's his Greek rubbish, isn't it? I always think it seems like an egg-race in which the young woman didn't keep her eyes in the boat. But I suppose it comes to the same thing.'

Mrs Duchemin said:

'My *dear*! Not a word against John Ruskin in *this* house!'

Miss Wannop screamed.

An immense voice had shouted:

'This way! This way ... The ladies will be here!'

Of Mr Duchemin's curates—he had three of them, for

he had three marshland parishes almost without stipend, so that no one but a very rich clergyman could have held them—it was observed that they were all very large men with the physiques rather of prize-fighters than of clergy. So that when by any chance at dusk, Mr Duchemin, who himself was of exceptional stature, and his three assistants went together along a road the hearts of any malefactors whom in the mist they chanced to encounter went pit-a-pat.

Mr Horsley—the number two—had in addition an enormous voice. He shouted four or five words, interjected tee-hee, shouted four or five words more and again interjected tee-hee. He had enormous wrist-bones that protruded from his clerical cuffs, an enormous Adam's apple, a large, thin, close-cropped, colourless face like a skull, with very sunken eyes, and when he was once started speaking it was impossible to stop him, because his own voice in his ears drowned every possible form of interruption.

This morning, as an inmate of the house, introducing to the breakfast-room Messrs Tietjens and Macmaster, who had driven up to the steps just as he was mounting them, he had a story to tell. The introduction was, therefore, not, as such, a success. . . .

'A STATE OF SIEGE, LADIES! Tee-hee!' he alternately roared and giggled. 'We're living in a regular state of siege. . . . What with . . .' It appeared that the night before, after dinner, Mr Sandbach and rather more than half a dozen of the young bloods who had dined at Mountby, had gone scouring the country lanes, mounted on motor bicycles and armed with loaded canes . . . for suffragettes! Every woman they had come across in the darkness they had stopped, abused, threatened with their loaded canes and subjected to cross-examination. The countryside was up in arms.

As a story this took, with the appropriate reflections and repetitions, a long time in telling, and afforded Tietjens and Miss Wannop the opportunity of gazing at each other. Miss Wannop was frankly afraid that this large, clumsy, unusual-looking man, now that he had found her again, might hand her over to the police whom she imagined to be searching for herself and her friend Gertie, Miss Wilson, at that moment in bed, under the care, as she also imagined, of Mrs Wannop. On the links he had seemed to her natural and in place; here, with his loosely hung clothes and immense hands, the white patch on the side of his rather cropped head and his masked, rather shapeless features, he affected her queerly as being both in and out of place. He seemed to go with the ham, the meat-pie, the galantine and even at a pinch with the roses; but the Turner pictures, the aesthetic curtain and Mrs Duchemin's flowing robes, amber and rose in the hair, did not go with him at all. Even the Chippendale chairs hardly did. And she felt herself thinking oddly, beneath her perturbations, of a criminal and the voice of the Rev. Mr Horsley that *his* Harris tweeds went all right with her skirt, and she was glad that she had on a clean, cream-coloured silk blouse, not a striped pink cotton.

She was right as to that.

In every man there are two minds that work side by side, the one checking the other; thus emotion stands against reason, intellect corrects passion and first impressions act just a little, but very little, before quick reflection. Yet first impressions have always a bias in their favour, and even quiet reflection has often a job to efface them.

The night before, Tietjens had given several thoughts to this young woman. General Campion had assigned her to him as *maîtresse du titre*. He was said to have ruined himself, broken up his home and spent his wife's money on her. Those were lies. On the other hand they were not inherent impossibilities. Upon occasion and given the right woman, quite sound men have done such things. He might, heaven knows, himself be so caught. But that he should have ruined himself over an unnoticeable young female who had announced herself as having been a domestic servant, and wore a pink cotton blouse ... that had seemed to go beyond the bounds of even the unreason of club gossip!

That was the strong, first impression! It was all very well for his surface mind to say that the girl was not by birth a tweeny maid; she was the daughter of Professor Wannop and she could jump! For Tietjens held very strongly the theory that what finally separated the classes was that the upper could lift its feet from the ground whilst common people couldn't.

... But the strong impression remained. Miss Wannop was a tweeny maid. Say a lady's help, by nature. She was of good family, for the Wannops were first heard of at Birdlip in Gloucestershire in the year 1417—no doubt enriched after Agincourt. But even brilliant men of good family will now and then throw daughters who are lady helps by nature. That was one of the queernesses of heredity. ... And, though Tietjens had even got as far as to realize that Miss Wannop must be a heroine who had sacrificed her young years to her mother's gifts, and no doubt to a brother at school—for he had guessed as far as that—even then Tietjens couldn't make her out as more than a lady help. Heroines are all very well; admirable, they may even be saints; but if they let themselves get careworn in face and go shabby. ... Well, they must wait for the gold that shall be amply stored for them in heaven. On this earth you could hardly accept them as wives for men of your own set. Certainly you wouldn't spend your own wife's money on them. That was what it really came to.

But, brightened up as he now suddenly saw her, with silk for the pink cotton, shining coiled hair for the white canvas hat, a charming young neck, good shoes beneath neat ankles, a healthy flush taking the place of yesterday's pallor of fear for her comrade; an obvious equal in the surroundings of quite good people; small, but well-shaped and healthy; immense blue eyes fixed without embarrassment on his own. ...

'By Jove . . .' he said to himself: 'It's true! What a jolly little mistress she'd make!'

He blamed Campion, Sandbach and the club gossips for the form the thought had taken. For the cruel, bitter and stupid pressure of the world has yet about it something selective; if it couples male and female in its inexorable rings of talk, it will be because there is something harmonious in the union. And there exists then the pressure of suggestion!

He took a look at Mrs Duchemin and considered her infinitely commonplace and probably a bore. He disliked her large-shouldered, many-yarded style of blue dress and considered that no woman should wear clouded amber, for which the proper function was the provision of cigarette holders for bounders. He looked back at Miss Wannop, and considered that she would make a good wife for Macmaster; Macmaster liked bouncing girls and this girl was quite lady enough.

He heard Miss Wannop shout against the gale to Mrs Duchemin:

'Do I sit beside the head of the table and pour out?'

Mrs Duchemin answered:

'No! I've asked Miss Fox to pour out. She's nearly stone deaf.' Miss Fox was the penniless sister of a curate deceased. 'You're to amuse Mr Tietjens.'

Tietjens noticed that Mrs Duchemin had an agreeable turret voice; it penetrated the noises of Mr Horsley as the missel-thrush's note a gale. It was rather agreeable. He noticed that Miss Wannop made a little grimace.

Mr Horsley, like a megaphone addressing a crowd, was turning from side to side, addressing his hearers by rotation. At the moment he was bawling at Macmaster; it would be Tietjens' turn again in a moment to hear a description of the heart attacks of old Mrs Haglen at Nobeys. But Tietjens' turn did not come. . . .

A high-complexioned, round-cheeked, forty-fivish lady, with agreeable eyes, dressed rather well in the black of the not-very-lately widowed, entered the room with precipita-

tion. She patted Mr Horsley on his declamatory right arm
and, since he went on talking, she caught him by the
hand and shook it. She exclaimed in high, commanding
tones:

'Which is Mr Macmaster, the critic?' and then, in the
dead lull to Tietjens: 'Are you Mr Macmaster, the critic?
No! . . . Then *you* must be.'

Her turning to Macmaster and the extinction of her
interest in himself had been one of the rudest things Tietjens had ever experienced, but it was an affair so strictly
businesslike that he took it without any offence. She was
remarking to Macmaster:

'Oh, Mr Macmaster, my new book will be out on Thursday week,' and she had begun to lead him towards a
window at the other end of the room.

Miss Wannop said:

'What have you done with Gertie?'

'Gertie!' Mrs Wannop exclaimed with the surprise of
one coming out of a dream. 'Oh yes! She's fast asleep.
She'll sleep till four. I told Hannah to give a look at her
now and then.'

Miss Wannop's hands fell open at her side.

'Oh, *mother!*' forced itself from her.

'Oh, yes,' Mrs Wannop said, 'we'd agreed to tell old
Hannah we didn't want her to-day. So we had!' She said
to Macmaster: 'Old Hannah is our charwoman,' wavered a
little and then went on brightly: 'Of course it will be of
use to you to hear about my new book. To you journalists
a little bit of previous explanation . . .' and she dragged off
Macmaster, who seemed to bleat faintly. . . .

That had come about because just as she had got into
the dog-cart to be driven to the rectory—for she herself
could not drive a horse—Miss Wannop had told her mother
that there would be two men at breakfast, one whose name
she didn't know; the other, a Mr Macmaster, a celebrated
critic. Mrs Wannop had called up to her:

'A critic? Of what?' her whole sleepy being electrified.

'I don't know,' her daughter had answered. 'Books, I daresay. . . .'

A second or so after, when the horse, a large black animal that wouldn't stand, had made twenty yards or so at several bounds, the handy man who drove had said:

'Yer mother's 'owlin' after yer.' But Miss Wannop had answered that it didn't matter. She was confident that she had arranged for everything. She was to be back to get lunch; her mother was to give an occasional look at Gertie Wilson in the garret; Hannah, the daily help, was to be told she could go for the day. It was of the highest importance that Hannah should not know that a completely strange young woman was asleep in the garret at eleven in the morning. If she did the news would be all over the neighbourhood at once, and the police instantly down on them.

But Mrs Wannop was a woman of business. If she heard of a reviewer within driving distance she called on him with eggs as a present. The moment the daily help had arrived, she had set out and walked to the rectory. No consideration of danger from the police would have stopped her; besides, she had forgotten all about the police.

Her arrival worried Mrs Duchemin a good deal, because she wished all her guests to be seated and the breakfast well begun before the entrance of her husband. And this was not easy. Mrs Wannop, who was uninvited, refused to be separated from Mr Macmaster. Mr Macmaster had told her that he never wrote reviews in the daily papers, only articles for the heavy quarterlies, and it had occurred to Mrs Wannop that an article on her new book in one of the quarterlies was just what was needed. She was, therefore, engaged in telling Mr Macmaster how to write about herself, and twice after Mrs Duchemin had succeeded in shepherding Mr Macmaster nearly to his seat, Mrs Wannop had conducted him back to the embrasure of the window. It was only by sitting herself firmly in her chair next to Macmaster that Mrs Duchemin was able to retain for her-

self this all-essential, strategic position. And it was only
by calling out:

'Mr Horsley, *do* take Mrs Wannop to the seat beside
you and feed her,' that Mrs Duchemin got Mrs Wannop
out of Mr Duchemin's own seat at the head of the table,
for Mrs Wannop, having perceived this seat to be vacant
next to Mr Macmaster, had pulled out the Chippendale
armchair and had prepared to sit down in it. This could
only have spelt disaster, for it would have meant turning
Mrs Duchemin's husband loose amongst the other guests.

Mr Horsley, however, accomplished his duty of leading
away this lady with such firmness that Mrs Wannop conceived of him as a very disagreeable and awkward person.
Mr. Horsley's seat was next to Miss Fox, a grey spinster,
who sat, as it were, within the fortification of silver urns
and deftly occupied herself with the ivory taps of these
machines. This seat, too, Mrs Wannop tried to occupy,
imagining that, by moving the silver vases that upheld the
tall delphiniums, she would be able to get a diagonal view
of Macmaster and so to shout to him. She found, however,
that she couldn't, and so resigned herself to taking the chair
that had been reserved for Miss Gertie Wilson, who was
to have been the eighth guest. Once there she sat in distracted gloom, occasionally saying to her daughter:

'I think it's very bad management. I think this party's
very badly arranged.' Mr Horsley she hardly thanked for
the sole that he placed before her; Tietjens she did not
even look at.

Sitting beside Macmaster, her eyes fixed on a small door
in the corner of the panelled wall, Mrs Duchemin became a
prey to a sudden and overwhelming fit of apprehension. It
forced her to say to her guest, though she had resolved to
chance it and say nothing:

'It wasn't perhaps fair to ask you to come all this way.
You may get nothing out of my husband. He's apt . . .
especially on Saturdays. . . .'

She trailed off into indecision. It was possible that
nothing might occur. On two Saturdays out of seven

nothing *did* occur. Then an admission would be wasted; this sympathetic being would go out of her life with a knowledge that he needn't have had—to be a slur on her memory in his mind. . . . But then, overwhelmingly, there came over her the feeling that, if he knew of her sufferings, he might feel impelled to remain and comfort her. She cast about for words with which to finish her sentence. But Macmaster said:

'Oh, dear lady!' (And it seemed to her to be charming to be addressed thus!) 'One understands . . . One is surely trained and adapted to understand . . . that these great scholars, these abstracted cognoscenti . . .'

Mrs Duchemin breathed a great 'Ah!' of relief. Macmaster had used the exactly right words.

'And,' Macmaster was going on, 'merely to spend a short hour; a swallow flight . . . "As when the swallow gliding from lofty portal to lofty portal!" . . . You know the lines . . . in these, your perfect surroundings . . .'

Blissful waves seemed to pass from him to her. It was in this way that men should speak; in that way—steel-blue tie, true-looking gold ring, steel-blue eyes beneath black brows!—that men should look. She was half-conscious of warmth; this suggested the bliss of falling asleep, truly, in perfect surroundings. The roses on the table were lovely; their scent came to her.

A voice came to her:

'You *do* do the thing in style, I must say.'

The large, clumsy but otherwise unnoticeable being that this fascinating man had brought in his train was setting up pretensions to her notice. He had just placed before her a small blue china plate that contained a little black caviare and a round of lemon; a small Sèvres, pinkish, delicate plate that held the pinkest peach in the room. She had said to him: 'Oh . . . a little caviare! A peach!' a long time before, with the vague underfeeling that the names of such comestibles must convey to her person a charm in the eyes of Caliban.

She buckled about her her armour of charm; Tietjens

was gazing with large, fishy eyes at the caviare before her.

'How do you get *that*, for instance?' he asked.

'Oh!' she answered: 'If it wasn't my husband's doing it would look like ostentation. I'd find it ostentatious for myself.' She found a smile, radiant, yet muted. 'He's trained Simpkins of New Bond Street. For a telephone message overnight special messengers go to Billingsgate at dawn for salmon, and red mullet, this, in ice, and great blocks of ice too. It's such pretty stuff ... and then by seven the car goes to Ashford Junction. . . . All the same, it's difficult to give a breakfast before ten.'

She didn't want to waste her careful sentences on this grey fellow; she couldn't, however, turn back, as she yearned to do, to the kindredly running phrases—as if out of books she had read!—of the smaller man.

'Ah, but it isn't,' Tietjens said, 'ostentation. It's the great Tradition. You mustn't ever forget that your husband's Breakfast Duchemin of Magdalen.'

He seemed to be gazing, inscrutably, deep into her eyes. But no doubt he meant to be agreeable.

'Sometimes I wish I could,' she said. 'He doesn't get anything out of it himself. He's ascetic to unreasonableness. On Fridays he eats nothing at all. It makes me quite anxious ... for Saturdays.'

Tietjens said:

'I know.'

She exclaimed—and almost with sharpness:

'You know!'

He continued to gaze straight into her eyes:

'Oh, of course one knows all about Breakfast Duchemin!' he said. 'He was one of Ruskin's road-builders. He was said to be the most Ruskin-like of them all!'

Mrs Duchemin cried out: 'Oh!' Fragments of the worst stories that in his worst moods her husband had told her of his old preceptor went through her mind. She imagined that the shameful parts of her intimate life must be known to this nebulous monster. For Tietjens, turned sideways and facing her, had seemed to grow monstrous, and as if with undefined outlines. He was the male, threatening, clumsily odious and external! She felt herself say to herself: 'I will do you an injury, if ever——' For already she had felt herself swaying the preferences, the thoughts and the future of the man on her other side. He was the male, tender, in-fitting; the complement of the harmony, the meat for consumption, like the sweet pulp of figs. . . . It was inevitable; it was essential to the nature of her relationship with her husband that Mrs Duchemin should have these feelings. . . .

She heard, almost without emotion, so great was her disturbance, from behind her back the dreaded, high, rasping tones:

'*Post coitum triste!* Ha! Ha! That's what it is?' The voice repeated the words and added sardonically: 'You know what *that* means?' But the problem of her husband had become secondary; the real problem was: 'What was this monstrous and hateful man going to say of her to his friend, when, for long hours, they were away?'

He was still gazing into her eyes. He said nonchalantly, rather low.

'I wouldn't look round if I were you. Vincent Macmaster is quite up to dealing with the situation.'

His voice had the familiarity of an elder brother's. And at once Mrs Duchemin knew—that *he* knew that already close ties were developing between herself and Macmaster. He was speaking as a man speaks in emergencies to the mistress of his dearest friend. He was then one of those formidable and to be feared males who possess the gift of right intuitions.

Tietjens said: 'You heard!'

To the gloating, cruel tones that had asked:

'You know what that means?' Macmaster had answered clearly, but with the snappy intonation of a reproving Don:

'Of course I know what it means. It's no discovery!' That was exactly the right note. Tietjens—and Mrs Duchemin too—could hear Mr Duchemin, invisible behind his rampart of blue spikes and silver, give the answering snuffle of a reproved schoolboy. A hard-faced, small man, in grey tweed that buttoned, collar-like, tight round his throat, standing behind the invisible chair, gazed straight forward into infinity.

Tietjens said to himself:

'By God! Parry! the Bermondsey light middle-weight! He's there to carry Duchemin off if he becomes violent!'

During the quick look that Tietjens took round the table, Mrs Duchemin gave, sinking lower in her chair, a short gasp of utter relief. Whatever Macmaster was going to think of her, he thought now. He knew the worst! It was settled, for good or ill. In a minute she would look round at him.

Tietjens said:

'It's all right, Macmaster will be splendid. We had a friend up at Cambridge with your husband's tendencies, and Macmaster could get him through *any* social occasion. ... Besides, we're all gentlefolk here!'

He had seen the Rev. Mr Horsley and Mrs Wannop both interested in their plates. Of Miss Wannop he was not so certain. He had caught, bent obviously on himself, from large, blue eyes, a glance that was evidently appealing. He said to himself: 'She must be in the secret. She's appealing to me not to show emotion and upset the applecart! It is a shame that she should be here: a girl!' and into his answering glance he threw the message: 'It's all right as far as this end of the table is concerned.'

But Mrs Duchemin had felt come into herself a little stiffening of morale. Macmaster by now knew the worst; Duchemin was quoting snufflingly to him the hot licentiousness of the *Trimalchio* of Petronius; snuffling into Macmaster's ear. She caught the phrase: *Froturianas, puer callide.* ... Duchemin, holding her wrist with the painful force of the maniac, had translated it to her over and over again. ... No doubt, that too, this hateful man beside her would have guessed!

She said: 'Of course we should be all gentlefolk here. One naturally arranges that. ...'

Tietjens began to say:

'Ah! But it isn't easy to arrange nowadays. All sorts of bounders get into all sorts of holies of holies!'

Mrs Duchemin turned her back on him right in the middle of his sentence. She devoured Macmaster's face with her eyes, in an infinite sense of calm.

Macmaster four minutes before had been the only one to see the entrance, from a small panelled door that had behind it another of green baize, of the Rev. Mr Duchemin, and following him a man whom Macmaster, too, recognized at once as Parry, the ex-prize-fighter. It flashed through his mind at once that this was an extraordinary conjunction. It flashed through his mind, too, that it was extraordinary that anyone so ecstatically handsome as Mrs Duchemin's husband should not have earned high preferment in a Church always hungry for male beauty. Mr Duchemin was extremely tall, with a slight stoop of the proper clerical type. His face was of alabaster; his grey hair, parted in the middle, fell brilliantly on his high brows; his glance was quick, penetrating, austere; his nose very hooked and chiselled. He was the exact man to adorn a lofty and gorgeous fane, as Mrs Duchemin was the exact woman to consecrate an episcopal drawing-room. With his great wealth, scholarship and tradition. . . . 'Why then,' went through Macmaster's mind in a swift pin-prick of suspicion, 'isn't he at least a dean?'

Mr Duchemin had walked swiftly to his chair which Parry, as swiftly walking behind him, drew out. His master slipped into it with a graceful, sideways motion. He shook his head at grey Miss Fox who had moved a hand towards an ivory urn-tap. There was a glass of water beside his plate, and round it his long, very white fingers closed. He stole a quick glance at Macmaster, and then looked at him steadily with laughingly glittering eyes. He said: 'Good morning, doctor,' and then, drowning Macmaster's quiet protest: 'Yes! Yes! The stethoscope meticulously packed into the top-hat and shining hat left in the hall.'

The prize-fighter, in tight box-cloth leggings, tight whip-cord breeches, and a short tight jacket that buttoned up at the collar to his chin—the exact stud-groom of a man of property—gave a quick glance of recognition to Macmaster and then to Mr Duchemin's back another quick look, raising his eyebrows. Macmaster, who knew him very well because he had given Tietjens boxing lessons at Cambridge, could almost hear him say: 'A queer change this, sir! Keep your eyes on him a second!' and, with the quick, light tip-toe of the pugilist he slipped away to the sideboard. Mac-master stole a quick glance on his own account at Mrs Duchemin. She had her back to him, being deep in con-versation with Tietjens. His heart jumped a little when, looking back again, he saw Mr Duchemin half raised to his feet, peering round the fortifications of silver. But he sank down again in his chair, and surveying Macmaster with an expression of singular cunning on his ascetic features, exclaimed:

'And your friend? Another medical man? All with stethoscope complete. It takes, of course, two medical men to certify ...'

He stopped and with an expression of sudden, distorted rage, pushed aside the arm of Parry, who was sliding a plate of sole fillets on to the table beneath his nose.

'Take away,' he was beginning to exclaim thunderously, 'these inducements to the filthy lusts of ...' But with another cunning and apprehensive look at Macmaster, he said: 'Yes! yes! Parry! That's right. Yes! Sole! A touch of kidney to follow. Another! Yes! Grapefruit! With sherry!' He had adopted an old Oxford voice, spread his napkin over his knees and hastily placed in his mouth a morsel of fish.

Macmaster with a patient and distinct intonation said that he must be permitted to introduce himself. He was Macmaster, Mr Duchemin's correspondent on the subject of his little monograph. Mr Duchemin looked at him, hard, with an awakened attention that gradually lost suspicion and became gloatingly joyful:

'Ah, yes, Macmaster!' he said. 'Macmaster. A budding critic. A little of a hedonist, perhaps? And yes . . . you wired that you were coming. Two friends! Not medical men! Friends!' He moved his face closer to Macmaster and said:

'How tired you look! Worn! Worn!'

Macmaster was about to say that he was rather hard-worked when, in a harsh, high cackle close to his face, there came the Latin words Mrs Duchemin—and Tietjens!—had heard. He knew then what he was up against. He took another look at the prize-fighter; moved his head to one side to catch a momentary view of the gigantic Mr Horsley, whose size took on a new meaning. Then he settled down in his chair and ate a kidney. The physical force present was no doubt enough to suppress Mr Duchemin should he become violent. And trained! It was one of the curious, minor coincidences of life that, at Cambridge, he had once thought of hiring this very Parry to follow round his dear friend Sim. Sim, the most brilliant of sardonic ironists, sane, decent, and ordinarily a little prudish on the surface, had been subject to just such temporary lapses as Mr Duchemin. On society occasions he would stand up and shout or sit down and whisper the most unthinkable indecencies. Macmaster, who had loved him very much, had run round with Sim as often as he could, and had thus gained skill in dealing with these manifestations. . . . He felt suddenly a certain pleasure! He thought he might gain prestige in the eyes of Mrs Duchemin if he dealt quietly and efficiently with this situation. It might even lead to an intimacy. He asked nothing better!

He knew that Mrs Duchemin had turned towards him: he could feel her listening and observing him; it was as if her glance was warm on his cheek. But he did not look round; he had to keep his eyes on the gloating face of her husband. Mr Duchemin was quoting Petronius, leaning towards his guest. Macmaster consumed kidneys stiffly.

He said:

'That isn't the amended version of the iambics. Wila-
movitz Möllendorf that we used . . .'

To interrupt him Mr Duchemin put his thin hand cour-
teously on Macmaster's arm. It had a great cornelian seal
set in red gold on the third finger. He went on, reciting in
ecstasy; his head a little on one side as if he were listening
to invisible choristers. Macmaster really disliked the Oxford
intonation of Latin. He looked for a short moment at Mrs
Duchemin; her eyes were upon him; large, shadowy, full
of gratitude. He saw, too, that they were welling over with
wetness.

He looked quietly back at Duchemin. And suddenly it
came to him; she was suffering! She was probably suffering intensely. It had not occurred to him that she would
suffer—partly because he was without nerves himself,
partly because he had conceived of Mrs Duchemin as
firstly feeling admiration for himself. Now it seemed to him
abominable that she should suffer.

Mrs Duchemin was in agony. Macmaster had looked at
her intently and looked away! She read into his glance
contempt for her situation, and anger that he should have
been placed in such a position. In her pain she stretched
out her hand and touched his arm.

Macmaster was aware of her touch; his mind seemed
filled with sweetness. But he kept his head obstinately
averted. For her sake he did not dare to look away from
the maniacal face. A crisis was coming. Mr Duchemin had
arrived at the English translation. He placed his hands on
the table-cloth in preparation for rising; he was going to
stand on his feet and shout obscenities to the other guests.
It was the exact moment.

Macmaster made his voice dry and penetrating to say:

' "Youth of tepid loves" is a lamentable rendering of
puer callide! It's lamentably antiquated. . . .'

Duchemin chewed and said:

'What? What? What's that?'

'It's just like Oxford to use an eighteenth-century crib. I
suppose that's Whiston and Ditton? Something like that.

... ' He observed Duchemin, brought out of his impulse, to be wavering—as if he were coming awake in a strange place! He added:

'Anyhow it's wretched schoolboy smut. Fifth form. Or not even that. Have some galantine. I'm going to. Your sole's cold.'

Mr Duchemin looked down at his plate.

'Yes! Yes!' he muttered. 'Yes! With sugar and vinegar sauce!' The prize-fighter slipped away to the sideboard, an admirable, quiet fellow; as unobtrusive as a burying beetle. Macmaster said:

'You were about to tell me something for my little monograph. What became of Maggie ... Maggie Simpson. The Scots girl who was model for *Alla Finestra del Cielo*?'

Mr Duchemin looked at Macmaster with sane, muddled, rather exhausted eyes:

'*Alla Finestra!*' he exclaimed: 'Oh yes! I've got the watercolour. I saw her sitting for it and bought it on the spot. . . .' He looked again at his place, started at sight of the galantine and began to eat ravenously: 'A beautiful girl!' he said. 'Very long necked ... She wasn't of course ... eh ... respectable! She's living yet, I think. Very old. I saw her two years ago. She had a lot of pictures. Relics of course! ... In the Whitechapel Road she lived. She was naturally of that class. . . . ' He went muttering on, his head over his plate. Macmaster considered that the fit was over. He was irresistibly impelled to turn to Mrs Duchemin; her face was rigid, stiff. He said swiftly:

'If he'll eat a little: get his stomach filled ... It calls the blood down from the head. . . .'

She said:

'Oh, forgive! It's dreadful for you! Myself I will never forgive!'

He said:

'No! No! ... Why, it's what I'm *for*!'

A deep emotion brought her whole white face to life:

'Oh, you *good* man!' she said in her profound tones, and they remained gazing at each other.

Suddenly, from behind Macmaster's back Mr Duchemin shouted:

'I say he made a settlement on her, *dum casta et sola*, of course. Whilst she remained chaste and alone!'

Mr Duchemin, suddenly feeling the absence of the powerful will that had seemed to overweigh his own like a great force in the darkness, was on his feet, panting and delighted:

'Chaste!' he shouted. 'Chaste you observe! What a world of suggestion in the word . . .' He surveyed the opulent broadness of his tablecloth; it spread out before his eyes as if it had been a great expanse of meadow in which he could gallop, relaxing his limbs after long captivity. He shouted three obscene words and went on in his Oxford Movement voice: 'But chastity . . .'

Mrs Wannop suddenly said:

'Oh!' and looked at her daughter, whose face grew slowly crimson as she continued to peel a peach. Mrs Wannop turned to Mr Horsley beside her and said:

'You write, too, I believe, Mr Horsley. No doubt something more learned than my poor readers would care for. . . .' Mr Horsley had been preparing, according to his instructions from Mrs Duchemin, to shout a description of an article he had been writing about the *Mosella* of Ausonius, but as he was slow in starting the lady got in first. She talked on serenely about the tastes of the large public. Tietjens leaned across to Miss Wannop and, holding in his right hand a half-peeled fig, said to her as loudly as he could:

'I've got a message for you from Mr Waterhouse. He says if you'll . . .'

The completely deaf Miss Fox—who had had her training by writing—remarked diagonally to Mrs Duchemin:

'I think we shall have thunder to-day. Have you remarked the number of minute insects . . .'

'When my revered preceptor,' Mr Duchemin thundered on, 'drove away in the carriage on his wedding day he said to his bride: "We will live like blessed angels!" How sublime! I, too, after my nuptials . . .'

Mrs Duchemin suddenly screamed:

'Oh . . . *no*!'

As if checked for a moment in their stride all the others paused—for a breath. Then they continued talking with polite animation and listening with minute attention. To Tietjens that seemed the highest achievement and justification of English manners!

Parry, the prize-fighter, had twice caught his master by the arm and shouted that breakfast was getting cold. He said now to Macmaster that he and the Rev. Mr Horsley could get Mr Duchemin away, but there'd be a hell of a fight. Macmaster whispered: 'Wait!' and, turning to Mrs Duchemin he said: 'I can stop him. Shall I?' She said:

'Yes! Yes! Anything!' He observed tears; isolated upon her cheeks, a thing he had never seen. With caution and with hot rage he whispered into the prize-fighter's hairy ear that was held down to him:

'Punch him in the kidney. With your thumb. As *hard* as you can without breaking your thumb . . .'

Mr Duchemin had just declaimed:

'I, too, after my nuptials . . .' He began to wave his arms, pausing and looking from unlistening face to unlistening face. Mrs Duchemin had just screamed.

Mr Duchemin thought that the arrow of God struck him. He imagined himself an unworthy messenger. In such pain as he had never conceived of he fell into his chair and sat huddled up, a darkness covering his eyes.

'He won't get up again,' Macmaster whispered to the appreciative pugilist. 'He'll want to. But he'll be afraid to.'

He said to Mrs Duchemin:

'Dearest lady! It's all over. I assure you of that. It's a scientific nerve counter-irritant.'

Mrs Duchemin said:

'Forgive!' with one deep sob: 'You can never respect . . .' She felt her eyes explore his face as the wretch in a cell

explores the face of his executioner for a sign of pardon.
Her heart stayed still: her breath suspended itself . . .

Then complete heaven began. Upon her left palm she
felt cool fingers beneath the cloth. This man knew always
the exact right action! Upon the fingers, cool, like spike-
nard and ambrosia, her fingers closed themselves.

In complete bliss, in a quiet room, his voice went on
talking. At first with great neatness of phrase, but with
what refinement! He explained that certain excesses being
merely nervous cravings, can be combated if not, indeed,
cured altogether, by the fear of, by the determination not
to endure, sharp physical pain—which of course is a nervous matter, too! . . .

Parry, at a given moment, had said into his master's ear:

'It's time you prepared for your sermon to-morrow, sir,'
and Mr Duchemin had gone as quietly as he had arrived,
gliding over the thick carpet to the small door.

Then Macmaster said to her:

'You come from Edinburgh? You'll know the Fifeshire
coast then.'

'Do I not?' she said. His hand remained in hers. He
began to talk of the whins on the links and the sanderlings
along the flats, with such a Scots voice and in phrases so
vivid that she saw her childhood again, and had in her eyes
a wetness of a happier order. She released his cool hand
after a long, gentle pressure. But when it was gone it was
as if much of her life went. She said: 'You'll be knowing
Kingussie House, just outside your town. It was there I
spent my holidays as a child.'

He answered:

'Maybe I played round it a barefoot lad and you in your
grandeur within.'

She said:

'Oh, no! Hardly! There would be the difference of our
ages! And . . . and indeed there are other things I will tell
you.'

She addressed herself to Tietjens, with all her heroic
armour of charm buckled on again:

'Only think! I find Mr Macmaster and I almost played together in our youth.'

He looked at her, she knew, with a commiseration that she hated:

'Then you're an older friend than I,' he said, 'though I've known him since I was fourteen, and I don't believe you could be a better. He's a good fellow. . . .'

She hated him for his condescension towards a better man and for his warning—she *knew* it was a warning—to her to spare his friend.

Mrs Wannop gave a distinct but not an alarming scream. Mr Horsley had been talking to her about an unusual fish that used to inhabit the Moselle in Roman times. The *Mosella* of Ausonius; the subject of the essay he was writing is mostly fish. . . .

'No,' he shouted, 'it's been said to be the roach. But there are no roach in the river now. *Vannulis viridis, oculisque*. No. It's the other way round: *Red* fins . . .'

Mrs Wannop's scream and her wide gesture: her hand, indeed, was nearly over his mouth and her trailing sleeve across his plate!—were enough to interrupt him.

'*Tietjens!*' she again screamed. 'Is it possible? . . .'

She pushed her daughter out of her seat and, moving round beside the young man, she overwhelmed him with vociferous love. As Tietjens had turned to speak to Mrs Duchemin she had recognized his aquiline half-profile as exactly that of his father at her own wedding breakfast. To the table that knew it by heart—though Tietjens himself didn't!—she recited the story of how his father had saved her life, and was her mascot. And she offered the son—for to the father she had never been allowed to make any return—her horse, her purse, her heart, her time, her all. She was so completely sincere that, as the party broke up, she just nodded to Macmaster and, catching Tietjens forcibly by the arm, said perfunctorily to the critic:

'Sorry I can't help you any more with the article, but my dear Chrissie must have the books he wants. At once! This very minute!'

She moved off, Tietjens grappled to her, her daughter following as a young swan follows its parents. In her gracious manner Mrs Duchemin had received the thanks of her guests for her wonderful breakfast and had hoped that now that they had found their ways there. . . .

The echoes of the dispersed festival seemed to whisper in the room. Macmaster and Mrs Duchemin faced each other, their eyes wary—and longing.

He said:

'It's dreadful to have to go now. But I have an engagement.'

She said:

'Yes! I know! With your great friends.'

He answered:

'Oh, only with Mr Waterhouse and General Campion . . . and Mr Sandbach, of course . . .'

She had a moment of fierce pleasure at the thought that Tietjens was not to be of the company: *her* man would be outsoaring the vulgarian of his youth, of his past that she didn't know. . . . Almost harshly she exclaimed:

'I don't want you to be mistaken about Kingussie House. It was just a holiday school. Not a grand place.'

'It was very costly,' he said, and she seemed to waver on her feet.

'Yes! yes!' she said, nearly in a whisper. 'But you're so grand now! I was only the child of very poor bodies. Johnstons of Midlothian. But very poor bodies. . . . I. . . . He bought me, you might say. You know. . . . Put me to very rich schools; when I was fourteen . . . my people were glad. . . . But I think if my mother had known when I married . . . ' She writhed her whole body. 'Oh, dreadful! dreadful!' she exclaimed. 'I want you to know . . .'

His hands were shaking as if he had been in a jolting cart. . . .

Their lips met in a passion of pity and tears. He removed his mouth to say: 'I must see you this evening. . . . I shall be mad with anxiety about you.' She whispered: 'Yes! yes! . . . In the yew walk.' Her eyes were closed, she

pressed her body fiercely into his. 'You are the . . . first . . .
man . . .' she breathed.

'I will be the only one for ever,' he said.

He began to see himself; in the tall room, with the long
curtains: a round, eagle mirror reflected them gleaming:
like a bejewelled picture with great depths: the entwined
figures.

They drew apart to gaze at each other: holding hands.
. . . The voice of Tietjens said:

'Macmaster! You're to dine at Mrs Wannop's to-night.
Don't dress; I shan't.' He was looking at them without any
expression, as if he had interrupted a game of cards; large,
grey, fresh-featured, the white patch glistening on the side
of his grizzling hair.

Macmaster said:

'All right. It's near here, isn't it? . . . I've got an engagement just after . . .' Tietjens said that that would be all
right: he would be working himself. All night probably.
For Waterhouse . . .

Mrs Duchemin said with swift jealousy:

'You let him order you about . . .' Tietjens was gone.

Macmaster said absently:

'Who? Chrissie! . . . Yes! Sometimes I him, sometimes
he me. . . . We make engagements. My best friend. The
most brilliant man in England, of the best stock too. Tietjens of Groby. . . .' Feeling that she didn't appreciate his
friend he was abstractedly piling on commendations: 'He's
making calculations now. For the Government that no
other man in England could make. But he's going . . .'

An extreme languor had settled on him, he felt weakened
but yet triumphant with the cessation of her grasp. It
occurred to him numbly that he would be seeing less of
Tietjens. A grief. He heard himself quote:

' "Since when we stand side by side!" ' His voice
trembled.

'Ah yes!' came in her deep tones: 'The beautiful lines
. . . They're true. We must part. In this world . . .' They
seemed to her lovely and mournful words to say; heavenly

to have them to say, vibratingly, arousing all sorts of images. Macmaster, mournfully too, said:

'We must wait.' He added fiercely: 'But to-night, at dusk!' He imagined the dusk, under the yew hedge. A shining motor drew up in the sunlight under the window.

'Yes! yes!' she said. 'There's a little white gate from the lane.' She imagined their interview of passion and mournfulness amongst dim objects half seen. That she could allow herself of glamour.

Afterwards he must come to the house to ask after her health and they would walk side by side on the lawn, publicly, in the warm light, talking of indifferent but beautiful poetries, a little wearily, but with what currents electrifying and passing between their flesh.... And then: long, circumspect years....

Macmaster went down the tall steps to the car that gleamed in the summer sun. The roses shone over the supremely levelled turf. His heel met the stones with the hard tread of a conqueror. He could have shouted aloud!

VI

Tietjens lit a pipe beside the stile, having first meticulously cleaned out the bowl and the stem with a surgical needle, in his experience the best of all pipe-cleaners, since, made of German silver, it is flexible, won't corrode and is indestructible. He wiped off methodically, with a great dock-leaf, the glutinous brown products of burnt tobacco, the young woman, as he was aware, watching him from behind his back. As soon as he had restored the surgical needle to the notebook in which it lived, and had put the notebook into its bulky pocket, Miss Wannop moved off down the path: it was only suited for Indian file, and had on the left hand a ten-foot, untrimmed quicken hedge, the hawthorn blossoms just beginning to blacken at the edges and small green haws to show. On the right the grass was above knee high and bowed to those that passed. The sun was exactly vertical; the chaffinches said 'Pink! Pink!'; the young woman had an agreeable back.

This, Tietjens thought, is England! A man and a maid walk through Kentish grass-fields: the grass ripe for the scythe. The man honourable, clean, upright; the maid virtuous, clean, vigorous: he of good birth; she of birth quite as good; each filled with a too good breakfast that each could yet capably digest. Each come just from an admirably appointed establishment: a table surrounded by the best people: their promenade sanctioned, as it were by the Church—two clergy—the State: two Government officials; by mothers, friends, old maids. . . . Each knew the names of birds that piped and grasses that bowed: chaffinch, greenfinch, yellow-ammer (*not*, my dear, hammer! *amonrer* from the Middle High German for 'finch'), garden warbler, Dartford warbler, pied-wagtail, known as 'dishwasher.' (These *charming* local dialect names.) Marguerites over the grass, stretching in an infinite white blaze: grasses purple in a haze to the far distant hedgerow: coltsfoot, wild white clover, sainfoin, Italian rye grass (all technical names that the best people must know: the best grass mixture for permanent pasture on the Wealden loam). In the hedge: our lady's bedstraw: dead-nettle: bachelor's button (but in *Sussex* they call it ragged robin, my dear): so interesting! Cowslip (paigle, you know from the old French *pasque*, meaning Easter); burr, burdock (farmer that thy wife may thrive, but not burr and burdock wive!); violet leaves, the flowers of course over; black bryony; wild clematis, later it's old man's beard; purple loose-strife. (That our young maid's long purples call and literal shepherds give a grosser name. *So* racy of the soil!!) . . . Walk, then, through the field, gallant youth and fair maid, minds cluttered up with all these useless anodynes for thought, quotation, imbecile epithets! Dead silent: unable to talk: from too good breakfast to probably extremely bad lunch. The young woman, so the young man is duly warned, to prepare it: pink india-rubber, half-cooked cold beef, no doubt: tepid potatoes, water in the bottom of willow-pattern dish.

(*No! Not* genuine willow-pattern, of *course*, Mr Tietjens.)
Overgrown lettuce with wood-vinegar to make the mouth
scream with pain; pickles, also preserved in wood-vinegar;
two bottles of public-house beer that, on opening, squirts
to the wall. A glass of invalid port ... for the *gentleman*!
... and the jaws hardly able to open after the too enormous
breakfast at 10.15. Midday now!

'God's England!' Tietjens exclaimed to himself in high
good humour. 'Land of Hope and Glory!—F natural descending to tonic C major: chord of 6–4, suspension over
dominant seventh to common chord of C major. ... All
absolutely correct! Double basses, cellos, all violins: all
wood wind: all brass. Full grand organ: all stops: special
vox humana and key-bugle effect. ... Across the counties
came the sound of bugles that his father knew. ... Pipe
exactly right. It must be: pipe of Englishman of good birth:
ditto tobacco. Attractive young woman's back. English
midday mid-summer. Best climate in the world! No day
on which man may not go abroad!' Tietjens paused and
aimed with his hazel stick an immense blow at a tall spike
of yellow mullein with its undecided, furry, glaucous leaves
and its undecided, buttony, unripe lemon-coloured flowers.
The structure collapsed, gracefully, like a woman killed
among crinolines!

'Now I'm a bloody murderer!' Tietjens said. 'Not gory!
Green-stained with vital fluid of innocent plant. ... And by
God! Not a woman in the country who won't let you rape
her after an hour's acquaintance!' He slew two more mul-
leins and a sow-thistle! A shadow, but not from the sun, a
gloom, lay across the sixty acres of purple grass bloom and
marguerites, white: like petticoats of lace over the grass!

'By God,' he said, 'Church! State! Army! H.M. Ministry: H.M. Opposition: H.M. City Man. ... All the governing class! All rotten! Thank God we've got a navy! ...
But perhaps that's rotten too! Who knows! Britannia needs
no bulwarks. ... Then thank God for the upright young
man and the virtuous maiden in the summer fields: he Tory
of the Tories as he should be: she suffragette of the mili-

tants: militant here on earth ... as she should be! As she
should be! In the early decades of the twentieth century
however else can a woman keep clean and wholesome!
Ranting from platforms, splendid for the lungs: bashing in
policemen's helmets.... No! It's I do that: my part, I
think, miss! ... Carrying heavy banners in twenty-mile
processions through streets of Sodom. All splendid! I bet
she's virtuous. But you can tell it in the eye. Nice eyes!
Attractive back. Virginal cockiness. ... Yes, better occupation for mothers or empire than attending on lewd husbands year in year out till you're as hysterical as a female
cat on heat.... You could see it in her: that woman: you
can see it in most of 'em! Thank God then for the Tory,
upright young married man and the suffragette kid ...
Backbone of England! ...'

He killed another flower.

'But by God! we're both under a cloud! Both! ... That
kid and I! And General Lord Edward Campion, Lady
Claudine Sandbach, and the Hon. Paul, M.P. (suspended)
to spread the tale.... And forty toothless fogies in the club
to spread it: and no end visiting books yawning to have
your names cut out of them, my boy! ... My dear boy: I
so regret: your father's oldest friend.... By Jove, the
pistachio nut of that galantine! Repeating! Breakfast gone
wrong: gloomy reflections! Thought I could stand anything: digestion of an ostrich.... But no! Gloomy reflections: I'm hysterical: like that large-eyed whore! For same
reason! Wrong diet and wrong life: diet meant for par-
tridge shooters over the turnips consumed by the sedentary.
England the land of pills.... *Das Pillen-Land*, the Germans call us. Very properly.... And, damn it: outdoor
diet: boiled mutton, turnips: sedentary life ... and forced
up against the filthiness of the world: your nose in it all day
long! ... Why, hang it, I'm as badly off as she. Sylvia's as
bad as Duchemin! ... I'd never have thought that.... No
wonder meat's turned to prussic acid ... prime cause of
neurasthenia.... What a beastly muddle! Poor Macmaster!
He's finished. Poor devil: he'd better have ogled this kid.

He could have sung: "Highland Mary" a better tune than "This is the end of every man's desire" . . . You can cut it on his tombstone, you can write it on his card that a young man tacked on to a paulo-post Pre-Raphaelite prostitute. . . .'

He stopped suddenly in his walk. It had occurred to him that he ought not to be walking with this girl!

'But damn it all,' he said to himself, 'she makes a good screen for Sylvia . . . who cares! She must chance it. She's probably struck off all their beastly visiting lists already . . . as a suffragette!'

Miss Wannop, a cricket pitch or so ahead of him, hopped over a stile: left foot on the step, right on the top bar, a touch of the left on the other steps, and down on the white, drifted dust of a road they no doubt had to cross. She stood waiting, her back still to him. . . . Her nimble footwork, her attractive back, seemed to him, now, infinitely pathetic. To let scandal attach to her was like cutting the wings of a goldfinch: the bright creature, yellow, white, golden and delicate, that in the sunlight makes a haze with its wings beside thistle-tops. No; damn it! it was worse; it was worse than putting out, as the bird-fancier does, the eyes of a chaffinch. . . . Infinitely pathetic!

Above the stile, in an elm, a chaffinch said: 'Pink! pink!'

The imbecile sound filled him with rage; he said to the bird:

'Damn your eyes! *Have* them put out, then!' The beastly bird that made the odious noise, when it had its eyes put out, at least squealed like any other skylark or tom-tit. Damn all birds, field naturalists, botanists! In the same way he addressed the back of Miss Wannop: 'Damn your eyes! *Have* your chastity impugned then! What do you speak to strange men in public for? You know you can't do it in this country. If it were a decent, straight land like Ireland where people cut each other's throats for clean issues: Papist versus Prot. . . . well, you could! You could walk through Ireland from east to west and speak to every man you met. . . . "Rich and rare were the gems she wore. . . ." To every

5*

man you met as long as he wasn't an Englishman of good birth: *that* would deflower you!' He was scrambling clumsily over the stile. 'Well! *be* deflowered then: *lose* your infantile reputation. You've spoken to strange pitch: you're defiled ... with the benefit of Clergy, Army, Cabinet, Administration, Opposition, mothers and old maids of England. . . . They'd all tell you you can't talk to a strange man, in the sunlight, on the links, without becoming a screen for some Sylvia or other. . . . Then *be* a screen for Sylvia: *get* struck off the visiting books! The deeper you're implicated, the more bloody villain I am! I'd like the whole lot to see us here: that would settle it. . . .'

Nevertheless, when at the roadside he stood level with Miss Wannop who did not look at him, and saw the white road running to right and left with no stile opposite, he said gruffly to her:

'Where's the next stile? I hate walking on roads!' She pointed with her chin along the opposite hedgerow. 'Fifty yards!' she said.

'Come along!' he exclaimed, and set off at a trot almost. It had come into his head that it would be just the beastly sort of thing that would happen if a car with General Campion and Lady Claudine and Paul Sandbach all aboard should come along that blinding stretch of road: or one alone: perhaps the General driving the dog-cart he affected. He said to himself:

'By God! If they cut this girl I'd break their backs over my knee!' and he hastened. 'Just the beastly thing that *would* happen.' The road probably led straight in at the front door of Mountby!

Miss Wannop trotted along a little in his rear. She thought him the most extraordinary man: as mad as he was odious. Sane people, if they're going to hurry—but *why* hurry!—do it in the shade of field hedgerows, not in the white blaze of county council roads. Well, he could go ahead. In the next field she was going to have it out with him: she didn't intend to be hot with running: let him be, his hateful, but certainly noticeable eyes, protruding at her

like a lobster's; but she was cool and denunciatory in her
pretty blouse. . . .

There was a dog-cart coming behind them!

Suddenly it came into her head: that fool had been
lying when he had said that the police meant to let them
alone: lying over the breakfast-table. . . . The dog-cart
contained the police: after them! She didn't waste time
looking round: she wasn't a fool like Atalanta in the egg-
race. She picked up her heels and sprinted. She beat him
by a yard and a half to the kissing-gate, white in the hedge:
panicked, breathing hard. He panted into it, after her: the
fool hadn't the sense to let her through first. They were
jammed in together: face to face, panting! An occasion on
which sweethearts kiss in Kent: the gate being made in
three, the inner flange of the V moving on hinges. It stops
cattle getting through: but this great lout of a Yorkshireman didn't know: trying to push through like a mad
bullock! Now they were caught. Three weeks in Wandsworth gaol. . . . Oh hang. . . .

The voice of Mrs Wannop—of course it was only
mother! Twenty feet on high or so behind the kicking
mare, with a good round face like a peony—said:

'Ah, you can jam my Val in a gate and hold her . . . but
she gave you seven yards in twenty and beat you to the
gate. That was her father's ambition!' She thought of
them as children running races. She beamed down, round-
faced and simple, on Tietjens from beside the driver, who
had a black, slouch hat and the grey beard of St Peter.

'My dear boy!' she said, 'my dear boy; it's such a
satisfaction to have you under my roof!'

The black horse reared on end, the patriarch sawing at
its mouth. Mrs Wannop said unconcernedly: 'Stephen
Joel! I haven't done talking.'

Tietjens was gazing enragedly at the lower part of the
horse's sweat-smeared stomach.

'You soon will have,' he said, 'with the girth in that
state. Your neck will be broken.'

'Oh, I don't think so,' Mrs Wannop said. 'Joel only bought the turn-out yesterday.'

Tietjens addressed the driver with some ferocity:

'Here, get down, you,' he said. He held, himself, the head of the horse whose nostrils were wide with emotion: it rubbed its forehead almost immediately against his chest. He said: 'Yes! yes! There! there!' Its limbs lost their tautness. The aged driver scrambled down from the high seat, trying to come down at first forward and then backwards. Tietjens fired indignant orders at him:

'Lead the horse into the shade of that tree. Don't touch her bit: her mouth's sore. Where did you get this job lot? Ashford market: thirty pounds: it's worth more.... But, blast you, don't you see you've got a thirteen hands pony's harness for a sixteen and a half hands horse. Let the bit out: three holes: it's cutting the animal's tongue in half. ... This animal's a rig. Do you know what a rig is? If you give it corn for a fortnight it will kick you and the cart and the stable to pieces in five minutes one day.' He led the conveyance, Mrs Wannop triumphantly complacent and all, into a patch of shade beneath elms.

'Loosen that bit, confound you,' he said to the driver. 'Ah! you're afraid.'

He loosened the bit himself, covering his fingers with greasy harness polish which he hated. Then he said:

'Can you hold her head or are you afraid of that too? You *deserve* to have her bite your hands off.' He addressed Miss Wannop: 'Can *you*?' She said: 'No! I'm afraid of horses. I can drive any sort of car: but I'm afraid of horses.' He said: 'Very proper!' He stood back and looked at the horse: it had dropped its head and lifted its near hind foot, resting the toe on the ground: an attitude of relaxation.

'She'll stand now!' he said. He undid the girth, bending down uncomfortably, perspiring and greasy: the girth-strap parted in his hand.

'It's true,' Mrs Wannop said. 'I'd have been dead in three

minutes if you hadn't seen that. The cart would have gone over backwards . . .'

Tietjens took out a large, complicated, horn-handled knife like a schoolboy's. He selected a punch and pulled it open. He said to the driver:

'Have you got any cobbler's thread? Any string? Any copper wire? A rabbit wire, now? Come, you've got a rabbit wire or you're not a handy-man.'

The driver moved his slouch hat circularly in negation. This seemed to be Quality who summons you for poaching if you own to possessing rabbit wires.

Tietjens laid the girth along the shaft and punched into it with his punch.

'Woman's work!' he said to Mrs Wannop, 'but it'll take you home and last you six months as well . . . But I'll sell this whole lot for you to-morrow.'

Mrs Wannop sighed:

'I suppose it'll fetch a ten-pound note . . .' She said: 'I ought to have gone to market myself.'

'No!' Tietjens answered: 'I'll get you fifty for it or I'm no Yorkshireman. This fellow hasn't been swindling you. He's got you deuced good value for money, but he doesn't know what's suited for ladies; a white pony and a basket-work chaise is what you want.'

'Oh, I like a bit of spirit,' Mrs Wannop said.

'Of course you do,' Tietjens answered: 'but this turn-out's too much.'

He sighed a little and took out his surgical needle.

'I'm going to hold this band together with this,' he said. 'It's so pliant it will make two stitches and hold for ever. . . .'

But the handy-man was beside him, holding out the contents of his pockets; a greasy leather pouch, a ball of beeswax, a knife, a pipe, a bit of cheese and a pale rabbit wire. He had made up his mind that *this* Quality was benevolent and he made offering of all his possessions.

Tietjens said: 'Ah,' and then, while he unknotted the wire:

'Well! Listen . . . you bought this turn-out off a higgler at the back door of the Leg of Mutton Inn.'

'Saracen's 'Ed!' the driver muttered.

'You got it for thirty pounds because the higgler wanted money bad. *I* know. And dirt cheap. . . . But a rig isn't everybody's driving. All right for a vet or a horse-coper. Like the cart that's too tall! . . . But you did damn well. Only you're not what you were, are you, at thirty? And the horse looked to be a devil and the cart so high you couldn't get out once you were in. And you kept it in the sun for two hours waiting for your mistress.'

'There wer' a bit o' lewth 'longside stable wall,' the driver muttered.

'Well! She didn't like waiting,' Tietjens said placably. 'You can be thankful your old neck's not broken. Do this band up, one hole less for the bit I've taken in.'

He prepared to climb into the driver's seat, but Mrs Wannop was there before him, at an improbable altitude on the sloping watch-box with strapped cushions.

'Oh, no, you don't,' she said, 'no one drives me and my horse but me or my coachman when I'm about. Not even you, dear boy.'

'I'll come with you then,' Tietjens said.

'Oh, no, you don't,' she answered. 'No one's neck to be broken in this conveyance but mine and Joel's,' she added: 'perhaps to-night if I'm satisfied the horse is fit to drive.'

Miss Wannop suddenly exclaimed:

'Oh, *no*, mother.' But the handy-man having climbed in, Mrs Wannop flirted her whip and started the horse. She pulled up at once and leaned over to Tietjens:

'*What* a life for that poor woman,' she said. 'We must *all* do all we can for her. She could have her husband put in a lunatic asylum to-morrow. It's sheer self-sacrifice that she doesn't.'

The horse went off at a gentle, regular trot.

Tietjens addressed Miss Wannop:

'What hands your mother's got,' he said, 'it isn't often

one sees a woman with hands like that on a horse's mouth.
. . . Did you see how she pulled up? . . .'

He was aware that, all this while, from the road-side,
the girl had been watching him with shining eyes: intently
even: with fascination.

'I suppose you think that a mighty fine performance,'
she said.

'I didn't make a very good job of the girth,' he said.
'Let's get off this road.'

'Setting poor, weak women in their places,' Miss Wannop continued. 'Soothing the horse like a man with a
charm. I suppose you soothe women like that, too. I pity
your wife. . . . The English country male! And making
a devoted vassal at sight of the handy-man. The feudal
system all complete. . . .'

Tietjens said:

'Well, you know, it'll make him all the better servant to
you if he thinks you've friends in the know. The lower
classes are like that. Let's get off this road.'

She said:

'You're in a mighty hurry to get behind the hedge. Are
the police after us or aren't they? Perhaps you were lying
at breakfast: to calm the hysterical nerves of a weak
woman.'

'I wasn't lying,' he said, 'but I hate roads when there
are field-paths . . .'

'That's a phobia, like any woman's,' she exclaimed.

She almost ran through the kissing-gate and stood awaiting him.

'I suppose,' she said, 'if you've stopped off the police
with your high and mighty male ways you think you've
destroyed my romantic young dream. You haven't. I don't
want the police after me. I believe I'd *die* if they put me
in Wandsworth . . . I'm a coward.'

'Oh, no, you aren't,' he said, but he was following his
own train of thought, just as she wasn't in the least listening to him. 'I daresay you're a heroine all right. *Not* because you persevere in actions the consequences of which

you fear. But I daresay you can touch pitch and not be defiled.'

Being too well brought up to interrupt she waited till he had said all he wanted to say, then she exclaimed:

'Let's settle the preliminaries. It's obvious mother means us to see a great deal of you. *You're* going to be a mascot, too, like your father. I suppose you think you are: you saved me from the police yesterday, you appear to have saved mother's neck to-day. You appear, too, to be going to make twenty pounds profit on a horse deal. You say you will and you seem to be that sort of a person... Twenty pounds is no end in a family like ours... Well, then, you appear to be going to be the regular *bel ami* of the Wannop family...'

Tietjens said:

'I hope not.'

'Oh, I don't mean,' she said, 'that you're going to rise to fame by making love to all the women of the Wannop family. Besides, there's only me. But mother will press you into all sorts of odd jobs: and there will always be a plate for you at the table. Don't shudder! I'm a regular good cook—*cuisine bourgeoise* of course. I learned under a real professed cook, though a drunkard. That meant I used to do half the cooking and the family was particular. Ealing people are: county councillors, half of them, and the like. So I know what men are...' She stopped and said good-naturedly: 'But do, for goodness' sake, get it over. I'm sorry I was rude to you. But it *is* irritating to have to stand like a stuffed rabbit while a man is acting like a regular Admiral Crichton, and cool and collected, with the English country gentleman air and all.'

Tietjens winced. The young woman had come a little too near the knuckle of his wife's frequent denunciations of himself. And she exclaimed:

'No! That's not fair! I'm an ungrateful pig! You didn't show a bit more side really than a capable workman must who's doing his job in the midst of a crowd of incapable duffers. But just get it out, will you? Say once and for all that—you know the proper, pompous manner: you are not without sympathy with our aims: but you disapprove —oh, immensely, strongly—of our methods.'

It struck Tietjens that the young woman was a good deal more interested in the cause—of votes for women— than he had given her credit for. He wasn't much in the mood for talking to young women, but it was with considerably more than the surface of his mind that he answered:

'I don't. I approve entirely of your methods: but your aims are idiotic.'

She said:

'You don't know, I suppose, that Gertie Wilson, who's in bed at our house, is wanted by the police: not only for yesterday, but for putting explosives in a whole series of letter-boxes?'

He said:

'I didn't ... but it was a perfectly proper thing to do. She hasn't burned any of my letters or I might be annoyed; but it wouldn't interfere with my approval.'

'You don't think,' she asked earnestly, 'that we ... mother and I ... are likely to get heavy sentences for shielding her? It would be beastly bad luck on mother. Because she's an anti ...'

'I don't know about the sentence,' Tietjens said, 'but we'd better get her off your premises as soon as we can. ...'

She said:

'Oh, you'll *help*?'

He answered:

'Of course, your mother can't be incommoded. She's written the only novel that's been fit to read since the eighteenth century.'

She stopped and said earnestly:

'Look here. Don't be one of those ignoble triflers who say the vote won't do women any good. Women have a rotten time. They do, really. If you'd seen what I've seen, I'm not talking through my hat.' Her voice became quite deep: she had tears in her eyes: '*Poor* women *do*!' she said, 'little insignificant creatures. We've *got* to change the divorce laws. We've *got* to get better conditions. *You* couldn't stand it if you knew what I know.'

Her emotion vexed him, for it seemed to establish a sort of fraternal intimacy that he didn't at the moment want. Women do not show emotion except before their families. He said drily:

'I daresay I shouldn't. But I don't know, so I can!'

She said with deep disappointment:

'Oh, you *are* a beast! And I shall never beg your pardon for saying that. I don't believe you mean what you say, but merely to say it is heartless.'

This was another of the counts of Sylvia's indictment and Tietjens winced again. She explained:

'You don't know the case of the Pimlico army clothing factory workers or you wouldn't say the vote would be no use to women.'

'I know the case perfectly well,' Tietjens said: 'It came under my official notice, and I remember thinking that there never was a more signal instance of the uselessness of the vote to anyone.'

'We can't be thinking of the same case,' she said.

'We are,' he answered. 'The Pimlico army clothing factory is in the constituency of Westminster; the Under-Secretary for War is member for Westminster; his majority at the last election was six hundred. The clothing factory employed seven hundred men at 1s. 6d. an hour, all these men having votes in Westminster. The seven hundred men wrote to the Under-Secretary to say that if their screw wasn't raised to two bob they'd vote solid against him at the next election. . . .'

Miss Wannop said: 'Well then!'

'So,' Tietjens said: 'The Under-Secretary had the seven hundred men at eighteenpence fired and took on seven hundred women at tenpence. What good did the vote do the seven hundred men? What good did a vote ever do anyone?'

Miss Wannop checked at that and Tietjens prevented
her exposure of his fallacy by saying quickly:

'Now, if the seven hundred women, backed by all the
other ill-used, sweated women of the country, had
threatened the Under-Secretary, burned the pillar-boxes,
and cut up all the golf greens round his country house,
they'd have had their wages raised to half a crown next
week. That's the only straight method. It's the feudal
system at work.'

'Oh, but we couldn't cut up *golf* greens,' Miss Wannop
said. 'At least the W.S.P.U. debated it the other day, and
decided that anything so unsporting would make us *too*
unpopular. I was for it personally.'

Tietjens groaned:

'It's maddening,' he said, 'to find women, as soon as they
get in Council, as muddleheaded and as afraid to face
straight issues as men! ...'

'You won't, by-the-by,' the girl interrupted, 'be able to
sell our horse to-morrow. You've forgotten that it will be
Sunday.'

'I shall have to on Monday, then,' Tietjens said. 'The
point about the feudal system ...'

Just after lunch—and it was an admirable lunch of the
cold lamb, new potatoes and mint-sauce variety, the mint-
sauce made with white wine vinegar and as soft as kisses,
the claret perfectly drinkable and the port much more
than that, Mrs Wannop having gone back to the late professor's wine merchants—Miss Wannop herself went to
answer the telephone....

The cottage had no doubt been a cheap one, for it was
old, roomy and comfortable; but effort had no doubt, too,
been lavished on its low rooms. The dining-room had
windows on each side and a beam across; the dining silver
had been picked up at sales, the tumblers were old cut
glass; on each side of the ingle was a grandfather's chair.
The garden had red brick paths, sunflowers, hollyhocks
and scarlet gladioli. There was nothing to it all, but the
garden-gate was well hung.

To Tietjens all this meant effort. Here was a woman who, a few years ago, was penniless, in the most miserable-off circumstances, supporting life with the most exiguous of all implements. What effort hadn't it meant! and what effort didn't it mean? There was a boy at Eton . . . a senseless, but a gallant effort.

Mrs Wannop sat opposite him in the other grandfather's chair; an admirable hostess, an admirable lady. Full of spirit in dashes; but tired. As an old horse is tired that, taking three men to harness it in the stable yard, starts out like a stallion, but soon drops to a jog-trot. The face tired, really; scarlet-cheeked with the good air, but seamed downward. She could sit there at ease, the plump hands covered with a black lace shawl, and descending on each side of her lap, as much at ease as any other Victorian great lady. But at lunch she had let drop that she had written for eight hours every day for the last four years—till that day —without missing a day. To-day being Saturday, she had no leader to write:

'And, my darling boy,' she had said to him. 'I'm giving it to you. I'd give it to no other soul but your father's son. Not even to . . .' And she had named the name that she most respected. 'And that's the truth,' she had added. Nevertheless, even over lunch, she had fallen into abstractions, heavily and deeply, and made fantastic mis-statements, mostly about public affairs. . . . It all meant a tremendous record. . . .

And there he sat, his coffee and port on a little table beside him; the house belonging to him. . . .

She said:

'My dearest boy . . . you've so much to do. Do you think you ought really to drive the girls to Plimsoll to-night? They're young and inconsiderate, work comes first.'

Tietjens said:

'It isn't the distance . . .'

'You'll find that it is,' she answered humorously. 'It's twenty miles beyond Tenterden. If you don't start till ten when the moon sets, you won't be back till five, even if you've no accidents ... The horse is all right, though. ...'

Tietjens said:

'Mrs Wannop, I ought to tell you that your daughter and I are being talked about. Uglily!'

She turned her head to him; rather stiffly. But she was only coming out of an abstraction.

'Eh?' she said, and then; 'Oh! About the golf-links episode. ... It must have looked suspicious. I daresay you made a fuss, too, with the police, to head them off her.' She remained pondering for a moment, heavily, like an old pope:

'Oh, you'll live it down,' she said.

'I ought to tell you,' he persisted, 'that it's more serious than you think. I fancy I ought not to be here.'

'Not here!' she exclaimed. 'Why, where else in the world should you be? You don't get on with your wife; I know. She's a regular wrong 'un. Who else could look after you as well as Valentine and I.'

In the acuteness of that pang, for, after all, Tietjens cared more for his wife's reputation than for any other factor in a complicated world, Tietjens asked rather sharply why Mrs Wannop had called Sylvia a wrong 'un. She said in rather a protesting, sleepy way:

'My dear boy, nothing! I've guessed that there are differences between you; give me credit for some perception. Then, as you're perfectly obviously a right 'un, she must be a wrong 'un. That's all, I assure you.'

In his relief Tietjens' obstinacy revived. He liked this house; he liked this atmosphere; he liked the frugality, the choice of furniture, the way the light fell from window to window; the weariness after hard work, the affection of mother and daughter; the affection, indeed, that they both had for himself, and he was determined, if he could help it, not to damage the reputation of the daughter of the house.

Decent men, he held, don't do such things, and he recounted with some care the heads of the conversation he had had with General Campion in the dressing-room. He

seemed to see the cracked wash-bowls in their scrubbed
oak settings. Mrs Wannop's face seemed to grow greyer,
more aquiline; a little resentful! She nodded from time to
time, either to denote attention or else in sheer drowsi-
ness:

'My dear boy,' she said at last, 'it's pretty damnable to
have such things said about you. I can see that. But I
seem to have lived in a bath of scandal all my life. Every
woman who has reached my age has that feeling. . . . Now
it doesn't seem to matter . . . ' She really nodded nearly off:
then she started. 'I don't see . . . I really don't see how
I can help you as to your reputation. I'd do it if I could:
believe me. . . . But I've other things to think of. . . . I've
this house to keep going and the children to keep fed and
at school. I can't give all the thought I ought to to other
people's troubles. . . . .

She started into wakefulness and right out of her chair.

'But what a beast I am!' she said, with a sudden intonation that was exactly that of her daughter; and, drifting
with a Victorian majesty of shawl and long skirt behind
Tietjens' high-backed chair, she leaned over it and stroked
the hair on his right temple:

'My dear boy,' she said. 'Life's a bitter thing. I'm an
old novelist and know it. There you are working yourself
to death to save the nation with a wilderness of cats and
monkeys howling and squalling your personal reputation
away. . . . It was Dizzy himself said these words to me at
one of our receptions. "Here I am, Mrs Wannop," he
said . . . And . . .' She drifted for a moment. But she made
another effort: 'My dear boy,' she whispered, bending
down her head to get it near his ear: 'My dear boy; it
doesn't matter; it doesn't really matter. You'll live it down.
The only thing that matters it to do good work. Believe an
old woman who has lived very hard; "Hard lying money"
as they call it in the navy. It sounds like cant, but it's the
only real truth. . . . You'll find consolation in that. And
you'll live it down. Or perhaps you won't; that's for God in
His mercy to settle. But it won't matter; believe me, as thy

days so shall thy strength be.' She drifted into other thoughts; she was much perturbed over the plot of a new novel and much wanted to get back to the consideration of it. She stood gazing at the photograph, very faded, of her husband in side-whiskers and an immense shirt-front, but she continued to stroke Tietjens' temple with a sublime tenderness.

This kept Tietjens sitting there. He was quite aware that he had tears in his eyes; this was almost too much tenderness to bear, and, at bottom his was a perfectly direct, simple and sentimental soul. He always had bedewed eyes at the theatre, after tender love scenes, and so avoided the theatre. He asked himself twice whether he should or shouldn't make another effort, though it was almost beyond him. He wanted to sit still.

The stroking stopped; he scrambled on to his feet.

'Mrs Wannop,' he said, facing her, 'it's perfectly true. I oughtn't to care what these swine say about me, but I do. I'll reflect about what you say till I get it into my system . . .'

She said:

'Yes, yes! my dear,' and continued to gaze at the photograph.

'But,' Tietjens said; he took her mittened hand and led her back to her chair: 'What I'm concerned for at the moment is not my reputation, but your daughter Valentine's.'

She sank down into the high chair, balloon-like, and came to rest:

'Val's reputation!' she said, 'Oh! you mean they'll be striking *her* off their visiting lists. It hadn't struck me. So they will!' She remained lost in reflection for a long time.

Valentine was in the room, laughing a little. She had been giving the handy-man his dinner, and was still amused at his commendations of Tietjens.

'You've got one admirer,' she said to Tietjens. ' "Punched that rotten strap," he goes on saying, "like a gret ol' yaffle punchin' a 'ollow log!" He's had a pint of beer and said it between each gasp.' She continued to narrate the quaintness of Joel which appealed to her; informed Tietjens that 'yaffle' was Kentish for great green woodpecker; and then said:

'You haven't got any friends in Germany, have you?' She was beginning to clear the table.

Tietjens said:

'Yes; my wife's in Germany; at a place called Lob-scheid.'

She placed a pile of plates on a black japanned tray.

'I'm so sorry,' she said, without an expression of any deep regret. 'It's the ingenious clever stupidities of the telephone. I've got a telegraph message for you then. I thought it was the subject for mother's leader. It always comes through with the initials of the paper which are not unlike Tietjens, and the girl who always sends it is called Hopside. It seemed rather inscrutable, but I took it to have to do with German politics and I thought mother would understand it. . . . You're not both asleep, are you?'

Tietjens opened his eyes, the girl was standing over him, having approached from the table. She was holding out a slip of paper on which she had transcribed the message. She appeared all out of drawing and the letters of the message ran together. The message was:

'Righto. But arrange for certain Hullo Central travels with you. Sylvia Hopside Germany.'

Tietjens leaned back for a long time looking at the words; they seemed meaningless. The girl placed the paper on his knee, and went back to the table. He imagined the girl wrestling with these incomprehensibilities on the telephone.

'Of course if I'd had any sense,' the girl said, 'I should have known it couldn't have been mother's leader note; she never gets one on a Saturday.'

Tietjens heard himself announce clearly, loudly and with between each word a pause:

'It means I go to my wife on Tuesday and take her maid with me.'

'Lucky you!' the girl said, 'I wish I was you. I've never been in the Fatherland of Goethe and Rosa Luxemburg.' She went off with her great tray load, the table-cloth over her forearm. He was dimly aware that she had before then removed the crumbs with a crumb-brush. It was extraordinary with what swiftness she worked, talking all the time. That was what domestic service had done for her; an ordinary young lady would have taken twice the time, and would certainly have dropped half her words if she had tried to talk. Efficiency! He had only just realized that he was going back to Sylvia, and of course to Hell! Certainly it was Hell. If a malignant and skilful devil . . . though the devil of course is stupid and uses toys like fireworks and sulphur; it is probably only God who can, very properly, devise the long ailings of mental oppressions . . . if God then desired (and one couldn't object but one hoped He would not!) to devise for him, Christopher Tietjens, a cavernous eternity of weary hopelessness. . . . But He had done it; no doubt as retribution. What for? Who knows what sins of his own are heavily punishable in the eyes of God, for God is just? . . . Perhaps God then, after all, visits thus heavily sexual offences.

There came back into his mind, burnt in, the image of their breakfast-room, with all the brass, electrical fixings, poachers, toasters, grillers, kettle-heaters, that he detested for their imbecile inefficiency; with gross piles of hothouse flowers—that he detested for their exotic waxennesses!— with white enamelled panels that he disliked and framed, weak prints—quite genuine of course, my dear, guaranteed so by Sotheby—pinkish women in sham Gainsborough hats, selling mackerel or brooms. A wedding present that he despised. And Mrs Satterthwaite, in negligé, but with an immense hat; reading *The Times* with an eternal rustle of leaves because she never could settle down to any one page; and Sylvia walking up and down because she could not sit still, with a piece of toast in her fingers or her hands behind her back. Very tall; fair; as graceful, as full of blood and as cruel as the usual degenerate Derby winner. Inbred

for generations for one purpose: to madden men of one
type. . . . Pacing backwards and forwards, exclaiming: 'I'm
bored! Bored!'; sometimes even breaking the breakfast
plates . . . And talking! For ever talking; usually, cleverly,
with imbecility; with maddening inaccuracy; with wicked
penetration, and clamouring to be contradicted; a gentleman has to answer his wife's questions . . . And in his forehead the continual pressure; the determination to sit put;
the *décor* of the room seeming to burn into his mind. It
was there, shadowy before him now. And the pressure
upon his forehead. . . .

Mrs Wannop was talking to him now, he did not know
what she said; he never knew afterwards what he had
answered.

'God!' he said within himself, 'if it's sexual sins God
punishes, He indeed is just and inscrutable!' . . . Because
he had had physical contact with this woman before he
married her! In a railway carriage; coming down from the
Dukeries. An extravagantly beautiful girl!

Where was the physical attraction of her gone to now?
Irresistible; reclining back as the shires rushed past. . . .
His mind said that she had lured him on. His intellect put
the idea from him. No gentleman thinks such things of
his wife.

No gentleman thinks. . . . By God; she must have been
with child by another man. . . . He had been fighting the
conviction down all the last four months. . . . He knew
now that he had been fighting the conviction all the last
four months, whilst, anaesthetized, he had bathed in
figures and wave-theories. . . . Her last words had been:
her very last words: late: all in white she had gone up to
her dressing-room, and he had never seen her again; her
last words had been about the child . . . 'Supposing,' she
had begun . . . He didn't remember the rest. But he
remembered her eyes. And her gesture as she peeled off
her long white gloves. . . .

He was looking at Mrs Wannop's ingle; he thought it a
mistake in taste, really, to leave logs in an ingle during the

summer. But then what are you to do with an ingle in summer? In Yorkshire cottages they shut the ingles up with painted doors. But that is stuffy, too!

He said to himself:

'By God! I've had a stroke!' and he got out of his chair to test his legs. . . . But he hadn't had a stroke. It must then, he thought, be that the pain of his last consideration must be too great for his mind to register as certain great physical pains go unperceived. Nerves, like weighing machines, can't register more than a certain amount, then they go out of action. A tramp who had had his leg cut off by a train had told him that he had tried to get up, feeling nothing at all. . . . The pain comes back though. . . .

He said to Mrs Wannop, who was still talking:

'I beg your pardon. I really missed what you said.'

Mrs Wannop said:

'I was saying that that's the best thing I can do for you.'

He said:

'I'm really very sorry: it was that that I missed. I'm a little in trouble, you know.'

She said:

'I know: I know. The mind wanders; but I wish you'd listen. I've got to go to work, so have you, I said: after tea you and Valentine will walk into Rye to fetch your luggage.'

Straining his intelligence, for, in his mind, he felt a sudden strong pleasure; sunlight on pyramidal red roof in the distance: themselves descending in a long diagonal, a green hill: God, yes, he wanted open air. Tietjens said:

'I see. You take us both under your protection. You'll bluff it out.'

Mrs Wannop said rather coolly:

'I don't know about you both. It's you I'm taking under my protection (it's *your* phrase!). As for Valentine: she's made her bed; she must lie on it. I've told you all that already. I can't go over it again.'

She paused, then made another effort:

'It's disagreeable,' she said, 'to be cut off the Mountby

visiting list. They give amusing parties. But I'm too old to care and they'll miss my conversation more than I do theirs. Of course, I back my daughter against the cats and monkeys. Of course, I back Valentine through thick and thin. I'd back her if she lived with a married man or had illegitimate children. But I don't approve, I don't approve of the suffragettes: I despise their aims: I detest their methods. I don't think young girls ought to talk to strange men. Valentine spoke to you, and look at the worry it has caused you. I disapprove. I'm a woman: but I've made my own way: other women could do it if they liked or had the energy. I disapprove! But don't believe that I will ever go back on any suffragette, individual, in gangs; my Valentine or any other. Don't believe that I will ever say a word against them that's to be repeated—*you* won't repeat them. Or that I will ever write a word against them. No, I'm a woman and I stand by my sex!'

She got up energetically:

'I must go and write my novel,' she said. 'I've Monday's instalment to send off by train to-night. You'll go into my study: Valentine will give you paper; ink; twelve different kinds of nibs. You'll find Professor Wannop's books all round the room. You'll have to put up with Valentine typing in the alcove. I've got two serials running, one typed, the other in manuscript.'

Tietjens said:

'But *you*!'

'I,' she exclaimed, 'I shall write in my bedroom on my knee. I'm a woman and can. You're a man and have to have a padded chair and sanctuary.... You feel fit to work? Then: you've got till five, Valentine will get tea then. At half-past five you'll set off to Rye. You'll be back with your luggage and your friend and your friend's luggage at seven.'

She silenced him imperiously with:

'Don't be foolish. Your friend will certainly prefer this house and Valentine's cooking to the pub and the pub's cooking. And he'll save on it.... It's *no* extra trouble. I suppose your friend won't inform against that wretched little suffragette girl upstairs.' She paused and said: 'You're *sure* you can do your work in the time and drive Valentine and her to that place. . . . Why it's necessary is that the girl daren't travel by train and we've relations there who've never been connected with the suffragettes. The girl can live hidden there for a bit. . . . But sooner than you shouldn't finish your work I'd drive them myself . . .'

She silenced Tietjens again: this time sharply:

'I tell you it's *no* extra trouble. Valentine and I *always* make our own beds. We don't like servants among our intimate things. We can get three times as much help in the neighbourhood as we want. We're liked here. The extra work you give will be met by extra help. We could have servants if we wanted. But Valentine and I like to be alone in the house together at night. We're very fond of each other.'

She walked to the door and then drifted back to say:

'You know, I can't get out of my head that unfortunate woman and her husband. We must *all* do what we can for them.' Then she started and exclaimed: 'But, good heavens, I'm keeping you from your work . . . The study's in there, through that door.'

She hurried through the other doorway and no doubt along a passage, calling out:

'Valentine! Valentine! Go to Christopher in the study. At once . . . at . . .' Her voice died away.

VII

Jumping down from the high step of the dog-cart the girl completely disappeared into the silver: she had on an otter-skin toque, dark, that should have been visible. But she was gone more completely than if she had dropped into deep water, into snow—or through tissue paper. More suddenly, at least! In darkness or in deep water a moving paleness would have been visible for a second: snow or a paper hoop would have left an opening. Here there had been nothing.

The constatation interested him. He had been watching her intently and with concern for fear she should miss the hidden lower step, in which case she would certainly bark her shins. But she had jumped clear of the cart: with unreasonable pluckiness, in spite of his: 'Look out how you get down.' He wouldn't have done it himself: he couldn't have faced jumping down into that white solidity . . .

He would have asked: 'Are you all right?' but to express more concern than the 'look out,' which he had expended already, would have detracted from his stolidity. He was Yorkshire and stolid: she south country and soft: emotional: given to such ejaculations as 'I hope you're not hurt,' when the Yorkshireman only grunts. But soft because she was south country. She was as good as a man—a south-country man. She was ready to acknowledge the superior woodenness of the north. . . . That was their convention: so he did not call down: 'I hope you're all right,' though he had desired to.

Her voice came, muffled, as if from the back of the top of his head: the ventriloquial effect was startling:

'Make a noise from time to time. It's ghostly down here and the lamp's no good at all. It's almost out.'

He returned to his constatations of the concealing effect of water vapour. He enjoyed the thought of the grotesque appearance he must present in that imbecile landscape. On his right an immense, improbably brilliant horn of a moon, sending a trail as if down the sea, straight to his neck: beside the moon a grotesquely huge star: in an extravagant position above them the Plough, the only constellation that he knew; for, though a mathematician, he despised astronomy. It was not theoretical enough for the pure mathematician and not sufficiently practical for daily life. He had of course calculated the movements of abstruse heavenly bodies: but only from given figures: he had never looked for the stars of his calculations. . . . Above his head and all over the sky were other stars; large and weeping with light, or as the dawn increased, so paling that at times, you saw them; then missed them. Then the eye picked them up again.

Opposite the moon was a smirch or two of cloud; pink below, dark purple above; on the more pallid, lower blue of the limpid sky.

But the absurd thing was this mist! ... It appeared to spread from his neck, absolutely level, absolutely silver, to infinity on each side of him. At great distances on his right black tree-shapes, in groups—there were four of them— were exactly like coral islands on a silver sea. He couldn't escape the idiotic comparison: there wasn't any other.

Yet it didn't exactly spread from his neck: when he now held his hands, nipple-high, like pallid fish they held black reins which ran downwards into nothingness. If he jerked the rein, the horse threw its head up. Two pricked ears were visible in greyness: the horse being sixteen two and a bit over, the mist might be ten foot high. Thereabouts. ... He wished the girl would come back and jump out of the cart again. Being ready for it, he would watch her disappearance more scientifically. He couldn't of course ask her to do it again: that was irritating. The phenomenon would have proved—or it might of course disprove—his idea of smoke screens. The Chinese of the Ming dynasty were said to have approached and overwhelmed their enemies under clouds of—of course, not acrid—vapour. He had read that the Patagonians, hidden by smoke, were accustomed to approach so near to birds or beasts as to be able to take them by hand. The Greeks under Paleologus the ...

Miss Wannop's voice said—from beneath the bottom board of the cart:

'I wish you'd make some noise. It's lonely down here, besides being possibly dangerous. There might be dicks on each side of the road.'

If they were on the marsh there certainly would be dykes —why did they call ditches 'dykes,' and why did she pronounce it 'dicks'?—on each side of the road. He could think of nothing to say that wouldn't express concern, and he couldn't do that by the rules of the game. He tried to whistle 'John Peel'! But he was no hand at whistling. He sang:

'D'ye ken, John Peel at the break of day . . .' and felt like a fool. But he kept on at it, the only tune that he knew. It was the Yorkshire Light Infantry quick-step: the regiment of his brothers in India. He wished he had been in the army; but his father hadn't approved of having more than two younger sons in the army. He wondered if he would ever run with John Peel's hounds again: he had once or twice. Or with any of the trencher-fed foot packs of the Cleveland district, of which there had been still several when he had been a boy. He had been used to think of himself as being like John Peel with his coat so grey . . . Up through the heather, over Wharton's place; the pack running wild; the heather dripping; the mist rolling up . . . another kind of mist than this south-country silver sheet. Silly stuff! Magical! That was the word. A silly word. . . . South country . . . In the north the old grey mists rolled together, revealing black hillsides.

He didn't suppose he'd have the wind now: this rotten bureaucratic life! . . . If he had been in the army like the two brothers, Ernest and James, next above him . . . But no doubt he would not have liked the army. Discipline! . . . He supposed he would have put up with the discipline: a gentleman had to. Because *noblesse oblige*: not for fear of consequences . . . But army officers seemed to him pathetic. They spluttered and roared: to make men jump smartly: at the end of apoplectic efforts the men jumped smartly. But there was the end of it. . . .

Actually, this mist was not silver, or was, perhaps, no longer silver: if you looked at it with the eye of the artist . . . With the exact eye! It was smirched with bars of purple; of red; or orange; delicate reflections: dark blue shadows from the upper sky where it formed drifts like snow. . . . The exact eye: exact observation: it was a man's work. The only work for a man. Why then were artists soft:

effeminate: not men at all: whilst the army officer, who had
the inexact mind of the schoolteacher, was a manly man?
Quite a manly man: until he became an old woman!

And the bureaucrat then? Growing fat and soft like himself, or dry and stringy like Macmaster or old Ingleby?
They did men's work: exact observation: return no. 17642
with figures exact. Yet they grew hysterical: they ran about
corridors or frantically rang table bells, asking with high
voices of querulous eunuchs why form ninety thousand and
two wasn't ready. Nevertheless men liked the bureaucratic
life: his own brother, Mark, head of the family: heir to
Groby.... Fifteen years older: a quiet stick: wooden:
brown: always in a bowler hat, as often as not with his
racing-glasses hung around him. Attending his first-class
office when he liked: too good a man for any administration
to lose by putting on the screw.... But heir to Groby:
what would that stick make of the place? ... Let it, no
doubt, and go on pottering from the Albany to race meetings—where he never betted—to Whitehall, where he was
said to be indispensable.... Why indispensable? Why in
heaven's name! That stick who had never hunted, never
shot: couldn't tell coulter from plough-handle and lived in
his bowler hat! ... A 'sound' man: the archetype of all
sound men. Never in his life had anyone shaken his head at
Mark and said:

'You're brilliant!' Brilliant! That stick! No, he was indispensable!

'Upon my soul!' Tietjens said to himself, 'that girl down
there is the only intelligent living soul I've met for years.'
... A little pronounced in manner sometimes; faulty in
reasoning naturally, but quite intelligent, with a touch of
wrong accent now and then. But if she was wanted anywhere, there she'd be! Of good stock, of course: on both
sides! ... But, positively, she and Sylvia were the only two
human beings he had met for years whom he could respect:
the one for sheer efficiency in killing: the other for having
the constructive desire and knowing how to set about it.
Kill or cure! The two functions of man. If you wanted

something killed you'd go to Sylvia Tietjens in the sure faith that she would kill it; emotion: hope: ideal: kill it quick and sure. If you wanted something kept alive you'd go to Valentine: she'd find something to do for it. . . . The two types of mind: remorseless enemy: sure screen: dagger . . . sheath!

Perhaps the future of the world then was to women? Why not? He hadn't in years met a man that he hadn't to talk down to—as you talk down to a child: as he had talked down to General Campion or to Mr Waterhouse . . . as he always talked down to Macmaster. All good fellows in their way. . . .

But why was he born to be a sort of lonely buffalo: outside the herd? Not artist: not soldier: not bureaucrat: not certainly indispensable anywhere: apparently not even sound in the eyes of these dim-minded specialists . . . An exact observer. . . .

Hardly even that for the last six and a half hours:

> *'Die Sommer Nacht hat mirs angethan*
> *Das war ein schweigsame Reiten . . .'*

he said aloud.

How could you translate that? You couldn't translate it: no one could translate Heine:

> 'It was the summer night came over me:
> That was silent riding . . .'

A voice cut into his warm, drowsy thought:

'Oh, you *do* exist. But you've spoken too late. I've run into the horse.' He must have been speaking aloud. He had felt the horse quivering at the end of the reins. The horse, too, was used to her by now. It had hardly stirred . . . He wondered when he had left off singing 'John Peel.' . . . He said:

'Come along, then: have you found anything?'

The answer came:

'Something . . . But you can't talk in this stuff . . . I'll just . . .'

The voice died away as if a door had shut. He waited: consciously waiting: as an occupation! Contritely and to make a noise he rattled the whip-stock in its bucket. The horse started and he had to check it quickly: a damn fool he was. Of course a horse would start if you rattled a whip-stock. He called out:

'Are you all right?' The cart might have knocked her down. He had, however, broken the convention. Her voice came from a great distance:

'I'm all right. Trying the other side . . .'

His last thought came back to him. He had broken their convention: he had exhibited concern: like any other man. . . . He said to himself:

'By God! Why not take a holiday: why not break all conventions?'

They erected themselves intangibly and irrefragably. He had not known this young women twenty-four hours: not to speak to: and already the convention existed between them that he must play stiff and cold, she warm and cling-ing. . . . Yet she was obviously as cool a hand as himself: cooler no doubt, for at bottom he was certainly a sentimen-talist.

A convention of the most imbecile type . . . Then break all conventions: with the young woman: with himself above all. For forty-eight hours . . . almost exactly forty-eight hours till he started for Dover. . . .

> 'And I must to the greenwood go,
> Alone: a banished man!'

Border ballad! Written not seven miles from Groby!

By the descending moon: it being then just after cock-crow of midsummer night—what sentimentality!—it must be half-past-four on Sunday. He had worked out that to catch the morning Ostend boat at Dover he must leave the Wannops' at 5.15 on Tuesday morning, in a motor for the junction. . . . What incredible cross-country train connec-tions! Five hours for not forty miles.

He had then forty-eight and three-quarter hours! Let

them be a holiday! A holiday from himself above all: a
holiday from his standards: from his convention with himself. From clear observation: from exact thought: from
knocking over all the skittles of the exactitudes of others:
from the suppression of emotions. . . . From all the weari-
nesses that made him intolerable to himself. . . . He felt his
limbs lengthen, as if they too had relaxed.

Well, already he had had six and a half hours of it. They
had started at 10 and, like any other man, he had enjoyed
the drive, though it had been difficult to keep the beastly
cart balanced, the girl had had to sit behind with her arm
round the other girl, who screamed at every oak tree. . . .
But he had—if he put himself to the question—mooned
along under the absurd moon that had accompanied them
down the heaven: to the scent of hay: to the sound of
nightingales, hoarse by now, of course—in June he changes
his tune; of corncrakes, of bats, of a heron twice, overhead.
They had passed the blue-black shadows of corn stacks, of
heavy, rounded oaks, of hop oasts that are half church
tower, half finger-post. And the road silver grey, and the
night warm. . . . It was midsummer night that had done
that to him. . . . *Hat mirs angethan.*
Das war ein schweigsame Reiten. . . .
Not absolutely silent of course: but silentish! Coming
back from the parson's, where they had dropped the little
London sewer rat, they had talked very little. . . . Not unpleasant people the parson's: an uncle of the girl's: three
girl cousins, not unpleasant, like the girl but without the
individuality . . . A remarkably good bite of beef: a truly
meritorious Stilton and a drop of whisky that proved the
parson to be a man. All in candlelight. A motherly mother
of the family to take the rat up some stairs . . . a great deal
of laughter of girls . . . then a re-start an hour later than
had been scheduled. . . . Well, it hadn't mattered: they had
the whole of eternity before them: the good horse—*really*
it was a good horse!—putting its shoulders into the
work. . . .

They had talked a little at first; about the safeness of the London girl from the police now; about the brickishness of the parson in taking her in. She certainly would never have reached Charing Cross by train. . . .

There had fallen long periods of silences. A bat had whirled very near their off-lamp.

'What a large bat!' she had said. '*Noctilux major* . . .'

He said:

'Where do you get your absurd Latin nomenclature from? Isn't it *phalæna* . . .' She had answered:

'From White . . . The *Natural History of Selborne* is the only natural history I ever read. . . .'

'He's the last English writer that could write,' said Tietjens.

'He calls the downs "those majestic and amusing mountains," ' she said. 'Where do you get your dreadful Latin pronunciation from? Phal . . . i . . . i . . . na! To rhyme with Dinah!'

'It's "*sublime* and amusing mountains," not "majestic and amusing," ' Tietjens said. 'I got my Latin pronunciation, like all public schoolboys of to-day, from the German.'

She answered:

'You would! Father used to say it made him sick.'

'Cæsar equals Kaiser,' Tietjens said. . . .

'Bother your Germans,' she said, 'they're no ethnologists; they're rotten at philology!' She added: 'Father used to say so,' to take away from an appearance of pedantry.

A silence then! She had right over her head a rug that her aunt had lent her; a silhouette beside him, with a cocky nose turned up straight out of the descending black mass. But for the square toque she would have had the silhouette of a Manchester cotton-hand: the toque gave it a different line; like the fillet of Diana. It was piquant and agreeable to ride beside a quite silent lady in the darkness of the thick Weald that let next to no moonlight through. The horse's hoofs went clock, clock: a good horse. The near lamp illuminated the russet figure of a man with a sack on his back, pressed into the hedge, a blinking lurcher beside him.

'Keeper between the blankets!' Tietjens said to himself:
'All these south-country keepers sleep all night. . . . And
then you give them a five-quid tip for the week-end shoot.
. . .' He determined that, as to that, too, he would put his
foot down. No more week-ends with Sylvia in the mansions
of the Chosen People. . . .

The girl said suddenly; they had run into a clearing of
the deep underwoods:

'I'm not stuffy with you over that Latin, though you were
unnecessarily rude. And I'm not sleepy. I'm loving it all.'

He hesitated for a minute. It was a silly-girl thing to say.
She didn't usually say silly-girl things. He ought to snub
her for her own sake. . . .

He said:

'I'm rather loving it, too!' She was looking at him; her
nose had disappeared from the silhouette. He hadn't been
able to help it; the moon had been just above her head;
unknown stars all round her; the night was warm. Besides,
a really manly man may condescend at times! He rather
owes it to himself. . . .

She said:

'That was nice of you! You might have hinted that the
rotten drive was taking you away from your so important
work. . . .'

'Oh, I can think as I drive,' he said. She said:

'Oh!' and then: 'The reason why I'm unconcerned over
your rudeness about my Latin is that I know I'm a much
better Latinist than you. You can't quote a few lines of
Ovid without sprinkling howlers in. . . . It's *vastum*, not
longum . . . "Terra tribus scopulis vastum procurrit" . . .
It's *alto*, not *coelo* . . . "Uvidus ex alto desilientis." . . .
How could Ovid have written *ex coelo*? The "c" after the
"x" sets your teeth on edge.'

Tietjens said:

'*Excogitabo!*'

'That's purely canine!' she said with contempt.

'Besides,' Tietjens said, '*longum* is much better than
vastum. I hate cant adjectives like "vast." . . .'

'It's like your modesty to correct Ovid,' she exclaimed. 'Yet you say Ovid and Catullus were the only two Roman poets to *be* poets. That's because they *were* sentimental and used adjectives like *vastum*. . . . What's "Sad tears mixed with kisses" but the sheerest sentimentality?'

'It ought, you know,' Tietjens said with soft dangerousness, 'to be "Kisses mingled with sad tears" . . . "Tristibus et lacrimis oscula mixta dabis." . . . '

'I'm hanged if ever I could,' she exclaimed explosively. 'A man like you could die in a ditch and I'd never come near. You're desiccated even for a man who has learned his Latin from the Germans.'

'Oh, well, I'm a mathematician,' Tietjens said. 'Classics is not my line!'

'It *isn't*,' she answered tartly.

A long time afterwards from her black figure came the words:

'You used "mingled" instead of "mixed" to translate *mixta*. I shouldn't think you took English at Cambridge, either! Though they're as rotten at that as at everything else, father used to say.'

'Your father was Balliol, of course,' Tietjens said with the snuffy contempt of a scholar of Trinity College, Cambridge. But having lived most of her life amongst Balliol people she took this as a compliment and an olive branch.

Some time afterwards Tietjens, observing that her silhouette was still between him and the moon, remarked:

'I don't know if you know that for some minutes we've been running nearly due west. We ought to be going south-east by a bit south. I suppose you *do* know this road. . . .'

'Every inch of it,' she said. 'I've been on it over and over again on my motor-bicycle with mother in the side-car. The next cross road is called Grandfather's Wantways. We've got eleven miles and a quarter to do. The road turns back here because of the old Sussex iron pits; it goes in and out amongst them; hundreds of them. You know the exports of the town of Rye in the eighteenth century were hops, cannon, kettles, and chimney backs. The railings round St Paul's are made of Sussex iron.'

'I knew that, of course,' Tietjens said: 'I come of an iron county myself. . . . Why didn't you let me run the girl over in the side-car, it would have been quicker?'

'Because,' she said, 'three weeks ago I smashed up the side-car on the milestone at Hog's Corner: doing forty.'

'It must have been a pretty tidy smash!' Tietjens said. 'Your mother wasn't aboard?'

'No,' the girl said, 'suffragette literature. The side-car was full. It *was* a pretty tidy smash. Hadn't you observed I still limp a little?'

A few minutes later she said:

'I haven't the least notion where we really are. I clean forgot to notice the road. And I don't care. . . . Here's a signpost though; pull in to it. . . .'

The lamps would not, however, shine on the arms of the post; they were burning dim and showing low. A good deal of fog was in the air. Tietjens gave the reins to the girl and got down. He took out the near light and, going back a yard or two to the signpost, examined its bewildering ghostlinesses. . . .

The girl gave a little squeak that went to his backbone; the hoofs clattered unusually; the cart went on. Tietjens went after it; it was astonishing; it had completely disappeared. Then he ran into it: ghostly, reddish and befogged. It must have got much thicker suddenly. The fog swirled all round the near lamp as he replaced it in its socket.

'Did you do that on purpose?' he asked the girl. 'Or can't you hold a horse?'

'I can't drive a horse,' the girl said; 'I'm afraid of them. I can't drive a motor-bike either. I made that up because I *knew* you'd say you'd rather have taken Gertie over in the side-car than driven with me.'

'Then do you mind,' Tietjens said, 'telling me if you know this road at all?'

'Not a bit!' she answered cheerfully. 'I never drove over it in my life. I looked it up on the map before we started because I'm sick to death of the road we went by. There's a one-horse bus from Rye to Tenterden, and I've walked from Tenterden to my uncle's over and over again. . . .'

'We shall probably be out all night then,' Tietjens said. 'Do you mind? The horse may be tired. . . .'

She said:

'Oh, the poor horse! . . . I *meant* us to be out all night. . . . But the poor horse. . . . What a brute I was not to think of it.'

'We're thirteen miles from a place called Brede; eleven and a quarter from a place whose name I couldn't read; six and three-quarters from somewhere called something like Uddlemere . . .' Tietjens said. 'This is the road to Uddlemere.'

'Oh, that was Grandfather's Wantways all right,' she declared. 'I know it well. It's called "Grandfather's" because an old gentleman used to sit there called Gran'fer Finn. Every Tenterden market day he used to sell fleed cakes from a basket to the carts that went by. Tenterden market was abolished in 1845—the effect of the repeal of the Corn Laws, you know. As a Tory you ought to be interested in that.'

Tietjens said patiently: He could sympathize with her mood; she had now a heavy weight off her chest; and, if long acquaintance with his wife had not made him able to put up with feminine vagaries, nothing ever would.

'Would you mind,' he said then, 'telling me . . .'

'If,' she interrupted, 'that was really Gran'fer's Wantways: midland English. "Vent" equals four crossroads: high French *carrefour*. . . . Or, perhaps, that isn't the right word. But it's the way your mind works. . . .'

'You have, of course, often walked from your uncle's to Gran'fer's Wantways,' Tietjens said, 'with your cousins, taking brandy to the invalid in the old toll-gate house. That's how you know the story of Grandfer. You said you had never driven it; but you *have* walked it. That's the way *your* mind works, isn't it?'

She said: '*Oh!*'

6*

'Then,' Tietjens went on, 'would you mind telling me—
for the sake of the poor horse—whether Uddlemere is or
isn't on our road home. I take it you don't know just this
stretch of road, but you know whether it is the right road.'

'The touch of pathos,' the girl said, 'is a wrong note. It's
you who're in mental trouble about the road. The horse
isn't. . . .'

Tietjens let the cart go on another fifty yards; then he
said:

'It *is* the right road. The Uddlemere turning *was* the
right one. You wouldn't let the horse go another five steps
if it wasn't. You're as soppy about horses as . . . as I am.'

'There's at least that bond of sympathy between us,' she
said drily. 'Gran'fer's Wantways is six and three-quarter
miles from Udimore; Udimore is exactly five from us; total,
eleven and three-quarters; twelve and a quarter if you add
half a mile for Udimore itself. The name is Udimore, not
Uddlemere. Local place-name enthusiasts derive this from
"O'er the mere." Absurd! Legend as follows: Church
builders desiring to put church with relic of St Rumwold in
wrong place, voice wailed: "O'er the mere." Obviously
absurd! . . . Putrid! *"O'er the"* by Grimm's law impossible
as *"Udi"*; *"mere"* not a middle low German word at
all. . . .'

'Why,' Tietjens said, 'are you giving me all this information?'

'Because,' the girl said, 'it's the way your mind works. . . .
It picks up useless facts as silver after you've polished it
picks up sulphur vapour; and tarnishes! It arranges the
useless facts in obsolescent patterns and makes Toryism out
of them. . . . I've never met a Cambridge Tory man before.
I thought they were all in museums, and you work them
up again out of bones. That's what father used to say; he
was an Oxford Disraelian Conservative Imperialist. . . .'

'I know, of course,' Tietjens said.

'Of course you know,' the girl said. 'You know everything. . . . And you've worked everything into absurd principles. You think father was unsound because he tried to

apply tendencies to life. *You* want to be a Nenglish country
gentleman and spin principles out of the newspapers and
the gossip of horse-fairs. And let the country go to hell,
you'll never stir a finger except to say I told you so.'

She touched him suddenly on the arm:

'*Don't* mind me!' she said. 'It's reaction. I'm so happy.
I'm so happy.'

He said:

'That's all right! That's all right!' But for a minute or
two it wasn't really. All feminine claws, he said to himself,
are sheathed in velvet; but they can hurt a good deal if
they touch you on the sore places of the defects of your
qualities—even merely with the velvet. He added: 'Your
mother works you very hard.'

She exclaimed:

'How you *understand*. You're amazing: for a man who
tries to be a sea-anemone!' She said: 'Yes, this is the first
holiday I've had for four solid months; six hours a day
typing; four hours a day work for the movement; three,
housework and gardening; three, mother reading out her
day's work for slips of the pen. . . . And on the top of it
the raid and the anxiety. . . . Dreadful anxiety, you know.
Suppose mother *had* gone to prison. . . . Oh, I'd have gone
mad. . . . Weekdays and Sundays. . . .' She stopped: 'I'm
apologizing, really,' she went on. 'Of course I ought not to
have talked to you like that. You a great Panjandrum;
saving the country with your statistics and all. . . . It *did*
make you a rather awful figure, you know . . . and the relief
to find you're . . . oh, a man like oneself with feet of clay.
. . . I'd dreaded this drive. . . . I'd have dreaded it dreadfully if I hadn't been in such a dread about Gertie and the
police. And if I hadn't let off steam I should have had to
jump out and run beside the cart. . . . I could still . . .'

'You couldn't,' Tietjens said. 'You couldn't see the cart.'

They had just run into a bank of solid fog that seemed to
encounter them with a soft, ubiquitous blow. It was blinding; it was deadening to sounds; it was in a sense mournful; but it was happy, too, in its romantic unusualness.

They couldn't see the gleam of the lamps; they could hardly hear the step of the horse; the horse had fallen at once to a walk. They agreed that neither of them could be responsible for losing the way; in the circumstances that was impossible. Fortunately the horse would take them somewhere; it had belonged to a local higgler: a man that used the roads buying poultry for re-sale. . . . They agreed that they had no responsibilities; and after that went on for unmeasured hours in silence; the mist growing, but very, very gradually, more luminous. . . . Once or twice, at a rise in the road, they saw again the stars and the moon, but mistily. On the fourth occasion they had emerged into the silver lake; like mermen rising to the surface of a tropical sea. . . .

Tietjens had said:

'You'd better get down and take the lamp. See if you can find a milestone; I'd get down myself, but you might not be able to hold the horse. . . .' She had plunged in . . .

And he had sat, feeling, he didn't know why, like a Guy Fawkes; up in the light, thinking by no means disagreeable thoughts—intent, like Miss Wannop herself, on a complete holiday of forty-eight hours; till Tuesday morning! He had to look forward to a long and luxurious day of figures; a rest after dinner; half a night more of figures; a Monday devoted to a horse-deal in the market-town where he happened to know the horse-dealer. The horse-dealer, indeed, was known to every hunting man in England! A luxurious, long argument in the atmosphere of stable-hartshorn and slow wranglings couched in ostler's epigrams. You couldn't have a better day; the beer in the pub probably good, too. Or if not that, the claret. . . . The claret in south-country inns was often quite good; there was no sale for it so it got well kept. . . .

On Tuesday it would close in again, beginning with the meeting of his wife's maid at Dover. . . .

He was to have, above all, a holiday from himself and to take it like other men, free of his conventions, his strait waistcoatings. . . .

The girl said:

'I'm coming up now! I've found out something....' He watched intently the place where she must appear; it would give him pointers about the impenetrability of mist to the eye.

Her otter-skin cap had beads of dew; beads of dew were on her hair beneath: she scrambled up, a little awkwardly: her eyes sparkled with fun: panting a little: her cheeks bright. Her hair was darkened by the wetness of the mist, but she appeared golden in the sudden moonlight.

Before she was quite up, Tietjens almost kissed her. Almost. An all but irresistible impulse! He exclaimed:

'Steady, the Buffs!' in his surprise.

She said:

'Well, you might as well have given me a hand. I found,' she went on, 'a stone that had I.R.D.C. on it, and there the lamp went out. We're not on the marsh because we are between quick hedges. That's all I have found.... But I've worked out what makes me so tart with you....'

He couldn't believe she could be so absolutely calm: the after-wash of that impulse had been so strong in him that it was as if he had tried to catch her to him and had been foiled by her.... She ought to be indignant, amused, even pleased.... She ought to show some emotion....

She said:

'It was your silencing me with that absurd non-sequitur about the Pimlico clothing factory. It was an insult to my intelligence.'

'You recognized that it was a fallacy!' Tietjens said. He was looking hard at her. He didn't know what had happened to him. She took a long look at him, cool, but with immense eyes. It was as if for a moment destiny, which usually let him creep past somehow, had looked at him. 'Can't,' he argued with destiny, 'a man want to kiss a schoolgirl in a scuffle....' His own voice, a caricature of his own voice, seemed to come to him: 'Gentlemen don't ...' He exclaimed:

'Don't gentlemen? . . .' and then stopped because he realized that he had spoken aloud.

She said:

'Oh, *gentlemen* do!' she said, 'use fallacies to glide over tight places in arguments. And they browbeat schoolgirls with them. It's that, that underneath, has been exasperating me with you. You regarded me at that date—three-quarters of a day ago—as a schoolgirl.'

Tietjens said:

'I don't now!' He added: 'Heaven knows, I don't now!'

She said: 'No, you don't now!'

He said:

'It didn't need your putting up all that blue-stocking erudition to convince me. . . .'

'Blue-stocking!' she exclaimed contemptuously. 'There's nothing of the blue-stocking about me. I know Latin because father spoke it with us. It was your pompous blue socks I was pulling.'

Suddenly she began to laugh. Tietjens was feeling sick, physically sick. She went on laughing. He stuttered:

'What is it?'

'The sun!' she said, pointing. Above the silver horizon was the sun; not a red sun: shining, burnished.

'I don't see . . .' Tietjens said.

'What there is to laugh at?' she asked. 'It's the day! . . . The longest day's begun . . . and to-morrow's as long. . . . The summer solstice, you know. . . . After to-morrow the days shorten towards winter. But to-morrow's as long. . . . I'm so glad . . .'

'That we've got through the night? . . .' Tietjens asked.

She looked at him for a long time. 'You're not so dreadfully ugly, really,' she said.

Tietjens said:

'What's that church?'

Rising out of the mist on a fantastically green knoll, a quarter of a mile away, was an unnoticeable place of worship: an oak shingle tower roof that shone grey like

lead: an impossibly bright weathercock, brighter than the
sun. Dark elms all round it, holding wetnesses of mist.

'Icklesham!' she cried softly. 'Oh, we're nearly home.
Just above Mountby.... That's the Mountby drive....'

Trees existed, black and hoary with the dripping mist.
Trees in the hedgerow and the avenue that led to Mountby:
it made a right-angle just before coming into the road and
the road went away at right-angles across the gate.

'You'll have to pull to the left before you reach the
avenue,' the girl said. 'Or as like as not the horse will walk
right up to the house. The higgler who had him used to
buy Lady Claudine's eggs....'

Tietjens exclaimed barbarously:

'Damn Mountby. I wish we'd never come near it,' and
he whipped the horse into a sudden trot. The hoofs
sounded suddenly loud. She placed her hand on his gloved
driving hand. Had it been his flesh she wouldn't have done
it.

She said:

'My dear, it couldn't have lasted for ever ... But you're
a good man. And very clever.... You will get through....'

Not ten yards ahead Tietjens saw a tea-tray, the underneath of a black-lacquered tea-tray, gliding towards them:
mathematically straight, just rising from the mist. He
shouted: mad: the blood in his head. His shout was
drowned by the scream of the horse: he had swung it to
the left. The cart turned up: the horse emerged from the
mist: head and shoulders: pawing. A stone sea-horse from
the fountain of Versailles! Exactly like that! Hanging in
air for an eternity: the girl looking at it, leaning slightly
forward.

The horse didn't come over backwards: he had loosened
the reins. It wasn't there any more. The damndest thing
that *could* happen! He had known it would happen. He
said:

'We're all right now!' There was a crash and scraping:
like twenty tea-trays: a prolonged sound. They must be
scraping along the mudguard of the invisible car. He had

the pressure of the horse's mouth: the horse was away: going hell for leather. He increased the pressure. The girl said:

'I know I'm all right with you.'

They were suddenly in bright sunlight: cart: horse: commonplace hedgerows. They were going uphill: a steep brae. He wasn't certain she hadn't said: 'Dear!' or 'My dear!' Was it possible after so short . . . ? But it had been a long night. He was, no doubt, saving her life, too. He increased his pressure on the horse's mouth gently: up to all his twelve stone: all his strength. The hill told, too. Steep, white road between shaven grass banks!

Stop, damn you! Poor beast . . . The girl fell out of the cart. No! jumped clear! Out to the animal's head. It threw its head up. Nearly off her feet: she was holding the bit. . . . She couldn't! Tender mouth . . . afraid of horses. . . . He said:

'Horse cut!' Her face like a little white blancmange!

'Come quick,' she said.

'I must hold a minute,' he said, 'might go off if I let go to get down. Badly cut?'

'Blood running down solid! Like an apron,' she said.

He was at last at her side. It was true. But not so much like an apron. More like a red, varnished stocking. He said:

'You've a white petticoat on. Get over the hedge; jump it, and take it off . . .'

'Tear it into strips?' she asked. 'Yes!'

He called to her; she was suspended halfway up the bank:

'Tear one half off first. The rest into strips.'

She said: 'All right!' She didn't go over the quickset as neatly as he had expected. No take off. But she was over. . . .

The horse, trembling, was looking down, its nostrils distended, at the blood pooling from its near foot. The cut was just on the shoulder. He put his left arm right over the horse's eyes. The horse stood it, almost with a sigh of relief. . . . A wonderful magnetism with horses. Perhaps with women, too? God knew. He was almost certain she had said 'Dear.'

She said: 'Here.' He caught a round ball of whitish stuff. He undid it. Thank God: what sense! A long, strong, white band. . . . What the devil was the hissing. . . . A small, closed car with crumpled mudguards: noiseless nearly: gleaming black . . . God curse it: it passed them: stopped ten yards down . . . the horse rearing back: mad! Clean mad . . . something like a scarlet and white cockatoo, fluttering out of the small car door . . . a general. In full tog. White feathers! Ninety medals! Scarlet coat! Black trousers with red stripes. Spurs, too, by God!

Tietjens said:

'God damn you, you bloody swine. Go away!'

The apparition, past the horse's blinkers, said:

'I can, at least, hold the horse for you. I went past to get you out of Claudine's sight.'

'Damn good-natured of you,' Tietjens said as rudely as he could. 'You'll have to pay for the horse.'

The General exclaimed:

'Damn it all! Why should I? You were driving your beastly camel right into my drive.'

'You never sounded your horn,' Tietjens said.

'I was on private ground,' the General shouted. 'Besides I did.' An enraged, scarlet scarecrow, very thin, he was holding the horse's bridle. Tietjens was extending the half petticoat, with a measuring eye, before the horse's chest. The General said:

'Look here! I've got to take the escort for the Royal party at St Peter-in-Manor, Dover. They're laying the Buffs' colours on the altar or something.'

'You never sounded your horn,' Tietjens said. 'Why didn't you bring your chauffeur? He's a capable man. . . . You talk very big about the widow and child. But when it comes to robbing them of fifty quid by slaughtering their horse . . .'

The General said:

'What the devil were you doing coming into our drive at five in the morning?'

Tietjens, who had applied the half petticoat to the horse's chest, exclaimed:

'Pick up that thing and give it to me.' A thin roll of linen was at his feet: it had rolled down from the hedge.

'Can I leave the horse?' the General asked.

'Of course you can,' Tietjens said. 'If I can't quiet a horse better than you can run a car . . .'

He bound the new linen strips over the petticoat: the horse dropped its head, smelling his hand. The General, behind Tietjens, stood back on his heels, grasping his gold-mounted sword. Tietjens went on twisting and twisting the bandage.

'Look here,' the General suddenly bent forward to whisper into Tietjens' ear, 'what am I to tell Claudine? I believe she saw the girl.'

'Oh, tell her we came to ask what time you cast off your beastly otter hounds,' Tietjens said; 'that's a matutinal job. . . .'

The General's voice had a really pathetic intonation:

'On a Sunday!' he exclaimed. Then in a tone of relief he added: 'I shall tell her you were going to early communion in Duchemin's church at Pett.'

'If you want to add blasphemy to horse-slaughtering as a profession, do,' Tietjens said. 'But you'll have to pay for the horse.'

'I'm damned if I will,' the General shouted. 'I tell you you were driving into my drive.'

'Then I *shall*,' Tietjens said, 'and you know the construction you'll put on *that*.'

He straightened his back to look at the horse.

'Go away,' he said, 'say what you like. Do what you like! But as you go through Rye send up the horse ambulance from the vet.'s. Don't forget that. I'm going to save this horse. . . .'

'You know, Chris,' the General said, 'you're the most

wonderful hand with a horse . . . There isn't another man in England . . .'

'I know it,' Tietjens said. 'Go away. And send up that ambulance. . . . There's your sister getting out of your car. . . .'

The General began:

'I've an awful lot to get explained . . . ' But, at a thin scream of: 'General! General!' he pressed on his sword hilt to keep it from between his long, black, scarlet-striped legs, and running to the car pushed back into its door a befeathered, black bolster. He waved his hand to Tietjens:

'I'll send the ambulance,' he called.

The horse, its upper leg swathed with criss-crosses of white through which a purple stain was slowly penetrating, stood motionless, its head hanging down, mule-like, under the blinding sun. To ease it Tietjens began to undo the trace. The girl hopped over the hedge and, scrambling down, began to help him.

'Well. My reputation's gone,' she said cheerfully. 'I know what Lady Claudine is. . . . Why did you try to quarrel with the General? . . .'

'Oh, you'd better,' Tietjens said wretchedly, 'have a law-suit with him. It'll account for . . . for your not going to Mountby . . .'

'You think of everything,' she said.

They wheeled the cart backwards off the motionless horse. Tietjens moved it two yards forward—to get it out of sight of its own blood. Then they sat down side by side on the slope of the bank.

'Tell me about Groby,' the girl said at last.

Tietjens began to tell her about his home. . . . There was, in front of it, an avenue that turned into the road at right angles. Just like the one at Mountby.

'My great-great-grandfather made it,' Tietjens said. 'He liked privacy and didn't want the house visible to vulgar people on the road . . . just like the fellow who planned Mountby, no doubt. . . . But it's beastly dangerous with motors. We shall have to alter it . . . just at the bottom of

a dip. We can't have horses hurt. . . . You'll see . . .' It came
suddenly into his head that he wasn't perhaps the father of
the child who was actually the heir to that beloved place
over which generation after generation had brooded. Ever
since Dutch William! A damn Nonconformist swine!

On the bank his knees were almost level with his chin.
He felt himself slipping down.

'If I ever take you there . . .' he began.

'Oh, but you never will,' she said.

The child wasn't his. The heir to Groby! All his brothers
were childless . . . There was a deep well in the stable yard.
He had meant to teach the child how, if you dropped a
pebble in, you waited to count sixty-three. And there
came up a whispering roar. . . . But not his child! Perhaps
he hadn't even the power to beget children. His married
brothers hadn't. . . . Clumsy sobs shook him. It was the
dreadful injury to the horse which had finished him. He
felt as if the responsibility were his. The poor beast had
trusted him and he had smashed it up. Miss Wannop had
her arm over his shoulder.

'My dear!' she said, 'you won't ever take me to Groby
. . . It's perhaps . . . oh . . . short acquaintance; but I feel
you're the splendidest . . .'

He thought: 'It *is* rather short acquaintance.'

He felt a great deal of pain, over which there presided
the tall, eel-skin, blonde figure of his wife. . . .

The girl said:

'There's a fly coming!' and removed her arm.

A fly drew up before them with a blear-eyed driver. He
said General Campion had kicked him out of bed, from
beside his old woman. He wanted a pound to take them to
Mrs Wannop's, waked out of his beauty sleep and all. The
knacker's cart was following.

'You'll take Miss Wannop home at once,' Tietjens said,
'she's got her mother's breakfast to see to. . . . I shan't leave
the horse till the knacker's van comes.'

The fly-driver touched his age-green hat with his whip.

'Aye,' he said thickly, putting a sovereign into his waistcoat pocket. 'Always the gentleman ... a merciful man is merciful also to his beast. ... But I wouldn't leave my little wooden 'ut, nor miss my breakfast, for no beast. ... Some do and some ... do not.'

He drove off with the girl in the interior of his antique conveyance.

Tietjens remained on the slope of the bank, in the strong sunlight, beside the drooping horse. It had done nearly forty miles and lost, at last, a lot of blood.

Tietjens said:

'I suppose I could get the governor to pay fifty quid for it. They want the money. . . .'

He said:

'But it wouldn't be playing the game!'

A long time afterwards he said:

'Damn all principles!' And then:

'But one has to keep on going. . . . Principles are like a skeleton map of a country—you know whether you're going east or north.'

The knacker's cart lumbered round the corner.

PART TWO

I

SYLVIA TIETJENS rose from her end of the lunch-table
and swayed along it, carrying her plate. She still wore her
hair in bandeaux and her skirts as long as she possibly
could: she didn't, she said, with her height, intend to be
taken for a girl guide. She hadn't, in complexion, in figure
or in the languor of her gestures, aged by a minute. You
couldn't discover in the skin of her face any deadness: in
her eyes the shade more of fatigue than she intended to
express, but she had purposely increased her air of scorn-
ful insolence. That was because she felt that her hold over
men increased to the measure of her coldness. Someone,
she knew, had once said of a dangerous woman, that when
she entered the room every woman kept her husband on
the leash. It was Sylvia's pleasure to think that, before she
went out of that room, all the women in it realized with
mortification—that they needn't! For if coolly and distinctly she had said on entering: 'Nothing doing!' as bar-
maids will to the enterprising, she couldn't more plainly
have conveyed to the other women that she had no use for
their treasured rubbish.

Once, on the edge of a cliff in Yorkshire where the
moors come above the sea, during one of the tiresome
shoots that are there the fashion, a man had bidden her
observe the demeanour of the herring gulls below. They
were dashing from rock to rock on the cliff face, screaming,
with none of the dignity of gulls. Some of them even let
fall the herrings that they had caught and she saw the
pieces of silver dropping into the blue motion. The man
told her to look up; high, circling and continuing for a

long time to circle; illuminated by the sunlight below, like
a pale flame against the sky was a bird. The man told her
that that was some sort of fish-eagle or hawk. Its normal
habit was to chase the gulls which, in their terror, would
drop their booty of herrings, whereupon the eagle would
catch the fish before it struck the water. At the moment
the eagle was not on duty, but the gulls were just as terrified as if it had been.

Sylvia stayed for a long time watching the convolutions
of the eagle. It pleased her to see that, though nothing
threatened the gulls, they yet screamed and dropped their
herrings ... The whole affair reminded her of herself in
her relationship to the ordinary women of the barnyard.
... Not that there was the breath of a scandal against herself; that she very well knew, and it was her preoccupation
just as turning down nice men—the 'really nice men' of
commerce—was her hobby.

She practised every kind of 'turning down' on these
creatures: the really nice ones, with the Kitchener mous-
taches, the seal's brown eyes, the honest, thrilling voices,
the clipped words, the straight backs and the admirable
records—as long as you didn't enquire *too* closely. Once,
in the early days of the Great Struggle, a young man—she
had smiled at him in mistake for someone more trustable—
had followed in a taxi, hard on her motor, and flushed with
wine, glory and the firm conviction that all women in that
lurid carnival had become common property, had burst
into her door from the public stairs ... She had over-
topped him by the forehead and before a few minutes were
up she seemed to him to have become ten foot high with
a gift of words that scorched his backbone and the voice
of a frozen marble statue: a *chaudfroid* effect. He had
come in like a stallion, red-eyed, and all his legs off the
ground: he went down the stairs like a half-drowned rat,
with dim eyes and really looking wet, for some reason or
other.

Yet she hadn't really told him more than the way one
should behave to the wives of one's brother officers then

actually in the line, a point of view that, with her intimates, she daily agreed was pure bosh. But it must have
seemed to him like the voice of his mother—when his
mother had been much younger, of course—speaking from
paradise, and his conscience had contrived the rest of his
general wetness. This, however, had been melodrama and
war stuff at that: it hadn't, therefore, interested her. She
preferred to inflict deeper and more quiet pains.

She could, she flattered herself, tell the amount of *em-
pressement* which a man could develop about herself at the
first glance—the amount and the quality too. And from
not vouchsafing a look at all, or a look of the barest and
most incurious to some poor devil who even on introduction couldn't conceal his desires, to letting, after dinner, a
measured glance travel from the right foot of a late dinner
partner, diagonally up the ironed fold of the right trouser
to the watch pocket, diagonally still, across the shirt front,
pausing at the stud and so, rather more quickly, away over
the left shoulder, while the poor fellow stood appalled, with
his dinner going wrong—from the milder note to the
more pronounced she ran the whole gamut of 'turnings
down.' The poor fellows next day would change their
bootmakers, their sock merchants, their tailors, the de-
signers of their dress-studs and shirts: they would sigh
even to change the cut of their faces, communing seriously
with their after-breakfast mirrors. But they knew in their
hearts that calamity came from the fact that she hadn't
deigned to look into their eyes. . . . Perhaps hadn't dared
was the right word!

Sylvia, herself, would have cordially acknowledged that
it might have been. She knew that, like her intimates—all
the Elizabeths, Alixs, and Lady Moiras of the smooth-
papered, be-photographed weekly journals—she was man-
mad. It was the condition, indeed, of their intimacy as of
their eligibilities for reproduction on hot-pressed paper.
They went about in bands with, as it were, a cornfield of
feather boas floating above them, though to be sure no one
wore feather boas; they shortened their hairs and their

skirts and flattened, as far as possible, their chest develop-
ments, which *does* give, oh, you know ... a *certain*. ...
They adopted demeanours as like as possible—and yet how
unlike—to those of waitresses in tea-shops frequented by
city men. And one reads in police court reports of raids
what *those* are! Probably they were, in action, as respectable as any body of women; *more* respectable, probably,
than the great middle class of before the war, and certainly
spotless by comparison with their own upper servants
whose morals, merely as recorded in the divorce court
statistics—*that* she had from Tietjens—would put to shame
even those of Welsh or lowland Scotch villages. Her mother
was accustomed to say that she was sure her butler would
get to heaven, simply because the Recording Angel, being
an angel—and, as such, delicately minded—wouldn't have
the face to put down, much less read out, the least venial
of Morgan's offences. ...

And, sceptical as she was by nature, Sylvia Tietjens
didn't really even believe in the capacity for immoralities
of her friends. She didn't believe that any one of them was
seriously what the French would call the *maîtresse en titre*
of any particular man. Passion wasn't, at least, their strong
suit; they left that to more—or to less—august circles. The
Duke of A ... and all the little A's ... might be the children of the morose and passion-stricken Duke of B ...
instead of the still more morose but less passionate late
Duke of A ... Mr C, the Tory statesman and late Foreign
Minister, might equally be the father of all the children of
the Tory Lord Chancellor E ... The Whig front benches,
the gloomy and disagreeable Russells and Cavendishes
trading off these—again French—*collages sérieux* against
the matrimonial divagations of their own Lord F and
Mr G. ... But those armours of heavily titled and born
front benchers were rather of august politics. The hot-
pressed weekly journals never got hold of them: the parties
to them didn't, for one thing, photograph well, being old,
uglyish and terribly badly dressed. They were matter

rather for the memoirs of the indiscreet, already written, but not to see the light for fifty years. . . .

The affairs of her own set, female front benchers of one side or other as they were, were more tenuous. If they ever came to heads, their affairs, they had rather the nature of promiscuity and took place at the country houses where bells rang at five in the morning. Sylvia had heard of such country houses, but she did not know of any. She imagined that they might be the baronial halls of such barons of the crown as had patronymics ending in schen . . . stein . . . and baum. There were getting to be a good many of these, but Sylvia did not visit them. She had in her that much of the papist.

Certain of her more brilliant girl friends certainly made very sudden marriages; but the averages of those were not markedly higher than in the case of the daughters of doctors, solicitors, the clergy, the lord mayors and common council-men. They were the product usually of the more informal type of dance, of inexperience and champagne—of champagne of unaccustomed strength or of champagne taken in unusual circumstances—fasting as often as not. They were, these hasty marriages, hardly ever the result of either passion or temperamental lewdness.

In her own case—years ago now—she had certainly been taken advantage of, after champagne, by a married man called Drake. A bit of a brute she acknowledged him now to be. But after the event passion had developed: intense on her side and quite intense enough on his. When, in a scare that had been as much her mother's as her own, she had led Tietjens on and married him in Paris to be out of the way—though it was fortunate that the English Catholic church in the Avenue Hoche had been the scene of her mother's marriage also, thus establishing a precedent and an ostensible reason!—there had been dreadful scenes right up to the very night of the marriage. She had hardly to close her eyes in order to see the Paris hotel bedroom, the distorted face of Drake, who was mad with grief and jealousy, against a background of white things, flowers and the like, sent in overnight for the wedding. She knew that she had been very near death. She had wanted death.

And even now she had only to see the name of Drake in the paper—her mother's influence with the pompous front bencher of the Upper House, her cousin, had put Drake in the way of colonial promotions that were recorded in gazettes—nay, she had only involuntarily to think of that night and she would stop dead, speaking or walking, drive her nails into her palms and groan slightly. ... She had to invent a chronic stitch in her heart to account for this groan, which ended in a mumble and seemed to herself to degrade her. ...

The miserable memory would come, ghost-like, at any time, anywhere. She would see Drake's face, dark against the white things; she would feel the thin night-gown ripping off her shoulder; but most of all she would seem, in darkness that excluded the light of any room in which she might be, to be transfused by the mental agony that there she had felt: the longing for the brute who had mangled her: the dreadful pain of the mind. The odd thing was that the sight of Drake himself, whom she had seen several times since the outbreak of the war, left her completely without emotion. She had no aversion, but no longing for him. ... She had, nevertheless, longing, but she knew it was longing merely to experience again that dreadful feeling. And not with Drake.

Her 'turnings down' then of the really nice men, if it were a sport, was a sport not without a spice of danger. She imagined that, after a success, she must feel much of the exhilaration that men told her they felt after bringing off a clean right and left, and no doubt she felt some of the emotions that the same young men felt when they were out shooting with beginners. Her personal chastity she now cherished much as she cherished her personal cleanliness and persevered in her Swedish exercises after her baths before an open window, her rides afterwards, and her long nights of dancing which she would pursue in any room that was decently ventilated. Indeed, the two sides of life were, in her mind, intimately connected: she kept herself attractive by her skilfully selected exercises and cleanlinesses: and the same fatigues, healthful as they were, kept her in the mood for chastity of life. She had done so ever since her return to her husband; and this not because of any attachment to her husband or to virtue as such, as because she had made the pact with herself out of caprice and meant to keep it. She *had* to have men at her feet: that was, as it were, the price of her—purely social— daily bread: as it was the price of the daily bread of her intimates. She was, and had been for many years, absolutely continent. And so very likely were, and had been, all her Moiras, and Megs, and Lady Marjories—but she was perfectly aware that they had to have, above their assemblies as it were, a light vapour of the airs and habits of the brothel. The public demanded that . . . a light vapour, like the slight traces of steam that she had seen, glutinously adhering to the top of the water in the crocodile-houses of the Zoo.

It was, indeed, the price; and she was aware that she had been lucky. Not many of the hastily married young women of her set really kept their heads above water *in* her set: for a season you would read that Lady Marjorie and Captain Hunt, after her presentation at Court on the occasion of her marriage, were to be seen at Roehampton, at Goodwood and the like: photographs of the young couple, striding along with the palings of the Row behind them, would appear for a month or so. Then the records of their fashionable doings would transfer themselves to the lists of the attendants and attachés of distant vice-regal courts in tropics bad for the complexion. 'And then no more of he and she,' as Sylvia put it.

In her case it hadn't been so bad, but it had been nearish. She had had the advantage of being an only daughter of a very rich woman: her husband wasn't just any Captain Hunt to stick on a vice-regal staff. He was in a first-class office and when Angélique wrote notes on the

young *ménage* she could—Angélique's ideas of these
things being hazy—always refer to the husband as the
future Lord Chancellor or Ambassador to Vienna. And
their little, frightfully expensive establishment—to which
her mother, who had lived with them, had very hand-
somely contributed—had floated them over the first
dangerous two years. They had entertained like mad, and
two much-canvassed scandals had had their beginnings in
Sylvia's small drawing-room. She had been quite established when she had gone off with Perowne. . . .

And coming back had not been so difficult. She had
expected it would be, but it hadn't. Tietjens had stipulated
for large rooms in Gray's Inn. That hadn't seemed to her
to be reasonable; but she imagined that he wanted to be
near his friend and, though she had no gratitude to Tietjens for taking her back and nothing but repulsion from the
idea of living in his house, as they were making a bargain,
she owed it to herself to be fair. She had never swindled
a railway company, brought dutiable scent past a custom-
house or represented to a second-hand dealer that her
clothes were less worn than they were, though with her
prestige she could actually have done this. It was fair that
Tietjens should live where he wished, and live there they
did, their very tall windows looking straight into those of
Macmaster across the Georgian quadrangle.

They had two floors of a great building, and that gave
them a great deal of space; the breakfast-room, in which
during the war they also lunched, was an immense room,
completely lined with books that were nearly all calf-
backed, with an immense mirror over an immense, carved,
yellow and white marble mantelpiece, and three windows
that, in their great height, with the spideriness of their
divisions and their odd, bulging glass—some of the panes
were faintly violet in age—gave to the room an eighteenth-
century distinction. It suited, she admitted, Tietjens, who
was an eighteenth-century figure of the Dr Johnson type
—the only eighteenth-century type of which she knew,
except for that of the beau something who wore white

satin and ruffles, went to Bath and must have been in-
describably tiresome.

Above, she had a great white drawing-room, with fixings
that she knew were eighteenth century and to be respected.
For Tietjens—again she admitted—had a marvellous gift
for old furniture: he despised it as such, but he knew it
down to the ground. Once when her friend Lady Moira
had been deploring the expense of having her new, little
house furnished from top to toe under the advice of Sir
John Robertson, the specialist (the Moiras had sold Arling-
ton Street lock, stock, and barrel to some American), Tietjens, who had come in to tea and had been listening without speaking, had said, with the soft good nature, rather
sentimental in tone, that once in a blue moon he would
bestow on her prettiest friends:

'You had better let me do it for you.'

Taking a look round Sylvia's great drawing-room, with
the white panels, the Chinese lacquer screens, the red
lacquer and ormolu cabinets and the immense blue and
pink carpet (and Sylvia knew that if only for the three
panels by a fellow called Fragonard, bought just before
Fragonards had been boomed by the late King, her
drawing-room was something remarkable), Lady Moira
had said to Tietjens, rather flutteringly and almost with
the voice with which she began one of her affairs:

'Oh, if only you *would*.'

He had done it, and he had done it for a quarter of the
estimate of Sir John Robertson. He had done it without
effort, as if with a roll or two of his elephantine shoulders,
for he seemed to know what was in every dealer's and auc-
tioneer's catalogue by looking at the green halfpenny stamp
on the wrapper. And, still more astonishingly, he had
made love to Lady Moira—they had stopped twice with
the Moiras in Gloucestershire and the Moiras had three
times week-ended with Mrs Satterthwaite as the Tietjens'
invités. . . . Tietjens had made love to Lady Moira quite
prettily and sufficiently to tide Moira over until she was
ready to begin her affair with Sir William Heathly.

For the matter of that, Sir John Robertson, the specialist in old furniture, challenged by Lady Moira to pick holes in her beautiful house, had gone there, poked his large spectacles against cabinets, smelt the varnish of table tops and bitten the backs of chairs in his ancient and short-sighted way, and had then told Lady Moira that Tietjens had bought her nothing that wasn't worth a bit more than he had given for it. This increased their respect for the old fellow: it explained his several millions. For, if the old fellow proposed to make out of a friend like Moira a profit of 300 per cent—limiting it to that out of sheer affection for a pretty woman—what wouldn't he make out of a natural—and national—enemy like a United States senator!

And the old man took a great fancy to Tietjens himself—which Tietjens, to Sylvia's bewilderment, did not resent. The old man would come in to tea and, if Tietjens were present, would stay for hours talking about old furniture. Tietjens would listen without talking. Sir John would expatiate over and over again about this to Mrs Tietjens. It was extraordinary. Tietjens went purely by instinct: by taking a glance at a thing and chancing its price. According to Sir John one of the most remarkable feats of the furniture trade had been Tietjens' purchase of the Hemingway bureau for Lady Moira. Tietjens, in his dislikeful way, had bought this at a cottage sale for £3 10s., and had told Lady Moira it was the best piece she would ever possess: Lady Moira had gone to the sale with him. Other dealers present had hardly looked at it: Tietjens certainly hadn't opened it. But at Lady Moira's, poking his spectacles into the upper part of the glazed piece, Sir John had put his nose straight on the little bit of inserted yellow wood by a hinge, bearing signature, name and date: 'Jno. Hemingway, Bath 1784.' Sylvia remembered them because Sir John told her so often. It was a lost 'piece' that the furnishing world had been after for many years.

For that exploit the old man seemed to love Tietjens.

That he loved Sylvia herself, she was quite aware. He
fluttered round her tremulously, gave fantastic entertain-
ments in her honour and was the only man she had never
turned down. He had a harem, so it was said, in an
enormous house at Brighton or somewhere. But it was
another sort of love he bestowed on Tietjens: the rather
pathetic love that the aged bestow on their possible
successors in office.

Once Sir John came in to tea and quite formally and
with a sort of portentousness announced that this was his
seventy-first birthday, and that he was a broken man. He
seriously proposed that Tietjens should come into partner-
ship with him with the reversion of the business—not, of
course, of his private fortune. Tietjens had listened
amiably, asking a detail or two of Sir John's proposed
arrangement. Then he had said, with the rather caressing
voice that he now and then bestowed on a pretty woman,
that he didn't think it would do. There would be too
much beastly money about it. As a career it would be
more congenial to him than his office... but there was
too much beastly money about it.

Once more, a little to Sylvia's surprise—but men are
queer creatures!—Sir John seemed to see this objection
as quite reasonable, though he heard it with regret and
combated it feebly. He went away with a relieved jaunti-
ness; for, if he couldn't have Tietjens he couldn't, and he
invited Sylvia to dine with him somewhere where they
were going to have something fabulous and very nasty at
about two guineas the ounce on the menu. Something like
that! And during dinner Sir John had entertained her by
singing the praises of her husband. He said that Tietjens
was much too great a gentleman to be wasted on the old-
furniture trade: that was why he hadn't persisted. But
he sent by Sylvia a message to the effect that if ever Tietjens *did* come to be in want of money...

Occasionally Sylvia was worried to know why people—
as they sometimes did—told her that her husband had
great gifts. To her he was merely unaccountable. His

actions and opinions seemed simply the products of caprice
—like her own; and, since she knew that most of her own
manifestations were a matter of contrariety, she abandoned
the habit of thinking much about him.

But gradually and dimly she began to see that Tietjens
had, at least, a consistency of character and a rather
unusual knowledge of life. This came to her when she had
to acknowledge that their move to the Inn of Court had
been a social success and had suited herself. When they
had discussed the change at Lobscheid—or rather when
Sylvia had unconditionally given in to every stipulation of
Tietjens!—he had predicted almost exactly what would
happen, though it had been the affair of her mother's
cousin's opera box that had most impressed her. He had
told her, at Lobscheid, that he had no intention of inter-
fering with her social level, and she was convinced that
he was not going to. He had thought about it a good deal.

She hadn't much listened to him. She had thought,
firstly, that he was a fool and, secondly, that he *did* mean
to hurt her. And she acknowledged that he had a certain
right. If, after she had been off with another man, she
asked this one still to extend to her the honour of his
name and shelter of his roof, she had no right to object to
his terms. Her only decent revenge on him was to live
afterwards with such equanimity as to let him know the
mortification of failure.

But at Lobscheid he had talked a lot of nonsense, as it
had seemed to her: a mixture of prophecy and politics.
The Chancellor of the Exchequer of that date had been
putting pressure on the great landlords; the great landlords had been replying by cutting down their establishments and closing their town houses—not to any great
extent, but enough to make a very effective gesture of it,
and so as to raise a considerable clamour from footmen and
milliners. The Tietjens—both of them—were of the great
land-owning class: they could adopt that gesture of shut-
ting up their Mayfair house and going to live in a wilder-

ness. All the more if they made their wilderness a thoroughly comfortable affair!

He had counselled her to present this aspect of the matter to her mother's cousin, the morosely portentous Rugeley. Rugely was a great landowner—almost the greatest of all; and he was a landowner obsessed with a sense of his duties both to his dependants and his even remote relatives. Sylvia had only, Tietjens said, to go to the Duke and tell him that the Chancellor's exactions had forced them to this move, but that they had done it partly as a protest, and the Duke would accept it almost as a personal tribute to himself. *He* couldn't, even as a protest, be expected to shut up Mexborough or reduce his expenses. But, if his humbler relatives spiritedly did, he would almost certainly make it up to them. And Rugeley's favours were on the portentous scale of everything about him. 'I shouldn't wonder,' Tietjens had said, 'if he didn't lend you the Rugeley box to entertain in.'

And that is exactly what had happened.

The Duke—who must have kept a register of his remotest cousins—had, shortly before their return to London, heard that this young couple had parted with every prospect of a large and disagreeable scandal. He had approached Mrs Satterthwaite—for whom he had a gloomy affection—and he had been pleased to hear that the rumour was a gross libel. So that, when the young couple actually turned up again—from Russia!—Rugeley, who perceived that they were not only together, but to all appearances quite united, was determined not only to make it up to them, but to show, in order to abash their libellers, as signal a mark of his favour as he could without inconvenience to himself. He, therefore, twice—being a widower—invited Mrs Satterthwaite to entertain for him, Sylvia to invite the guests, and then had Mrs Tietjens' name placed on the roll of those who could have the Rugeley box at the opera, on application at the Rugeley estate office, when it wasn't wanted. This was a very great

privilege and Sylvia had known how to make the most of
it.

On the other hand, on the occasion of their conversation
at Lobscheid, Tietjens had prophesied what at the time
seemed to her a lot of tosh. It had been two or three years
before, but Tietjens had said that about the time grouse-
shooting began, in 1914, a European conflagration would
take place which would shut up half the houses in Mayfair and beggar their inhabitants. He had patiently supported his prophecy with financial statistics as to the
approaching bankruptcy of various European powers and
the growingly acquisitive skill and rapacity of the inhabitants of Great Britain. She had listened to that with some
attention: it had seemed to her rather like the usual nonsense talked in country houses—where, irritatingly, he
never talked. But she liked to be able to have a picturesque
fact or two with which to support herself when she too,
to hold attention, wanted to issue moving statements as to
revolutions, anarchies and strife in the offing. And she
had noticed that when she magpied Tietjens' conversations
more serious men in responsible positions were apt to
argue with her and to pay her more attention than
before. . . . .

And now, walking along the table with her plate in her
hand, she could not but acknowledge that, triumphantly—
and very comfortably for her!—Tietjens had been right!
In the third year of the war it was very convenient to have
a dwelling, cheap, comfortable, almost august and so easy
to work that you could have, at a pinch, run it with one
maid, though the faithful Hullo Central had not let it
come to that yet. . . .

Being near Tietjens she lifted her plate, which contained two cold cutlets in aspic and several leaves of salad:
she wavered a little to one side and, with a circular motion
of her hand, let the whole contents fly at Tietjens' head.
She placed the plate on the table and drifted slowly towards the enormous mirror over the fireplace.

'I'm bored,' she said. 'Bored! Bored!'

Tietjens had moved slightly as she had thrown: the
cutlets and most of the salad leaves had gone over his
shoulder. But one, couched, very green leaf was on his
shoulder-strap, and the oil and vinegar from the plate—
Sylvia *knew* that she took too much of all condiments—
had splashed from the revers of his tunic to his green
staff-badges. She was glad that she had hit him as much
as that: it meant that her marksmanship had not been
quite rotten. She was glad, too, that she had missed him.
She was also supremely indifferent. It had occurred to her
to do it and she had done it. Of that she was glad!

She looked at herself for some time in the mirror of
bluish depths. She pressed her immense bandeaux with
both hands on to her ears. She was all right: high-
featured: alabaster complexion—but that was mostly the
mirror's doing—beautiful, long, cool hands—what man's
forehead wouldn't long for them? . . . And that hair! What
man wouldn't think of it unloosed on white shoulders!
. . . Well, Tietjens wouldn't! Or, perhaps, he did . . . she
hoped he did, curse him, for he never saw that sight.
Obviously sometimes, at night, with a little whisky taken
he must want to!

She rang the bell and bade Hullo Central sweep the
plateful from the carpet; Hullo Central, tall and dark,
looking with wide-open eyes, motionless at nothing.

Sylvia went along the bookshelves, pausing over a book
back, '*Vitare Hominum Notiss* . . .' in gilt, irregular capi-
tals pressed deep into the old leather. At the first long
window she supported herself by the blind-cord. She
looked out and back into the room.

'There's that veiled woman!' she said, 'going into
eleven. . . . It's two o'clock, of course. . . .'

She looked at her husband's back hard, the clumsy
khaki back that was getting round-shouldered now. Hard!
She wasn't going to miss a motion or a stiffening.

'I've found out who it is!' she said, 'and who she goes
to. I got it out of the porter.' She waited. Then she
added:

'It's the woman you travelled down from Bishop Auck-land with. On the day war was declared.'

Tietjens turned solidly round in his chair. She knew he would do that out of stiff politeness, so it meant nothing.

His face was whitish in the pale light, but it was always whitish since he had come back from France and passed his day in a tin hut among dust heaps. He said:

'So you saw me!' But that, too, was mere politeness.

She said:

'Of course the whole crowd of us from Claudine's saw you! It was old Campion who said she was a Mrs . . . I've forgotten the name.'

Tietjens said:

'I imagined he would know her. I saw him looking in from the corridor!'

She said:

'Is she your mistress, or only Macmaster's, or the mistress of both of you? It would be like you to have a mistress in common. . . . She's got a mad husband, hasn't she? A clergyman.'

Tietjens said:

'She hasn't!'

Sylvia checked suddenly in her next questions, and Tietjens, who in these discussions never manoeuvred for position, said:

'She has been Mrs Macmaster over six months.'

Sylvia said:

'She married him then the day after her husband's death.'

She drew a long breath and added:

'I don't care. . . . She has been coming here every Friday for three years. . . . I tell you I shall expose her unless that little beast pays you to-morrow the money he owes you. . . . God knows you need it!' She said then hurriedly, for she didn't know how Tietjens might take that proposition:

'Mrs Wannop rang up this morning to know who was . . . oh! . . . the evil genius of the Congress of Vienna.

Who, by the by, is Mrs Wannop's secretary? She wants to
see you this afternoon. About war babies!'

Tietjens said:

'Mrs Wannop hasn't got a secretary. It's her daughter
who does the ringing-up.'

'The girl,' Sylvia said, 'you were so potty about at that
horrible afternoon Macmaster gave. Has she had a war
baby by you? They all say she's your mistress.'

Tietjens said:

'No, Miss Wannop isn't my mistress. Her mother has
had a commission to write an article about war babies. I
told her yesterday there weren't any war babies to speak
of, and she's upset because she won't be able to make a
sensational article. She wants to try to make me change
my mind.'

'It *was* Miss Wannop at that beastly affair of your
friend's?' Sylvia asked. 'And I suppose the woman who
received was Mrs What's-er-name: your other mistress.
An unpleasant show. I don't think much of your taste. The
one where all the horrible geniuses in London were? There
was a man like a rabbit talked to me about how to write
poetry.'

'That's no good as an identification of the party,' Tietjens said. 'Macmaster gives a party every Friday, not
Saturday. He has for years. Mrs Macmaster goes there
every Friday. To act as hostess. She has for years. Miss
Wannop goes there every Friday after she has done work
for her mother. To support Mrs Macmaster. . . .'

'She has for years!' Sylvia mocked him. 'And you go
there every Friday! to croodle over Miss Wannop. Oh,
Christopher!'—she adopted a mock pathetic voice—'I
never did have much opinion of your taste . . . but not
that! Don't let it be that. Put her back. She's too young
for you. . . .'

'All the geniuses in London,' Tietjens continued
equably, 'go to Macmaster's every Friday. He has been
trusted with the job of giving away Royal Literary Bounty

money: that's why they go. They go: that's why he was
given his C.B.'

'I should not have thought they counted,' Sylvia said.

'Of course they count,' Tietjens said. 'They write for
the Press. They can get anybody anything . . . except themselves!'

'Like you!' Sylvia said; 'exactly like you! They're a lot
of bribed squits.'

'Oh, no,' Tietjens said. 'It isn't done obviously or dis-
creditably. Don't believe that Macmaster distributes forty-
pounders yearly of bounty on condition that he gets
advancement. He hasn't, himself, the least idea of how it
works, except by his atmosphere.'

'I never knew a beastlier atmosphere,' Sylvia said. 'It
reeked of rabbit's food.'

'You're quite mistaken,' Tietjens said; 'that is the Russian leather of the backs of the specially bound presentation copies in the *large* bookcase.'

'I don't know what you're talking about,' Sylvia said.
'What *are* presentation copies? I should have thought
you'd had enough of the beastly Russian smells Kiev stunk
of.'

Tietjens considered for a moment.

'No! I don't remember it,' he said. 'Kiev? . . . Oh, it's
where we were . . .'

'You put half your mother's money,' Sylvia said, 'into
the Government of Kiev 12½ per cent. City Tram-
ways. . . .'

At that Tietjens certainly winced, a type of wincing that
Sylvia hadn't wanted.

'You're not fit to go out to-morrow,' she said. 'I shall
wire to old Campion.'

'Mrs Duchemin,' Tietjens said woodenly. 'Mrs Macmaster that is, also used to burn a little incense in the
room before the parties. . . . Those Chinese stinks . . . what
do they call them? Well, it doesn't matter,' he added
resignedly. Then he went on: 'Don't you make any mistake. Mrs Macmaster is a very superior woman. Enor-

mously efficient! Tremendously respected. I shouldn't advise even you to come up against her, now she's in the saddle.'

Mrs Tietjens said:

'*That* sort of woman!'

Tietjens said:

'I don't say you ever will come up against her. Your spheres differ. But, if you do, don't. . . . I say it because you seem to have got your knife into her.'

'I don't like that sort of thing going on under my windows,' Sylvia said.

Tietjens said:

'What sort of thing? . . . I was trying to tell you a little about Mrs Macmaster . . . she's like the woman who was the mistress of the man who burned the other fellow's horrid book. . . . I can't remember the names.'

Sylvia said quickly:

'Don't try!' In a slower tone she added: 'I don't in the least want to know. . . .'

'Well, she was an Egeria!' Tietjens said. 'An inspiration to the distinguished. Mrs Macmaster is all that. The geniuses swarm round her, and with the really select ones she corresponds. She writes superior letters, about the Higher Morality usually; very delicate in feeling. Scotch naturally. When they go abroad she sends them snatches of London literary happenings; well done, mind you! And then, every now and then, she slips in something she wants Macmaster to have. But with great delicacy. . . . Say it's this C.B. . . . she transfuses into the minds of Genius One, Two and Three the idea of a C.B. for Macmaster. . . . Genius No. One lunches with the Deputy Sub-Patronage Secretary, who looks after literary honours and lunches with geniuses to get the gossip. . . .'

'Why,' Sylvia said, 'did you lend Macmaster all that money?'

'Mind you,' Tietjens continued his own speech, 'it's perfectly proper. That's the way patronage *is* distributed in this country; it's the way it should be. The only clean

way. Mrs Duchemin backs Macmaster because he's a
first-class fellow for his job. And *she* is an influence over
the geniuses because she's a first-class person for hers. . . .
She represents the higher, nicer morality for really nice
Scots. Before long she will be getting tickets stopped from
being sent to people for the Academy soirées. She already
does it for the Royal Bounty dinners. A little later, when
Macmaster is knighted for bashing the French in the eye,
she'll have a tiny share in auguster assemblies. . . . Those
people have to ask *somebody* for advice. Well, one day
you'll want to present some débutante. And you won't get
a ticket. . . .'

'Then I'm glad,' Sylvia exclaimed, 'that I wrote to
Brownie's uncle about the woman. I was a little sorry this
morning because, from what Glorvina told me, you're in
such a devil of a hole. . . .'

'Who's Brownie's uncle?' Tietjens asked. 'Lord . . . Lord
. . . The banker! I know Brownie's in his uncle's bank.'

'Port Scatho!' Sylvia said. 'I wish you wouldn't act forgetting people's names. You overdo it.'

Tietjens' face went a shade whiter. . . .

'Port Scatho,' he said, 'is the chairman of the Inn
Billeting Committees, of course. And you wrote to
him? . . .'

'I'm sorry,' Sylvia said. 'I mean, I'm sorry I said that
about your forgetting. . . . I wrote to him and said that as
a resident of the Inn I objected to your mistress—he knows
the relationship, of course!—creeping in every Friday
under a heavy veil and creeping out every Saturday at four
in the morning.'

'Lord Port Scatho knows about my relationship,' Tietjens began.

'He saw her in your arms in the train,' Sylvia said. 'It
upset Brownie so much he offered to shut down your
overdraft and return any cheques you had out marked
R.D.'

'To please you?' Tietjens asked. '*Do* bankers do that
sort of thing? It's a new light on British society. . . .'

'I suppose bankers try to please their women friends, like other men,' Sylvia said. 'I told him very emphatically it wouldn't please me ... But ...' she hesitated, 'I wouldn't give him a chance to get back on you. I don't want to interfere in your affairs. But Brownie doesn't like you. ...'

'He wants you to divorce me and marry him?' Tietjens asked.

'How did you know?' Sylvia asked indifferently. 'I let him give me lunch now and then because it's convenient to have him manage my affairs, you being away.... But of course he hates you for being in the army. All the men who aren't hate all the men that are. And, of course, when there's a woman between them, the men who aren't do all they can to do the others in. When they're bankers they have a pretty good pull. ...'

'I suppose they have,' Tietjens said vaguely; 'of course they would have. ...'

Sylvia abandoned the blind-cord on which she had been dragging with one hand. In order that light might fall on her face and give more impressiveness to her words, for, in a minute or two, when she felt brave enough, she meant really to let him have her bad news!—she drifted to the fireplace. He followed her round, turning on his chair to give her his face.

She said:

'Look here, it's all the fault of this beastly war, isn't it? Can you deny it? ... I mean that decent, gentlemanly fellows like Brownie have turned into beastly squits!'

'I suppose it is,' Tietjens said dully. 'Yes, certainly it is. You're quite right. It's the incidental degeneration of the heroic impulse: if the heroic impulse has too even a strain put on it the incidental degeneration gets the upper hand. That accounts for the Brownies ... all the Brownies ... turning squits. ...'

'Then why do you go on with it?' Sylvia said. 'God knows, I could wangle you out if you'd back me in the least little way.'

Tietjens said:

'Thanks! I prefer to remain in it. . . . How else am I to get a living? . . .'

'You know then,' Sylvia exclaimed almost shrilly. 'You know that they won't have you back in the office if they can find a way of getting you out. . . .'

'Oh, they'll find that!' Tietjens said. . . . He continued his other speech: 'When we go to war with France,' he said dully. . . . And Sylvia knew he was only now formulating his settled opinion so as not to have his active brain to give to the discussion. He must be thinking hard of the Wannop girl! With her littleness; her tweed-skirtishness. . . . A provincial miniature of herself, Sylvia Tietjens. . . . If she, then, had been miniature, provincial. . . . But Tietjens' words cut her as if she had been lashed with a dog-whip. 'We shall behave more creditably,' he had said, 'because there will be less heroic impulse about it. We shall . . . half of us . . . be ashamed of ourselves. So there will be much less incidental degeneration.'

Sylvia, who by that was listening to him, abandoned the consideration of Miss Wannop and the pretence that obsessed her of Tietjens saying four words, against a background of books at Macmaster's party. She exclaimed:

'Good God! What are you talking about? . . .'

Tietjens went on:

'About our next war with France. . . . We're the natural enemies of the French. We have to make our bread either by robbing them or making cat's-paws of them. . . .'

Sylvia said:

'We can't! We couldn't . . .'

'We've got to!' Tietjens said. 'It's the condition of our existence. We're a practically bankrupt, over-populated, northern country: they're rich southerners, with a falling population. Towards 1930 we shall have to do what Prussia did in 1914. Our conditions will be exactly those of Prussia then. It's the . . . what is it called? . . .

'But . . .' Sylvia cried out, 'you're a Franco-maniac. . . .

You're thought to be a French agent. . . . That's what's
bitching your career!'

'I am?' Tietjens asked uninterestedly. He added: 'Yes,
that probably *would* bitch my career. . . .' He went on,
with a little more animation and a little more of his mind:

'Ah! *that* will be a war worth seeing. . . . None of their
drunken rat-fighting for imbecile boodlers . . .'

'It would drive mother mad!' Sylvia said.

'Oh, no it wouldn't,' Tietjens said. 'It will stimulate her
if she is still alive. . . . Our heroes won't be drunk with
wine and lechery: our squits won't stay at home and stab
the heroes in the back. Our Minister for Water-closets
won't keep two and a half million men in any base in
order to get the votes of their women at a General Election—that's been the first evil effects of giving women
the vote! With the French holding Ireland and stretching
in a solid line from Bristol to Whitehall, we should hang
the Minister before he had time to sign the papers. And
we should be decently loyal to our Prussian allies and
brothers. . . . Our Cabinet won't hate them as they hate
the French for being frugal and strong in logic and well-
educated and remorselessly practical. Prussians are the
sort of fellows you can be hoggish with when you want
to. . . .'

Sylvia interjected violently:

'For God's sake stop it. You almost make me believe
what you say is true. I tell you mother would go mad. Her
greatest friend is the Duchesse Tonnerre Château-
Herault. . . .'

'Well!' Tietjens said. 'Your greatest friends are the Med
. . . Med . . . the Austrian officers you take chocolates and
flowers to. That there was all the row about . . . We're at
war with *them* and you haven't gone mad!'

'I don't know,' Sylvia said. 'Sometimes I think I am going mad!' She drooped. Tietjens, his face very strained,
was looking at the tablecloth. He muttered: 'Med . . . Met
. . . Kos . . .' Sylvia said:

'Do you know a poem called *Somewhere*? It begins: "Somewhere or other there must surely be..."'

Tietjens said:

'I'm sorry. No! I haven't been able to get up my poetry again.'

Sylvia said:

'*Don't!*' She added: 'You've got to be at the War Office at 4.15, haven't you? What's the time now?' She extremely wanted to give him her bad news before he went; she extremely wanted to put off giving it as long as she could. She wanted to reflect on the matter first; she wanted also to keep up a desultory conversation, or he might leave the room. She didn't want to have to say to him: 'Wait a minute, I've something to say to you!' for he might not, at that moment, be in the mood. He said it was not yet two. He could give her an hour and a half more.

To keep the conversation going, she said:

'I suppose the Wannop girl is making bandages or being a Waac. Something forceful.'

Tietjens said:

'No; she's a pacifist. As pacifist as you. Not so impulsive; but, on the other hand, she has more arguments. I should say she'll be in prison before the war's over....'

'A nice time you must have between the two of us,' Sylvia said. The memory of her interview with the great lady nicknamed Glorvina—though it was not at all a good nickname—was coming over her forcibly.

She said:

'I suppose you're always talking it over with her? You see her every day.'

She imagined that that might keep him occupied for a minute or two. He said—she caught the sense of it only—and quite indifferently that he had tea with Mrs Wannop every day. She had moved to a place called Bedford Park, which was near his office: not three minutes' walk. The War Office had put up a lot of huts on some public green in that neighbourhood. He only saw the daughter once a week, at most. They never talked about the war; it was too disagreeable a subject for the young woman. Or rather, too painful. . . . His talk gradually drifted into unfinished sentences. . . .

They played that comedy occasionally, for it is impossible for two people to live in the same house and not have some common meeting ground. So they would each talk: sometimes talking at great length and with politeness, each thinking his or her thoughts till they drifted into silence.

And, since she had acquired the habit of going into retreat—with an Anglican sisterhood in order to annoy Tietjens, who hated convents and considered that the communions should not mix—Sylvia had acquired also the habit of losing herself almost completely in reveries. Thus she was now vaguely conscious that a greyish lump, Tietjens, sat at the head of a whitish expanse: the lunch-table. There were also books . . . actually she was seeing a quite different figure and other books—the books of Glorvina's husband, for the great lady had received Sylvia in that statesman's library.

Glorvina, who was the mother of two of Sylvia's absolutely most intimate friends, had sent for Sylvia. She wished, kindly and even wittily, to remonstrate with Sylvia because of her complete abstention from any patriotic activity. She offered Sylvia the address of a place in the city where she could buy wholesale and ready-made diapers for babies which Sylvia could present to some charity or other as being her own work. Sylvia said she would do nothing of the sort, and Glorvina said she would present the idea to poor Mrs Pilsenhauser. She—Glorvina—said she spent some time every day thinking out acts of patriotism for the distressed rich with foreign names, accents or antecedents. . . .

Glorvina was a fiftyish lady with a pointed, grey face and a hard aspect; but when she was inclined to be witty or to plead earnestly she had a kind manner. The room in which they were was over a Belgravia back garden. It was lit by

a skylight, and the shadows from above deepened the lines
of her face, accentuating the rather dusty grey of the hair
as well as both the hardness and the kind manner. This
very much impressed Sylvia, who was used to seeing the
lady by artificial light. . . .

She said, however:

'You don't suggest, Glorvina, that I'm the distressed
rich with a foreign name!'

The great lady had said:

'My dear Sylvia; it isn't so much you as your husband.
Your last exploit with the Esterhazys and Metternichs has
pretty well done for *him*. You forget that the present
powers that be are not logical. . . .'

Sylvia remembered that she had sprung up from her
leather saddle-back chair, exclaiming:

'You mean to say that those unspeakable swine think
that I'm . . .'

Glorvina said patiently:

'My dear Sylvia, I've already said it's not you. It's your
husband that suffers. He appears to be too good a fellow
to suffer. Mr Waterhouse says so. I don't know him myself,
well.'

Sylvia remembered that she had said:

'And who in the world is Mr Waterhouse?' and hearing
that Mr Waterhouse was a late Liberal Minister, had lost
interest. She couldn't, indeed, remember any of the further
words of her hostess, as words. The sense of them had too
much overwhelmed her. . . .

She stood now, looking at Tietjens and only occasionally
seeing him, her mind completely occupied with the effort
to recapture Glorvina's own words in the desire for exact-
ness. Usually she remembered conversations pretty well;
but on this occasion her mad fury, her feeling of nausea,
the pain of her own nails in her palms, an unrecoverable
sequence of emotions, had overwhelmed her.

She looked at Tietjens now with a sort of gloating
curiosity. How was it possible that the most honourable
man she knew should be so overwhelmed by foul and

baseless rumours? It made you suspect that honour had,
in itself, a quality of the evil eye. . . .

Tietjens, his face pallid, was fingering a piece of toast.
He muttered:

'Met . . Met . . . It's Met . . .' He wiped his brow with
a table-napkin, looked at it with a start, threw it on the
floor and pulled out a handkerchief. . . . He muttered:
'Mett . . . Metter . . .' His face illuminated itself like the
face of a child listening at a shell.

Sylvia screamed with a passion of hatred:

'For God's sake say *Metternich* . . . you're driving me
mad!'

When she looked at him again his face had cleared and
he was walking quickly to the telephone in the corner of
the room. He asked her to excuse him and gave a number
at Ealing. He said after a moment:

'Mrs Wannop? Oh! My wife has just reminded me that
Metternich was the evil genius of the Congress of Vienna.
. . .' He said: 'Yes! Yes!' and listened. After a time he
said: 'Oh, you could put it stronger than that. You could
put it that the Tory determination to ruin Napoleon at
all costs was one of those pieces of party imbecility that,
etc. . . . Yes; Castlereagh. And of course Wellington. . . .
I'm very sorry, I must ring off. . . . Yes; to-morrow at 8.30
from Waterloo. . . . No; I *shan't* be seeing her again. . . .
No; she's made a mistake. . . . Yes; give her my love . . .
good-bye.' He was reversing the earpiece to hang it up,
but a high-pitched series of yelps from the instrument
forced it back to his ear: 'Oh! *War babies!*' he exclaimed.
'I've already sent the statistics off to you! No! there *isn't*
a marked increase of the illegitimacy rate, except in
patches. The rate's appallingly high in the lowlands of
Scotland; but it always *is* appallingly high there . . .' He
laughed and said good-naturedly: 'Oh, you're an old
journalist: you won't let fifty quid go for that . . .' He was
breaking off. But: '*Or,*' he suddenly exclaimed, 'here's
another idea for you. The rate's about the same, probably
because of this: half the fellows who go out to France are

reckless because it's the last chance, as they see it. But the other half are made twice as conscientious. A decent Tommie thinks twice about leaving a girl in trouble just before he's killed. . . . The divorce statistics are up, of course, because people will chance making new starts within the law. . . . Thanks . . . thanks . . .' He hung up the earpiece. . . .

Listening to that conversation had extraordinarily cleared Sylvia's mind. She said, almost sorrowfully:

'I suppose that that's why you don't seduce that girl.' And she knew—she knew at once from the suddenly changed inflection of Tietjens' voice when he had said 'a decent Tommie thinks twice before leaving his girl in trouble!'—that Tietjens himself had thought twice.

She looked at him now almost incredulously, but with great coolness. Why *shouldn't* he, she asked herself, give himself a little pleasure with his girl before going to almost certain death. . . . She felt a real, sharp pain at her heart. . . . A poor wretch in such a devil of a hole. . . .

She had moved to a chair close beside the fireplace and now sat looking at him, leaning interestedly forward, as if at a garden party she had been finding—*par impossible!*— a pastoral play not so badly produced. Tietjens was a fabulous monster. . . .

He was a fabulous monster not because he was honourable and virtuous. She had known several very honourable and very virtuous men. If she had never known an honourable or virtuous woman except among her French or Austrian friends, that was, no doubt, because virtuous and honourable women did not amuse her or because, except just for the French and Austrians, they were not Roman Catholics. . . . But the honourable and virtuous men she had known had usually prospered and been respected. They weren't the great fortunes, but they were well-offish: well spoken of: of the country gentleman type . . . Tietjens. . . .

She arranged her thoughts. To get one point settled in her mind, she asked:

'What really happened to you in France? What is really the matter with your memory? Or your brain, is it?'

He said carefully:

'It's half of it, an irregular piece of it, dead. Or rather pale. Without a proper blood supply.... So a great portion of it, in the shape of memory, has gone.'

She said:

'But *you*!... without a brain!...' As this was not a question, he did not answer.

His going at once to the telephone, as soon as he was in the possession of the name 'Metternich,' had at last convinced her that he had not been, for the last four months, acting the hypochondriac or merely lying to obtain sympathy or extended sick leave. Amongst Sylvia's friends a wangle known as shell-shock was cynically laughed at and quite approved of. Quite decent and, as far as she knew, quite brave menfolk of her women would openly boast that, when they had had enough of it over there, they would wangle a little leave or get a little leave extended by simulating this purely nominal disease, and in the general carnival of lying, lechery, drink, and howling that this affair was, to pretend to a little shell-shock had seemed to her to be almost virtuous. At any rate if a man passed his time at garden parties—or, as for the last months Tietjens had done, passed his time in a tin hut amongst dust heaps, going to tea every afternoon in order to help Mrs Wannop with her newspaper articles—when men were so engaged they were, at least, not trying to kill each other.

She said now:

'Do you mind telling me what actually happened to you?'

He said:

'I don't know that I can very well.... Something burst —or "exploded" is probably the right word—near me, in the dark. I expect you'd rather not hear about it? ...'

'I want to!' Sylvia said.

He said:

'The point about it is that I don't *know* what happened

and I don't remember what I did. There are three weeks of my life dead. . . . What I remember is being in a C.C.S. and not being able to remember my own name.'

'You *mean* that?' Sylvia asked. 'It's not just a way of talking?'

'No, it's not just a way of talking,' Tietjens answered. 'I lay in bed in the C.C.S. . . . Your friends were dropping bombs on it.'

'You might not call them my friends,' Sylvia said.

Tietjens said:

'I beg your pardon. One gets into a loose way of speaking. The poor bloody Huns, then, were dropping bombs from aeroplanes on the hospital huts. . . . I'm not suggesting they knew it was a C.C.S.; it was, no doubt, just carelessness. . . .'

'You needn't spare the Germans for me!' Sylvia said. 'You needn't spare any man who has killed another man.'

'I was, then, dreadfully worried,' Tietjens went on. 'I was composing a preface for a book on Arminianism. . . .'

'You haven't written a book!' Sylvia exclaimed eagerly, because she thought that if Tietjens took to writing a book there might be a way of his earning a living. Many people had told her that he ought to write a book.

'No, I hadn't written a book,' Tietjens said, 'and I didn't know what Arminianism was. . . .'

'You know perfectly well what the Arminian heresy is,' Sylvia said sharply; 'you explained it all to me years ago.'

'Yes,' Tietjens exclaimed. 'Years ago I could have, but I couldn't then. I could now, but I was a little worried about it then. It's a little awkward to write a preface about a subject of which you know nothing. But it didn't seem to me to be discreditable in an army sense. . . . Still it worried me dreadfully not to know my own name. I lay and worried and worried, and thought how discreditable it would appear if a nurse came along and asked me and I didn't know. Of course my name was on a luggage label tied to my collar; but I'd forgotten they did that to casualties. . . . Then a lot of people carried pieces of a nurse down the hut: the

Germans' bombs had done that of course. They were still dropping about the place.'

'But good heavens,' Sylvia cried out, 'do you mean they carried a dead nurse past you? . . .'

'The poor dear wasn't dead,' Tietjens said. 'I wish she had been. Her name was Beatrice Carmichael . . . the first name I learned after my collapse. She's dead now of course. . . . That seemed to wake up a fellow on the other side of the room with a lot of blood coming through the bandages on his head. . . . He rolled out of his bed and, without a word, walked across the hut and began to strangle me. . . .'

'But this isn't believable,' Sylvia said. 'I'm sorry, but I can't believe it. . . . You were an officer: they *couldn't* have carried a wounded nurse under your nose. They must have known your sister Caroline was a nurse and was killed. . . .'

'Carrie,' Tietjens said, 'was drowned on a hospital ship. I thank God I didn't have to connect the other girl with her. . . . But you don't suppose that in addition to one's name, rank, unit, and date of admission they'd put that I'd lost a sister and two brothers in action and a father—of a broken heart, I dare say. . . .'

'But you only lost one brother,' Sylvia said. 'I went into mourning for him and your sister. . . .'

'No, two,' Tietjens said; 'but the fellow who was strangling me was what I wanted to tell you about. He let out a number of ear-piercing shrieks and lots of orderlies came and pulled him off me and sat all over him. Then he began to shout "*Faith!*" He shouted: "Faith! . . . Faith! . . . Faith!' . . ." at intervals of two seconds, as far as I could tell by my pulse, until four in the morning, when he died. . . . I don't know whether it was a religious exhortation or a woman's name, but I disliked him a good deal because he started my tortures, such as they were. . . . There had been a girl I knew called Faith. Oh, not a love affair: the daughter of my father's head gardener, a Scotsman. The point is that every time he said Faith I asked myself "Faith . . . Faith what?" I couldn't remember the name of my father's head gardener.'

Sylvia, who was thinking of other things, asked:

'What *was* the name?'

Tietjens answered:

'I don't know, I don't know to this day. . . . The point is that when I knew that I didn't know *that* name, I was as ignorant, as *uninstructed*, as a new-born babe and much more worried about it. . . . The Koran says—I've got as far as K in my reading of the *Encyclopaedia Britannica* every afternoon at Mrs Wannop's—"The strong man when smitten is smitten in his pride!" . . . Of course I got King's Regs. and the M.M.L. and Infantry Field Training and all the A.C.I.s to date by heart very quickly. And that's all a British officer is really encouraged to know. . . .'

'Oh, Christopher!' Sylvia said. '*You* read that encyclopaedia; it's pitiful. You used to despise it so.'

'That's what's meant by "smitten in his pride," ' Tietjens said. 'Of course what I read or hear now I remember. . . . But I haven't got to M, much less V. That was why I was worried about Metternich and the Congress of Vienna. I *try* to remember things on my own, but I haven't yet done so. You see, it's as if a certain area of my brain had been wiped white. Occasionally one name suggests another. You noticed, when I got Metternich it suggested Castlereagh and Wellington—and even other names. . . . But that's what the Department of Statistics will get me on. When they fire me out. The real reason will be that I've served. But they'll pretend it's because I've no more general knowledge than is to be found in the encyclopaedia: or two-thirds more or less—according to the duration of the war. . . . Or, of course, the real reason will be that I won't fake statistics to dish the French with. They asked me to, the other day, as a holiday task. And when I refused, you should have seen their faces.'

'Have you *really*,' Sylvia asked, 'lost two brothers in action?'

'Yes,' Tietjens answered. 'Curly and Longshanks. You never saw them because they were always in India. And they weren't noticeable. . . .'

'*Two!*' Sylvia said. 'I only wrote to your father about one called Edward. And your sister Caroline. In the same letter. . . .'

'Carrie wasn't noticeable either,' Tietjens said. 'She did Charity Organization Society work. . . . But I remember: you didn't like her. She was the born old maid. . . .'

'Christopher!' Sylvia asked, 'do you still think your mother died of a broken heart because I left you?'

Tietjens said:

'Good God, no. I never thought so and I don't think so. I *know* she didn't.'

'*Then!*' Sylvia exclaimed, 'she died of a broken heart because I came back. . . . It's no good protesting that you don't think so. I remember your face when you opened the telegram at Lobscheid. Miss Wannop forwarded it from Rye. I remember the postmark. She was born to do me ill. The moment you got it I could see you thinking that you must conceal from me that you thought it was because of me she died. I could see you wondering if it wouldn't be practicable to conceal from me that she was dead. You couldn't, of course, do that because, you remember, we were to have gone to Wiesbaden and show ourselves; and we couldn't do that because we should have to be in mourning. So you took me to Russia to get out of taking me to the funeral.'

'I took you to Russia,' Tietjens said. 'I remember it all now—because I had an order from Sir Robert Ingleby to assist the British Consul-General in preparing a Blue Book statistical table of the Government of Kiev. . . . It appeared to be the most industrially promising region in the world in those days. It isn't now, naturally. I shall never see back a penny of the money I put into it. I thought I was clever in those days. . . . And of course, yes, the money was my mother's settlement. It comes back . . . yes, of course. . . .'

'Did you,' Sylvia asked, 'get out of taking me to your mother's funeral because you thought I should defile your mother's corpse by my presence? Or because you were afraid that in the presence of your mother's body you wouldn't be able to conceal from me that you thought I killed her? . . . Don't deny it. And don't get out of it by saying that you can't remember those days. You're remembering now: that I killed your mother: that Miss Wannop sent the telegram—why don't you score it against her, that she sent the news? . . . Or, good God, why don't you score it against yourself, as the wrath of the Almighty, that your mother was dying while you and that girl were croodling over each other? . . . At Rye! Whilst I was at Lobscheid. . . .'

Tietjens wiped his brow with his handkerchief.

'Well, let's drop that,' Sylvia said. 'God knows, I've no right to put a spoke in that girl's wheel or in yours. If you love each other you've a right to happiness and I daresay she'll make you happy. I can't divorce you, being a Catholic; but I won't make it difficult for you in other ways, and self-contained people like you and her will manage somehow. You'll have learned the way from Macmaster and his mistress. . . . But, oh, Christopher Tietjens, have you ever considered how foully you've used *me*!"

Tietjens looked at her attentively, as if with magpie anguish.

'If,' Sylvia went on with her denunciation, 'you had once in our lives said to me: "You whore! You bitch! You killed my mother. May you rot in hell for it. . . ." If you'd only once said something like it . . . about the child! About Perowne! . . . you might have done something to bring us together. . . .'

Tietjens said:

'That's, of course, true!'

'I know,' Sylvia said, 'you can't help it. . . . But when, in your famous county family pride—though a youngest son! —you say to yourself: And I daresay if . . . Oh, Christ! . . . you're shot in the trenches you'll say it . . . oh, between the saddle and the ground! that you never did a dishonourable action. . . . And, mind you, I believe that no other man save one has ever had more right to say it than you. . . .'

Tietjens said:

'You believe that!'

'As I hope to stand before my Redeemer,' Sylvia said, 'I believe it.... But, in the name of the Almighty, how could any woman live beside you ... and be for ever forgiven? Or no: not forgiven: ignored! ... Well, be proud when you die because of your honour. But, God, be humble about ... your errors in judgment. *You* know what it is to ride a horse for miles with too tight a curb-chain and its tongue cut almost in half.... You remember the groom your father had who had the trick of turning the hunters out like that.... And you horse-whipped him, and you've told me you've almost cried ever so often afterwards for thinking of that mare's mouth.... Well! Think of *this* mare's mouth sometimes! You've ridden me like that for seven years....'

She stopped and then went on again:

'Don't you know, Christopher Tietjens, that there is only one man from whom a woman could take *"Neither do I condemn thee"* and not hate him more than she hates the fiend! ...'

Tietjens so looked at her that he contrived to hold her attention.

'I'd like you to let me ask you,' he said, 'how I could throw stones at you? I have never disapproved of your actions.'

Her hands dropped dispiritedly to her sides.

'Oh, Christopher,' she said, 'don't carry on that old play-acting. I shall never see you again, very likely, to speak to. You'll sleep with the Wannop girl to-night: you're going out to be killed to-morrow. *Let's* be straight for the next ten minutes or so. And give me your attention. The Wannop girl can spare that much if she's to have all the rest....'

She could see that he was giving her his whole mind.

'As you said just now,' he exclaimed slowly, 'as I hope to meet my Redeemer, I believe you to be a good woman. One that never did a dishonourable thing.'

She recoiled a little in her chair.

'Then!' she said, 'you're the wicked man I've always made believe to think you, though I didn't.'

Tietjens said:

'No! . . . Let me try to put it to you as I see it.'

She exclaimed:

'No! . . . I've been a wicked woman. I have ruined you. I am not going to listen to you.'

He said:

'I daresay you have ruined me. That's nothing to me. I am completely indifferent.'

She cried out:

'Oh! Oh! . . . Oh!' on a note of agony.

Tietjens said doggedly:

'I don't care. I can't help it. Those are—those *should* be —the conditions of life amongst decent people. When our next war comes I hope it will be fought out under those conditions. Let us, for God's sake, talk of the gallant enemy. Always. We have *got* to plunder the French or millions of our people must starve: they have *got* to resist us successfully or be wiped out. . . . It's the same with you and me. . . .'

She exclaimed:

'You mean to say that you don't think I was wicked when I . . . when I trepanned is what mother calls it? . . .'

He said loudly:

'*No!* . . . You had been let in for it by some brute. I have always held that a woman who has been let down by one man has the right—has the duty for the sake of her child— to let down a man. It becomes woman against man: against one man. I happened to be that one man: it was the will of God. But you were within your rights. I will never go back on that. Nothing will make me, ever!'

She said:

'And the others! And Perowne. . . . I know you'll say that anyone is justified in doing anything as long as they are open enough about it. . . . But it killed your mother. Do you disapprove of my having killed your mother? Or you consider that I have corrupted the child. . . .'

Tietjens said:

'I don't . . . I want to speak to you about that.'

She exclaimed:

'You *don't*. . . .'

He said calmly:

'You know I don't . . . while I was certain that I was going to be here to keep him straight and an Anglican, I fought your influence over him. I'm obliged to you for having brought up of yourself the considerations that I may be killed and that I am ruined. I am. I could not raise a hundred pounds between now and tomorrow. I am, therefore, obviously not the man to have sole charge of the heir of Groby.'

Sylvia was saying:

'Every penny I have is at your disposal. . . .' when the maid, Hullo Central, marched up to her master and placed a card in his hand. He said:

'Tell him to wait five minutes in the drawing-room.'

Sylvia said:

'Who is it?'

Tietjens answered:

'A man . . . Let's get this settled. I've never thought you corrupted the boy. You tried to teach him to tell white lies. On perfectly straight Papist lines. I have no objection to Papists and no objection to white lies for Papists. You told him once to put a frog in Marchant's bath. I've no objection to a boy putting a frog in his nurse's bath, as such. But Marchant is an old woman, and the heir to Groby should respect old women always and old family servants in particular. . . . It hasn't, perhaps, struck you that the boy is heir to Groby. . . .'

Sylvia said:

'If . . . if your second brother is killed. . . . But your eldest brother. . . .'

'He,' Tietjens said, 'has got a French woman near Euston station. He's lived with her for over fifteen years, of afternoons, when there were no race meetings. She'll never let him marry and she's past the child-bearing stage. So there's no one else. . . .'

Sylvia said:

'You mean that I may bring the child up as a Catholic.'

Tietjens said:

'A *Roman* Catholic. . . . You'll teach him, please, to use that term before myself if I ever see him again. . . .'

Sylvia said:

'Oh, I thank God that He has softened your heart. This will take the curse off this house.'

Tietjens shook his head:

'I think not,' he said, 'off you perhaps. Off Groby very likely. It was, perhaps, time that there should be a Papist owner of Groby again. You've read Spelden on sacrilege about Groby? . . .'

She said:

'Yes! The first Tietjens who came over with Dutch William, the swine, was pretty bad to the Papist owners. . . .'

'He was a tough Dutchman,' Tietjens said, 'but let us get on! There's enough time, but not too much. . . . I've got this man to see.'

'Who is he?' Sylvia asked.

Tietjens was collecting his thoughts.

'My dear!' he said. 'You'll permit me to call you "my dear"? We're old enemies enough and we're talking about the future of our child.'

Sylvia said:

'You said "our" child, not "the" child. . . .'

Tietjens said with a great deal of concern:

'You will forgive me for bringing it up. You might prefer to think he was Drake's child. He can't be. It would be outside the course of nature. . . . I'm as poor as I am because . . . forgive me . . . I've spent a great deal of money on tracing the movements of you and Drake before our marriage. And if it's a relief to you to know . . .'

'It *is*,' Sylvia said. 'I . . . I've always been too beastly shy to put the matter before a specialist, or even before mother. . . . And we women are so ignorant. . . .'

Tietjens said:

'I know ... I know you were too shy even to think about it yourself, hard.' He went into months and days; then he continued: 'But it would have made no difference: a child born in wedlock is by law the father's, and if a man who's a gentleman suffers the begetting of his child he must, in decency, take the consequences: the woman and the child must come before the man, be he who he may. And worse-begotten children than ours have inherited statelier names. And I loved the little beggar with all my heart and with all my soul from the first minute I saw him. That may be the secret clue, or it may be sheer sentimentality. ... So I fought your influence because it was Papist, while I was a whole man. But I'm not a whole man any more, and the evil eye that is on me might transfer itself to him.'

He stopped and said:

'For I must to the greenwood go. Alone a broken man. ... But have him well protected against the evil eye. ...'

'Oh, Christopher,' she said, 'it's true I've not been a bad woman to the child. And I never will be. And I will keep Marchant with him till she dies. You'll tell her not to interfere with his religious instruction, and she won't. ...'

Tietjens said with a friendly weariness:

'That's right ... and you'll have Father ... Father ... the priest that was with us for a fortnight before he was born to give him his teachings. He was the best man I ever met and one of the most intelligent. It's been a great comfort to me to think of the boy as in his hands. ...'

Sylvia stood up, her eyes blazing out of a pallid face of stone:

'Father Consett,' she said, 'was hung on the day they shot Casement. They dare not put it into the papers because he was a priest and all the witnesses Ulster witnesses. ... And yet I may not say this is an accursed war.'

Tietjens shook his head with the slow heaviness of an aged man.

'You may for me . . .' he said. 'You might ring the bell, will you? Don't go away. . . .'

He sat with the blue gloom of that enclosed space all over him, lumped heavily in his chair.

'Spelden on sacrilege,' he said, 'may be right after all. You'd say so from the Tietjenses. There's not been a Tietjens since the first Lord Justice cheated the Papist Loundeses out of Groby, but died of a broken neck or of a broken heart: for all the fifteen thousand acres of good farming land and iron land, and for all the heather on the top of it. . . . What's the quotation: "Be ye something as something and something and ye shall not escape. . . ." What is it?'

'Calumny!' Sylvia said. She spoke with intense bitterness. . . . 'Chaste as ice and cold as . . . as you are. . . .'

Tietjens said:

'Yes! Yes. . . . And mind you none of the Tietjens were ever soft. Not one! They had reason for their broken hearts. . . . Take my poor father. . . .'

Sylvia said:

'*Don't!*'

'Both my brothers were killed in Indian regiments on the same day and not a mile apart. And my sister in the same week: out at sea, not so far from them. . . . Unnoticeable people. But one can be fond of unnoticeable people. . . .'

Hullo Central was at the door. Tietjens told her to ask Lord Port Scatho to step down. . . .

'You must, of course, know these details,' Tietjens said, 'as the mother to my father's heir. . . . My father got the three notifications on the same day. It was enough to break his heart. He only lived a month. I saw him . . .'

Sylvia screamed piercingly:

'Stop! stop! stop!' She clutched at the mantelpiece to hold herself up. 'Your father died of a broken heart,' she said, 'because your brother's best friend, Ruggles, told him you were a squit who lived on women's money and had got the daughter of his oldest friend with child. . . .'

Tietjens said:

'Oh! Ah! Yes! . . . I suspected that. I know it, really. I suppose the poor dear knows better now. Or perhaps he doesn't. . . . It doesn't matter.'

II

It has been remarked that the peculiarly English habit of self-suppression in matters of the emotion puts the Englishman at a great disadvantage in moments of unusual stresses. In the smaller matters of the general run of life he will be impeccable and not to be moved; but in sudden confrontations of anything but physical dangers he is apt—he is, indeed, almost certain—to go to pieces very badly. This, at least, was the view of Christopher Tietjens, and he very much dreaded his interview with Lord Port Scatho—because he feared that he must be near breaking point.

In electing to be peculiarly English in habits and in as much of his temperament as he could control—for, though no man can choose the land of his birth or his ancestry, he can, if he have industry and determination, so watch over himself as materially to modify his automatic habits—Tietjens had quite advisedly and of set purpose adopted a habit of behaviour that he considered to be the best in the world for the normal life. If every day and all day long you chatter at high pitch and with the logic and lucidity of the Frenchman; if you shout in self-assertion, with your hat on your stomach, bowing from a stiff spine and by implication threaten all day long to shoot your interlocutor, like the Prussian; if you are as lachrymally emotional as the Italian, or as drily and epigrammatically imbecile over inessentials as the American, you will have a noisy, troublesome and thoughtless society without any of the surface calm that should distinguish the atmosphere of men when they are together. You will never have deep arm-chairs in which to sit for hours in clubs, thinking of nothing at all—or of the off-theory in bowling. On the other hand, in the face of death—except at sea, by fire, railway accident, or acciden-

tal drowning in rivers; in the face of madness, passion, dishonour or—and particularly—prolonged mental strain, you
will have all the disadvantages of the beginner at any game
and may come off very badly indeed. Fortunately death,
love, public dishonour and the like are rare occurrences in
the life of the average man, so that the great advantage
would seem to have lain with English society; at any rate
before the later months of the year 1914. Death for man
came but once: the danger of death so seldom as to be
practically negligible: love of a distracting kind was a
disease merely of the weak: public dishonour for persons of
position, so great was the hushing-up power of the ruling
class and the power of absorption of the remoter Colonies,
was practically unknown.

Tietjens found himself now faced by all these things,
coming upon him cumulatively and rather suddenly, and
he had before him an interview that might cover them all
and with a man whom he much respected and very much
desired not to hurt. He had to face these, moreover, with
a brain two-thirds of which felt numb. It was exactly like
that.

It was not so much that he couldn't use what brain he
had as trenchantly as ever: it was that there were whole
regions of fact upon which he could no longer call in support of his argument. His knowledge of history was still
practically negligible: he knew nothing whatever of the
humaner letters and, what was far worse, nothing at all of
the higher and more sensuous phrases of mathematics. And
the coming back of these things was much slower than he
had confessed to Sylvia. It was with these disadvantages
that he had to face Lord Port Scatho.

Lord Port Scatho was the first man of whom Sylvia
Tietjens had thought when she had been considering of
men who were absolutely honourable, entirely benevolent
... and rather lacking in constructive intelligence. He had
inherited the management of one of the most respected of
the great London banks, so that his commercial and social
influences were very extended: he was extremely inter-

ested in promoting Low Church interests, the reform of the
divorce laws and sports for the people, and he had a great
affection for Sylvia Tietjens. He was forty-five, beginning
to put on weight, but by no means obese; he had a large,
quite round head; very high-coloured cheeks that shone
as if with frequent ablutions; an uncropped, dark moustache, dark, very cropped, smooth hair; brown eyes; a very
new grey tweed suit, a very new grey Trilby hat, a black tie
in a gold ring, and very new patent leather boots that had
white calf tops. He had a wife almost the spit of himself in
face, figure, probity, kindliness, and interests, except that
for his interest in sports for the people she substituted that
for maternity hospitals. His heir was his nephew, Mr
Brownlie, known as Brownie, who would also be physically
the exact spit of his uncle, except that, not having put on
flesh, he appeared to be taller and that his moustache and
hair were both a little longer and more fair. This gentleman
entertained for Sylvia Tietjens a gloomy and deep passion
that he considered to be perfectly honourable because he
desired to marry her after she had divorced her husband.
Tietjens he desired to ruin because he considered Tietjens
to be an undesirable person of no great means. Of this
passion Lord Port Scatho was ignorant.

He now came into the Tietjens' dining-room, behind the
servant, holding an open letter: he walked rather stiffly
because he was very much worried. He observed that
Sylvia had been crying and was still wiping her eyes. He
looked round the room to see if he could see in it anything
to account for Sylvia's crying. Tietjens was still sitting at
the head of the lunch-table: Sylvia was rising from a chair
beside the fireplace.

Lord Port Scatho said:

'I want to see you, Tietjens, for a minute on business.'

Tietjens said:

'I can give you ten minutes. . . .'

Lord Port Scatho said:

'Mrs Tietjens perhaps . . . '

8 + F.M.F. III

He waved the open letter towards Mrs Tietjens. Tietjens said:

'No! Mrs Tietjens will remain.' He desired to say something more friendly. He said: 'Sit down.'

Lord Port Scatho said:

'I shan't be stopping a minute. But really...' and he moved the letter, but not with so wide a gesture, towards Sylvia.

'I have no secrets from Mrs Tietjens,' Tietjens said. 'Absolutely none....'

Lord Port Scatho said:

'No.... No, of course not ... But ...'

Tietjens said:

'Similarly, Mrs Tietjens has no secrets from me. Again absolutely none.'

Sylvia said:

'I don't, of course, tell Tietjens about my maid's love affairs or what the fish costs every day.'

Tietjens said:

'You'd better sit down.' He added on an impulse of kindness: 'As a matter of fact, I was just clearing up things for Sylvia to take over ... this command.' It was part of the disagreeableness of his mental disadvantages that upon occasion he could not think of other than military phrases. He felt intense annoyance. Lord Port Scatho affected him with some of the slight nausea that in those days you felt at contact with the civilian who knew none of your thoughts, phrases or preoccupations. He added, nevertheless equably:

'One has to clear up. I'm going out.'

Lord Port Scatho said hastily:

'Yes; yes, I won't keep you. One has so many engagements in spite of the war....' His eyes wandered in bewilderment. Tietjens could see them at last fixing themselves on the oil stains that Sylvia's salad dressing had left on his collar and green tabs. He said to himself that he must remember to change his tunic before he went to the War Office. He must not forget. Lord Port Scatho's bewilderment at these oil stains was such that he had lost himself

in the desire to account for them.... You could see the
slow thoughts moving inside his square, polished brown
forehead. Tietjens wanted very much to help him. He
wanted to say: 'It's about Sylvia's letter that you've got in
your hand, isn't it?' But Lord Port Scatho had entered the
room with the stiffness, with the odd, high-collared sort of
gait that on formal and unpleasant occasions Englishmen
use when they approach each other; braced up, a little like
strange dogs meeting in the street. In view of that, Tietjens
couldn't say 'Sylvia.'... But it would add to the formality
and unpleasantness if he said again 'Mrs Tietjens!' *That*
wouldn't help Port Scatho....

Sylvia said suddenly:

'You don't understand, apparently. My husband is going
out to the front line. To-morrow morning. It's for the
second time.'

Lord Port Scatho sat down suddenly on a chair beside
the table. With his fresh face and brown eyes suddenly
anguished he exclaimed:

'But, my dear fellow! You! Good God!' and then to
Sylvia: 'I beg your pardon!' To clear his mind he said
again to Tietjens: '*You!* Going out to-morrow!' And, when
the idea was really there, his face suddenly cleared. He
looked with a swift, averted glance at Sylvia's face and then
for a fixed moment at Tietjens' oil-stained tunic. Tietjens
could see him explaining to himself with immense enlight-
enment that *that* explained both Sylvia's tears and the oil
on the tunic. For Port Scatho might well imagine that
officers went to the conflict in their oldest clothes....

But, if his puzzled brain cleared, his distressed mind
became suddenly distressed doubly. He had to add to the
distress he had felt on entering the room and finding himself in the midst of what he took to be a highly emotional
family parting. And Tietjens knew that during the whole
war Port Scatho had never witnessed a family parting at
all. Those that were not inevitable he would avoid like the
plague, and his own nephew and all his wife's nephews
were in the bank. That was quite proper, for if the en-

nobled family of Brownlie were not of the Ruling Class—
who had to go!—they were of the Administrative Class,
who were privileged to stay. So he had seen no partings.

Of his embarrassed hatred of them he gave immediate
evidence. For he first began several sentences of praise of
Tietjens' heroism which he was unable to finish and then,
getting quickly out of his chair, exclaimed:

'In the circumstances then . . . the little matter I came
about . . . I couldn't of course think . . .'

Tietjens said:

'No; don't go. The matter you came about—I know all
about it of course—had better be settled.'

Port Scatho sat down again: his jaw fell slowly: under
his bronzed complexion his skin became a shade paler. He
said at last:

'You know what I came about? But then . . .'

His ingenuous and kindly mind could be seen to be
working with reluctance: his athletic figure drooped. He
pushed the letter that he still held along the tablecloth
towards Tietjens. He said, in the voice of one awaiting a
reprieve:

'But you *can't* be . . . aware . . . Not of this letter. . . .'

Tietjens left the letter on the cloth, from there he could
read the large handwriting on the blue-grey paper:

'Mrs Christopher Tietjens presents her compliments to
Lord Port Scatho and the Honourable Court of Benchers
of the Inn. . . .' He wondered where Sylvia had got hold of
that phraseology: he imagined it to be fantastically wrong.
He said:

'I have already told you that I know about this letter, as
I have already told you that I know—and I will add that I
approve!—of all Mrs Tietjens' actions. . . .' With his hard
blue eyes he looked browbeatingly into Port Scatho's soft
brown orbs, knowing that he was sending the message:
'Think what you please and be damned to you!'

The gentle brown things remained on his face; then
they filled with an expression of deep pain. Port Scatho
cried:

'But good God! Then . . . '

He looked at Tietjens again. His mind, which took refuge from life in the affairs of the Low Church, of Divorce Law Reform and of Sports for the People, became a sea of pain at the contemplation of strong situations. His eyes said:

'For heaven's sake do not tell me that Mrs Duchemin, the mistress of your dearest friend, is the mistress of yourself, and that you take this means of wreaking a vulgar spite on them.'

Tietjens, leaning heavily forward, made his eyes as enigmatic as he could; he said very slowly and very clearly:

'Mrs Tietjens is, of course, not aware of *all* the circumstances.'

Port Scatho threw himself back in his chair.

'I don't understand!' he said. 'I do not understand. How am I to act? You do not wish me to act on this letter? You can't!'

Tietjens, who found himself, said:

'You had better talk to Mrs Tietjens about that. I will say something myself later. In the meantime let me say that Mrs Tietjens would seem to me to be quite within her rights. A lady, heavily veiled, comes here every Friday and remains until four on the Saturday morning. . . . If you are prepared to palliate the proceeding you had better do so to Mrs Tietjens. . . .'

Port Scatho turned agitatedly on Sylvia.

'I can't, of course, palliate,' he said. 'God forbid. . . . But, my dear Sylvia . . . my dear Mrs Tietjens. . . . In the case of two people so much esteemed! . . . We have, of course, argued the matter of principle. It is a part of a subject I have very much at heart: the granting of divorce . . . civil divorce, at least . . . in cases in which one of the parties to the marriage is in a lunatic asylum. I have sent you the pamphlets of E. S. P. Haynes that we publish. I know that as a Roman Catholic you hold strong views. . . . I do not, I assure you, stand for latitude. . . .' He became then simply eloquent: he really had the matter at heart, one of his sisters having been for many years married to a lunatic. He expatiated on the agonies of this situation all the more eloquently in that it was the only form of human distress which he had personally witnessed.

Sylvia took a long look at Tietjens: he imagined for counsel. He looked at her steadily for a moment, then at Port Scatho, who was earnestly turned to her, then back at her. He was trying to say:

'Listen to Port Scatho for a minute. I need time to think of my course of action!'

He needed, for the first time in his life, time to think of his course of action.

He had been thinking with his under mind ever since Sylvia had told him that she had written her letter to the benchers denouncing Macmaster and his woman; ever since Sylvia had reminded him that Mrs Duchemin in the Edinburgh to London express of the day before the war had been in his arms he had seen, with extraordinary clearness, a great many north country scenes though he could not affix names to all the places. The forgetfulness of the names was abnormal: he ought to know the names of places from Berwick down to the vale of York—but that he should have forgotten the incidents was normal enough. They had been of little importance: he preferred not to remember the phases of his friend's love affair; moreover, the events that happened immediately afterwards had been of a nature to make one forget quite normally what had just preceded them. That Mrs Duchemin should be sobbing on his shoulder in a locked corridor carriage hadn't struck him as in the least important: she was the mistress of his dearest friend: she had had a very trying time for a week or so, ending in a violent, nervous quarrel with her agitated lover. She was, of course, crying off the effects of the quarrel which had been all the more shaking in that Mrs Duchemin, like himself, had always been almost too self-contained. As a matter of fact, he did not himself like Mrs Duchemin, and he was pretty certain that she herself more than a little disliked him; so that nothing but their common feeling for Mac-

master had brought them together. General Campion,
however, was not to know that.... He had looked into
the carriage in the way one does in a corridor just after the
train had left.... He couldn't remember the name....
Doncaster ... No! ... Darlington; it wasn't that. At Darlington there was a model of the Rocket ... or perhaps it
isn't the Rocket. An immense clumsy leviathan of a loco-
motive by ... by ... The great gloomy stations of the
north-going trains ... Durham ... No! Alnwick.... No!
... Wooler ... By God! Wooler! The junction for Bamborough....

It had been in one of the castles at Bamborough that he
and Sylvia had been staying with the Sandbachs. Then
... a name had come into his mind spontaneously! ...
Two names! ... It was, perhaps, the turn of the tide! For
the first time ... To be marked with a red stone ... after
this: some names, sometimes, on the tip of the tongue,
might come over! He had, however, to get on....

The Sandbachs, then, and he and Sylvia ... others too
... had been in Bamborough since mid-July: Eton and
Harrow at Lord's, waiting for the real house parties that
would come with the 12th.... He repeated these names
and dates to himself for the personal satisfaction of knowing that, amongst the repairs effected in his mind, these
two remained: Eton and Harrow, the end of the London
season: 12th of August, grouse shooting begins.... It was
pitiful....

When General Campion had come up to rejoin his sister
he, Tietjens, had stopped only two days. The coolness
between the two of them remained; it was the first time
they had met, except in Court, after the accident.... For
Mrs Wannop, with grim determination, had sued the
General for the loss of her horse. It had lived all right—
but it was only fit to draw a lawn-mower for cricket pitches.
... Mrs Wannop, then, had gone bald-headed for the
General, partly because she wanted the money, partly
because she wanted a public reason for breaking with the
Sandbachs. The General had been equally obstinate and

had undoubtedly perjured himself in Court: not the best, not the most honourable, the most benevolent man in the world would not turn oppressor of the widow and orphan when his efficiency as a chauffeur was impugned or the fact brought to light that at a very dangerous turning he hadn't sounded his horn. Tietjens had sworn that he hadn't: the General that he had. There *could* not be any question of doubt, for the horn was a beastly thing that made a prolonged noise like that of a terrified peacock. ... So Tietjens had not, till the end of that July, met the General again. It had been quite a proper thing for gentlemen to quarrel over and was quite convenient, though it had cost the General fifty pounds for the horse and, of course, a good bit over for costs. Lady Claudine had refused to interfere in the matter: she was privately of opinion that the General *hadn't* sounded his horn, but the General was both a passionately devoted and explosive brother. She had remained closely intimate with Sylvia, mildly cordial with Tietjens and had continued to ask the Wannops to such of her garden parties as the General did not attend. She was also very friendly with Mrs Duchemin.

Tietjens and the General had met with the restrained cordiality of English gentlemen who had some years before accused each other of perjury in a motor accident. On the second morning a violent quarrel had broken out between them on the subject of whether the General had or hadn't sounded his horn. The General had ended up by shouting ... really shouting:

'By God! If I ever get you under my command. . . .'

Tietjens remembered that he had quoted and given the number of a succinct paragraph in King's Regs. dealing with the fate of general or higher field officers who gave their subordinates bad confidential reports because of private quarrels. The General had exploded into noise that ended in laughter.

'What a rag-bag of a mind you have, Chrissie!' he said. 'What's King's Regs. to you? And how do you know it's

paragraph 66 or whatever you say it is? I don't.' He added
more seriously: '*What* a fellow you are for getting into
obscure rows! What in the world do you do it for?'

That afternoon Tietjens had gone to stop, a long way
up in the moors, with his son, the nurse, his sister Effie
and her children. They were the last days of happiness he
was to know and he hadn't known so many. He was then
content. He played with his boy, who, thank God, was
beginning to grow healthy at last. He walked about the
moors with his sister Effie, a large, plain, parson's wife,
who had no conversation at all, though at times they
talked of their mother. The moors were like enough to
those above Groby to make them happy. They lived in a
bare, grim farmhouse, drank great quantities of butter-
milk and ate great quantities of Wensleydale. It was the
hard, frugal life of his desire, and his mind was at rest.

His mind was at rest because there was going to be a
war. From the first moment of his reading the paragraph
about the assassination of the Archduke Franz Ferdinand
he had known that, calmly and with assurance. Had he
imagined that his country would come in he would not
have known a mind at rest. He loved this country for the
run of its hills, the shape of its elm trees and the way the
heather, running uphill to the skyline, meets the blue of
heavens. War for this country could only mean humiliation,
spreading under the sunlight, an almost invisible pall,
over the elms, the hills, the heather, like the vapour that
spread from ... oh, Middlesbrough! We were fitted
neither for defeat nor for victory: we could be true to
neither friend nor foe. Not even to ourselves!

But of war for us he had no fear. He saw our Ministry
sitting tight till the opportune moment and then grabbing
a French channel port or a few German colonies as the
price of neutrality. And he was thankful to be out of it;
for his back-doorway out—his second!—was the French
Foreign Legion. First Sylvia: then that! Two tremendous
disciplines: for the soul and for the body.

The French he admired: for their tremendous efficiency,

8*

for their frugality of life, for the logic of their minds, for their admirable achievements in the arts, for their neglect of the industrial system, for their devotion, above all, to the eighteenth century. It would be restful to serve, if only as a slave, people who saw clearly, coldly, straight, not obliquely and with hypocrisy only, such things as should deviously conduce to the standard of comfort of hogs and to lecheries winked at. . . . He would rather sit for hours on a bench in a barrack-room polishing a badge in preparation for the cruellest of route marches of immense lengths under the Algerian sun.

For, as to the Foreign Legion, he had had no illusion. You were treated not as a hero but as a whipped dog; he was aware of all the *asticoteries,* the cruelties, the weight of the rifle, the cells. You would have six months of training in the desert and then be hurtled into the line to be massacred without remorse . . . as foreign dirt. But the prospect seemed to him one of deep peace: he had never asked for soft living and now was done with it. . . . The boy was healthy; Sylvia, with the economies they had made, very rich . . . and even at that date he was sure that if the friction of himself, Tietjens, were removed, she would make a good mother. . . .

Obviously he might survive; but after that tremendous physical drilling what survived would not be himself, but a man with cleaned, sand-dried bones: a clear mind. His private ambition had always been for saintliness: he must be able to touch pitch and not be defiled. That he knew marked him off as belonging to the sentimental branch of humanity. He couldn't help it: Stoic or Epicurean: Caliph in the harem or Dervish desiccating in the sand: one or the other you must be. And his desire was to be a saint of the Anglican variety . . . as his mother had been, without convent, ritual, vows, or miracles to be performed by your relics! That sainthood, truly, the Foreign Legion might give you. . . . The desire of every English gentleman from Colonel Hutchinson upwards. . . . A mysticism. . . .

Remembering the clear sunlight of those naïvetés—

though in his blue gloom he had abated no jot of the
ambition—Tietjens sighed deeply as he came back for a
moment to regard his dining-room. Really, it was to see
how much time he had left in which to think out what to
say to Port Scatho. . . . Port Scatho had moved his chair
over to beside Sylvia and, almost touching her, was leaning over and recounting the griefs of his sister who was
married to a lunatic. Tietjens gave himself again for a
moment to the luxury of self-pity. He considered that he
was dull-minded, heavy, ruined, and so calumniated that
at times he believed in his own infamy, for it is impossible
to stand up for ever against the obloquy of your kind and
remain unhurt in the mind. If you hunch your shoulders
too long against a storm your shoulders will grow
bowed. . . .

His mind stopped for a moment and his eyes gazed
dully at Sylvia's letter which lay open on the tablecloth.
His thoughts came together, converging on the loosely
written words:

'For the last nine months a woman . . .'

He wondered swiftly what he had already said to Port
Scatho: only that he had known of his wife's letter; not
when! And that he approved! Well, on principle! He
sat up. To think that one could be brought down to
thinking so slowly!

He ran swiftly over what had happened in the train from
Scotland and before. . . .

Macmaster had turned up one morning beside their
breakfast table in the farm house, much agitated, looking
altogether too small in a cloth cap and a new grey tweed
suit. He had wanted £50 to pay his bill with: at some
place up the line above . . . above . . . Berwick suddenly
flashed into Tietjens' mind. . . .

That was the geographic position. Sylvia was at Bamborough on the coast (junction Wooler); he, himself, to
the north-west, on the moors. Macmaster to the north-
east of him, just over the border: in some circumspect

beauty spot where you did not meet people. Both Mac-master and Mrs Duchemin would know that country and gurgle over its beastly literary associations. . . . The Shirra! Maida! Pet Marjorie . . . Faugh! Macmaster would, no doubt, turn an honest penny by writing articles about it and Mrs Duchemin would hold his hand. . . .

She had become Macmaster's mistress, as far as Tiet-jens knew, after a dreadful scene in the rectory, Duchemin having mauled his wife like a savage dog, and Macmaster in the house. . . . It was natural: a Sadix reaction as it were. But Tietjens rather wished they hadn't. Now it appeared they had been spending a week together . . . or more. Duchemin by that time was in an asylum. . . .

From what Tietjens had made out they had got out of bed early one morning to take a boat and see the sunrise on some lake and had passed an agreeable day together quoting, 'Since when we stand side by side only hands may meet' and other poems of Gabriel Charles Dante Rossetti, no doubt to justify their sin. On coming home they had run their boat's nose into the tea-table of the Port Scathos with Mr Brownlie, the nephew, just getting out of a motor to join them. The Port Scatho group were spending the night at the Macmasters' hotel which backed on to the lake. It was the ordinary damn sort of thing that must happen in these islands that are only a few yards across.

The Macmasters appear to have lost their heads fright-fully, although Lady Port Scatho had been as motherly as possible to Mrs Duchemin; so motherly, indeed, that if they had not been unable to observe anything, they might have recognized the Port Scathos as backers rather than spies upon themselves. It was, no doubt, however, Brown-lie who had upset them: he wasn't very civil to Mac-master, whom he knew as a friend of Tietjens. He had dashed up from London in his motor to consult his uncle, who was dashing down from the west of Scotland, about the policy of the bank in that moment of crisis. . . .

Macmaster, anyhow, did not spend the night in the

hotel, but went to Jedburgh or Melrose or some such place,
turning up again almost before it was light to have a frightful interview about five in the morning with Mrs Duchemin, who, towards three, had come to a disastrous conclusion as to her condition. They had lost their nerves for
the first time in their association, and they had lost them
very badly indeed, the things that Mrs Duchemin said to
Macmaster seeming almost to have passed belief. . . .

Thus, when Macmaster turned up at Tietjens' breakfast,
he was almost out of his mind. He wanted Tietjens to go
over in the motor he had brought, pay the bill at the
hotel, and travel down to town with Mrs Duchemin, who
was certainly in no condition to travel alone. Tietjens was
also to make up the quarrel with Mrs Duchemin and to
lend Macmaster £50 in cash, as it was then impossible to
change cheques anywhere. Tietjens got the money from his
old nurse, who, because she distrusted banks, carried great
sums in £5 notes in a pocket under her under-petticoat.

Macmaster, pocketing the money, had said:

'That makes exactly two thousand guineas that I owe
you. I'm making arrangements to repay you next week. . . .'

Tietjens remembered that he had rather stiffened and
had said: 'For God's sake don't. I beg you not to. Have
Duchemin properly put under trustee in lunacy, and
leave his capital alone. I really beg you. You don't know
what you'll be letting yourselves in for. You don't owe me
anything and you can always draw on me.'

Tietjens never knew what Mrs Duchemin had done
about her husband's estate over which she had at that date
had a power of attorney; but he had imagined that, from
that time on, Macmaster had felt a certain coldness for
himself and that Mrs Duchemin had hated him. During
several years Macmaster had been borrowing hundreds at
a time from Tietjens. The affair with Mrs Duchemin had
cost her lover a good deal; he had week-ended almost
continuously in Rye at the expensive hostel. Moreover,
the famous Friday parties for geniuses had been going on

for several years now, and these had meant new furnishings, bindings, carpets, and loans to geniuses—at any rate
before Macmaster had had the ear of the Royal Bounty.
So the sum had grown to £2,000, and now to guineas.
And, from that date, the Macmasters had not offered any
repayment.

Macmaster had said that he dare not travel with Mrs
Duchemin because all London would be going south by
that train. All London had. It pushed in at every conceiv-
able and inconceivable station all down the line—it was the
great rout of the 3-8-14. Tietjens had got on board at
Berwick, where they were adding extra coaches, and by
giving a £5 note to the guard, who hadn't been able to
promise isolation for any distance, had got a locked carriage. It hadn't remained locked for long enough to let
Mrs Duchemin have her cry out—but it had apparently
served to make some mischief. The Sandbach party had
got on, no doubt at Wooler; the Port Scatho party somewhere else. Their petrol had run out somewhere and sales
were stopped, even to bankers. Macmaster, who after all
had travelled by the same train, hidden beneath two blue-
jackets, had picked up Mrs Duchemin at King's Cross and
that had seemed the end of it.

Tietjens, back in his dining-room, felt relief and also
anger. He said:

'Port Scatho. Time's getting short. I'd like to deal with
this letter if you don't mind.'

Port Scatho came as if up out of a dream. He had
found the process of attempting to convert Mrs Tietjens to
divorce law reform very pleasant—as he always did. He
said:

'Yes! ... Oh, yes!'

Tietjens said slowly:

'If you can listen. ... Macmaster has been married to
Mrs Duchemin exactly nine months. ... Have you got
that? Mrs Tietjens did not know this till this afternoon.
The period Mrs Tietjens complains of in her letter is nine
months. She did perfectly right to write the letter. As

such I approve of it. If she had known that the Macmasters
were married she would not have written it. I didn't know
she was going to write it. If I had known she was going to
write it, I should have requested her not to. If I had
requested her not to she would, no doubt, have done so.
I did know of the letter at the moment of your coming
in. I had heard of it at lunch only ten minutes before. I
should, no doubt, have heard of it before, but this is the
first time I have lunched at home in four months. I have
to-day had a day's leave as being warned for foreign service. I have been doing duty at Ealing. To-day is the first
opportunity I have had for serious business conversation
with Mrs Tietjens. . . . Have you got all that? . . .'

Port Scatho was running towards Tietjens, his hand
extended, and over his whole shining personage the air of
an enraptured bridegroom. Tietjens moved his right hand
a little to the right, thus eluding the pink, well-fleshed
hand of Port Scatho. He went on frigidly:

'You had better, in addition, know as follows: The late
Mr Duchemin was a scatological—afterwards a homicidal
—lunatic. He had recurrent fits, usually on a Saturday
morning. That was because he fasted—not abstained
merely—on Fridays. On Fridays he also drank. He had
acquired the craving for drink when fasting, from finishing the sacramental wine after communion services. That
is a not unknown occurrence. He behaved latterly with
great physical violence to Mrs Duchemin. Mrs Duchemin,
on the other hand, treated him with the utmost consideration and concern: she might have had him certified much
earlier, but, considering the pain that confinement must
cause him during his lucid intervals, she refrained. I have
been an eye-witness of the most excruciating heroisms on
her part. As for the behaviour of Macmaster and Mrs
Duchemin, I am ready to certify—and I believe society
accepts—that it has been most . . . oh, circumspect and
right! . . . There has been no secret of their attachment
to each other. I believe that their determination to behave

with decency during their period of waiting has not been questioned. . . .'

Lord Port Scatho said:

'No! no! Never . . . Most . . . as you say . . . circumspect and, yes . . . right!'

'Mrs Duchemin,' Tietjens continued, 'has presided at Macmaster's literary Fridays for a long time; of course since long before they were married. But, as you know, Macmaster's Fridays have been perfectly open: you might almost call them celebrated. . . .'

Lord Port Scatho said:

'Yes! yes! indeed . . . I sh'd be only too glad to have a ticket for Lady Port Scatho. . . .'

'She's only got to walk in,' Tietjens said. 'I'll warn them: they'll be pleased. . . . If, perhaps, you don't look in to-night! They have a special party. . . . But Mrs Macmaster was always attended by a young lady who saw her off by the last train to Rye. Or I very frequently saw her off myself, Macmaster being occupied by the weekly article that he wrote for one of the papers on Friday nights. . . . They were married on the day after Mr Duchemin's funeral. . . .'

'You can't blame 'em!' Lord Port Scatho proclaimed.

'I don't propose to,' Tietjens said. 'The really frightful tortures Mrs Duchemin had suffered justified—and indeed necessitated—her finding protection and sympathy at the earliest possible moment. They have deferred this announcement of their union partly out of respect for the usual period of mourning, partly because Mrs Duchemin feels very strongly that, with all the suffering that is now abroad, wedding feasts and signs of rejoicing on the part of non-participants are eminently to be deprecated. Still, the little party of to-night is by the way of being an announcement that they are married. . . .' He paused to reflect for a moment.

'I perfectly understand!' Lord Port Scatho exclaimed. 'I perfectly approve. Believe me, I and Lady Port Scatho will do everything. . . . Everything! . . . Most admirable people.

... Tietjens, my dear fellow, your behaviour ... most handsome. ...'

Tietjens said:

'Wait a minute. ... There was an occasion in August, '14. In a place on the border. I can't remember the name. ...'

Lord Port Scatho burst out:

'My dear fellow ... I beg you won't. ... I beseech you not to ...'

Tietjens went on:

'Just before then Mr Duchemin had made an attack on his wife of an unparalleled violence. It was that that caused his final incarceration. She was not only temporarily disfigured, but she suffered serious internal injuries and, of course, great mental disturbance. It was absolutely necessary that she should have change of scene. ... But I think you will bear me out that, in that case too, their behaviour was ... again, circumspect and right. ...'

Port Scatho said:

'I know; I know ... Lady Port Scatho and I agreed—even without knowing what you have just told me—that the poor things almost exaggerated it. ... He slept, of course, at Jedburgh? ...

Tietjens said:

'Yes! They almost exaggerated it. ... I had to be called in to take Mrs Duchemin home. ... It caused, apparently, misunderstandings. ...'

Port Scatho—full of enthusiasm at the thought that at least two unhappy victims of the hateful divorce laws had, with decency and circumspectness, found the haven of their desires—burst out:

'By God, Tietjens, if I ever hear a man say a word against you. ... Your splendid championship of your friend. ... Your ... your unswerving devotion ...'

Tietjens said:

'Wait a minute, Port Scatho, will you?' He was unbuttoning the flap of his breast pocket.

'A man who can act so splendidly in one instance,' Port
Scatho said. . . . 'And your going to France. . . . If any
one . . . if *any* one . . . dares . . .'

At the sight of a vellum-coloured, green-edged book in
Tietjens' hand Sylvia suddenly stood up; as Tietjens took
from an inner flap a cheque that had lost its freshness she
made three great strides over the carpet to him.

'Oh, Chrissie! . . .' she cried out. 'He hasn't . . . That
beast hasn't . . .'

Tietjens answered:

'He has . . .' He handed the soiled cheque to the banker.
Port Scatho looked at it with slow bewilderment.

' "Account overdrawn," ' he read. 'Brownie's . . . my
nephew's handwriting. . . . To the club . . . It's . . .'

'You aren't going to take it lying down?' Sylvia said.
'Oh, thank goodness, you aren't going to take it lying
down.'

'No! I'm not going to take it lying down,' Tietjens said.
'Why should I?' A look of hard suspicion came over the
banker's face.

'You appear,' he said, 'to have been overdrawing your
account. People should not overdraw their accounts. For
what sum are you overdrawn?'

Tietjens handed his pass-book to Port Scatho.

'I don't understand on what principle you work,' Sylvia
said to Tietjens. 'There are things you take lying down;
this you don't.'

Tietjens said:

'It doesn't matter, really. Except for the child.'

Sylvia said:

'I guaranteed an overdraft for you up to a thousand
pounds last Thursday. You can't be overdrawn over a
thousand pounds.'

'I'm not overdrawn at all,' Tietjens said. 'I was for about
fifteen pounds yesterday. I didn't know it.'

Port Scatho was turning over the pages of the pass-
book, his face completely blank.

'I simply don't understand,' he said. 'You appear to be

in credit.... You appear always to have been in credit except for a small sum now and then. For a day or two.'

'I was overdrawn,' Tietjens said, 'for fifteen pounds yesterday. I should say for three or four hours: the course of a post, from my army agent to your head office. During these two or three hours your bank selected two out of six of my cheques to dishonour—both being under two pounds. The other one was sent back to my mess at Ealing, who won't, of course, give it back to me. That also is marked "account overdrawn," and in the same handwriting.'

'But good God,' the banker said. 'That means your ruin.'

'It certainly means my ruin,' Tietjens said. 'It was meant to.'

'But,' the banker said—a look of relief came into his face which had begun to assume the aspect of a broken man's—'you must have other accounts with the bank ... a speculative one, perhaps, on which you are heavily down. ... I don't myself attend to clients' accounts, except the very huge ones, which affect the bank's policy.'

'You ought to,' Tietjens said. 'It's the very little ones you ought to attend to, as a gentleman making his fortune out of them. I have no other account with you. I have never speculated in anything in my life. I have lost a great deal in Russian securities—a great deal for me. But so, no doubt, have you.'

'Then ... betting!' Port Scatho said.

'I never put a penny on a horse in my life,' Tietjens said. 'I know too much about them.'

Port Scatho looked at the faces first of Sylvia, then of Tietjens. Sylvia, at least, was his very old friend. She said:

'Christopher never bets and never speculates. His personal expenses are smaller than those of any man in town. You could say he had *no* personal expenses.'

Again the swift look of suspicion came into Port Scatho's open face.

'Oh,' Sylvia said, 'you couldn't suspect Christopher and me of being in a plot to blackmail you.'

'No; I couldn't suspect that,' the banker said. 'But the other explanation is just as extraordinary.... To suspect the bank ... the *bank*.... How do *you* account? ...' He was addressing Tietjens; his round head seemed to become square, below; emotion worked on his jaws.

'I'll tell you simply this,' Tietjens said. 'You can then repair the matter as you think fit. Ten days ago I got my marching orders. As soon as I had handed over to the officer who relieved me I drew cheques for everything I owed—to my military tailor, the mess—for one pound twelve shillings. I had also to buy a compass and a revolver, the Red Cross orderlies having annexed mine when I was in hospital....'

Port Scatho said: 'Good God!'

'Don't you know they annex things?' Tietjens asked. He went on: 'The total, in fact, amounted to an overdraft of fifteen pounds, but I did not think of it as such because my army agents ought to have paid my month's army pay over to you on the first. As you perceive, they have only paid it over this morning, the 13th. But, as you will see from my pass-book, they have always paid about the 13th, not the 1st. Two days ago I lunched at the club and drew that cheque for one pound fourteen shillings and sixpence: one ten for personal expenses and the four and six for lunch....'

'You were, however, actually overdrawn,' the banker said sharply.

Tietjens said:

'Yesterday, for two hours.'

'But then,' Port Scatho said, 'what do you want done? We'll do what we can.'

Tietjens said:

'I don't know. Do what you like. You'd better make what explanation you can to the military authority. If they court-martialled me it would hurt you more than me. I assure you of that. There *is* an explanation.'

Port Scatho began suddenly to tremble.

'What ... what ... what explanation?' he said. 'You ... damn it ... you draw this out.... Do you dare to say my bank....' He stopped, drew his hand down his face and said: 'But yet ... you're a sensible, sound man. ... I've heard things against you. But I don't believe them. ... Your father always spoke very highly of you.... I remember he said if you wanted money you could always draw on him through us for three or four hundred.... That's what makes it so incomprehensible.... It's ... it's ...' His agitation grew on him. 'It seems to strike at the very heart ...'

Tietjens said:

'Look here, Port Scatho.... I've always had a respect for you. Settle it how you like. Fix the mess up for both our sakes with any formula that's not humiliating for your bank. I've already resigned from the club....'

Sylvia said: 'Oh, *no*, Christopher ... not from the *club*!'

Port Scatho started back from beside the table.

'But if you're in the right!' he said. 'You *couldn't* ... Not resign from the club.... I'm on the committee.... I'll explain to them, in the fullest, in the most generous ...'

'You couldn't explain,' Tietjens said. 'You can't get ahead of rumour.... It's half over London at this moment. You know what the toothless old fellows of your committee are.... Anderson! ffolliott ... And my brother's friend, Ruggles....'

Port Scatho said:

'Your brother's friend, Ruggles.... But look here.... He's something about the Court, isn't he? But look here. ...' His mind stopped. He said: 'People shouldn't over-draw.... But if your father said you could draw on him, I'm really much concerned.... You're a first-rate fellow. ... I can tell that from your pass-book alone.... Nothing but cheques drawn to first-class tradesmen for reasonable amounts. The sort of pass-book I liked to see when I was a junior clerk in the bank....' At that early reminiscence feelings of pathos overcame him and his mind once more stopped.

Sylvia came back into the room; they had not perceived her going. She in turn held in her hand a letter.

Tietjens said:

'Look here, Port Scatho, don't get into this state. Give me your word to do what you can when you've assured yourself the facts are as I say. I wouldn't bother you at all, it's not my line, except for Mrs Tietjens. A man alone can live that sort of thing down, or die. Bue there's no reason why Mrs Tietjens should live, tied to a bad hat, while he's living it down or dying.'

'But that's not *right*,' Port Scatho said, 'it's not the right way to look at it. You can't pocket . . . I'm simply bewildered. . . .'

'You've no right to be bewildered,' Sylvia said. 'You're worrying your mind for expedients to save the reputation of your bank. We know your bank is more to you than a baby. You should look after it better, then.'

Port Scatho, who had already fallen two paces away from the table, now fell two paces back, almost on top of it. Sylvia's nostrils were dilated.

She said:

'Tietjens shall not resign from your beastly club. He shall not! Your committee will request him formally to withdraw his resignation. You understand? He will withdraw it. Then he will resign for good. He is too good to mix with people like you. . . .' She paused, her chest working fast. 'Do you understand what you've got to do?' she asked.

An appalling shadow of a thought went through Tietjens' mind: he would not let it come into words.

'I don't know . . .' the banker said. 'I don't know that I can get the committee . . .'

'You've got to,' Sylvia answered. 'I'll tell you why . . . Christopher was never overdrawn. Last Thursday I instructed your people to pay a thousand pounds to my husband's account. I repeated the instruction by letter,

and I kept a copy of the letter, witnessed by my confidential maid. I also registered the letter and have the receipt
for it. . . . You can see them.'

Port Scatho mumbled from over the letter:

'It's to Brownlie . . . Yes, a receipt for a letter to Brownlie . . .' She examined the little green slip on both sides. He
said: 'Last Thursday. . . . To-day's Monday. . . . An instruction to sell North-Western stock to the amount of
one thousand pounds and place to the account of . . .
Then . . .'

Sylvia said:

'That'll do. . . . You can't angle for time any more. . . .
Your nephew has been in an affair of this sort before. . . .
I'll tell you. Last Thursday at lunch your nephew told me
that Christopher's brother's solicitors had withdrawn all
the permissions for overdrafts on the books of the Groby
estate. There were several to members of the family. Your
nephew said that he intended to catch Christopher on the
hop—that's his own expression—and dishonour the next
cheque of his that came in. He said he had been waiting
for the chance ever since the war and the brother's with-
drawal had given it him. I begged him not to . . .'

'But, good God,' the banker said, 'this is unheard of . . .'

'It isn't,' Sylvia said. 'Christopher has had five snotty,
little, miserable subalterns to defend at courts-martial for
exactly similar cases. One was an exact reproduction of
this . . . .'

'But, good God,' the banker exclaimed again, 'men giving their lives for their country. . . . Do you mean to say
Brownlie did this out of revenge for Tietjens' defending
at courts-martial. . . . And then . . . your thousand pounds
is not shown in your husband's pass-book. . . .'

'Of course it's not,' Sylvia said. 'It has never been paid
in. On Friday I had a formal letter from your people
pointing out that North-Westerns were likely to rise and
asked me to reconsider my position. The same day I sent
an express telling them explicitly to do as I said. . . . Ever
since then your nephew has been on the 'phone begging

me not to save my husband. He was there, just now, when
I went out of the room. He was also beseeching me to fly
with him.'

Tietjens said:

'Isn't that enough, Sylvia? It's rather torturing.'

'Let them be tortured,' Sylvia said. 'But it appears to be
enough.'

Port Scatho had covered his face with both his pink
hands. He had exclaimed:

'Oh, my God! Brownlie again. . . .'

Tietjens' brother Mark was in the room. He was smaller,
browner, and harder than Tietjens and his blue eyes protruded more. He had in one hand a bowler hat, in the other
an umbrella, wore a pepper-and-salt suit and had race-
glasses slung across him. He disliked Port Scatho, who
detested him. He had lately been knighted. He said:

'Hullo, Port Scatho,' neglecting to salute his sister-in-
law. His eyes, whilst he stood motionless, rolled a look
round the room and rested on a miniature bureau that
stood on a writing-table, in a recess, under and between
bookshelves.

'I see you've still got that cabinet,' he said to Tietjens.

Tietjens said:

'I haven't. I've sold it to Sir John Robertson. He's
waiting to take it away till he has room in his collection.'

Port Scatho walked, rather unsteadily, round the lunch-
table and stood looking down from one of the long
windows. Sylvia sat down on her chair beside the fireplace.
The two brothers stood facing each other, Christopher
suggesting wheat-sacks, Mark carved wood. All round
them, except for the mirror that reflected bluenesses, the
gilt backs of books. Hullo Central was clearing the table.

'I hear you're going out again to-morrow,' Mark said.
'I want to settle some things with you.'

'I'm going at nine from Waterloo,' Christopher said. 'I've
not much time. You can walk with me to the War Office
if you like.'

Mark's eyes followed the black and white of the maid

round the table. She went out with the tray. Christopher suddenly was reminded of Valentine Wannop clearing the table in her mother's cottage. Hullo Central was no faster about it. Mark said:

'Port Scatho! As you're there we may as well finish one point. I have cancelled my father's security for my brother's overdraft.'

Port Scatho said, to the window, but loud enough:

'We all know it. To our cost.'

'I wish you, however,' Mark Tietjens went on, 'to make over from my own account a thousand a year to my brother as he needs it. Not more than a thousand in any one year.'

Port Scatho said:

'Write a letter to the bank. I don't look after clients' accounts on social occasions.'

'I don't see why you don't,' Mark Tietjens said. 'It's the way you make your bread and butter, isn't it?'

Tietjens said:

'You may save yourself all this trouble, Mark. I am closing my account, in any case.'

Port Scatho spun round on his heel.

'I beg that you won't,' he exclaimed. 'I beg that we . . . that we may have the honour of continuing to have you draw upon us.' He had the trick of convulsively working jaws: his head against the light was like the top of a rounded gatepost. He said to Mark Tietjens: 'You may tell your friend, Mr Ruggles, that your brother is empowered by me to draw on my private account . . . on my personal and private account up to any amount he needs. I say that to show my estimate of your brother; because I know he will incur no obligations he cannot discharge.'

Mark Tietjens stood motionless; leaning slightly on the crook of his umbrella on the one side; on the other displaying, at arm's length, the white silk lining of his bowler hat, the lining being the brightest object in the room.

'That's your affair,' he said to Port Scatho. 'All I'm con-

cerned with is to have a thousand a year paid to my
brother's account till further notice.'

Christopher Tietjens spoke, with what he knew was a
sentimental voice, to Port Scatho. He was very touched; it
appeared to him that with the spontaneous appearance of
several names in his memory, and with this estimate of
himself from the banker, his tide was turning and that this
day might indeed be marked by a red stone:

'Of course, Port Scatho, I won't withdraw my wretched
little account from you if you want to keep it. It flatters me
that you should.' He stopped and added: 'I only wanted
to avoid these ... these family complications. But I suppose you can stop my brother's money being paid into my
account. I don't want his money.'

He said to Sylvia:

'You had better settle the other matter with Port Scatho.'

To Port Scatho:

'I'm intensely obliged to you, Port Scatho. . . . You'll get
Lady Port Scatho round to Macmaster's this evening if
only for a minute; before eleven. . . .' And to his brother:

'Come along, Mark. I'm going down to the War Office.
We can talk as we walk.'

Sylvia said very nearly with timidity—and again a dark
thought went over Tietjens' mind:

'Do we meet again then? ... I know you're very
busy. . . .'

Tietjens said:

'Yes. I'll come and pick you out from Lady Job's, if
they don't keep me too long at the War Office. I'm dining,
as you know, at Macmaster's; I don't suppose I shall stop
late.'

'I'd come,' Sylvia said, 'to Macmaster's, if you thought
it was appropriate. I'd bring Claudine Sandbach and
General Wade. We're only going to the Russian dancers.
We'd cut off early.'

Tietjens could settle that sort of thought very quickly.

'Yes, do,' he said hurriedly. 'It would be appreciated.'

He got to the door: he came back: his brother was

nearly through. He said to Sylvia, and for him the occasion was a very joyful one:

'I've worried out some of the words of that song. It runs:

> "Somewhere or other there must surely be
> The face not seen: the voice not heard . . ."

Probably it's "the voice not ever heard" to make up the metre. . . . I don't know the writer's name. But I hope I'll worry it all out during the day.'

Sylvia had gone absolutely white.

'Don't!' she said. 'Oh . . . *don't.*' She added coldly: 'Don't take the trouble,' and wiped her tiny handkerchief across her lips as Tietjens went away.

She had heard the song at a charity concert and had cried as she heard it. She had read, afterwards, the words in the programme and had almost cried again. But she had lost the programme and had never come across the words again. The echo of them remained with her like something terrible and alluring: like a knife she would someday take out and with which she would stab herself.

III

The two brothers walked twenty steps from the door along the empty Inn pavements without speaking. Each was completely expressionless. To Christopher it seemed like Yorkshire. He had a vision of Mark, standing on the lawn at Groby, in his bowler hat and with his umbrella, whilst the shooters walked over the lawn, and up the hill to the butts. Mark probably never had done that; but it was so that his image always presented itself to his brother. Mark was considering that one of the folds of his umbrella was disarranged. He seriously debated with himself whether he should unfold it at once and refold it—which was a great deal of trouble to take!—or whether he should leave it till he got to his club, where he would tell the porter to have it done at once. That would mean that he would have to

walk for a mile and a quarter through London with a disarranged umbrella, which was disagreeable.

He said :

'If I were you I wouldn't let that banker fellow go about
giving you testimonials of that sort.'

Christopher said:

'Ah!'

He considered that, with a third of his brain in action, he
was over a match for Mark, but he was tired of discussions.
He supposed that some unpleasant construction would be
put by his brother's friend, Ruggles, on the friendship of
Port Scatho for himself. But he had no curiosity. Mark felt
a vague discomfort. He said:

'You had a cheque dishonoured at the club this morning?'

Christopher said:

'Yes.'

Mark waited for explanations. Christopher was pleased
at the speed with which the news had travelled: it confirmed what he had said to Port Scatho. He viewed his case
from outside. It was like looking at the smooth working
of a mechanical model.

Mark was more troubled. Used as he had been for thirty
years to the vociferous south, he had forgotten that there
were taciturnities still. If at his Ministry he laconically
accused a transport clerk of remissness, or if he accused his
French mistress—just as laconically—of putting too many
condiments on his nightly mutton chop, or too much salt in
the water in which she boiled his potatoes, he was used to
hearing a great many excuses or negations, uttered with
energy and continued for long. So he had got into the
habit of considering himself the only laconic being in the
world. He suddenly remembered with discomfort—but
also with satisfaction—that his brother was his brother.

He knew nothing about Christopher, for himself. He
had seemed to look at his little brother down avenues from
a distance, the child misbehaving himself. Not a true Tietjens: born very late: a mother's child, therefore, rather

than a father's. The mother an admirable woman, but
from the South Riding. Soft, therefore, and ample. The
elder Tietjens' children, when they had experienced
failures, had been wont to blame their father for not
marrying a woman of their own Riding. So, for himself,
he knew nothing of this boy. He was said to be brilliant:
an un-Tietjens-like quality. Akin to talkativeness! . . . Well,
he wasn't talkative. Mark said:

'What have you done with all the brass our mother left
you? Twenty thousand, wasn't it?'

They were just passing through a narrow way between
Georgian houses. In the next quadrangle Tietjens stopped
and looked at his brother. Mark stood still to be looked at.
Christopher said to himself:

'This man has the right to ask these questions!'

It was as if a queer slip had taken place in a moving-
picture. This fellow had become the head of the house:
he, Christopher, was the heir. At that moment, their father,
in the grave four months now, was for the first time dead.

Christopher remembered a queer incident. After the
funeral, when they had come back from the churchyard
and had lunched, Mark—and Tietjens could now see the
wooden gesture—had taken out his cigar-case and, select-
ing one cigar for himself, had passed the rest round the
table. It was as if people's hearts had stopped beating.
Groby had never, till that day, been smoked in: the father
had his twelve pipes filled and put in the rose-bushes in the
drive. . . .

It had been regarded merely as a disagreeable incident:
a piece of bad taste. . . . Christopher, himself, only just
back from France, would not even have known it as such,
his mind was so blank, only the parson had whispered to
him: 'And Groby never smoked in till this day.'

But now! It appeared a symbol, and an absolutely right
symbol. Whether they liked it or not, here were the head
of the house and the heir. The head of the house must
make his arrangements, the heir agree or disagree; but the
elder brother had the right to have his enquiries answered.

Christopher said:

'Half the money was settled at once on my child. I lost seven thousand in Russian securities. The rest I spent. . . .'

Mark said:

'Ah!'

They had just passed under the arch that leads into Holborn. Mark, in turn, stopped and looked at his brother, and Christopher stood still to be inspected, looking into his brother's eyes. Mark said to himself:

'The fellow isn't, at least, afraid to look at you!' He had been convinced that Christopher would be. He said:

'You spent it on women? Or where do you get the money that you spend on women?'

Christopher said:

'I never spent a penny on a woman in my life.'

Mark said:

'Ah!'

They crossed Holborn and went by the backways towards Fleet Street.

Christopher said:

'When I say "woman" I'm using the word in the ordinary sense. Of course I've given women of our own class tea or lunch and paid for their cabs. Perhaps I'd better put it that I've never—either before or after marriage—had connection with any woman other than my wife.'

Mark said:

'Ah!'

He said to himself:

'Then Ruggles must be a liar.' This neither distressed nor astonished him. For twenty years he and Ruggles had shared a floor of a large and rather gloomy building in Mayfair. They were accustomed to converse whilst shaving in a joint toilet-room, otherwise they did not often meet except at the club. Ruggles was attached to the Royal Court in some capacity, possibly as sub-deputy gold-stick-in-waiting. Or he might have been promoted in the twenty years. Mark Tietjens had never taken the trouble to enquire. Enormously proud and shut in on himself, he was without curiosity of any sort. He lived in London because it was immense, solitary, administrative and apparently without curiosity as to its own citizens. If he could have found, in the north, a city as vast and as distinguished by the other characteristics, he would have preferred it.

Of Ruggles he thought little or nothing. He had once heard a phrase 'agreeable rattle,' and he regarded Ruggles as an agreeable rattle, though he did not know what the phrase meant. Whilst they shaved Ruggles gave out the scandal of the day. He never, that is to say, mentioned a woman whose virtue was not purchasable, or a man who would not sell his wife for advancement. This matched with Mark's ideas of the south. When Ruggles aspersed the fame of a man of family from the north, Mark would stop him with:

'Oh, no. That's not true. He's a Craister of Wantley Fells,' or another name, as the case might be. Half Scotchman, half Jew, Ruggles was very tall and resembled a magpie, having his head almost always on one side. Had he been English Mark would never have shared his rooms with him: he knew indeed few Englishmen of sufficient birth and position to have that privilege, and, on the other hand, few Englishmen of birth and position would have consented to share rooms so grim and uncomfortable, so furnished with horse-hair-seated mahogany, or so lit with ground-glass skylights. Coming up to town at the age of twenty-five, Mark had taken these rooms with a man called Peebles, long since dead, and he had never troubled to make any change, though Ruggles had taken the place of Peebles. The remote similarity of the names had been less disturbing to Mark Tietjens than would have been the case had the names been more different. It would have been very disagreeable, Mark often thought, to share with a man called, say, Granger. As it was, he still often called Ruggles Peebles, and no harm was done. Mark knew nothing of Ruggles' origins, then—so that, in a remote way, their union resembled that of Christopher with Macmaster. But whereas Christopher would have given his

satellite the shirt off his back, Mark would not have lent
Ruggles more than a five-pound note, and would have
turned him out of their rooms if it had not been returned
by the end of the quarter. But, since Ruggles never had
asked to borrow anything at all, Mark considered him an
entirely honourable man. Occasionally Ruggles would talk
of his determination to marry some widow or other with
money, or of his influence with people in exalted stations,
but, when he talked like that, Mark would not listen to him
and he soon returned to stories of purchasable women
and venial men.

About five months ago Mark had said one morning to
Ruggles:

'You might pick up what you can about my youngest
brother Christopher and let me know.'

The evening before that Mark's father had called Mark
to him from over the other side of the smoking-room and
had said:

'You might find out what you can about Christopher.
He may be in want of money. Has it occurred to you that
he's the heir to the estate! After you, of course.' Mr Tietjens had aged a good deal after the deaths of his children.
He said: 'I suppose you won't marry?' and Mark had
answered:

'No; I shan't marry. But I suppose I'm a better life than
Christopher. He appears to have been a good deal knocked
about out there.'

Armed then with this commission, Mr Ruggles appears
to have displayed extraordinary activity in preparing a
Christopher Tietjens dossier. It is not often that an inveterate gossip gets a chance at a man whilst being at the
same time practically shielded against the law of libel. And
Ruggles disliked Christopher Tietjens with the inveterate
dislike of a man who revels in gossip for the man who
never gossips. And Christopher Tietjens had displayed
more than his usual insolence to Ruggles. So Ruggles' coat-
tails flashed round an unusual number of doors and his

top-hat gleamed before an unusual number of tall portals
during the next week.

Amongst others he had visited the lady known as
Glorvina.

There is said to be a book, kept in a holy of holies, in
which bad marks are set down against men of family and
position in England. In this book Mark Tietjens and his
father—in common with a great number of hard-headed
Englishmen of county rank—implicitly believed. Christopher Tietjens didn't: he imagined that the activities of
gentlemen like Ruggles were sufficient to stop the careers
of people whom they disliked. On the other hand, Mark
and his father looked abroad upon English society and saw
fellows, apparently with every qualification for successful
careers in one service or the other; and these fellows got
no advancements, orders, tithes or preferments of any kind.
Just, rather mysteriously, they didn't make their marks.
This they put down to the workings of the book.

Ruggles, too, not only believed in the existence of that
compilation of the suspect and doomed, but believed that
his hand had a considerable influence over the inscriptions
in its pages. He believed that if, with more moderation and
with more grounds than usual, he uttered denigrations of
certain men before certain personages, it would at least
do those men a great deal of harm, And, quite steadily
and with, indeed, real belief in much of what he said,
Ruggles had denigrated Tietjens before these personages.
Ruggles could not see why Christopher had taken Sylvia
back after her elopement with Perowne: he could not see
why Christopher had, indeed, married Sylvia at all when
she was with child by a man called Drake—just as he
wasn't going to believe that Christopher could get a testi-
monial out of Lord Port Scatho except by the sale of
Sylvia to the banker. He couldn't see anything but money
or jobs at the bottom of these things: he couldn't see how
Tietjens otherwise got the money to support Mrs Wannop, Miss Wannop and her child, and to maintain Mrs
Duchemin and Macmaster in the style they affected, Mrs

Duchemin being the mistress of Christopher. He simply could see no other solution. It is, in fact, asking for trouble if you are more altruist than the society that surrounds you.

Ruggles, however, hadn't any pointers as to whether or no or to what degree he had really damaged his roommate's brother. He had talked in what he considered to be the right quarters, but he hadn't any evidence that what he had said had got through. It was to ascertain that he had called on the great lady, for if anybody knew, she would.

He hadn't definitely ascertained anything, for the great lady was—and he knew it—a great deal cleverer than himself. The great lady, he was allowed to discover, had a real affection for Sylvia, her daughter's close friend, and she expressed real concern to hear that Christopher Tietjens wasn't getting on. Ruggles had gone to visit her quite openly to ask whether something better couldn't be done for the brother of the man with whom he lived. Christopher had, it was admitted, great liabilities; yet neither in his office—in which he would surely have remained had he been satisfied with his prospects—nor in the army did he occupy anything but a very subordinate position. Couldn't, he asked, Glorvina do anything for him? And he added: 'It's almost as if he had a bad mark against him. . . .'

The great lady had said, with a great deal of energy, that she could not do anything at all. The energy was meant to show how absolutely her party had been downed, outed and jumped on by the party in power, so that she had no influence of any sort anywhere. That was an exaggeration; but it did Christopher Tietjens no good, since Ruggles chose to take it to mean that Glorvina said she could do nothing because there *was* a black mark against Tietjens in the book of the inner circle to which—if anyone had—the great lady must have had access.

Glorvina, on the other hand, had been awakened to concern for Tietjens. In the existence of a book she didn't believe: she had never seen it. But that a black mark of a metaphorical nature might have been scored against him she was perfectly ready to believe and, when occasion served, during the next five months, she made enquiries about Tietjens. She came upon a Major Drake, an intelligence officer, who had access to the central depôt of confidential reports upon officers, and Major Drake showed her, with a great deal of readiness, as a specimen, the report on Tietjens. It was of a most discouraging sort and peppered over with hieroglyphics, the main point being Tietjens' impecuniosity and his predilection for the French; and apparently for the French Royalists. There being at that date and with that Government a great deal of friction with our Allies, this characteristic which earlier had earned him a certain number of soft jobs had latterly done him a good deal of harm. Glorvina carried away the definite information that Tietjens had been seconded to the French artillery as a liaison officer and had remained with them for some time, but, having been shell-shocked, had been sent back. After that a mark had been added against him: 'Not to be employed as liaison officer again.'

On the other hand, Sylvia's visits to Austrian officer-prisoners had also been noted to Tietjens' account and a final note added: 'Not to be entrusted with any confidential work.'

To what extent Major Drake himself compiled these records the great lady didn't know and didn't want to know. She was acquainted with the relationships of the parties and was aware that in certain dark, full-blooded men the passion for sexual revenge is very lasting, and she let it go at that. She discovered, however, from Mr Waterhouse—now also in retreat—that he had a very high opinion of Tietjens' character and abilities, and that just before Waterhouse's retirement he had especially recommended Tietjens for very high promotion. That alone, in the then state of Ministerial friendships and enmities, Glorvina knew to be sufficient to ruin any man within range of Governmental influence.

She had, therefore, sent for Sylvia and had put all these

matters before her, for she had too much wisdom to believe
that, even supposing there should be differences between
the young people of which she had no evidence at all,
Sylvia could wish to do anything but promote her husband's material interests. Moreover, sincerely benevolent
as the great lady was towards this couple, she also saw
that here was a possibility of damaging, at least, individuals
of the party in power. A person in a relatively unimportant official position can sometimes make a very nasty
stink if he is unjustly used, has determination and a small
amount of powerful backing. This Sylvia, at least, certainly had.

And Sylvia had received the great lady's news with so
much emotion that no one could have doubted that she
was utterly devoted to her husband and would tell him
all about it. This Sylvia had not as yet managed to do.

Ruggles in the meantime had collected a very full budget
of news and inferences to present to Mark Tietjens whilst
shaving. Mark had been neither surprised nor indignant.
He had been accustomed to call all his father's children,
except the brother immediately next him, 'the whelps,' and
their concerns had been no concerns of his. They would
marry, beget unimportant children who would form collateral lines of Tietjens and disappear as is the fate of
sons of younger sons. And the deaths of the intermediate
brothers had been so recent that Mark was not yet used to
thinking of Christopher as anything but a whelp, a person
whose actions might be disagreeable but couldn't matter.
He said to Ruggles:

'You had better talk to my father about this. I don't
know that I could keep all these particulars accurately in
my head.'

Ruggles had been only too pleased to, and—with to
give him weight, his intimacy with the eldest son, who
certified to his reliability in money matters and his quali-
fications for amassing details as to personalities, acts, and
promotions—that day, at tea at the club, in a tranquil
corner, Ruggles had told Mr. Tietjens senior that Chris-

topher's wife had been with child when he had married her; he had hushed up her elopement with Perowne and connived at other love affairs of hers to his own dishonour, and was suspected in high places of being a French agent, thus being marked down as suspect in the great book. . . . All this in order to obtain money for the support of Miss Wannop, by whom he had had a child, and to maintain Macmaster and Mrs Duchemin on a scale unsuited to their means, Mrs Duchemin being his mistress. The story that Tietjens had had a child by Miss Wannop was first suggested, and then supported, by the fact that in Yorkshire he certainly had a son who never appeared in Gray's Inn.

Mr Tietjens was a reasonable man: not reasonable enough to doubt Ruggles' circumstantial history. He believed implicitly in the great book—which has been believed in by several generations of country gentlemen: he perceived that his brilliant son had made no advancement commensurate with either his brilliance or his influence: he suspected that brilliance was synonymous with reprehensible tendencies. Moreover, his old friend, General ffolliott, had definitely told him some days before that he ought to enquire into the goings on of Christopher. On being pressed ffolliott had, also definitely, stated that Christopher was suspected of very dishonourable dealings, both in money and women. Ruggles' allegations came, therefore, as a definite confirmation of suspicions that appeared only too well backed up.

He bitterly regretted that, knowing Christopher to be brilliant, he had turned the boy—as is the usual portion of younger sons—adrift, with what of a competence could be got together, to sink or swim. He had, he said to himself, always wished to keep at home and under his own eyes this boy for whom he had had especial promptings of tenderness. His wife, to whom he had been absolutely attached by a passionate devotion, had been unusually wrapped up in Christopher, because Christopher had been her youngest son, born very late. And, since his wife's

death, Christopher had been especially dear to him, as if
he had carried about his presence some of the radiance
and illumination that had seemed to attach to his mother.
Indeed, after his wife's death, Mr Tietjens had very nearly
asked Christopher and his wife to come and keep house for
him at Groby, making, of course, special testamentary provision for Christopher in order to atone for his giving up
his career at the Department of Statistics. His sense of
justice to his other children had prevented him doing this.

What broke his heart was that Christopher should not
only have seduced but should have had a child by Valentine Wannop. Very grand seigneur in his habits, Mr Tietjens had always believed in his duty to patronise the arts
and, if he had actually done little in this direction beyond
purchasing some chocolate-coloured pictures of the French
historic school, he had for long prided himself on what
he had done for the widow and children of his old friend,
Professor Wannop. He considered, and with justice, that
he had made Mrs Wannop a novelist, and he considered
her to be a very great novelist. And his conviction of the
guilt of Christopher was strengthened by a slight tinge of
jealousy of his son: a feeling that he would not have
acknowledged to himself. For, since Christopher, he didn't
know how, for he had given his son no introduction, had
become an intimate of the Wannop household, Mrs
Wannop had completely given up asking him, Mr Tietjens, clamorously and constantly for advice. In return she
had sung the praises of Christopher in almost extravagant
terms. She had, indeed, said that if Christopher had not
been almost daily in the house or at any rate at the end
of the phone she would hardly have been able to keep on
working at full pressure. This had not overpleased Mr
Tietjens. Mr Tietjens entertained for Valentine Wannop
an affection of the very deepest, the same qualities appealing to the father as appealed to the son. He had even, in
spite of his sixty odd years, seriously entertained the idea
of marrying the girl. She was a lady: she would have
managed Groby very well; and, although the entail on the

property was very strict indeed, he would, at least, have been able to put her beyond the reach of want after his death. He had thus no doubt of his son's guilt, and he had to undergo the additional humiliation of thinking that not only had his son betrayed this radiant personality, but he had done it so clumsily as to give the girl a child and let it be known. That was unpardonable want of management in the son of a gentleman. And now this boy was his heir with a misbegotten brat to follow. Irrevocably!

All his four tall sons, then, were down. His eldest tied for good to—a quite admirable!—trollop: his two next dead: his youngest worse than dead: his wife dead of a broken heart.

A soberly but deeply religious man, Mr Tietjens' very religion made him believe in Christopher's guilt. He knew that it is as difficult for a rich man to go to heaven as it is for a camel to go through the gate in Jerusalem called the Needle's Eye. He humbly hoped that his Maker would receive him amongst the pardoned. Then, since he was a rich—an enormously rich—man, his sufferings on this earth must be very great. . . .

From tea-time that day until it was time to catch the midnight train for Bishop Auckland, he had been occupied with his son Mark in the writing-room of the club. They had made many notes. He had seen his son Christopher, in uniform, looking broken and rather bloated, the result, no doubt, of debauch. Christopher had passed through the other end of the room and Mr Tietjens had avoided his eye. He had caught the train and reached Groby, travelling alone. Towards dusk he had taken out a gun. He was found dead next morning, a couple of rabbits beside his body, just over the hedge from the little church-yard. He appeared to have crawled through the hedge, dragging his loaded gun, muzzle forward, after him. Hundreds of men, mostly farmers, die from that cause every year in England. . . .

With these things in his mind—or as much of them as he could keep at once—Mark was now investigating his brother's affairs. He would have let things go on longer, for his father's estate was by no means wound up, but that morning Ruggles had told him that the club had had a cheque of his brother's returned and that his brother was going out to France next day. It was five months exactly since the death of their father. That had happened in March, it was now August: a bright, untidy day in narrow, high courts.

Mark arranged his thoughts.

'How much of an income,' he said, 'do you need to live in comfort? If a thousand isn't enough, how much? Two?'

Christopher said that he needed no money and didn't intend to live in comfort. Mark said:

'I am to let you have three thousand, if you'll live abroad. I'm only carrying out our father's instructions. You could cut a hell of a splash on three thousand in France.'

Christopher did not answer.

Mark began again:

'The remaining three thousand then: that was over from our mother's money. Did you settle it on your girl, or just spend it on her?'

Christopher repeated with patience that he hadn't got a girl.

Mark said:

'The girl who had a child by you. I'm instructed, if you haven't settled anything already—but father took it that you would have—I was to let her have enough to live on in comfort. How much do you suppose she'll need to live in comfort? I allow Charlotte four hundred. Would four hundred be enough? I suppose you want to go on keeping her? Three thousand isn't a great lot for her to live on with a child.'

Christopher said:

'Hadn't you better mention names?'

Mark said:

'No! I never mention names. I mean a woman writer and her daughter. I suppose the girl is father's daughter, isn't she?'

Christopher said:

'No. She couldn't be. I've thought of it. She's twenty-seven. We were all in Dijon for the two years before she was born. Father didn't come into the estate till next year. The Wannops were also in Canada at the time. Professor Wannop was principal of a university there. I forget the name.'

Mark said:

'So we were. In Dijon! For my French!' He added: 'Then she can't be father's daughter. It's a good thing. I thought, as he wanted to settle money on them, they were very likely his children. There's a son, too. He's to have a thousand. What's he doing?'

'The son,' Tietjens said, 'is a conscientious objector. He's on a mine-sweeper. A bluejacket. His idea is that picking up mines is saving life, not taking it.'

'Then he won't want the brass yet,' Mark said, 'it's to start him in any business. What's the full name and address of your girl? Where do you keep her?'

They were in an open space, dusty, with half-timber buildings whose demolition had been interrupted. Christopher halted close to a post that had once been a cannon; up against this he felt that his brother could lean in order to assimilate ideas. He said slowly and patiently:

'If you're consulting with me as to how to carry out our father's intentions, and as there's money in it, you had better make an attempt to get hold of the facts. I wouldn't bother you if it wasn't a matter of money. In the first place, no money is wanted at this end. I can live on my pay. My wife is a rich woman, relatively. Her mother is a very rich woman. . . .'

'She's Rugeley's mistress, isn't she?' Mark asked.

Christopher said:

'No, she isn't. I should certainly say she wasn't. Why should she be? She's his cousin.'

'Then it's your wife who was Rugeley's mistress?' Mark asked. 'Or why should she have the loan of his box?'

'Sylvia also is Rugeley's cousin, of course, a degree

9*

further removed,' Tietjens said. 'She isn't anyone's mistress. You can be certain of that.'

'They *say* she is,' Mark answered. 'They say she's a regular tart. . . . I suppose you think I've insulted you.'

Christopher said:

'No, you haven't. . . . It's better to get all this out. We're practically strangers, but you've a right to ask.'

Mark said:

'Then you haven't got a girl and don't need money to keep her. . . . You could have what you liked. There's no reason why a man shouldn't have a girl, and if he has he ought to keep her decently. . . .'

Christopher did not answer. Mark leaned against the half-buried cannon and swung his umbrella by its crook.

'But,' he said, 'if you don't keep a girl, what do you do for . . .' He was going to say 'for the comforts of home,' but a new idea had come into his mind. 'Of course,' he said, 'one can see that your wife's soppily in love with you.' He added: 'Soppily . . . one can see that with half an eye. . . .'

Christopher felt his jaw drop. Not a second before—that very second!—he had made up his mind to ask Valentine Wannop to become his mistress that night. It was no good, any more, he said to himself. She loved him, he knew, with a deep, an unshakable passion, just as his passion for her was a devouring element that covered his whole mind as the atmosphere envelops the earth. Were they, then, to go down to death separated by years, with no word ever spoken? To what end? For whose benefit? The whole world conspired to force them together! To resist became a weariness!

His brother Mark was talking on. 'I know all about women,' he had announced. Perhaps he did. He had lived with exemplary fidelity to a quite unpresentable woman, for a number of years. Perhaps the complete study of one woman gave you a map of all the rest!

Christopher said:

'Look here, Mark. You had better go through all my

pass-books for the last ten years. Or ever since I had an account. This discussion is no good if you don't believe what I say.'

Mark said:

'I don't want to see your pass-books. I believe you.'

He added, a second later:

'Why the devil shouldn't I believe you? It's either believing you're a gentleman or Ruggles a liar. It's only common sense to believe Ruggles a liar, in that case. I didn't before because I had no grounds to.'

Christopher said:

'I doubt if liar is the right word. He picked up things that were said against me. No doubt he reported them faithfully enough. Things *are* said against me. I don't know why.'

'Because,' Mark said with emphasis, 'you treat these south country swine with the contempt that they deserve. They're incapable of understanding the motives of a gentleman. If you live among dogs they'll think you've the motives of a dog. What other motives can they give you?' He added: 'I thought you'd been buried so long under their muck that you were as mucky as they!'

Tietjens looked at his brother with the respect one has to give to a man ignorant but shrewd. It was a discovery: that his brother was shrewd.

But, of course, he would be shrewd. He was the indispensable head of a great department. He had to have some qualities. . . . Not cultivated, not even instructed. A savage! But penetrating!

'We must move on,' he said, 'or I shall have to take a cab.' Mark detached himself from his half-buried cannon.

'What did you do with the other three thousand?' he asked. 'Three thousand is a hell of a big sum to chuck away. For a younger son.'

'Except for some furniture I bought for my wife's rooms,' Christopher said, 'it went mostly in loans.'

'Loans!' Mark exclaimed. 'To that fellow Macmaster?'

'Mostly to him,' Christopher answered. 'But about seven hundred to Dicky Swipes, of Cullercoats.'

'Good God! Why to him?' Mark ejaculated.

'Oh, because he was Swipes, of Cullercoats,' Christopher said, 'and asked for it. He'd have had more, only that was enough for him to drink himself to death on.'

Mark said:

'I suppose you don't give money to every fellow that asks for it?'

Christopher said:

'I do. It's a matter of principle.'

'It's lucky,' Mark said, 'that a lot of fellows don't know that. You wouldn't have much brass left for long.'

'I didn't have it for long,' Christopher said.

'You know,' Mark said, 'you couldn't expect to do the princely patron on a youngest son's portion. It's a matter of taste. I never gave a ha'penny to a beggar myself. But a lot of the Tietjens were princely. One generation to addle brass: one to keep: one to spend. That's all right.... I suppose Macmaster's wife *is* your mistress? That'll account for it not being the girl. They keep an arm-chair for you.'

Christopher said:

'No. I just backed Macmaster for the sake of backing him. Father lent him money to begin with.'

'So he did,' Mark exclaimed.

'His wife,' Christopher said, 'was the widow of Breakfast Duchemin. *You* knew Breakfast Duchemin?'

'Oh, *I* knew Breakfast Duchemin,' Mark said. 'I suppose Macmaster's a pretty warm man now. Done himself proud with Duchemin's money.'

'Pretty proud!' Christopher said. 'They won't be knowing me long now.'

'But damn it all!' Mark said, 'You've Groby to all intents and purposes. *I'm* not going to marry and beget children to hinder you.'

Christopher said:

'Thanks. I don't want it.'

'Got your knife into me?' Mark asked.

'Yes. I've got my knife into you,' Christopher answered. 'Into the whole bloody lot of you, and Ruggles and ffolliot and our father!'

Mark said: 'Ah!'

'You don't suppose I wouldn't have?' Christopher asked.

'Oh, *I* don't suppose you wouldn't have,' Mark answered. 'I thought you were a soft sort of bloke. I see you aren't.'

'I'm as North Riding as yourself!' Christopher answered.

They were in the tide of Fleet Street, pushed apart by foot passengers and separated by traffic. With some of the imperiousness of the officer of those days, Christopher barged across through motor-buses and paper lorries. With the imperiousness of the head of a department, Mark said:

'Here, policeman, stop these damn things and let me get over.' But Christopher was over much the sooner and waited for his brother in the gateway of the Middle Temple. His mind was completely swallowed up in the endeavour to imagine the embraces of Valentine Wannop. He said to himself that he had burnt his boats.

Mark, coming alongside him, said:

'You'd better know what our father wanted.'

Christopher said:

'Be quick then. I must get on.' He had to rush through his War Office interview to get to Valentine Wannop. They would have only a few hours in which to recount the loves of two lifetimes. He saw her golden head and her enraptured face. He wondered how her face would look, enraptured. He had seen on it humour, dismay, tenderness, in the eyes—and fierce anger and contempt for his, Christopher's, political opinions. His militarism!

Nevertheless they halted by the Temple fountain. That respect was due to their dead father. Mark had been explaining. Christopher had caught some of his words and divined the links. Mr Tietjens had left no will, confident that his desires as to the disposal of his immense fortune would be carried out meticulously by his eldest son. He would have left a will, but there was the vague case of

Christopher to be considered. Whilst Christopher had been
a youngest son you arranged that he had a good lump sum
and went, with it, to the devil how he liked. He was no
longer a youngest son: by the will of God.

'Our father's idea,' Mark said by the fountain, 'was that
no settled sum could keep you straight. His idea was that
if you were a bloody pimp living on women. . . . You don't
mind?'

'I don't mind your putting it straightforwardly,' Christopher said. He considered the base of the fountain that
was half full of leaves. This civilization had contrived a
state of things in which leaves rotted by August. Well, it
was doomed!

'If you were a pimp living on women,' Mark repeated,
'it was no good making a will. You might need uncounted
thousands to keep you straight. You were to have 'em.
You were to be as debauched as you wanted, but on clean
money. I was to see how much in all probability that would
be and arrange the other legacies to scale. . . . Father had
crowds of pensioners. . . .'

'How much did father cut up for?' Christopher asked.
Mark said:

'God knows. . . . You saw we proved the estate at a
million and a quarter as far as ascertained. But it might be
twice that. Or five times! . . . With steel prices what they
have been for the last three years it's impossible to say
what the Middlesbrough district property won't produce.
. . . The death duties even can't catch it up. And there are
all the ways of getting round *them*.'

Christopher inspected his brother with curiosity. This
brown-complexioned fellow with bulging eyes, shabby on
the whole, tightly buttoned into a rather old pepper-and-
salt suit, with a badly rolled umbrella, old race-glasses, and
his bowler hat the only neat thing about him, was, indeed,
a prince. With a rigid outline! All real princes must look
like that. He said:

'Well! You won't be a penny the poorer by me.'

Mark was beginning to believe this. He said:

'You won't forgive father?'

Christopher said:

'I won't forgive father for not making a will. I won't forgive him for calling in Ruggles. I saw him and you in the writing-room the night before he died. He never spoke to me. He could have. It was clumsy stupidity. That's unforgiveable.'

'The fellow shot himself,' Mark said. 'You usually forgive a fellow who shoots himself.'

'I don't,' Christopher said. 'Besides, he's probably in heaven and don't need my forgiveness. Ten to one he's in heaven. He was a good man.'

'One of the best,' Mark said. 'It was I that called in Ruggles though.'

'I don't forgive you either,' Christopher said.

'But you *must*,' Mark said—and it was a tremendous concession to sentimentality—'take enough to make you comfortable.'

'By God!' Christopher exclaimed. 'I loathe your whole beastly buttered toast, mutton-chopped, carpet-slippered, rum-negused comfort as much as I loathe your beastly Riviera-palaced, chauffeured, hydraulic-lifted, hot-house aired beastliness of fornication. . . .' He was carried away, as he seldom let himself be, by the idea of his amours with Valentine Wannop, which should take place on the empty boards of a cottage, without draperies, fat meats, gummy aphrodisiacs. . . . 'You won't,' he repeated, 'be a penny the poorer by me.'

Mark said:

'Well, you needn't get shirty about it. If you won't you won't. We'd better move on. You've only just time. We'll say that settles it. . . . Are you, or aren't you, overdrawn at your bank? I'll make that up, whatever you damn well do to stop it.'

'I'm not overdrawn,' Christopher said. 'I'm over thirty pounds in credit, and I've an immense overdraft guaranteed by Sylvia. It was a mistake of the bank's.'

Mark hesitated for a moment. It was to him almost un-
believable that a bank could make a mistake. One of the
great banks. The props of England.

They were walking down towards the Embankment.
With his precious umbrella Mark aimed a violent blow at
the railings above the tennis lawns, where whitish figures,
bedrabbled by the dim atmosphere, moved like mario-
nettes practising crucifixions.

'By God!' he said, 'this is the last of England. . . .
There's only my department where they never make mistakes. I tell you, if there were any mistakes made there
there would be some backs broken!' He added: 'But don't
you think that I'm going to give up comfort, I'm not. My
Charlotte makes better buttered toast than they can at the
club. And she's got a tap of French rum that's saved my
life over and over again after a beastly wet day's racing.
And she does it all on the five hundred I give her and keeps
herself clean and tidy on top of it. Nothing like a French-
woman for managing. . . . By God, I'd marry the doxy if
she wasn't a Papist. It would please her and it wouldn't
hurt me. But I couldn't stomach marrying a Papist.
They're not to be trusted.'

'You'll have to stomach a Papist coming into Groby,'
Christopher said. 'My son's to be brought up as a Papist.'

Mark stopped and dug his umbrella into the ground.

'Eh, but that's a bitter one,' he said. 'Whatever made ye
do that? . . . I suppose the mother made you do it. She
tricked you into it before you married her.' He added: 'I'd
not like to sleep with that wife of yours. She's too athletic.
It'd be like sleeping with a bundle of faggots. I suppose,
though, you're a pair of turtle doves. . . . Eh, but I'd not
have thought ye would have been so weak.'

'I only decided this morning,' Christopher said, 'when
my cheque was returned from the bank. You won't have
read Spelden on sacrilege, about Groby.'

'I can't say I have,' Mark answered.

'It's no good trying to explain that side of it then,' Christopher said, 'there isn't time. But you're wrong in thinking

Sylvia made it a condition of our marriage. Nothing would have made me consent then. It has made her a happy woman that I have. The poor thing thought our house was under a curse for want of a Papist heir.'

'What made ye consent now?' Mark asked.

'I've told you,' Christopher said, 'it was getting my cheque returned to the club; that on the top of the rest of it. A fellow who can't do better than that had better let the mother bring up the child. . . . Besides, it won't hurt a Papist boy to have a father with dishonoured cheques as much as it would a Protestant. They're not quite English.'

'That's true too,' Mark said.

He stood still by the railings of the public garden near the Temple station.

'Then,' he said, 'if I'd let the lawyers write and tell you the guarantee for your overdraft from the estate was stopped as they wanted to, the boy wouldn't be a Papist? You wouldn't have overdrawn.'

'I didn't overdraw,' Christopher said. 'But if you had warned me I should have made enquiries at the bank and the mistake wouldn't have occurred. Why didn't you?'

'I meant to,' Mark said. 'I meant to do it myself. But I hate writing letters. I put it off. I didn't much like having dealings with the fellow I thought you were. I suppose that's another thing you won't forgive me for?'

'No. I shan't forgive you for not writing to me,' Christopher said. 'You ought to write business letters.'

'I hate writing 'em,' Mark said. Christopher was moving on. 'There's one thing more,' Mark said. 'I suppose the boy is your son?'

'Yes, he's my son,' Christopher said.

'Then that's all,' Mark said. 'I suppose if you're killed you won't mind my keeping an eye on the youngster?'

'I'll be glad,' Christopher said.

They strolled along the Embankment side by side, walking rather slowly, their backs erected and their shoulders squared because of their satisfaction of walking together, desiring to lengthen the walk by going slow. Once or twice they stopped to look at the dirty silver of the river, for both liked grim effects of landscape. They felt very strong, as if they owned the land!

Once Mark chuckled and said:

'It's too damn funny. To think of our both being . . . what is it? . . . monogamists? Well, it's a good thing to stick to one woman . . . you can't say it isn't. It saves trouble. And you know where you are.'

Under the lugubrious arch that leads into the War Office quadrangle Christopher halted.

'No. I'm coming in,' Mark said. 'I want to speak to Hogarth. I haven't spoken to Hogarth for some time. About the transport waggon parks in Regent's Park. I manage all those beastly things and a lot more.'

'They say you do it damn well,' Christopher said. 'They say you're indispensable.' He was aware that his brother desired to stay with him as long as possible. He desired it himself.

'I damn well am!' Mark said. He added: 'I suppose you couldn't do that sort of job in France? Look after transport and horses.'

'I could,' Christopher said, 'but I suppose I shall go back to liaison work.'

'I don't think you will,' Mark said. 'I could put in a word for you with the transport people.'

'I wish you would,' Christopher said. 'I'm not fit to go back into the front line. Besides, I'm no beastly hero! And I'm a rotten infantry officer. No Tietjens was ever a soldier worth talking of.'

They turned the corner of the arch. Like something fitting in, exact and expected, Valentine Wannop stood looking at the lists of casualties that hung beneath a cheaply green-stained deal shelter against the wall, a tribute at once to the weaker art movements of the day and the desire to save the ratepayers' money.

With the same air of finding Christopher Tietjens fit in exactly to an expected landscape she turned on him. Her face was blue-white and distorted. She ran upon him and exclaimed:

'Look at this horror! And you in that foul uniform can support it!'

The sheets of paper beneath the green roof were laterally striped with little serrated lines: each line meant the death of a man, for the day.

Tietjens had fallen back a step off the kerb of the pavement that ran round the quadrangle. He said:

'I support it because I have to. Just as you decry it because you have to. They're two different patterns that we see.' He added: 'This is my brother Mark.'

She turned her head stiffly upon Mark: her face was perfectly waxen. It was as if the head of a shopkeeper's lay-figure had been turned. She said to Mark:

'I didn't know Mr Tietjens had a brother. Or hardly. I've never heard him speak of you.'

Mark grinned feebly, exhibiting to the lady the brilliant lining of his hat.

'I don't suppose anyone has ever heard me speak of *him*,' he said, 'but he's my brother all right!'

She stepped on to the asphalt carriage-way and caught between her fingers and thumb a fold of Christopher's khaki sleeve.

'I must speak to you,' she said; 'I'm going then.'

She drew Christopher into the centre of the enclosed, hard and ungracious space, holding him still by the stuff of his tunic. She pushed him round until he was facing her. She swallowed hard; it was as if the motion of her throat took an immense time. Christopher looked round the skyline of the buildings of sordid and besmirched stone. He had often wondered what would happen if an air-bomb of some size dropped into the mean, grey stoniness of that cold heart of an embattled world.

The girl was devouring his face with her eyes: to see him flinch. Her voice was hard between her little teeth. She said:

'Were you the father of the child Ethel was going to have? Your wife says you were.'

Christopher considered the dimensions of the quadrangle. He said vaguely:

'Ethel! Who's she?' In pursuance of the habits of the painter-poet Mr and Mrs Macmaster called each other always 'Gug Gums!' Christopher had in all probability never heard Mrs Duchemin's Christian names. Certainly he had never heard them since his disaster had swept all names out of his head.

He came to the conclusion that the quadrangle was not a space sufficiently confined to afford much bursting resistance to a bomb.

The girl said:

'Edith Ethel Duchemin! Mrs Macmaster that is!' She was obviously waiting intensely. Christopher said with vagueness:

'No! Certainly not! . . . What was said?'

Mark Tietjens was leaning forward over the kerb in front of the green-stained shelter, like a child over a brookside. He was obviously waiting, quite patient, swinging his umbrella by the hook. He appeared to have no other means of self-expression. The girl was saying that when she had rung up Christopher that morning a voice had said, without any preparation at all: the girl repeated, without any preparation at all:

'You'd better keep off the grass if you're the Wannop girl. Mrs Duchemin is my husband's mistress already. You keep off!'

Christopher said:

'She said that, did she?' He was wondering how Mark kept his balance, really. The girl said nothing more. She was waiting. With an insistence that seemed to draw him: a sort of sucking in of his personality. It was unbearable. He made his last effort of that afternoon.

He said:

'Damn it all. How could you ask such a tomfool question? *You!* I took you to be an intelligent person. The only intelligent person I know. Don't you *know* me?'

She made an effort to retain her stiffening.

'Isn't Mrs Tietjens a truthful person?' she asked. 'I thought she looked truthful when I saw her at Vincent and Ethel's.'

He said:

'What she says she believes. But she only believes what she wants to, for the moment. If you call that truthful, she's truthful. I've nothing against her.' He said to himself: 'I'm not going to appeal to her by damning my wife.'

She seemed to go all of a piece, as the hard outline goes suddenly out of a piece of lump sugar upon which you drop water.

'Oh,' she said, 'it *isn't* true. I *knew* it wasn't true.' She began to cry.

Christopher said:

'Come along. I've been answering tomfool questions all day. I've got another tomfool to see here, then I'm through.'

She said:

'I can't come with you, crying like this.'

He answered:

'Oh, yes you can. This is the place where women cry.' He added: 'Besides, there's Mark. He's a comforting ass.'

He delivered her over to Mark.

'Here, look after Miss Wannop,' he said. 'You want to talk to her anyhow, don't you?' and he hurried ahead of them like a fussy shopwalker into the lugubrious hall. He felt that, if he didn't come soon to an unemotional ass in red, green, blue, or pink tabs, who would have fish-like eyes and would ask the sort of questions that fishes ask in tanks, he, too, must break down and cry. With relief! However, that was a place where men cried, too!

He got through at once by sheer weight of personality, down miles of corridors, into the presence of a quite intelligent, thin, dark person with scarlet tabs. That meant a superior staff affair: not dustbins.

The dark man said to him at once:

'Look here! What's the matter with the Command Depôts? You've been lecturing a lot of them. In economy. What are all these damn mutinies about? Is it rotten old colonels in command?'

Tietjens said amiably:

'Look here! I'm not a beastly spy, you know! I've had hospitality from the rotten old colonels.'

The dark man said:

'I daresay you have. But that's what you were sent round for. General Campion said you were the brainiest chap in his command. He's gone out now, worse luck. . . . What's the matter with the Command Depôts? Is it the men? Or is it the officers! You needn't mention names.'

Tietjens said:

'Kind of Campion. It isn't the officers and it isn't the men. It's the foul system. You get men who think they've deserved well of their country—and they damn well have! —and you crop their heads. . . .'

'That's the M.O.s,' the dark man said. 'They don't want lice.'

'If they prefer mutinies . . .' Tietjens said. 'A man wants to walk with his girl and have a properly oiled quiff. They don't like being regarded as convicts. That's how they are regarded.'

The dark man said:

'All right. Go on. Why don't you sit down?'

'I'm a little in a hurry,' Tietjens said. 'I'm going out to-morrow and I've got a brother and people waiting below.'

The dark man said:

'Oh, I'm sorry. . . . But damn. You're the sort of man we want at home. Do you want to go? We can, no doubt, get you stopped if you don't.'

Tietjens hesitated for a moment.

'Yes!' he said eventually. 'Yes, I want to go.'

For the moment he had felt temptation to stay. But it came into his discouraged mind that Mark had said that Sylvia was in love with him. It had been underneath his

thoughts all the while: it had struck him at the time like
a kick from the hind leg of a mule in his subliminal con-
sciousness. It was the impossible complication. It might
not be true; but whether or no the best thing for him was
to go and get wiped out as soon as possible. He meant,
nevertheless, fiercely, to have his night with the girl who
was crying downstairs. . . .

He heard in his ear, perfectly distinctly, the lines:

'The voice that never yet
Made answer to my word . . .'

He said to himself:
'That was what Sylvia wanted! I've got that much!'
The dark man had said something. Tietjens repeated:
'I'd take it very unkindly if you stopped my going . . .
I want to go.'
The dark man said:
'Some do. Some do not. I'll make a note of your name
in case you come back. . . . You won't mind going on with
your cinder-sifting, if you do? . . . Get on with your story
as quick as you can. And get what fun you can before
you go. They say it's rotten out there. Damn awful!
There's a hell of a strafe on. That's why they want all of
you.'

For a moment Tietjens saw the grey dawn at rail-head
with the distant sound of a ceaselessly boiling pot from
miles away. The army feeling re-descended upon him. He
began to talk about Command Depôts, at great length and
with enthusiasm. He snorted with rage at the way men
were treated in these gloomy places. With ingenious
stupidity!

Every now and then the dark man interrupted him
with:
'Don't forget that a Command Depôt is a place where
sick and wounded go to get made fit. We've got to get 'em
back as soon as we can.'
'And do you?' Tietjens would ask.

'No, we don't,' the other would answer. 'That's what this enquiry is about.'

'You've got,' Tietjens would continue, 'on the north side of a beastly clay hill nine miles from Southampton three thousand men from the Highlands, North Wales, Cumberland. . . . God knows where, as long as it's three hundred miles from home to make them rather mad with nostalgia. . . . You allow 'em out for an hour a day during the pub's closing time; you shave their heads to prevent 'em appealing to local young women who don't exist, and you don't let 'em carry the swagger-canes! God knows why! To prevent their poking their eyes out if they fall down, I suppose. Nine miles from anywhere, with chalk down roads to walk on and not a bush for shelter or shade. . . . And, damn it, if you get two men, chums, from the Seaforths or the Argylls you don't let them sleep in the same hut, but shove 'em in with a lot of fat Buffs or Welshmen, who stink of leeks and can't speak English. . . .'

'That's the infernal medicals' orders to stop 'em talking all night.'

'To make 'em conspire all night not to turn out for parade,' Tietjens said. 'And there's a beastly mutiny begun. . . . And, damn it, they're fine men. They're first-class fellows. Why don't you—as this is a Christian land—let 'em go home to convalesce with their girls and pubs and friends and a little bit of swank, for heroes? Why in God's name don't you? Isn't there suffering enough?'

'I wish you wouldn't say "you," ' the dark man said. 'It isn't me. The only A.C.I. I've drafted was to give every Command Depôt a cinema and a theatre. But the beastly medicals got it stopped . . . for fear of infection. And, of course, the parsons and Nonconformist magistrates. . . .'

'Well, you'll have to change it all,' Tietjens said, 'or you'll just have to say: thank God we've got a navy. You won't have an army. The other day three fellows—Warwicks—asked me at question time, after a lecture, why they were shut up there in Wiltshire whilst Belgian refugees were getting bastards on their wives in Birmingham. And

when I asked how many men made that complaint over
fifty stood up. All from Birmingham. . . .'

The dark man said:

'I'll make a note of that. . . . Go on.'

Tietjens went on; for as long as he stayed there he felt
himself a man, doing work that befitted a man, with the
bitter contempt for fools that a man should have and
express. It was a letting up: a real last leave.

IV

Mark Tietjens, his umbrella swinging sheepishly, his
bowler hat pushed firmly down on to his ears to give him
a sense of stability, walked beside the weeping girl in the
quadrangle.

'I say,' he said, 'don't give it to old Christopher too
beastly hard about his militarist opinions. . . . Remember,
he's going out to-morrow and he's one of the best.'

She looked at him quickly, tears remaining upon her
cheeks, and then away.

'One of the best,' Mark said. 'A fellow who never told
a lie or did a dishonourable thing in his life. Let him down
easy, there's a good girl. You ought to, you know.'

The girl, her face turned away, said:

'I'd lay down my life for him!'

Mark said:

'I know you would. I know a good woman when I see
one. And think! He probably considers that he *is* . . . offering his life, you know, for you. And me, too, of course! . . .
It's a different way of looking at things.' He gripped her
awkwardly but irresistibly by the upper arm. It was very
thin under her blue cloth coat. He said to himself:

'By Jove! Christopher likes them skinny. It's the athletic
sort that attracts him. This girl is as clean run as . . .' He
couldn't think of anything as clean run as Miss Wannop,
but he felt a warm satisfaction at having achieved an intimacy with her and his brother. He said:

'You aren't going away? Not without a kinder word to
him. You think! He might be killed. . . . Besides. Probably
he's never killed a German. He was a liaison officer. Since
then he's been in charge of a dump where they sift army
dustbins. To see how they can give the men less to eat.
That means that the civilians get more. You don't object to
his giving civilians more meat? . . . It isn't even helping to
kill Germans. . . .'

He felt her arm press his hand against her warm side.

'What's he going to do now?' she asked. Her voice
wavered.

'That's what I'm here about,' Mark said. 'I'm going in
to see old Hogarth. You don't know Hogarth? Old General
Hogarth? I think I can get him to give Christopher a job
with the transport. A safe job. Safeish! No beastly glory
business about it. No killing beastly Germans either. . . . I
beg your pardon, if you like Germans.'

She drew her arm from his hand in order to look him
in the face.

'Oh!' she said, '*you* don't want him to have any beastly
military glory!' The colour came back into her face: she
looked at him open-eyed.

He said:

'No! Why the devil should he?' He said to himself:
'She's got enormous eyes: a good neck: good shoulders:
good breasts: clean hips: small hands. She isn't knock-
kneed: neat ankles. She stands well on her feet. Feet not too
large! Five foot four, say! A real good filly!' He went on
aloud: 'Why in the world should he want to be a beastly
soldier? He's the heir to Groby. That ought to be enough
for one man.'

Having stood still sufficiently long for what she knew
to be his critical inspection, she put her hand in turn, precipitately, under his arm and moved him towards the
entrance steps.

'Let's be quick then,' she said. 'Let's get him into your
transport at once. Before he goes to-morrow. Then we'll
know he's safe.'

He was puzzled by her dress. It was very business-like, dark blue and very short. A white blouse with a black silk, man's tie. A wide-awake, with, on the front of the band, a cipher.

'You're in uniform yourself,' he said. 'Does your conscience let you do war work?'

She said:

'No. We're hard up. I'm taking the gym classes in a great big school to turn an honest penny. . . . *Do* be quick!'

Her pressure on his elbow flattered him. He resisted it a little, hanging back, to make her more insistent. He liked being pleaded with by a pretty woman: Christopher's girl at that.

He said:

'Oh, it's not a matter of minutes. They keep 'em weeks at the base before they send 'em up. . . . We'll fix him up all right, I've no doubt. We'll wait in the hall till he comes down.'

He told the benevolent commissionaire, one of two in a pulpit in the crowded grim hall, that he was going up to see General Hogarth in a minute or two. But not to send a bellboy. He might be some time yet.

He sat himself beside Miss Wannop, clumsily, on a wooden bench, humanity surging over their toes as if they had been on a beach. She moved a little to make room for him and that, too, made him feel good. He said:

'You said just now: "we" are hard up. Does "we" mean you and Christopher?'

She said:

'I and Mr Tietjens. Oh, no! I and mother! The paper she used to write for stopped. When your father died, I believe. He found money for it, I think. And mother isn't suited to free-lancing. She's worked too hard in her life.'

He looked at her, his round eyes protruding.

'I don't know what that is, free-lancing,' he said. 'But you've got to be comfortable. How much do you and your mother need to keep you comfortable? And put in a bit more so that Christopher could have a mutton-chop now and then!'

She hadn't really been listening. He said with some insistence: 'Look here! I'm here on business. Not like an elderly admirer forcing himself on you. Though, by God, I do admire you too. . . . But my father wanted your mother to be comfortable. . . .'

Her face, turned to him, became rigid.

'You don't mean . . .' she began. He said:

'You won't get it any quicker by interrupting. I have to tell my stories in my own way. My father wanted your mother to be comfortable. He said so that she could write books, not papers. I don't know what the difference is: that's what he said. He wants you to be comfortable too. . . . You've not got any encumbrances! Not . . . oh, say a business: a hat shop that doesn't pay? Some girls have. . . .'

She said: 'No. I just teach . . . oh, *do* be quick. . . .'

For the first time in his life he dislocated the course of his thoughts to satisfy a longing in someone else.

'You may take it to go on with,' he said, 'as if my father had left your mother a nice little plum.' He cast about to find his scattered thoughts.

'He has! He *has!* After all!' the girl said. 'Oh, thank God!'

'There'll be a bit for you, if you like,' Mark said, 'or perhaps Christopher won't let you. He's ratty with me. And something for your brother to buy a doctor's business with.' He asked: 'You haven't fainted, have you?' She said:

'No. I don't faint. I cry.'

'That'll be all right,' he answered. He went on: 'That's your side of it. Now for mine. I want Christopher to have a place where he'll be sure of a mutton-chop and an arm-chair by the fire. And someone to be good for him. *You're* good for him. I can see that. I know women!'

The girl was crying, softly and continuously. It was the first moment of the lifting of strain that she had known since the day before the Germans crossed the Belgian frontier, near a place called Gemmenich.

It had begun with the return of Mrs Duchemin from Scotland. She had sent at once for Miss Wannop to the rectory, late at night. By the light of candles in tall silver stocks, against oak panelling she had seemed like a mad block of marble, with staring, dark eyes and mad hair. She had exclaimed in a voice as hard as a machine's:

'How do you get rid of a baby? You've been a servant. You ought to know!'

That had been the great shock, the turning-point, of Valentine Wannop's life. Her last years before that had been of great tranquillity, tinged of course with melancholy because she loved Christopher Tietjens. But she had early learned to do without, and the world as she saw it was a place of renunciations, of high endeavour, and sacrifice. Tietjens had to be a man who came to see her mother and talked wonderfully. She had been happy when he had been in the house—she in the housemaid's pantry, getting the tea-things. She had, besides, been very hard-worked for her mother; the weather had been, on the whole, good, the corner of the country in which they lived had continued to seem fresh and agreeable. She had had excellent health, got an occasional ride on the *qui-tamer* with which Tietjens had replaced Joel's rig; and her brother had done admirably at Eton, taking such a number of exhibitions and things that, once at Magdalen, he had been nearly off his mother's hands. An admirable, gay boy, not unlikely to run for, as well as being a credit to, his university, if he didn't get sent down for his political extravagances. He was a Communist!

And at the rectory there had been the Duchemins, or rather Mrs Duchemin and, during most week-ends, Macmaster somewhere about.

The passion of Macmaster for Edith Ethel and of Edith Ethel for Macmaster had seemed to her one of the beautiful things of life. They seemed to swim in a sea of renunciations, of beautiful quotations, and of steadfast waiting. Macmaster did not interest her personally much, but she took him on trust because of Edith Ethel's romantic passion and because he was Christopher Tietjens' friend. She had never heard him say anything original; when he used quotations they would be apt rather than striking. But she took it for granted that he was the right man—much as you take it for granted that the engine of an express train in which you are is reliable. The right people have chosen it for you. . . .

With Mrs Duchemin, mad before her, she had the first intimation that her idolized friend, in whom she had believed as she had believed in the firmness of the great sunny earth, had been the mistress of her lover—almost since the first day she had seen him. . . . And that Mrs Duchemin had, stored somewhere, a character of an extreme harshness and great vulgarity of language. She raged up and down in the candlelight, before the dark oak panelling, screaming coarse phrases of the deepest hatred for her lover. Didn't the oaf know his business better than to . . . ? The dirty little Port of Leith fish-handler. . . .

What, then, were tall candles in silver sticks for? And polished panelling in galleries?

Valentine Wannop couldn't have been a little ashcat in worn cotton dresses, sleeping under the stairs, in an Ealing household with a drunken cook, an invalid mistress, and three over-fed men, without acquiring a considerable knowledge of the sexual necessities and excesses of humanity. But, as all the poorer helots of great cities hearten their lives by dreaming of material beauties, elegance and suave wealth, she had always considered that, far from the world of Ealing and its county councillors who over-ate and neighed like stallions, there were bright colonies of beings, chaste, beautiful in thought, altruist and circumspect.

And, till that moment, she had imagined herself on the skirts of such a colony. She presupposed a society of beautiful intellects centring in London round her friends. Ealing she just put out of her mind. She considered: she had, indeed, once heard Tietjens say that humanity was made up of exact and constructive intellects on the one hand and on the other of stuff to fill graveyards. . . . Now, what had become of the exact and constructive intellects?

Worst of all, what became of her beautiful inclination towards Tietjens, for she couldn't regard it as anything more? Couldn't her heart sing any more whilst she was in the housemaid's pantry and he in her mother's study? And what became, still more, of what she knew to be Tietjens' beautiful inclination towards her? She asked herself the eternal question—and she knew it to be the eternal question—whether no man and woman can ever leave it at the beautiful inclination. And, looking at Mrs Duchemin, rushing backwards and forwards in the light of candles, blue-white of face and her hair flying, Valentine Wannop said: 'No! no! The tiger lying in the reeds will always raise its head!' But tiger . . . it was more like a peacock. . . .

Tietjens, raising his head from the other side of the teatable and looking at her with his long, meditative glance from beside her mother: ought he then, instead of blue and protruding, to have eyes divided longitudinally in the blacks of them—that should divide, closing or dilating, on a yellow ground, with green glowings of furtive light?

She was aware that Edith Ethel had done her an irreparable wrong, for you cannot suffer a great sexual shock and ever be the same. Or not for years. Nevertheless she stayed with Mrs Duchemin until far into the small hours, when she fell, a mere parcel of bones in a peacock-blue wrapper, into a deep chair and refused to move or speak; nor did she afterwards slacken in her faithful waiting on her friend. . . .

On the next day came the war. That was a nightmare of pure suffering, with never a let-up, day or night. It began on the morning of the fourth with the arrival of her brother from some sort of Oxford Communist Summer School on the Broads. He was wearing a German corps student's cap and was very drunk. He had been seeing German friends off from Harwich. It was the first time she had ever seen a drunken man, so that was a good present for her.

Next day, and sober, he was almost worse. A handsome, dark boy like his father, he had his mother's hooked nose and was always a little unbalanced: not mad, but always over-violent in any views he happened for the moment to hold. At the Summer School he had been under very vitriolic teachers of all sorts of notions. That hadn't hitherto mattered. Her mother had written for a Tory paper: her brother, when he had been at home, had edited some sort of Oxford organ of disruption. But her mother had only chuckled.

The war changed that. Both seemed to be filled with a desire for blood and to torture: neither paid the least attention to the other. It was as if—so for the rest of those years the remembrance of that time lived with her—in one corner of the room her mother, ageing, and on her knees, from which she only with difficulty rose, shouted hoarse prayers to God, to let her, with her own hands, strangle, torture and flay off all his skin, a being called the Kaiser, and as if, in the other corner of the room, her brother, erect, dark, scowling and vitriolic, one hand clenched above his head, called down the curse of heaven on the British soldier, so that in thousands, he might die in agony, the blood spouting from his scalded lungs. It appeared that the Communist leader whom Edward Wannop affected had had ill-success in his attempts to cause disaffection among some units or other of the British army, and had failed rather gallingly, being laughed at or ignored rather than being ducked in a horse-pond, shot, or otherwise martyrized. That made it obvious that the British man in the ranks was responsible for the war. If those ignoble hirelings had refused to fight all the other embattled and terrorized millions would have thrown down their arms!

Across that dreadful phantasmagoria went the figure of Tietjens. He was in doubt. She heard him several times voice his doubts to her mother, who grew every day more vacant. One day Mrs Wannop had said:

'What does your wife think about it?'

Tietjens had answered:

'Oh, Mrs Tietjens is a pro-German. . . . Or no, that isn't exact! She has German prisoner-friends and looks after them. But she spends nearly all her time in retreat in a convent reading novels of before the war. She can't bear the thought of physical suffering. I can't blame her.'

Mrs Wannop was no longer listening: her daughter was.

For Valentine Wannop the war had turned Tietjens into far more of a man and far less of an inclination—the war and Mrs Duchemin between them. He had seemed to grow less infallible. A man with doubts is more of a man, with eyes, hands, the need for food and for buttons to be sewn on. She had actually tightened up a loose glove button for him.

One Friday afternoon at Macmaster's she had had a long talk with him: the first she had had since the drive and the accident.

Ever since Macmaster had instituted his Friday afternoons—and that had been some time before the war—Valentine Wannop had accompanied Mrs Duchemin to town by the morning train and back at night to the rectory. Valentine poured out the tea, Mrs Duchemin drifting about the large book-lined room amongst the geniuses and superior journalists.

On this occasion—a November day of very chilly wet—there had been next to nobody present, the preceding Friday having been unusually full. Macmaster and Mrs Duchemin had taken a Mr Spong, an architect, into the dining-room to inspect an unusually fine set of Piranesi's *Views of Rome* that Tietjens had picked up somewhere and had given to Macmaster. A Mr Jegg and a Mrs Haviland were sitting close together in the far window-seat. They were talking in low tones. From time to time Mr Jegg used the word 'inhibition.' Tietjens rose from the fire-seat on which he had been sitting and came to her.

He ordered her to bring her cup of tea over by the fire and talk to him. She obeyed. They sat side by side on the leather fire-seat that stood on polished brass rails, the fire warming their backs. He said:

'Well, Miss Wannop. What have you been doing?' and they drifted into talking of the war. You couldn't not. She was astonished not to find him so loathsome as she had expected, for, just at that time, with the facts that were always being driven into her mind by the pacifist friends of her brother and with continual brooding over the morals of Mrs Duchemin, she had an automatic feeling that all manly men were lust-filled devils, desiring nothing better than to stride over battlefields, stabbing the wounded with long daggers in frenzies of sadism. She knew that this view of Tietjens was wrong, but she cherished it.

She found him—as subconsciously she knew he was—astonishingly mild. She had too often watched him whilst he listened to her mother's tirades against the Kaiser, not to know that. He did not raise his voice, he showed no emotion. He said at last:

'You and I are like two people . . .' He paused and began again more quickly: 'Do you know these soap advertisement signs that read differently from several angles? As you come up to them you read "Monkey's Soap"; if you look back when you've passed it's "Needs no Rinsing." . . . You and I are standing at different angles, and though we both look at the same thing we read different messages. Perhaps if we stood side by side we should see yet a third. . . . But I hope we respect each other. We're both honest. I, at least, tremendously respect you and I hope you respect me.'

She kept silent. Behind their backs the fire rustled. Mr Jegg, across the room, said: 'The failure to co-ordinate . . .' and then dropped his voice.

Tietjens looked at her attentively.

'You don't respect me?' he asked. She kept obstinately silent.

'I'd have liked you to have said it,' he repeated.

'Oh,' she cried out, 'how can I respect you when there is all this suffering? So much pain! Such torture...I can't sleep...Never...I haven't slept a whole night since...Think of the immense spaces, stretching out under the night...I believe pain and fear must be worse at night....' She knew she was crying out like that because her dread had come true. When he had said: 'I'd have liked you to have said it,' using the past, he had said his valedictory. Her man, too, was going.

And she knew too: she had always known under her mind and now she confessed it: her agony had been, half of it, because one day he would say farewell to her: like that, using the inflexion of a verb. As, just occasionally, using the word 'we'—and perhaps without intention—he had let her know that he loved her.

Mr Jegg drifted across from the window: Mrs Haviland was already at the door.

'We'll leave you to have your war talk out,' Mr Jegg said. He added: 'For myself, I believe it's one's sole duty to preserve the beauty of things that's preservable. I can't help saying that.'

She was alone with Tietjens and the quiet day. She said to herself:

'Now he must take me in his arms. He must. He *must*!' The deepest of her instincts came to the surface, from beneath layers of thought hardly known to her. She could feel his arms round her: she had in her nostrils the peculiar scent of his hair—like the scent of the skin of an apple, but very faint. 'You must! You *must*!' she said to herself. There came back to her overpoweringly the memory of their drive together and the moment, the overwhelming moment, when, climbing out of the white fog into the blinding air, she had felt the impulse of his whole body towards her and the impulse of her whole body towards him. A sudden lapse: like the momentary dream when you fall.... She saw the white disk of the sun over the silver mist and behind them was the long, warm night....

Tietjens sat, huddled rather together, dejectedly, the firelight playing on the silver places of his hair. It had grown nearly dark outside: they had a sense of the large room that, almost week by week, had grown, for its gleams of gilding and hand-polished dark woods, more like the great dining-room at the Duchemins'. He got down from the fire-seat with a weary movement, as if the fire-seat had been very high. He said, with a little bitterness, but as if with more fatigue:

'Well, I've got the business of telling Macmaster that I'm leaving the office. That, too, won't be an agreeable affair! Not that what poor Vinnie thinks matters.' He added: 'It's queer, dear ...' In the tumult of her emotions she was almost certain that he had said 'dear.' ... 'Not three hours ago my wife used to me almost the exact words you have just used. Almost the exact words. She talked of her inability to sleep at night for thinking of immense spaces full of pain that was worse at night. .... And she, too, said that she could not respect me. ...'

She sprang up.

'Oh,' she said, 'she didn't meant it. I didn't mean it. Almost every man who is a man must do as you are doing. But don't you see it's a desperate attempt to get you to stay: an attempt on moral lines? How can we leave any stone unturned that could keep us from losing our men?' She added, and it was another stone that she didn't leave unturned: 'Besides, how can you reconcile it with your sense of duty, even from your point of view! You're more useful—you know you're more useful to your country here than ...'

He stood over her, stooping a little, somehow suggesting great gentleness and concern.

'I can't reconcile it with my conscience,' he said. 'In this affair there is nothing that any man can reconcile with his conscience. I don't mean that we oughtn't to be in this affair and on the side we're on. We ought. But I'll put to you things I have put to no other soul.'

The simplicity of his revelation seemed to her to put

to shame any of the glibnesses she had heard. It appeared to her as if a child were speaking. He described the disillusionment it had cost him personally as soon as this country had come into the war. He even described the sunlit heather landscape of the north, where naïvely he had made his tranquil resolution to join the French Foreign Legion as a common soldier and his conviction that that would give him, as he called it, clean bones again.

That, he said, had been straightforward. Now there was nothing straightforward: for him or for any man. One could have fought with a clean heart for a civilization: if you like for the eighteenth century against the twentieth, since that was what fighting for France against the enemy countries meant. But our coming in had changed the aspect at once. It was one part of the twentieth century using the eighteenth as a cat's-paw to bash the other half of the twentieth. It was true there was nothing else for it. And as long as we did it in a decent spirit it was just bearable. One could keep at one's job—which was faking statistics against the other fellow—until you were sick and tired of faking and your brain reeled. And then some!

It was probably impolitic to fake—to overstate!—a case against enemy nations. The chickens would come home to roost in one way or another, probably. Perhaps they wouldn't. That was a matter for one's superiors. Obviously! And the first gang had been simple, honest fellows. Stupid, but relatively disinterested. But now! ... What was one to do? ... He went on, almost mumbling. ...

She had suddenly a clear view of him as a man extraordinarily clear-sighted in the affairs of others, in great affairs, but in his own so simple as to be almost a baby. And gentle! And extraordinarily unselfish. He didn't betray one thought of self-interest ... not one!

He was saying:

'But now! ... with this crowd of boodlers! ... Supposing one's asked to manipulate the figures of millions of pairs of boots in order to force someone else to send

some miserable general and his troops to, say, Salonika—
when they and you and common sense and everyone and
everything else, know it's disastrous? ... And from that to
monkeying with our own forces.... Starving particular
units for political...' He was talking to himself, not to
her. And indeed he said:

'I can't, you see, talk really before you. For all I know
your sympathies, perhaps your activities, are with the
enemy nations.'

She said passionately.

'They're not! They're not! How dare you say such a thing?'

He answered:

'It doesn't matter.... No! I'm sure you're not.... But,
anyhow, these things are official. One can't, if one's
scrupulous, even talk about them ... And then ... You see
it means such infinite deaths of men, such an infinite prolongation ... all this interference for side-ends! ... I seem
to see these fellows with clouds of blood over their heads.
... And then ... I'm to carry out their orders because
they're my superiors.... But helping them means un-
numbered deaths....'

He looked at her with a faint, almost humorous smile:

'You see!' he said, 'we're perhaps not so very far
apart! You mustn't think you're the only one that sees all
the deaths and all the sufferings. All, you see: I, too, am a
conscientious objector. My conscience won't let me continue any longer with these fellows....'

She said:

'But isn't there any other ...'

He interrupted:

'No! There's no other course. One is either a body or a
brain in these affairs. I suppose I'm more brain than body.
I suppose so. Perhaps I'm not. But my conscience won't
let me use my brain in this service. So I've a great, hulking
body! I'll admit I'm probably not much good. But I've
nothing to live for: what I stand for isn't any more in this
world. What I want, as you know, I can't have. So ...'

She exclaimed bitterly:

'Oh, say it! Say it! Say that your large hulking body
will stop two bullets in front of two small anaemic fellows.
And how can you say you'll have nothing to live for?
You'll come back. You'll do your good work again. You
know you did good work ...'

He said:

'Yes! I believe I did. I used to despise it, but I've come
to believe I did. ... But no! They'll never let me back.
They've got me out, with all sorts of bad marks against
me. They'll pursue me systematically. ... You see, in such
a world as this, an idealist—or perhaps it's only a senti-
mentalist—must be stoned to death. He makes the others
so uncomfortable. He haunts them at their golf. ... No;
they'll get me, one way or the other. And some fellow—
Macmaster here—will do my jobs. He won't do them so
well, but he'll do them more dishonestly. Or no. I oughtn't
to say dishonestly. He'll do them with enthusiasm and
righteousness. He'll fulfil the orders of his superiors with
an immense docility and unction. He'll fake figures against
our allies with the black enthusiasm of a Calvin and, when
that war comes, he'll do the requisite faking with the
righteous wrath of Jehovah smiting the priests of Baal.
And he'll be right. It's all we're fitted for. We ought never
to have come into this war. We ought to have snaffled other
peoples' colonies as the price of neutrality. ...'

'Oh!' Valentine Wannop said, 'how can you so hate
your country?'

He said with great earnestness:

'Don't say it! Don't believe it! Don't even for a
moment think it! I love every inch of its fields and every
plant in the hedgerows: comfrey, mullein, paigles, long red
purples, that liberal shepherds give a grosser name ... and
all the rest of the rubbish—you remember the field between the Duchemins' and your mother's—and we have
always been boodlers and robbers and reivers and pirates
and cattle thieves, and so we've built up the great tradition
that we love. ... But, for the moment, it's painful. Our
present crowd is not more corrupt than Walpole's. But

one's too near them. One sees of Walpole that he consolidated the nation by building up the National Debt: one doesn't see his methods. . . . My son, or his son, will only see the glory of the boodle we make out of this show. Or rather out of the next. He won't know about the methods. They'll teach him at school that across the counties went the sound of bugles that his father knew. . . . Though that was another discreditable affair. . . .'

'But you!' Valentine Wannop exclaimed. '*You*! what will *you* do! After the war!'

'I!' he said rather bewilderedly. 'I! . . Oh, I shall go into the old furniture business. I've been offered a job. . . .'

She didn't believe he was serious. He hadn't, she knew, ever thought about his future. But suddenly she had a vision of his white head and pale face in the back glooms of a shop full of dusty things. He would come out, get heavily on to a dusty bicycle and ride off to a cottage sale. She cried out:

'Why don't you do it at once? Why don't you take the job at once?' for in the back of the dark shop he would at least be safe.

He said:

'Oh, no! Not at this time! Besides the old furniture trade's probably not itself for the minute. . . .' He was obviously thinking of something else.

'I've probably been a low cad,' he said, 'wringing your heart with my doubts. But I wanted to see where our similarities come in. We've always been—or we've seemed always to me—so alike in our thoughts. I daresay I wanted you to respect me. . . .'

'Oh, I respect you! I respect you!' she said. 'You're as innocent as a child.'

He went on:

'And I wanted to get some thinking done. It hasn't been often of late that one has had a quiet room and a fire and . . . you! To think in front of. You *do* make one collect one's thoughts. I've been very muddled till to-day . . . till five minutes ago! Do you remember our drive? You

analysed my character. I'd never have let another soul ...
But you see ... Don't you see?'
 She said:
 'No! What am I to see? I remember ...'
 He said:
 'That I'm certainly not an English country gentleman
now; picking up the gossip of the horse markets and say-
ing: let the country go to hell, for me!'
 She said:
 'Did I say that? ... Yes, I said that!'
 The deep waves of emotion came over her: she
trembled. She stretched out her arms. ... She thought she
stretched out her arms. He was hardly visible in the firelight. But she could see nothing: she was blind for tears.
She could hardly be stretching out her arms, for she had
both hands to her handkerchief on her eyes. He said something: it was no word of love or she would have held it!
it began with: 'Well, I must be ...' He was silent for a
long time: she imagined herself to feel great waves coming from him to her. But he wasn't in the room. ...
 The rest, till that moment at the War Office, had been
pure agony, and unrelenting. Her mother's paper cut down
her money; no orders for serials came in: her mother,
obviously, was failing. The eternal diatribes of her brother
were like lashes upon her skin. He seemed to be praying
Tietjens to death. Of Tietjens she saw and heard nothing.
At the Macmasters she heard, once, that he had just
gone out. It added to her desire to scream when she saw a
newspaper. Poverty invaded them. The police raided the
house in search of her brother and his friends. Then her
brother went to prison: somewhere in the Midlands. The
friendliness of their former neighbours turned to surly
suspicion. They could get no milk. Food became almost
unprocurable without going to long distances. For three
days Mrs Wannop was clean out of her mind. Then she
grew better and began to write a new book. It promised
to be rather good. But there was no publisher. Edward

came out of prison, full of good-humour and boisterous-
ness. They seemed to have had a great deal to drink in
prison. But, hearing that his mother had gone mad over
that disgrace, after a terrible scene with Valentine, in
which he accused her of being the mistress of Tietjens
and therefore militarist, he consented to let his mother use
her influence—of which she had still some—to get him
appointed as an A.B. on a mine-sweeper. Great winds became an agony to Valentine Wannop in addition to the
unbearable sounds of firing that came continuously over
the sea. Her mother grew much better: she took pride in
having a son in a Service. She was then the more able to
appreciate the fact that her paper stopped payment altogether. A small mob on the fifth of November burned
Mrs Wannop in effigy in front of their cottage and broke
their lower windows. Mrs Wannop ran out and in the
illumination of the fire knocked down two farm labourer
hobbledehoys. It was terrible to see Mrs Wannop's grey
hair in the firelight. After that the butcher refused them
meat altogether, ration card or no ration card. It was
imperative that they should move to London.

The marsh horizon became obscured with giant stilts:
the air above it filled with aeroplanes: the roads covered
with military cars. There was then no getting away from
the sounds of the war.

Just as they had decided to move Tietjens came back.
It was for a moment heaven to have him in this country.
But when, a month later, Valentine Wannop saw him for a
minute, he seemed very heavy, aged and dull. It was then
almost as bad as before, for it seemed to Valentine as if he
hardly had his reason.

On hearing that Tietjens was to be quartered—or, at any
rate, occupied—in the neighbourhood of Ealing, Mrs Wannop at once took a small house in Bedford Park, whilst, to
make ends meet—for her mother made terribly little—
Valentine Wannop took a post as athletic mistress in a
great school in a not very near suburb. Thus, though Tietjens came in for a cup of tea almost every afternoon with

Mrs Wannop in the dilapidated little suburban house, Valentine Wannop hardly ever saw him. The only free afternoon she had was the Friday, and on that day she still regularly chaperoned Mrs Duchemin: meeting her at Charing Cross towards noon and taking her back to the same station in time to catch the last train to Rye. On Saturdays and Sundays she was occupied all day in typing her mother's manuscript.

Of Tietjens, then, she saw almost nothing. She knew that his poor mind was empty of facts and of names; but her mother said he was a great help to her. Once provided with facts his mind worked out sound Tory conclusions—or quite startling and attractive theories—with extreme rapidity. This Mrs Wannop found of the greatest use to her whenever—though it wasn't now very often—she had an article to write for an excitable newspaper. She still, however, contributed to her failing organ of opinion, though it paid her nothing. . . .

Mrs Duchemin, then, Valentine Wannop still chaperoned, though there was no bond any more between them. Valentine knew, for instance, perfectly well that Mrs Duchemin, after she had been seen off by train from Charing Cross, got out at Clapham Junction, took a taxi-cab back to Gray's Inn after dark and spent the night with Macmaster, and Mrs Duchemin knew quite well that Valentine knew. It was a sort of parade of circumspection and rightness, and they kept it up even after, at a sinister registry office, the wedding had taken place, Valentine being the one witness and an obscure-looking substitute for the usual pew opener another. There seemed to be, by then, no very obvious reason why Valentine should support Mrs Macmaster any more on these rather dreary occasions, but Mrs Macmaster said she might just as well, until they saw fit to make the marriage public. There were, Mrs Macmaster said, censorious tongues, and even if these were confuted afterwards it is difficult, if not impossible, to outrun scandal. Besides, Mrs Macmaster was of opinion that the Macmaster afternoons with these geniuses must be a liberal education for Valentine. But, as Valentine sat most of the time at the tea-table near the door, it was the backs and side faces of the distinguished rather than their intellects with which she was most acquainted. Occasionally, however, Mrs Duchemin would show Valentine, as an enormous privilege, one of the letters to herself from men of genius: usually North British, written, as a rule, from the Continent or more distant and peaceful climates, for most of them believed it their duty in these hideous times to keep alive in the world the only glimmering spark of beauty. Couched in terms so eulogistic as to resemble those used in passionate love-letters by men more profane, these epistles recounted, or consulted Mrs Duchemin as to, their love affairs with foreign princesses, the progress of their ailments or the progresses of their souls towards those higher regions of morality in which floated their so beautiful-souled correspondent.

The letters entertained Valentine and, indeed, she was entertained by that whole mirage. It was only the Macmasters' treatment of her mother that finally decided Valentine that this friendship had died; for the friendships of women are very tenacious things, surviving astonishing disillusionments, and Valentine Wannop was a woman of more than usual loyalty. Indeed, if she couldn't respect Mrs Duchemin on the old grounds, she could very really respect her for her tenacity of purpose, her determination to advance Macmaster and for the sort of ruthlessness that she put into these pursuits.

Valentine's affection had, indeed, survived even Edith Ethel's continued denigrations of Tietjens—for Edith Ethel regarded Tietjens as a clog round her husband's neck, if only because he was a very unpopular man, grown personally rather unpresentable and always extremely rude to the geniuses on Fridays. Edith Ethel, however, never made these complaints that grew more and more frequent as more and more the distinguished flocked to the Fridays, before Macmaster. And they ceased very suddenly and in a way that struck Valentine as odd.

Mrs Duchemin's grievance against Tietjens was that, Macmaster being a weak man, Tietjens had acted as his banker until, what with interest and the rest of it, Macmaster owed Tietjens a great sum: several thousand pounds. And there had been no real reason: Macmaster had spent most of the money either on costly furnishings for his rooms or on his costly journeys to Rye. On the one hand Mrs Duchemin could have found Macmaster all the bric-à-brac he could possibly have wanted from amongst the things at the rectory, where no one would have missed them and, on the other, she, Mrs Duchemin, would have paid all Macmaster's travelling expenses. She had had unlimited money from her husband, who never asked for accounts. But, whilst Tietjens still had influence with Macmaster, he had used it uncompromisingly against this course, giving him the delusion—it enraged Mrs Duchemin to think!—that it would have been dishonourable. So that Macmaster had continued to draw upon him.

And, most enraging of all, at a period when she had had a power of attorney over all Mr Duchemin's fortune and could, perfectly easily, have sold out something that no one would have missed for the couple of thousand or so that Macmaster owed, Tietjens had very forcibly refused to allow Macmaster to agree to anything of the sort. He had again put into Macmaster's weak head that it would be dishonourable. But Mrs Duchemin—and she closed her lips determinedly after she had said it—knew perfectly well Tietjens' motive. So long as Macmaster owed him money he imagined that they couldn't close their doors upon him. And their establishment was beginning to be a place where you met people of great influence who might well get for a person as lazy as Tietjens a sinecure that would suit him. Tietjens, in fact, knew which side his bread was buttered.

For what, Mrs Duchemin asked, could there have been dishonourable about the arrangements she had proposed? Practically the whole of Mr Duchemin's money was to come to her: he was by then insane; it was therefore,

morally, her own. But immediately after that, Mr Duchemin having been certified, the estate had fallen into the
hands of the Lunacy Commissioners and there had been no
further hope of taking the capital. Now, her husband
being dead, it was in the hands of trustees, Mr Duchemin
having left the whole of his property to Magdalen College
and merely the income to his widow. The income was very
large; but where, with their expenses, with the death
duties and taxation, which were by then merciless, was
Mrs. Duchemin to find the money? She was to be allowed,
under her husband's will, enough capital to buy a pleasant
little place in Surrey, with rather a nice lot of land—
enough to let Macmaster know some of the leisures of a
country gentleman's lot. They were going in for Short-
horns, and there was enough land to give them a small
golf-course and, in the autumn, a little—oh, mostly rough!
—shooting for Macmaster to bring his friends down to. It
would just run to that. Oh, no ostentation. Merely a nice
little place. As an amusing detail the villagers there already
called Macmaster 'squire' and the women curtsied to him.
But Valentine Wannop would understand that, with all
these expenses, they couldn't find the money to pay off
Tietjens. Besides, Mrs Macmaster said she wasn't going to
pay off Tietjens. He had had his chance once: now he
could go without, for her. Macmaster would have to pay
it himself, and he would never be able to, his contribu-
tion to their housekeeping being what it was. And there
were going to be complications. Macmaster wondered
about their little place in Surrey, saying that he would
consult Tietjens about this and that alteration. But over
the doorsill of that place the foot of Tietjens was never
going to go! Never! It would mean a good deal of unpleasantness; or rather it would mean one sharp:
'C-r-r-unch!' And then: Napoo finny! Mrs Duchemin
sometimes, and with great effect, condescended to use one
of the more picturesque phrases of the day.

   To all these diatribes Valentine Wannop answered
hardly anything. It was no particular concern of hers; even

if, for a moment, she felt proprietarily towards Christopher as she did now and then, she felt no particular desire that his intimacy with the Macmasters should be prolonged, because she knew he could have no particular desire for its prolongation. She imagined him turning them down with an unspoken and good-humoured gibe. And, indeed, she agreed on the whole with Edith Ethel. It *was* demoralising for a weak little man like Vincent to have a friend with an ever-open purse beside him. Tietjens ought not to have been princely: it was a defect, a quality that she did not personally admire in him. As to whether it would or wouldn't have been dishonourable for Mrs Duchemin to take her husband's money and give it to Macmaster, she kept an open mind. To all intents and purposes the money was Mrs Duchemin's, and if Mrs Duchemin had then paid Christopher off it would have been sensible. She could see that later it had become very inconvenient. There were, however, male standards to be considered, and Macmaster, at least, passed for a man. Tietjens, who was wise enough in the affairs of others, had, in that, probably been wise; for there might have been great disagreeablenesses with trustees and heirs-in-law had Mrs Duchemin's subtraction of a couple of thousand pounds from the Duchemin estate afterwards come to light. The Wannops had never been large property owners as a family, but Valentine had heard enough of collateral wranglings over small family dishonesties to know how very disagreeable these could be.

So she had made little or no comment; sometimes she had even faintly agreed as to the demoralisation of Macmaster, and that had sufficed. For Mrs Duchemin had been certain of her rightness and cared nothing at all for the opinion of Valentine Wannop, or else took it for granted.

And when Tietjens had gone to France for a little time Mrs Duchemin seemed to forget the matter, contenting herself with saying that he might very likely not come back. He was the sort of clumsy man who generally got killed. In that case, since no I.O.U.s or paper had passed, Mrs Tietjens would have no claim. So that would be all right.

But two days after the return of Christopher—and that was how Valentine knew he had come back!—Mrs Duchemin with a lowering brow exclaimed:

'That oaf, Tietjens, is in England, perfectly safe and sound. And now the whole miserable business of Vincent's indebtedness . . . Oh!'

She had stopped so suddenly and so markedly that even the stoppage of Valentine's own heart couldn't conceal the oddness from her. Indeed it was as if there were an interval before she completely realised what the news was and as if, during that interval, she said to herself:

'It's very queer. It's exactly as if Edith Ethel has stopped abusing him on my account . . . As if she *knew*!' But how could Edith Ethel know that she loved the man who had returned? It was impossible! She hardly knew herself. Then the great wave of relief rolled over her: he was in England. One day she would see him, there: in the great room. For these colloquies with Edith Ethel always took place in the great room where she had last seen Tietjens. It looked suddenly beautiful, and she was resigned to sitting there, waiting for the distinguished.

It was indeed a beautiful room: it had become so during the years. It was long and high—matching the Tietjens'. A great cut-glass chandelier from the rectory hung dimly coruscating in the centre, reflected and re-reflected in convex gilt mirrors, topped by eagles. A great number of books had gone to make place on the white panelled walls for the mirrors, and for the fair orange and brown pictures by Turner, also from the rectory. From the rectory had come the immense scarlet and lapis lazuli carpet, the great brass fire-basket and appendages, the great curtains that, in the three long windows, on their peacock-blue Chinese silk showed parti-coloured cranes ascending in long flights—and all the polished Chippendale arm-chairs. Amongst all these, gracious, trailing, stopping with a tender

gesture to rearrange very slightly the crimson roses in the
famous silver bowls, still in dark blue silks, with an amber
necklace and her elaborate black hair, waved exactly like
that of Julia Domna in the Musée Lapidaire at Arles,
moved Mrs Macmaster—also from the rectory. Macmaster had achieved his desire: even to the shortbread
cakes and the peculiarly scented tea that came every Friday morning from Princes Street. And, if Mrs Macmaster
hadn't the pawky, relishing humour of the great Scots
ladies of past days, she had in exchange her deep aspect
of comprehension and tenderness. An astonishingly
beautiful and impressive woman: dark hair; dark, straight
eyebrows; a straight nose; dark blue eyes in the shadows
of her hair and bowed, pomegranate lips in a chin curved
like the bow of a Greek boat. . . .

The etiquette of the place on Fridays was regulated as
if by a royal protocol. The most distinguished and, if possible, titled person was led to a great walnut wood fluted
chair that stood askew by the fire-place, its back and seat
of blue velvet, heaven knows how old. Over him would
hover Mrs Duchemin: or, if he were *very* distinguished,
both Mr and Mrs Macmaster. The not so distinguished
were led up by turns to be presented to the celebrity and
would then arrange themselves in a half-circle in the
beautiful arm-chairs; the less distinguished still, in outer
groups in chairs that had no arms; the almost undis-
tinguished stood, also in groups, or languished, awe-struck,
on the scarlet leather window seats. When all were there
Macmaster would establish himself on the incredibly
unique hearthrug and would address wise sayings to the
celebrity; occasionally, however, saying a kind thing to the
youngest man present—to give him a chance of distin-
guishing himself. Macmaster's hair, at that date, was still
black, but not quite so stiff or so well brushed; his beard
had in it greyish streaks, and his teeth, not being quite
so white, looked less strong. He wore also a single eyeglass, the retaining of which in his right eye gave him a
slightly agonised expression. It gave him, however, the

privilege of putting his face very close to the face of anyone upon whom he wished to make a deep impression. He
had lately become much interested in the drama, so that
there were usually several large—and, of course, very
reputable and serious—actresses in the room. On rare
occasions Mrs Duchemin would say across the room in
her deep voice:

'Valentine, a cup of tea for his highness,' or 'Sir
Thomas,' as the case might be, and when Valentine had
threaded her way through the chairs with a cup of tea,
Mrs Duchemin, with a kind, aloof smile, would say:
'Your highness, this is my little brown bird.' But as a rule
Valentine sat alone at the tea-table, the guests fetching
from her what they wanted.

Tietjens came to the Fridays twice during the five
months of his stay at Ealing. On each occasion he accompanied Mrs Wannop.

In earlier days—during the earliest Fridays—Mrs Wannop, if she ever came, had always been installed, with her
flowing black, in the throne and, like an enlarged Queen
Victoria, had sat there whilst suppliants were led up to this
great writer. But now: on the first occasion Mrs Wannop
got a chair without arms in the outer ring, whilst a general
officer commanding lately in chief somewhere in the East
whose military success had not been considered, but whose
despatches were considered very literary, occupied, rather
blazingly, the throne. But Mrs Wannop had chatted very
contentedly all the afternoon with Tietjens, and it had
been comforting to Valentine to see Tietjens' large, un-
couth, but quite collected figure, and to observe the affection that these two had for each other.

But, on the second occasion, the throne was occupied
by a very young woman who talked a great deal and with
great assurance. Valentine didn't know who she was. Mrs
Wannop, very gay and distracted, stood nearly the whole
afternoon by a window. And even at that, Valentine was
contented, quite a number of young men crowding round

the old lady and leaving the younger one's circle rather
bare.

There came in a very tall, clean-run and beautiful, fair
woman, dressed in nothing in particular. She stood with
extreme—with noticeable—unconcern near the doorway.
She let her eyes rest on Valentine, but looked away before
Valentine could speak. She must have had an enormous
quantity of fair tawny hair, for it was coiled in a great
surface over her ears. She had in her hand several visiting
cards which she looked at with a puzzled expression and
then laid on a card table. She was no one who had ever
been there before.

Edith Ethel—it was for the second time!—had just
broken up the ring that surrounded Mrs Wannop, bearing
the young men tributary to the young woman in the walnut chair and leaving Tietjens and the older woman high
and dry in a window: thus Tietjens saw the stranger, and
there was no doubt left in Valentine's mind. He came,
diagonally, right down the room to his wife and marched
her straight up to Edith Ethel. His face was perfectly
without expression.

Macmaster, perched on the centre of the hearthrug, had
an emotion that was extraordinarily comic to witness, but
that Valentine was quite unable to analyse. He jumped two
paces forward to meet Mrs Tietjens, held out a little hand,
half withdrew it, retreated half a step. The eyeglass fell
from his perturbed eye: this gave him actually an expression less perturbed, but, in revenge, the hairs on the back
of his scalp grew suddenly untidy. Sylvia, wavering along
beside her husband, held out her long arm and careless
hand. Macmaster winced almost at the contact, as if his
fingers had been pinched in a vice. Sylvia wavered desultorily towards Edith Ethel, who was suddenly small,
insignificant and relatively coarse. As for the young woman
celebrity in the arm-chair, she appeared to be about the
size of a white rabbit.

A complete silence had fallen on the room. Every
woman in it was counting the pleats of Sylvia's skirt and

the amount of material in it. Valentine Wannop knew that because she was doing it herself. If one had that amount of material and that number of pleats one's skirt might hang like that. . . . For it was extraordinary: it fitted close round the hips, and gave an effect of length and swing—yet it did not descend as low as the ankles. It was, no doubt, the amount of material that did that, like the Highlander's kilt that takes twelve yards to make. And from the silence Valentine could tell that every woman and most of the men—if they didn't know that this was Mrs Christopher Tietjens—knew that this was a personage of *Illustrated Weekly*, as who should say of county family, rank. Little Mrs Swan, lately married, actually got up, crossed the room and sat down beside her bridegroom. It was a movement with which Valentine could sympathize.

And Sylvia, having just faintly greeted Mrs Duchemin. and completely ignored the celebrity in the arm-chair—in spite of the fact that Mrs Duchemin had tried half-heartedly to effect an introduction—stood still, looking round her. She gave the effect of a lady in a nurseryman's hothouse considering what flower should interest her, collectively ignoring the nurserymen who bowed round her. She had just dropped her eyelashes, twice, in recognition of two small staff officers with a good deal of scarlet streak about them who were tentatively rising from their chairs. The staff officers who came to the Tietjens were not of the first vintages; still they had the labels and passed as such.

Valentine was by that time beside her mother, who had been standing all alone between two windows. She had dispossessed, in hot indignation, a stout musical critic of his chair and had sat her mother in it. And, just as Mrs Duchemin's deep voice sounded, yet a little waveringly:

'Valentine . . . a cup of tea for . . .' Valentine was carrying a cup of tea to her mother.

Her indignation had conquered her despairing jealousy, if you could call it jealousy. For what was the good of living or loving when Tietjens had beside him, for ever, the radiant, kind and gracious perfection. On the other hand, of her two deep passions, the second was for her mother.

Rightly or wrongly, Valentine regarded Mrs Wannop as a great, an august figure: a great brain, a high and generous intelligence. She had written, at least, one great book, and if the rest of her time had been frittered away in the desperate struggle to live that had taken both their lives, that could not detract from that one achievement that should last and for ever take her mother's name down time. That this greatness should not weigh with the Macmasters had hitherto neither astonished nor irritated Valentine. The Macmasters had their game to play and, for the matter of that, they had their predilections. Their game kept them amongst the officially influential, the semi-official and the officially accredited. They moved with such C.B.s, knights, presidents and the rest as dabbled in writing or the arts: they went upwards with such reviewers, art critics, musical writers and archaeologists as had posts in, if possible, first-class public offices or permanent positions on the more august periodicals. If an imaginative author seemed assured of position and lasting popularity Macmaster would send out feelers towards him, would make himself dumbly useful, and sooner or later either Mrs Duchemin would be carrying on with him one of her high-souled correspondences—or she wouldn't.

Mrs Wannop they had formerly accepted as permanent leader writer and chief critic of a great organ, but the great organ having dwindled and now disappeared the Macmasters no longer wanted her at their parties. That was the game—and Valentine accepted it. But that it should have been with such insolence, so obviously meant to be noted—for in twice breaking up Mrs Wannop's little circle Mrs Duchemin had not even once so much as said: 'How d'ye do?' to the elder lady!—that was almost more than Valentine could, for the moment, bear, and she would have taken her mother away at once and would never have re-entered the house, but for the compensations.

Her mother had lately written and even found a publisher for a book—and the book had showed no signs of failing powers. On the contrary, having been perforce stopped off the perpetual journalism that had dissipated her energies, Mrs Wannop had turned out something that Valentine knew was sound, sane and well done. Abstractions of failing attention to the outside world are not necessarily in a writer signs of failing, as a writer. It may mean merely that she is giving so much thought to her work that her outside contacts suffer. If that is the case her work will gain. That this might be the case with her mother was Valentine's great and secret hope. Her mother was barely sixty: many great works have been written by writers aged between sixty and seventy. . . .

And the crowding of youngish men round the old lady had given Valentine a little confirmation of that hope. The book naturally, in the maelstrom flux and reflux of the time, had attracted no attention, and poor Mrs Wannop had not succeeded in extracting a penny for it from her adamantine publisher: she hadn't, indeed, made a penny for several months, and they existed almost at starvation point in their little den of a villa—on Valentine's earnings as athletic teacher. . . . But that little bit of attention in that semi-public place had seemed, at least, as a confirmation to Valentine: there probably was something sound, sane and well done in her mother's work. That was almost all she asked of life.

And, indeed, while she stood by her mother's chair, thinking with a little bitter pathos that if Edith Ethel had left the three or four young men to her mother the three or four might have done her poor mother a little good, with innocent puffs and the like—and heaven knew they needed that little good badly enough!—a very thin and untidy young man *did* drift back to Mrs Wannop and asked, precisely, if he might make a note or two for publication as to what Mrs Wannop was doing. 'Her book,' he said, 'had attracted so much attention. They hadn't known that they had still writers among them. . . .'

A singular, triangular drive had begun through the chairs from the fireplace. That was how it had seemed to Valentine! Mrs Tietjens had looked at them, had asked Christopher a question and, immediately, as if she were coming through waist-high surf, had borne down Macmaster and Mrs Duchemin, flanking her obsequiously, setting aside chairs and their occupants, Tietjens and the two, rather bashfully following staff officers, broadening out the wedge.

Sylvia, her long arm held out from a yard or so away, was stretching out her hand to Valentine's mother. With her clear, high, unembarrassed voice she exclaimed, also from a yard or so away, so as to be heard by everyone in the room:

'You're Mrs Wannop. The great writer. I'm Christopher Tietjens' wife.'

The old lady, with her dim eyes, looked up at the younger woman towering above her.

'You're Christopher's wife!' she said. 'I must kiss you for all the kindness he has shown me.'

Valentine felt her eyes filling with tears. She saw her mother stand up, place both her hands on the other woman's shoulders. She heard her mother say:

'You're a most beautiful creature. I'm sure you're good!'

Sylvia stood, smiling faintly, bending a little to accept the embrace. Behind the Macmasters, Tietjens and the staff officers, a little crowd of goggle eyes had ranged itself.

Valentine was crying. She slipped back behind the tea-urns, though she could hardly feel the way. Beautiful! The most beautiful woman she had ever seen! And good! Kind! You could see it in the lovely way she had given her cheek to that poor old woman's lips.... And to live all day, for ever, beside him...she, Valentine, ought to be ready to lay down her life for Sylvia Tietjens....

The voice of Tietjens said, just above her head:

'Your mother seems to be having a regular triumph,' and, with his good-natured cynicism, he added, 'it seems to have upset some apple-carts!' They were confronted with the spectacle of Macmaster conducting the young celebrity from her deserted arm-chair across the room to be lost in the horseshoe of crowd that surrounded Mrs Wannop.

Valentine said:

'You're quite gay to-day. Your voice is different. I suppose you're better?' She did not look at him. His voice came:

'Yes! I'm relatively gay!' It went on: 'I thought you might like to know. A little of my mathematical brain seems to have come to life again. I've worked out two or three silly problems. . . .'

She said:

'Mrs Tietjens will be pleased.'

'Oh!' the answer came. 'Mathematics don't interest her any more than cock-fighting.' With immense swiftness, between word and word, Valentine read into that a hope! This splendid creature did not sympathise with her husband's activities. But he crushed it heavily by saying: 'Why should she? She's so many occupations of her own that she's unrivalled at!'

He began to tell her, rather minutely, of a calculation he had made only that day at lunch. He had gone into the Department of Statistics and had had rather a row with Lord Ingleby of Lincoln. A pretty title the fellow had taken! They had wanted him to ask to be seconded to his old department for a certain job. But he had said he'd be damned if he would. He detested and despised the work they were doing.

Valentine, for the first time in her life, hardly listened to what he said. Did the fact that Sylvia Tietjens had so many occupations of her own mean that Tietjens found her unsympathetic? Of their relationships she knew nothing. Sylvia had been so much of a mystery as hardly to exist as a problem hitherto. Macmaster, Valentine knew, hated her. She knew that through Mrs Duchemin; she had heard it ages ago, but she didn't know why. She had never come to the Macmasters' afternoons; but that was natural. Macmaster passed for a bachelor, and it was excusable for a young woman of the highest fashion not to come to bachelor teas of literary and artistic people. On the other hand, Macmaster dined at the Tietjens' quite often enough to make it public that he was a friend of that family. Sylvia, too, had never come down to see Mrs Wannop. But then it would, in the old days, have been a long way to come for a lady of fashion with no especial literary interests. And no one, in mercy, could have been expected to call on poor them in their dog-kennel in an outer suburb. They had had to sell almost all their pretty things.

Tietjens was saying that after his tempestuous interview with Lord Ingleby of Lincoln—she wished he would not be so rude to powerful people!—he had dropped in on Macmaster in his private room, and finding him puzzled over a lot of figures had, in the merest spirit of bravado, taken Macmaster and his papers out to lunch. And, he said, chancing to look, without any hope at all, at the figures, he had suddenly worked out an ingenious mystification. It had just come!

His voice had been so gay and triumphant that she hadn't been able to resist looking up at him. His cheeks were fresh coloured, his hair shining; his blue eyes had a little of their old arrogance—and tenderness! Her heart seemed to sing with joy! He was, she felt, her man. She imagined the arms of his mind stretching out to enfold her.

He went on explaining. He had rather, in his recovered self-confidence, gibed at Macmaster. Between themselves, wasn't it easy to do what the Department, under orders, wanted done? They had wanted to rub into our allies that their losses by devastation had been nothing to write home about—so as to avoid sending reinforcements to their lines! Well, if you took just the bricks and mortar of the devastated districts, you could prove that the loss in bricks, tiles, woodwork, and the rest didn't—and the figures with a little manipulation would prove it!—amount to more than a normal year's dilapidations spread over the whole country in peace time. . . . House repairs in a normal year had cost several million sterling. The enemy had only destroyed just about so many million sterling in bricks and mortar. And what was a mere year's dilapidations in house property! You just neglected to do them and did them next year.

So, if you ignored the lost harvests of three years, the lost industrial output of the richest industrial region of the country, the smashed machinery, the barked fruit trees, the three years' loss of four and a half-tenths of the coal output for three years—and the loss of life!—we could go to our allies and say:

'All your yappings about losses are the merest bulls. You can perfectly well afford to reinforce the weak places of your own lines. We intend to send our new troops to the Near East, where lies our true interest!' And, though they might sooner or later point out the fallacy, you would by so much have put off the abhorrent expedient of a single command.

Valentine, though it took her away from her own thoughts, couldn't help saying:

'But weren't you arguing about your own convictions?'

He said:

'Yes, of course I was. In the lightness of my heart! It's always a good thing to formulate the other fellow's objections.'

She had turned half round in her chair. They were gazing into each other's eyes, he from above, she from below. She had no doubt of his love: he, she knew, could have no doubt of hers. She said:

'But isn't it dangerous? To show these people how to do it?'

He said:

'Oh, no, no. No! You don't know what a good soul little Vinnie is. I don't think you've ever been quite just to Vincent Macmaster! He'd as soon think of picking my pocket as of picking my brains. The soul of honour!'

Valentine had felt a queer, queer sensation. She was not

sure afterwards whether she had felt it before she had
realized that Sylvia Tietjens was looking at them. She stood
there, very erect, a queer smile on her face. Valentine
could not be sure whether it was kind, cruel, or merely
distantly ironic; but she was perfectly sure it showed, whatever was behind it, that its wearer knew all that there was
to know of her, Valentine's, feelings for Tietjens and for
Tietjens' feelings for her. . . . It was like being a woman
and man in adultery in Trafalgar Square.

Behind Sylvia's back, their mouths agape, were the two
staff officers. Their dark hairs were too untidy for them to
amount to much, but, such as they were, they were the
two most presentable males of the assembly—and Sylvia
had snaffled them.

Mrs Tietjens said:

'Oh, Christopher! I'm going on to the Basils'.'

Tietjens said:

'All right. I'll pop Mrs Wannop into the tube as soon as
she's had enough of it, and come along and pick you up!'

Sylvia had just drooped her long eyelashes, in sign of
salutation, to Valentine Wannop, and had drifted through
the door, followed by her rather unmilitary military escort
in khaki and scarlet.

From that moment Valentine Wannop never had any
doubt. She knew that Sylvia Tietjens knew that her husband loved her, Valentine Wannop, and that she, Valentine
Wannop, loved her husband—with a passion absolute and
ineffable. The one thing she, Valentine, didn't know, the
one mystery that remained impenetrable, was whether
Sylvia Tietjens was good to her husband!

A long time afterwards Edith Ethel had come to her
beside the tea-cups and had apologized for not having
known, earlier than Sylvia's demonstration, that Mrs
Wannop was in the room. She hoped that they might see
Mrs Wannop much more often. She added after a moment
that she hoped Mrs Wannop wouldn't, in future, find it
necessary to come under the escort of Mr Tietjens. They
were too old friends for that, surely.

Valentine said:

'Look here, Ethel, if you think that you can keep friends with mother and turn on Mr Tietjens after all he's done for you, you're mistaken. You are really. And mother's a great deal of influence. I don't want to see you making any mistakes: just at this juncture. It's a mistake to make nasty rows. And you'd make a very nasty one if you said anything against Mr Tietjens to mother. She knows a great deal. Remember. She lived next door to the rectory for a number of years. And she's got a dreadfully incisive tongue. . . .'

Edith Ethel coiled back on her feet as if her whole body were threaded by a steel spring. Her mouth opened, but she bit her lower lip and then wiped it with a very white handkerchief. She said:

'I hate that man! I detest that man! I shudder when he comes near me.'

'I know you do!' Valentine Wannop answered. 'But I wouldn't let other people know it if I were you. It doesn't do you any real credit. He's a good man.'

Edith Ethel looked at her with a long, calculating glance. Then she went to stand before the fireplace.

That had been five—or at most six—Fridays before Valentine sat with Mark Tietjens in the War Office waiting-hall, and, on the Friday immediately before that again, all the guests being gone, Edith Ethel had come to the tea-table and, with her velvet kindness, had placed her right hand on Valentine's left. Admiring the gesture with a deep fervour, Valentine knew that that was the end.

Three days before, on the Monday, Valentine, in her school uniform, in a great store to which she had gone to buy athletic paraphernalia, had run into Mrs Duchemin, who was buying flowers. Mrs Duchemin had been horribly distressed to observe the costume. She had said:

'But do you go *about* in that? It's really dreadful.'

Valentine had answered:

'Oh, yes. When I'm doing business for the school in school hours I'm expected to wear it. And I wear it if I'm going anywhere in a hurry after school hours. It saves my dresses. I haven't got too many.'

'But *any* one might meet you,' Edith Ethel said in a note of agony. 'It's very inconsiderate. Don't you *think* you've been very inconsiderate? You might meet any of the people who come to our Fridays!'

'I frequently do,' Valentine said. 'But they don't seem to mind. Perhaps they think I'm a Waac officer. That would be quite respectable. . . .'

Mrs Duchemin drifted away, her arms full of flowers and real agony upon her face.

Now, beside the tea-table she said, very softly:

'My dear, we've decided not to have our usual Friday afternoon next week.' Valentine wondered whether this was merely a lie to get rid of her. But Edith Ethel went on: 'We've decided to have a little evening festivity. After a great deal of thought we've come to the conclusion that we ought, now, to make our union public.' She paused to await comment, but Valentine making none she went on: 'It coincides very happily—I can't help feeling it coincides very happily!—with another event. Not that *we* set much store by these things. . . . But it has been whispered to Vincent that next Friday. . . . Perhaps, my dear Valentine, you, too, will have heard . . .'

Valentine said:

'No, I haven't. I suppose he's got the O.B.E. I'm very glad.'

'The Sovereign,' Mrs Duchemin said, 'is seeing fit to confer the honour of knighthood on him.'

'Well!' Valentine said. 'He's had a quick career. I've no doubt he deserves it. He's worked very hard. I do sincerely congratulate you. It'll be a great help to you.'

'It's,' Mrs Duchemin said, 'not for mere plodding. That's what makes it so gratifying. It's for a special piece of brilliance, that has marked him out. It's, of course, a secret. But . . .'

'Oh, I know!' Valentine said. 'He's worked out some calculations to prove that losses in the devastated districts, if you ignore machinery, coal output, orchard trees, harvests, industrial products, and so on, don't amount to more than a year's household dilapidations for the . . .'

Mrs Duchemin said with real horror:

'But how did you know? How on *earth* did you know? . . .' She paused. 'It's such a *dead* secret. . . . That fellow must have told you. . . . But how on earth could *he* know?'

'I haven't seen Mr Tietjens to speak to since the last time he was here,' Valentine said. She saw, from Edith Ethel's bewilderment, the whole situation. The miserable Macmaster hadn't even confided to his wife that the practically stolen figures weren't his own. He desired to have a little prestige in the family circle; for once a little prestige! Well! Why shouldn't he have it? Tietjens, she knew, would wish him to have all he could get. She said therefore:

'Oh, it's probably in the air. . . . It's known the Government want to break their claims to the higher command. And anyone who could help them to that would get a knighthood. . . .'

Mrs Duchemin was more calm.

'It's certainly,' she said, 'Burke'd, as you call it, those beastly people.' She reflected for a moment. 'It's probably that,' she went on. 'It's in the air. Anything that can help to influence public opinion against those horrible people is to be welcomed. That's known pretty widely. . . . No! It could hardly be Christopher Tietjens who thought of it and told you. It wouldn't enter his head. He's their friend! He would be. . . .'

'He's certainly,' Valentine said, 'not a friend of his country's enemies. I'm not, myself.'

Mrs Duchemin exclaimed sharply, her eyes dilated.

'What do you mean? What on earth do you dare to mean? I thought you were a pro-German!'

Valentine said:

'I'm not! I'm not! . . . I hate men's deaths. . . . I hate any men's deaths. . . . Any men. . . .' She calmed herself by

main force. 'Mr Tietjens says that the more we hinder our
allies the more we drag the war on and the more lives are
lost. . . . More lives, do you understand? . . .'

Mrs Duchemin assumed her most aloof, tender, and high
air: 'My poor child,' she said, 'what possible concern can
the opinions of that broken fellow cause anyone! You can
warn him from me that he does himself no good by going
on uttering these discredited opinions. He's a marked man.
Finished! It's no good Guggums, my husband, trying to
stand up for him.'

'He *does* stand up for him?' Valentine asked. 'Though
I don't see why it's needed. Mr Tietjens is surely able to
take care of himself.'

'My good child,' Edith Ethel said, 'you may as well
know the worst. There's not a more discredited man in
London than Christopher Tietjens, and my husband does
himself infinite harm in standing up for him. It's our one
quarrel.'

She went on again:

'It was all very well whilst that fellow had brains. He was
said to have some intellect, though I could never see it.
But now that, with his drunkenness and debaucheries, he
has got himself into the state he is in; for there's no other
way of accounting for his condition! They're striking him,
I don't mind telling you, off the roll of his office. . . .'

It was there that, for the first time, the thought went
through Valentine Wannop's mind, like a mad inspiration:
this woman must at one time have been in love with
Tietjens. It was possible, men being what they were, that
she had even once been Tietjens' mistress. For it was impossible otherwise to account for this spite, which to Valentine seemed almost meaningless. She had, on the other
hand, no impulse to defend Tietjens against accusations
that could not have any possible grounds.

Mrs Duchemin was going on with her kind loftiness:

'Of course a fellow like that—in that condition!—could
not understand matters of high policy. It is imperative that
these fellows should not have the higher command. It

would pander to their insane spirit of militarism. They *must* be hindered. I'm talking, of course, between ourselves, but my husband says that that is the conviction in the very highest circles. To let them have their way, even if it led to earlier success, would be to establish a precedent —so my husband says!—compared with which the loss of a few lives. . . .'

Valentine sprang up, her face distorted.

'For the sake of Christ,' she cried out, 'as you believe that Christ died for you, try to understand that millions of men's lives are at stake. . . .'

Mrs Duchemin smiled.

'My poor child,' she said, 'if you moved in the higher circles you would look at these things with more aloofness. . . .'

Valentine leant on the back of a high chair for support.

'You don't move in the higher circles,' she said. 'For Heaven's sake—for your own—remember that you are a woman, not for ever and for always a snob. You were a good woman once. You stuck to your husband for quite a long time. . . .'

Mrs Duchemin, in her chair, had thrown herself back.

'My good girl,' she said, 'have you gone mad?'

Valentine said:

'Yes, very nearly. I've got a brother at sea; I've had a man I loved out there for an infinite time. You can understand that, I suppose, even if you can't understand how one can go mad merely at the thoughts of suffering at all. . . . And I know, Edith Ethel, that you are afraid of my opinion of you, or you wouldn't have put up all the subterfuges and concealments of all these years. . . .'

Mrs Duchemin said quickly:

'Oh, my good girl. . . . If you've got personal interests at stake you can't be expected to take abstract views of the higher matters. We had better change the subject.'

Valentine said:

'Yes, do. Get on with your excuses for not asking me and mother to your knighthood party.'

Mrs Duchemin, too, rose at that. She felt at her amber beads with long fingers that turned very slightly at the tips. She had behind her all her mirrors, the drops of her lustres, shining points of gilt and of the polish of dark woods. Valentine thought that she had never seen anyone so absolutely impersonate kindness, tenderness, and dignity. She said:

'My dear, I was going to suggest that it was the sort of party to which you might not care to come. . . . The people will be stiff and formal and you probably haven't got a frock.'

Valentine said:

'Oh, I've got a frock all right. But there's a Jacob's ladder in my party stockings and that's the sort of ladder you can't kick down.' She couldn't help saying that.

Mrs Duchemin stood motionless and very slowly redness mounted into her face. It was most curious to see against that scarlet background the vivid white of the eyes and the dark, straight eyebrows that nearly met. And slowly again her face went perfectly white; then her dark blue eyes became marked. She seemed to wipe her long, white hands one in the other, inserting her right hand into her left and drawing it out again.

'I'm sorry,' she said in a dead voice. 'We had hoped that, if that man went to France—or if other things happened— we might have continued on the old friendly footing. But you yourself must see that, with our official position, we can't be expected to connive . . .'

Valentine said:

'I don't understand!'

'Perhaps you'd rather I didn't go on!' Mrs Duchemin retorted. 'I'd much rather not go on.'

'You'd probably better,' Valentine answered.

'We had meant,' the elder woman said, 'to have a quiet little dinner—we two and you, before the party—for auld lang syne. But that fellow has forced himself in, and you see for yourself that we can't have you as well.'

Valentine said:

'I don't see why not. I always like to see Mr Tietjens!'

Mrs Duchemin looked hard at her.

'I don't see the use,' she said, 'of your keeping on that mask. It is surely bad enough that your mother should go about with that man and that terrible scenes like that of the other Friday should occur. Mrs Tietjens was heroic; nothing less than heroic. But you have no right to subject us, your friends, to such ordeals.'

Valentine said:

'You mean . . . Mrs Christopher Tietjens. . . .'

Mrs Duchemin went on:

'My husband insists that I should ask you. But I will not. I simply will not. I invented for you the excuse of the frock. Of course we could have given you a frock if that man is so mean or so penniless as not to keep you decent. But I repeat, with our official position we cannot—we cannot; it would be madness!—connive at this intrigue. And all the more as the wife appears likely to be friendly with us. She has been once: she may well come again.' She paused and went on solemnly: 'And I warn you, if the split comes—as it must, for what woman could stand it?—it is Mrs Tietjens we shall support. She will always find a home here.'

An extraordinary picture of Sylvia Tietjens standing beside Edith Ethel and dwarfing her as a giraffe dwarfs an emu, came into Valentine's head. She said:

'Ethel! Have I gone mad? Or is it you? Upon my word I can't understand. . . .'

Mrs Duchemin exclaimed:

'For God's sake hold your tongue, you shameless thing! You've had a child by the man, haven't you?'

Valentine saw suddenly the tall silver candlesticks, the dark polished panels of the rectory, and Edith Ethel's mad face and mad hair whirling before them.

She said:

'No! I certainly haven't. Can you get that into your head? I certainly haven't.' She made a further effort over immense fatigue. 'I assure you—I beg you to believe if it

will give you any ease—that Mr Tietjens has never
addressed a word of love to me in his life. Nor have I to
him. We have hardly talked to each other in all the time we
have known each other.'

Mrs Duchemin said in a harsh voice:

'Seven people in the last five weeks have told me you
have had a child by that beast: he's ruined because he has
to keep you and your mother and the child. You won't
deny that he has a child somewhere hidden away? . . .'

Valentine exclaimed suddenly:

'Oh, Ethel, you mustn't . . . you *mustn't* be jealous of
me! If you only knew you wouldn't be jealous of me. . . .
I suppose the child you were going to have was by Christopher? Men are like that. . . . But not of me! You need
never, never. I've been the best friend you can ever have
had. . . .'

Mrs Duchemin exclaimed harshly, as if she were being
strangled:

'A sort of blackmail! I knew it would come to that! It
always does with your sort. Then do your damnedest, you
harlot. You never set foot in this house again! Go you and
rot. . . .' Her face suddenly expressed extreme fear and with
great swiftness she ran up the room. Immediately afterwards she was tenderly bending over a great bowl of roses
beneath the lustre. The voice of Vincent Macmaster from
the door had said:

'Come in, old man. Of course I've got ten minutes. The
book's in here somewhere. . . .'

Macmaster was beside her, rubbing his hands, bending
with his curious, rather abject manner, and surveying her
agonisedly with his eyeglass, which enormously magnified
his lashes, his red lower lid and the veins in his cornea.

'Valentine!' he said, 'my dear Valentine. . . . You've
heard? We've decided to make it public. . . . Guggums
will have invited you to our little feast. And there will be a
surprise, I believe. . . .'

Edith Ethel looked, as she bent, lamentably and sharply,
over her shoulder at Valentine.

'Yes,' she said bravely, aiming her voice at Edith Ethel, 'Ethel has invited me. I'll try to come. . . .'

'Oh, but you must,' Macmaster said, 'just you and Christopher, who've been so kind to us. For old times' sake. You could not . . .'

Christopher Tietjens was ballooning slowly from the door, his hand tentatively held out to her. As they practically never shook hands at home, it was easy to avoid his hand. She said to herself: 'Oh, how is it possible! How could he have . . .' And the terrible situation poured itself over her mind: the miserable little husband, the desperately nonchalant lover—and Edith Ethel mad with jealousy! A doomed household. She hoped Edith Ethel had seen her refuse her hand to Christopher.

But Edith Ethel, bent over her rose bowl, was burying her beautiful face in flower after flower. She was accustomed to do this for many minutes on end: she thought that, so, she resembled a picture by the subject of her husband's first little monograph. And so, Valentine thought, she did. She was trying to tell Macmaster that Friday evenings were difficult times for her to get away. But her throat ached too much. That, she knew, was her last sight of Edith Ethel, whom she had loved very much. That also, she hoped, would be her last sight of Christopher Tietjens—whom also she had loved very much. . . . He was browsing along a bookshelf, very big and very clumsy.

Macmaster pursued her into the stony hall with clamorous repetitions of his invitation. She couldn't speak. At the great iron-lined door he held her hand for an eternity, gazing lamentably, his face close up against hers. He exclaimed in accents of great fear:

'Has Guggums? . . . She *hasn't* . . .' His face, which when you saw it so closely was a little blotched, distorted itself with anxiety: he glanced aside with panic at the drawing-room door.

Valentine burst a voice through her agonised throat.

'Ethel,' she said, 'has told me she's to be Lady Mac-

master. I'm so glad. I'm so truly glad for you. You've got
what you wanted, haven't you?'

His relief let him get out distractedly, yet as if he were
too tired to be any more agitated:

'Yes! yes! ... It's, of course, a secret.... I don't want
him told till Friday next ... so as to be a sort of *bonne
bouche* ... He's practically certain to go out again on
Saturday.... They're sending out a great batch of them
... for the big push....' At that she tried to draw her
hand from his: she missed what he was saying. It was
something to the effect that he would give it all for a
happy little party. She caught the rather astonishing
words: '*Wie im alten schönen Zeit.*' She couldn't tell
whether it was his or her eyes that were full of tears. She
said:

'I believe ... I believe you're a kind man!'

In the great stone hall, hung, with long Japanese paint-
ings on silk, the electric light suddenly jumped; it was at
best a sad, brown place.

He exclaimed:

'I, too, beg you to believe that I will never abandon ...'
He glanced again at the inner door and added: 'You both
... I will never abandon .. you both!' he repeated.

He let go her hand: she was on the stone stairs in the
damp air. The great door closed irresistibly behind her,
sending a whisper of air downwards.

V

Mark Tietjens' announcement that his father had after all
carried out his long-standing promise to provide for Mrs
Wannop in such a way as to allow her to write for the rest
of her life only the more lasting kind of work, delivered
Valentine Wannop of all her problems except one. That
one loomed, naturally and immediately, immensely large.

She had passed a queer, unnatural week, the feeling
dominating its numbness having been, oddly, that she

would have nothing to do on Friday! The feeling recurred
to her whilst she was casting her eyes over a hundred girls
all in their cloth jumpers and men's black ties, aligned
upon asphalt; whilst she was jumping on trams; whilst she
was purchasing the tinned or dried fish that formed the
staple diet of herself and her mother; whilst she was
washing-up the dinner-things; upbraiding the house agent
for the state of the bath, or bending closely over the large
but merciless handwriting of the novel of her mother's
that she was typing. It came, half as a joy, half mournfully
across her familiar businesses; she felt as a man might feel
who, luxuriating in the anticipation of leisure, knew that
it was obtained by being compulsorily retired from some
laborious but engrossing job. There would be nothing to do
on Fridays!

It was, too, as if a novel had been snatched out of her
hand so that she would never know the end. Of the fairy-
tale she knew the end: the fortunate and adventurous
tailor had married his beautiful and be-princessed goose
girl, and was well on the way to burial in Westminster
Abbey—or at any rate to a memorial service, the squire
being actually buried amongst his faithful villagers. But
she would never know whether they, in the end, got together all the blue Dutch tiles they wanted to line their
bathroom. . . . She would never know. Yet witnessing
similar ambitions had made up a great deal of her life.

And, she said to herself, there was another tale ended.
On the surface the story of her love for Tietjens had been
static enough. It had begun in nothing and in nothing it
had ended. But, deep down in her being—ah! it had pro-
gressed enough. Through the agency of two women! Before the scene with Mrs Duchemin there could, she
thought, have been few young women less preoccupied
than she with the sexual substrata, either of passion or of
life. Her months as a domestic servant had accounted for
that, sex, as she had seen it from a back kitchen, having
been a repulsive affair, whilst the knowledge of its manifestations that she had thus attained had robbed it of the

mystery which caused most of the young women whom she knew to brood upon these subjects.

Her convictions as to the moral incidence of sex were, she knew, quite opportunist. Brought up amongst rather 'advanced' young people, had she been publicly challenged to pronounce her views she would probably, out of loyalty to her comrades, have declared that neither morality nor any ethical aspects were concerned in the matter. Like most of her young friends, influenced by the advanced teachers and tendential novelists of the day, she would have stated herself to advocate an—of course, enlightened!—promiscuity. That, before the revelations of Mrs Duchemin! Actually she had thought very little about the matter.

Nevertheless, even before that date, had her deeper feelings been questioned, she would have reacted with the idea that sexual incontinence was extremely ugly and chastity to be prized in the egg and spoon race that life was. She had been brought up by her father—who, perhaps, was wiser than appeared on the surface—to admire athleticism, and she was aware that proficiency of the body calls for chastity, sobriety, cleanliness and the various qualities that group themselves under the heading of abnegation. She couldn't have lived amongst the Ealing servant-class—the eldest son of the house in which she had been employed had been the defendant in a peculiarly scabrous breach of promise case, and the comments of the drunken cook on this and similar affairs had run the whole gamut from the sentimentally reticent to the extreme of coarseness according to the state of her alcoholic barometer—she couldn't then have lived among the Ealing servant-class and come to any other subliminal conclusion. So that, dividing the world into bright beings on the one hand and, on the other, into the mere stuff to fill graveyards whose actions during life couldn't matter, she had considered that the bright beings must be people whose public advocating of enlightened promiscuity went along with an absolute continence. She was aware that enlightened beings occasionally fell away from these standards in order to become

portentous Egerias; but the Mary Wollstonecrafts, the Mrs
Taylors, and the George Eliots of the last century she had
regarded humorously as rather priggish nuisances. Indeed,
being very healthy and very hard-worked, she had been in
the habit of regarding the whole matter, if not humorously,
then at least good-humouredly, as a nuisance.

But being brought right up against the sexual necessities
of a first-class Egeria had been for her a horrible affair. For
Mrs Duchemin had revealed the fact that her circumspect,
continent and suavely aesthetic personality was doubled
by another at least as coarse as, and infinitely more incisive
in expression than, that of the drunken cook. The language
that she had used about her lover—calling him always
'that oaf' or 'that beast'!—had seemed literally to pain
the girl internally, as if it had caused so many fallings
away of internal supports at each two or three words. She
had hardly been able to walk home through the darkness
from the rectory.

And she had never heard what had become of Mrs
Duchemin's baby. Next day Mrs Duchemin had been as
suave, as circumspect, and as collected as ever. Never a
word more had passed between them on the subject. This
left in Valentine Wannop's mind a dark patch—as it were
of murder—at which she must never look. And across the
darkened world of her sexual tumult there flitted continually the quick suspicion that Tietjens might have been
the lover of her friend. It was a matter of the simplest
analogy. Mrs Duchemin had appeared a bright being: so
had Tietjens. But Mrs Duchemin was a foul whore. . . .
How much more then must Tietjens, who was a man,
with the larger sexual necessities of the male . . . Her mind
always refused to complete the thought.

Its suggestion wasn't to be combated by the idea of
Vincent Macmaster himself: he was, she felt, the sort of
man that it was almost a necessity for either mistress or
comrade to betray. He seemed to ask for it. Because, she
once put it to herself, how could any woman, given the
choice and the opportunity—and God knows there was

opportunity enough—choose that shadowy, dried leaf, if there were the splendid masculinity of Tietjens in whose arms to lie. She so regarded these two men. And that shadowy conviction was at once fortified and appeased when, a little later, Mrs Duchemin herself began to apply to Tietjens the epithets of 'oaf' and 'beast'—the very ones that she had used to designate the father of her putative child!

But then Tietjens must have abandoned Mrs Duchemin; and, if he had abandoned Mrs Duchemin, he must be available for her, Valentine Wannop! The feeling, she considered, made her ignoble; but it came from depths of her being that she could not control and, existing, it soothed her. Then, with the coming of the war, the whole problem died out, and between the opening of hostilities and what she had known to be the inevitable departure of her lover, she had surrendered herself to what she thought to be the pure physical desire for him. Amongst the terrible, crashing anguishes of that time, there had been nothing for it but surrender! With the unceasing—the never ceasing—thought of suffering; with the never ceasing idea that her lover, too, must soon be so suffering, there was in the world no other refuge. No other!

She surrendered. She waited for him to speak the word, or look the look that should unite them. She was finished. Chastity: napoo finny! Like everything else!

Of the physical side of love she had neither image nor conception. In the old days when she had been with him, if he had come into the room in which she was, or if he had merely been known to be coming down to the village, she had hummed all day under her breath and had felt warmer, little currents passing along her skin. She had read somewhere that to take alcohol was to send the blood into the surface vessels of the body, thus engendering a feeling of warmth. She had never taken alcohol, or not enough to produce recognisably that effect; but she imagined that it was thus love worked upon the body—and that it would stop for ever at that!

But, in these later days, much greater convulsions had
overwhelmed her. It sufficed for Tietjens to approach her
to make her feel as if her whole body was drawn towards
him as, being near a terrible height, you are drawn towards
it. Great waves of blood rushed across her being as if
physical forces as yet undiscovered or invented attracted
the very fluid itself. The moon so draws the tides.

Once before, for a fraction of a second, after the long,
warm night of their drive, she had felt that impulsion.
Now, years after, she was to know it all the time, waking
or half waking; and it would drive her from her bed. She
would stand all night at the open window till the stars
paled above a world turned grey. It could convulse her
with joy; it could shake her with sobs and cut through her
breast like a knife.

The day of her long interview with Tietjens, amongst
the amassed beauties of Macmaster furnishings, she
marked in the calendar of her mind as her great love
scene. That had been two years ago: he had been going
into the army. Now he was going out again. From that she
knew what a love scene was. It passed without any mention of the word 'love'; it passed in impulses; warmths;
rigors of the skin. Yet with every word they had said to
each other they had confessed their love: in that way,
when you listen to the nightingale you hear the expressed
craving of your lover beating upon your heart.

Every word that he had spoken amongst the amassed
beauties of Macmaster furnishings had been a link in a
love-speech. It was not merely that he had confessed to
her as he would have to no other soul in the world—'To
no other soul in the world,' he had said!—his doubts, his
misgivings and his fears: it was that every word he uttered
and that came to her, during the lasting of that magic,
had sung of passion. If he had uttered the word 'Come' she
would have followed him to the bitter ends of the earth;
if he had said, 'There is no hope,' she would have known
the finality of despair. Having said neither, he said she
knew: 'This is our condition; so we must continue!' And

she knew, too, that he was telling her that he, like her, was ... oh, say on the side of the angels. She was then, she knew, so nicely balanced that, had he said, 'Will you to-night be my mistress?' she would have said 'Yes'; for it was as if they had been, really, at the end of the world.

But his abstention not only strengthened her in her predilection for chastity; it restored to her her image of the world as a place of virtues and endeavours. For a time at least she again hummed beneath her breath upon occasion, for it seemed as if her heart sang within her. And there was restored to her her image of her lover as a beautiful spirit. She had been able to look at him across the tea-table of their dog-kennel in Bedford Park, during the last months, almost as she had looked across the more shining table of the cottage near the rectory. The deterioration that she knew Mrs Duchemin to have worked in her mind was assuaged. It could even occur to her that Mrs Duchemin's madness had been no more than a scare to be followed by no necessary crime. Valentine Wannop had re-become her confident self in a world of at least straight problems.

But Mrs Duchemin's outbreak of a week ago had driven the old phantoms across her mind. For Mrs Duchemin she had still had a great respect. She could not regard her Edith Ethel as merely a hypocrite; or, indeed, as a hypocrite at all. There was her great achievement of making something like a man of that miserable little creature—as there had been her other great achievement of keeping her unfortunate husband for so long out of a lunatic asylum. That had been no mean feat; neither feat had been mean. And Valentine knew that Edith Ethel really loved beauty, circumspection, urbanity. It was no hypocrisy that made her advocate the Atalanta race of chastity. But, also, as Valentine Wannop saw it, humanity has these doublings of strong natures; just as the urbane and grave Spanish nation must find its outlet in the shrieking lusts of the bull-ring or the circumspect, laborious and admirable city typist must find her derivative in the cruder lusts of certain novelists, so Edith Ethel must break down into physical sexualities—and into shrieked coarseness of fishwives. How else, indeed, do we have saints? Surely, alone, by the ultimate victory of the one tendency over the other!

But now after her farewell scene with Edith Ethel a simple rearrangement of the pattern had brought many of the old doubts at least temporarily back. Valentine said to herself that, just because of the very strength of her character, Edith Ethel couldn't have been brought down to uttering her fantastic denunciation of Tietjens, the merely mad charges of debauchery and excesses and finally the sexually lunatic charge against herself, except under the sting of some such passion as jealousy. She, Valentine, couldn't arrive at any other conclusion. And, viewing the matter as she believed she now did, more composedly, she considered with seriousness that, men being what they are, her lover respecting, or despairing of, herself had relieved the grosser necessities of his being— at the expense of Mrs Duchemin, who had, no doubt, been only too ready.

And in certain moods during the past week she had accepted this suspicion; in certain other moods she had put it from her. Towards the Thursday it had no longer seemed to matter. Her lover was going from her; the long pull of the war was on; the hard necessities of life stretched out; what could an infidelity more or less matter in the long, hard thing that life is? And on the Thursday two minor, or major, worries came to disturb her level. Her brother announced himself as coming home for several days' leave, and she had the trouble of thinking that she would have forced upon her a companionship and a point of view that would be coarsely and uproariously opposed to anything that Tietjens stood for—or for which he was ready to sacrifice himself. Moreover she would have to accompany her brother to a number of riotous festivities whilst all the time she would have to think of Tietjens as getting hour by hour nearer to the horrible circumstances of troops in contact with enemy forces. In addition her

mother had received an enviably paid for commission
from one of the more excitable Sunday papers to write a
series of articles on extravagant matters connected with the
hostilities. They had wanted the money so dreadfully—
more particularly as Edward was coming home—that
Valentine Wannop had conquered her natural aversion
from the waste of time of her mother. . . . It would have
meant very little waste of time, and the £60 that it would
have brought in would have made all the difference to them
for months and months.

But Tietjens, whom Mrs Wannop had come to rely on as
her right-hand man in these matters, had, it appeared,
shown an unexpected recalcitrancy. He had, Mrs Wannop
said, hardly seemed himself and had gibed at the two first
subjects proposed—that of 'war babies' and the fact that
the Germans were reduced to eating their own corpses—as
being below the treatment of any decent pen. The illegitimacy rate, he had said, had shown very little increase; the
French-derived German word '*Kadaver*' meant bodies of
horses or cattle; *Leichnam* being the German for the
word 'corpse.' He had practically refused to have anything
to do with the affair.

As to the *Kadaver* business, Valentine agreed with him,
as to the 'war babies' she kept a more open mind. If there
weren't any war babies it couldn't, as far as she could see,
matter whether one wrote about them; it couldn't certainly
matter as much as to write about them, supposing the poor
little things to exist. She was aware that this was immoral,
but her mother needed the money desperately and her
mother came first.

There was nothing for it, therefore, but to plead with
Tietjens; for Valentine knew that without so much of
moral support from him as would be implied by a good-
natured or an enforced sanction of the article, Mrs Wannop would drop the matter and so would lose her
connection with the excitable paper which paid well. It
happened that on the Friday morning Mrs Wannop received
a request that she would write for a Swiss review a propa-

ganda article about some historical matter connected with the peace after Waterloo. The pay would be practically nothing, but the employment was at least relatively dignified, and Mrs Wannop—which was quite in the ordinary course of things!—told Valentine to ring Tietjens up and ask him for some details about the Congress of Vienna at which, before and after Waterloo, the peace terms had been wrangled out.

Valentine rang up—as she had done hundreds of times; it was to her a great satisfaction that she was going to hear Tietjens speak once more at least. The telephone was answered from the other end, and Valentine gave her two messages, the one as to the Congress of Vienna, the other as to war babies. The appalling speech came back:

'Young woman! You'd better keep off the grass. Mrs Duchemin is already my husband's mistress. You keep off.' There was about the voice no human quality; it was as if from an immense darkness the immense machine had spoken words that dealt blows. She answered; and it was as if a substratum of her mind of which she knew nothing must have been prepared for that very speech; so that it was not her own 'she' that answered levelly and coolly:

'You have probably mistaken the person you are speaking to. Perhaps you will ask Mr Tietjens to ring up Mrs Wannop when he is at liberty.'

The voice said:

'My husband will be at the War Office at 4.15. He will speak to you there—about your war babies. But I'd keep off the grass if I were you!' The receiver at the other end was hung up.

She went about her daily duties. She had heard of a kind of pine kernel that was very cheap and very nourishing, or at least very filling. They had come to it that it was a matter of pennies balanced against the feeling of satiety, and she visited several shops in search of this food. When she had found it she returned to the dog-kennel; her brother Edward had arrived. He was rather subdued. He brought with him a piece of meat which was part of his

leave ration. He occupied himself with polishing up his
sailor's uniform for a rag-time party to which they were to
go that evening. They were to meet plenty of conchies, he
said. Valentine put the meat—it was a godsend, though
very stringy!—on to stew with a number of chopped vege-
tables. She went up to her room to do some typing for her
mother.

The nature of Tietjens' wife occupied her mind. Before,
she had barely thought about her: she had seemed unreal;
so mysterious as to be a myth! Radiant and high-stepping:
like a great stag! But she must be cruel! She must be vin-
dictively cruel to Tietjens himself, or she could not have
revealed his private affairs! Just broadcast; for she could
not, bluff it how she might, have been certain of to whom
she was speaking! A thing that wasn't done! But she had
delivered her cheek to Mrs Wannop; a thing, too, that
wasn't done! Yet so kindly! The telephone bell rang
several times during the morning. She let her mother
answer it.

She had to get the dinner, which took three-quarters of
an hour. It was a pleasure to see her mother eat so well; a
good stew, rich and heavy with haricot beans. She herself
couldn't eat, but no one noticed, which was a good thing.
Her mother said that Tietjens had not yet telephoned,
which was very inconsiderate. Edward said: 'What! The
Huns haven't killed old Feather Bolster yet? But of course
he's been found a safe job.' The telephone on the sideboard became a terror to Valentine; at any moment his
voice might . . . Edward went on telling anecdotes of how
they bamboozled petty officers on mine-sweepers. Mrs
Wannop listened to him with the courteous, distant interest
of the great listening to commercial travellers. Edward
desired draught ale and produced a two-shilling piece. He
seemed very much coarsened; it was, no doubt, only on
the surface. In these days everyone was very much
coarsened on the surface.

She went with a quart jug to the jug and bottle department of the nearest public-house—a thing she had never

done before. Even at Ealing the mistress hadn't allowed
her to be sent to a public-house; the cook had had to fetch
her dinner beer herself or have it sent in. Perhaps the
Ealing mistress had exercised more surveillance than
Valentine had believed; a kind woman, but an invalid.
Nearly all day in bed. Blind passion overcame Valentine
at the thought of Edith Ethel in Tietjens' arms. Hadn't she
got her own eunuch? Mrs Tietjens had said: 'Mrs Duchemin is his mistress!' *Is!* Then she might be there now!

In the contemplation of that image, she missed the
thrills of buying beer in a bottle and jug department.
Apparently it was like buying anything else, except for the
smell of beer on the sawdust. You said: 'A quart of the
best bitter!' and a fat, quite polite man, with an oily head
and a white apron, took your money and filled your jug.
. . . But Edith Ethel had abused Tietjens so foully! The
more foully the more certain it made it! . . . Draught beer
in a jug had little marblings of burst foam on its brown
surface. It mustn't be spilt at the kerbs of crossings!—
the more certain it made it! Some women did so abuse
their lovers after sleeping with them, and the more violent
the transports the more frantic the abuse. It was the *'post-
dash-triste'* of the Rev. Mr Duchemin! Poor devil! Triste!
Triste!

Terra tribus scopulis vastum . . . Not longum!

Brother Edward began communing with himself, long
and unintelligibly, as to where he should meet his sister
at 19.30 and give her a blow-out! The names of restaurants
fell from his lips into her panic. He decided hilariously
and not quite steadily—a quart is a lot to a fellow from a
mine-sweeper carrying no booze at all!—on meeting her
at 7.20 at High Street and going to a pub. he knew; they
would go on to the dance afterwards. In a studio. 'Oh,
God!' her heart said, 'if Tietjens should want her then!'
To be his; on his last night. He might! Everybody was
coarsened then; on the surface. Her brother rolled out of
the house, slamming the door so that every tile on the
jerry-built dog-kennel rose and sat down again.

She went upstairs and began to look over her frocks. She couldn't tell what frocks she looked over; they lay like aligned rags on the bed, the telephone bell ringing madly. She heard her mother's voice, suddenly assuaged: 'Oh! oh! . . . It's you!' She shut her door and began to pull open and to close drawer after drawer. As soon as she ceased that exercise her mother's voice became half audible; quite audible when she raised it to ask a question. She heard her say: 'Not get her into trouble . . . Of course!' then it died away into mere high sounds.

She heard her mother calling:

'Valentine! Valentine! Come down. . . . Don't you want to speak to Christopher? . . . Valentine! Valentine! . . .' And then another burst: 'Valentine . . . Valentine . . . Valentine . . .' As if she had been a puppy dog! Mrs Wannop, thank God, was on the lowest step of the creaky stairs. She had left the telephone. She called up:

'Come down. I want to tell you! The dear boy has saved me! He always saves me! What shall I do now he's gone?'

'He saved others: himself he could not save!' Valentine quoted bitterly. She caught up her wideawake. She wasn't going to prink herself for him. He must take her as she was. . . . Himself he could not save! But he did himself proud! With women! . . . Coarsened! But perhaps only on the surface! She herself! . . . She was running downstairs!

Her mother had retreated into the little parlour: nine feet by nine; in consequence, at ten feet it was too tall for its size. But there was in it a sofa with cushions. . . . With her head upon those cushions, perhaps. . . . If he came home with her! Late! . . .

Her mother was saying: He's a splendid fellow. . . . A root idea for a war baby article. . . . If a Tommy was a decent fellow he abstained because he didn't want to leave his girl in trouble. . . . If he wasn't he chanced it because it might be his last chance. . . .

'A message to me!' Valentine said to herself. 'But which sentence. . . .' She moved, absently, all the cushions to one end of the sofa. Her mother exclaimed:

11*

'He sent his love! His mother was lucky to have such a son!' and turned into her tiny hole of a study.

Valentine ran down over the broken tiles of the garden path, pulling her wideawake firmly on. She had looked at her wrist-watch: it was two and twelve: 14.45. If she was to walk to the War Office by 4.15—16.15—a sensible innovation!—she must step out. Five miles to Whitehall. God knows what, then! Five miles back! Two and a half diagonally, to High Street Station by half-past 19! Twelve and a half miles in five hours or less. And three hours dancing on the top of it. And to dress! ... She needed to be fit ... And, with violent bitterness, she said:

'Well! I'm fit ...' She had an image of the aligned hundreds of girls in blue jumpers and men's ties keeping whom fit had kept her super-fit. She wondered how many of them would be men's mistresses before the year was out. It was August then. But perhaps none! Because she had kept them fit....

'Ah!' she said, 'if I had been a loose woman, with flaccid breasts and a soft body. All perfumed!' ... But neither Sylvia Tietjens nor Ethel Duchemin were soft. They might be scented on occasion! But they would not contemplate with equanimity doing a twelve-mile walk to save a few pence and dancing all night on top of it! She could! And perhaps the price she paid was just that; she was in such hard condition she hadn't moved him to ... She perhaps exhaled such an aura of sobriety, chastity and abstinence as to suggest to him that ... that a decent fellow didn't get his girl into trouble before going to be killed.... Yet if he were such a town bull! ... She wondered how she knew such phrases....

The sordid and aligned houses seemed to rush past her in the mean August sunshine. That was because if you thought hard time went quicker; or because after you noticed the paper shop at this corner you would be up to the boxes of onions outside the shop of the next corner before you noticed anything else.

She was in Kensington Gardens, on the north side; she

had left the poor shops behind. . . . In sham country, with sham lawns, sham avenues, sham streams. Sham people pursuing their ways across the sham grass. Or no! Not sham! in a vacuum! No! 'Pasteurised' was the word! Like dead milk. Robbed of their vitamins. . . .

If she saved a few coppers by walking it would make a large pile to put into the leering—or compassionate—taxi-cabman's hand after he had helped her support her brother into the dog-kennel door. Edward would be dead drunk. She had fifteen shillings for the taxi. . . . If she gave a few coppers more it seemed generous. . . . What a day to look forward to still! Some days were lifetimes!

She would rather die than let Tietjens pay for the cab! Why? Once a taximan had refused payment for driving her and Edward all the way to Chiswick, and she hadn't felt insulted. She had paid him; but she hadn't felt insulted! A sentimental fellow; touched at the heart by the pretty sister—or perhaps he didn't really believe it was a sister—and her incapable bluejacket brother! Tietjens was a sentimental fellow too. . . . What was the difference! . . . And then! The mother a dead, heavy sleeper; the brother dead drunk. One in the morning! He couldn't refuse her! Blackness: cushions! She had arranged the cushions, she remembered. Arranged them subconsciously! Blackness! Heavy sleep; dead drunkenness! . . . Horrible! . . . A disgusting affair! An affair of Ealing. . . . It shall make her one with all the stuff to fill graveyards. . . . Well, what else was she, Valentine Wannop: daughter of her father? And of her mother? Yes! But she herself . . . Just a little nobody!

They were no doubt wirelessing from the Admiralty. . . . But her brother was at home, or getting a little more intoxicated and talking treason. At any rate the flickering intermittences over the bitter seas couldn't for the moment concern him. . . . That bus touched her skirt as she ran for the island. . . . It might have been better. . . . But one hadn't the courage!

She was looking at patterned deaths under a little green

roof, such as they put over bird shelters. Her heart stopped! Before, she had been breathless! She was going mad. She was dying. . . . All these deaths! And not merely the deaths. . . . The waiting for the approach of death; the contemplation of the parting from life! This minute you were; that, and you weren't! What was it like? Oh heaven, she knew. . . . She stood there contemplating parting from . . . One minute you were; the next . . . Her breath fluttered in her chest. . . . Perhaps he wouldn't come . . .

He was immediately framed by the sordid stones. She ran upon him and said something; with a mad hatred. All these deaths and he and his like responsible! . . . He had apparently a brother, a responsible one too! Browner complexioned! . . . But he! He! He! He! completely calm; with direct eyes. . . . It wasn't possible. '*Holde Lippen: klaare Augen: heller Sinn.* . . .' Oh, a little bit wilted, the clear intellect! And the lips? No doubt too. But he couldn't look at you so, unless . . .

She caught him fiercely by the arm; for the moment he belonged—more than to any browner, mere civilian, brother!—to her! She was going to ask him! If he answered: 'Yes, I am such a man!' she was going to say: 'Then you must take me too! If them, why not me? I must have a child. I too!' She desired a child. She would overwhelm those hateful lodestones with a flood of argument; she imagined—she felt—the words going between her lips. . . . She imagined her fainting mind; her consenting limbs. . . .

His looks were wandering round the cornice of these stone buildings. Immediately she was Valentine Wannop again; it needed no word from him. Words passed, but words could no more prove an established innocence than words can enhance a love that exists. He might as well have recited the names of railway stations. His eyes, his unconcerned face, his tranquil shoulders; they were what acquitted him. The greatest love speech he had ever made and could ever make her was when, harshly and angrily, he said something like:

'Certainly not. I imagined you knew me better'—brushing her aside as if she had been a midge. And, thank God, he had hardly listened to her!

She was Valentine Wannop again; in the sunlight the chaffinches said 'Pink! pink!' The seed-heads of the tall grasses were brushing against her skirt. She was clean-limbed, clear-headed.... It was just a problem whether Sylvia Tietjens was good to him.... Good *for* him was, perhaps, the more exact way of putting it. Her mind cleared, like water that goes off the boil.... 'Waters stilled at even.' Nonsense. It was sunlight, and he had an adorable brother! He could save *his* brother.... Transport! There was another meaning to the word. A warm feeling settled down upon her; this was *her* brother; the next to the best ever! It was as if you had matched a piece of stuff so nearly with another piece of stuff as to make no odds. Yet just not the real stuff! She must be grateful to this relative for all he did for her; yet, ah, never so grateful as to the other—who had done nothing!

Providence is kind in great batches! She heard mounting the steps the blessed word Transport! 'They,' so Mark said: he and she—the family feeling again—were going to get Christopher into the Transport.... By the kindness of God the First Line Transport was the only branch of the Services of which Valentine knew anything. Their charwoman, who could not read and write, had a son, a sergeant in a line regiment. 'Hooray!' he had written to his mother, 'I've been off my feed; recommended for the D.C.M. too. So they're putting me senior N.C.O. of First Line Transport for a rest; the safest soft job of the whole bally front line caboodle!' Valentine had had to read this letter in the scullery amongst black-beetles. Aloud! She had hated reading it as she had hated reading anything that gave details of the front line. But charity begins surely with the char! She had had to. Now she could thank God. The sergeant, in direct, perfectly sincere language, to comfort his mother, had described his daily work, detailing horses and G.S. limber wagons for jobs and super-

intending the horse-standings. 'Why,' one sentence
ran, 'our O.C. Transport is one of those fishing lunatics.
Wherever we go he has a space of grass cleared out and
pegged and b——y hell to the man who walks across it!'
There the O.C. practised casting with trout and salmon
rods by the hour together. 'That'll show you what a soft
job it is!' the sergeant had finished triumphantly. . . .

So that there she, Valentine Wannop, sat on a hard
bench against a wall; downright, healthy middle-class—or
perhaps upper middle-class—for the Wannops were, if
impoverished, yet of ancient family! Over her sensible,
moccasined shoes the tide of humanity flowed before her
hard bench. There were two commissionaires, the one
always benevolent, the other perpetually querulous, in a
pulpit on one side of her; on the other, a brown-visaged
sort of brother-in-law with bulging eyes, who in his shy
efforts to conciliate her was continually trying to thrust into
his mouth the crook of his umbrella. As if it had been a
knob. She could not, at the moment, imagine why he
should want to conciliate her; but she knew she would
know in a minute.

For just then she was occupied with a curious pattern;
almost mathematically symmetrical. *Now* she was an English middle-class girl—whose mother had a sufficient income—in blue cloth, a wideawake hat, a black silk tie;
without a thought in her head that she shouldn't have.
And with a man who loved her: of crystal purity. Not
ten, not five minutes ago, she had been . . . She could not
even remember what she had been! And he had been, he
had assuredly appeared a town . . . No, she could not
think the words. . . . A raging stallion then! If now he
should approach her, by the mere movement of a hand
along the sable, she would retreat.

It was a godsend; yet it was absurd. Like the weather
machine of the old man and the old woman on opposite
ends of the stick. . . . When the old man came out the
old woman went in and it would rain; when the old
woman came out . . . It was exactly like that! She hadn't

time to work out the analogy. But it was like that. . . . In rainy weather the whole world altered. Darkened! . . . The cat-gut that turned them slackened . . . slackened. . . . But, always, they remained at opposite ends of the stick!

Mark was saying, the umbrella crook hindering his utterance:

'We buy then an annuity of five hundred for your mother. . . .'

It was astonishing, though it spread tranquillity through her, how little this astonished her. It was the merely retarded expected. Mr. Tietjens senior, an honourable man, had promised as much years ago. Her mother, an august genius, was to wear herself out putting, Mr Tietjens alive, his political views in his paper. He was to make it up to her. He was making it up. In no princely fashion, but adequately, as a gentleman.

Mark Tietjens, bending over, held a piece of paper. A bell-boy came up to him and said: 'Mr Riccardo?' Mark Tietjens said: 'No! He's gone!' He continued:

'Your brother. . . . Shelved for the moment. But enough to buy a practice, a good practice! When he's a full-fledged sawbones.' He stopped, he directed upon her his atrabilarian eyes, biting his umbrella handle; he was extremely nervous.

'Now you!' he said. 'Two or three hundred. A year of course! The capital absolutely your own. . . .' He paused: 'But I warn you! Christopher won't like it. He's got his knife into me. I wouldn't grudge you . . . oh, any sum!' . . . He waved his hand to indicate an amount boundless in its figures. 'I know you keep Christopher straight,' he said. 'The only person that could!' He added: 'Poor devil!'

She said:

'He's got his knife into you? Why?'

He answered vaguely:

'Oh, there's been all this talk. . . . Untrue, of course.'

She said:

'People have been saying things against you? To him? Perhaps because there's been delay in settling the estate.'

He said:

'Oh, no! The other way round, in fact!'

'Then they have been saying,' she exclaimed, 'things against . . . against me. And him!'

He exclaimed in anguish:

'Oh, but I ask you to believe . . . I beg you to believe that I believe . . . *you!* Miss Wannop!' He added grotesquely: 'As pure as dew that lies within Aurora's suntipped . . .' His eyes stuck out like those of a suffocating fish. He said: 'I beg you not on that account to hand the giddy mitten to . . .' He writhed in his tight double collar. 'His wife!' he said . . . 'She's no good to . . . *for* him! . . . She's soppily in love with him. But no *good* . . .' He very nearly sobbed. 'You're the only . . .' he said, 'I *know* . . .'

It came into her head that she was losing too much time in this Salle des Pas Perdus! She would have to take the train home! Fivepence! But what did it matter. Her mother had five hundred a year. . . . Two hundred and forty times five. . . .

Mark said brightly:

'If now we bought your mother an annuity of five hundred. . . . You say that's ample to give Christopher his chop. . . . And settled on her three . . . four . . . I like to be exact . . . hundred a year. . . . The capital of it: with remainder to you . . .' His interrogative face beamed.

She saw now the whole situation with perfect plainness. She understood Mrs Duchemin's:

'You couldn't expect us, with our official position . . . to connive . . .' Edith Ethel had been perfectly right. She *couldn't* be expected. . . . She had worked too hard to appear circumspect and right! You can't ask people to lay down their whole lives for their friends! . . . It was only of Tietjens you could ask that! She said—to Mark:

'It's as if the whole world had conspired . . . like a carpenter's vice—to force us . . .' she was going to say 'together. . . .' But he burst in, astonishingly:

'He must have his buttered toast . . . and his mutton

chop . . . and Rhum St James!' He said: 'Damn it all. . . .
You were made for him. . . . You can't blame people for
coupling you. . . . They're forced to it. . . . If you hadn't
existed they'd have had to invent you . . . Like Dante for
. . . who was it? . . . Beatrice? There *are* couples like that.'

She said:

'Like a carpenter's vice. . . . Pushed together. Irresistibly.
Haven't we resisted?'

His face became panic-stricken; his bulging eyes pushed
away towards the pulpit of the two commissionaires. He
whispered:

'You won't . . . because of my ox's hoof . . . desert. . . .'

She said:—she heard Macmaster whispering it hoarsely.

'I ask you to believe that I will never . . . abandon . . .'

It was what Macmaster had said. He must have got it
from Mrs. Micawber!

Christopher Tietjens—in his shabby khaki, for his wife
had spoilt his best uniform—said suddenly from behind her
back, since he had approached her from beyond the pulpit
of the two commissionaires and she had been turned towards Mark on his bench:

'Come along! Let's get out of this!' He was, she asked
herself, getting out of this! Towards what?

Like mutes from a funeral—or as if she had been, between the brothers, a prisoner under escort—they walked
down steps; half righted towards the exit arch; one and a
half righted to face Whitehall. The brothers grunted in-
audible but satisfied sounds over her head. They crossed,
by the islands, Whitehall, where the bus had brushed her
skirt. Under an archway—

In a stony, gravelled majestic space the brothers faced
each other. Mark said:

'I suppose you won't shake hands!'

Christopher said:

'No! Why should I?' She herself had cried out to
Christopher:

'Oh, *do*!' (The wireless squares overhead no longer concerned her. Her brother was, no doubt, getting drunk in a bar in Piccadilly. . . . A surface coarseness!)

Mark said:

'Hadn't you better? You might get killed! A fellow just getting killed would not like to think he had refused to shake his brother by the hand!'

Christopher had said: 'Oh . . . well!'

During her happiness over this hyperborean sentimentality he had gripped her thin upper arm. He had led her past swans—or possibly huts; she never remembered which —to a seat that had over it, or near it, a weeping willow. He had said, gasping too, like a fish:

'Will you be my mistress to-night? I am going out to-morrow at 8.30 from Waterloo.'

She had answered:

'Yes! Be at such and such a studio just before twelve. . . . I have to see my brother home. . . . He will be drunk. . . . .' She meant to say: 'Oh, my darling, I have wanted you so much. . . .'

She said instead:

'I have arranged the cushions. . . .'

She said to herself:

'Now whatever made me say that? It's as if I had said: "You'll find the ham in the larder under a plate. . . ." No tenderness about it. . . .'

She went away, up a cockle-shelled path, between ankle-high railings, crying bitterly. An old tramp, with red weeping eyes and a thin white beard, regarded her curiously from where he lay on the grass. He imagined himself the monarch of that landscape.

'That's women!' he said with the apparently imbecile enigmaticality of the old and the hardened. 'Some do!' He spat into the grass; said 'Ah!' then added: 'Some do not!'

VI

He let himself in at the heavy door; when he closed it behind him, in the darkness, the heaviness of the door sent long surreptitious whisperings up the great stone stairs. These sounds irritated him. If you shut a heavy door on an enclosed space it will push air in front of it and there will be whisperings; the atmosphere of mystery was absurd. He was just a man, returning after a night out. . . . Two-thirds, say, of a night out! It must be half-past three. But what the night had lacked in length it had made up in fantastic aspects. . . .

He laid his cane down on the invisible oak chest and, through the tangible and velvety darkness that had always in it the chill of the stone of walls and stairs, he felt for the handle of the breakfast-room door.

Three long parallelograms existed: pale glimmerings above, cut two-thirds of the way down by the serrations of chimney-pot and roof-shadows! Nine full paces across the heavy piled carpet; then he ought to reach his round-backed chair, by the left-hand window. He sank into it; it fitted exactly his back. He imagined that no man had ever been so tired and that no man had ever been so alone! A small, alive sound existed at the other end of the room; in front of him existed one and a half pale parallelograms. They were the reflection of the windows in the mirror; the sound was no doubt Calton, the cat. Something alive, at any rate! Possibly Sylvia at the other end of the room, waiting for him, to see what he looked like. Most likely! It didn't matter!

His mind stopped! Sheer weariness!

When it went on again it was saying:

'Naked shingles and surges drear . . .' and, 'On these debatable borders of the world!' He said sharply: 'Non-sense!' The one was either *Calais beach* or *Dover sands* of the whiskered man: Arnold. . . . He would be seeing them both within the twenty-four hours. . . . But no! He was going from Waterloo. Southampton, Havre, therefore! . . . The other was by that detestable fellow: 'the subject of our little monograph!' . . . What a long time ago! . . . He saw a pile of shining despatch cases: the inscription *'This rack is reserved for . . .'*: a coloured—pink and blue!—photograph of Boulogne sands and the held up squares, the proofs of 'our little . . . ' What a long time ago! He heard his own voice saying in the new railway carriage, proudly, clearly and with male hardness:

'*I stand for monogamy and chastity. And for no talking about it. Of course if a man who's a man wants to have a woman he has her. And again no talking about it. . . .*' His voice—his own voice—came to him as if from the other end of a long-distance telephone. A damn long-distance one! Ten years . . .

If then a man who's a man wants to have a woman. . . . Damn it, he doesn't! In ten years he had learnt that a Tommie who's a decent fellow. . . . His mind said at one and the same moment, the two lines running one over the other like the two subjects of a fugue:

'Some beguiling virgins with the broken seals of perjury,' and:

'Since when we stand side by side, only hands may meet!'

He said:

'But damn it; damn it again! The beastly fellow was wrong! Our hands didn't meet. . . . I don't believe I've shaken hands. . . . I don't believe I've touched the girl . . . in my life. . . . Never once! . . . Not the hand-shaking sort. . . . A nod! . . . A meeting and parting! . . . English, you know . . . But yes! she put her arm over my shoulders. . . . On the bank! . . . *On such short acquaintance!* I said to myself then . . . Well, we've made up for it since then. Or no! Not made up! . . . Atoned. . . . As Sylvia so aptly put it; at that moment mother was dying. . . .'

He, his conscious self, said:

'But it was probably the drunken brother. . . . You don't beguile virgins with the broken seals of perjury in Kensington High Street at two at night supporting, one on each side, a drunken bluejacket with intermittent legs. . . .'

'Intermittent!' was the word. 'Intermittently functioning!'

At one point the boy had broken from them and run

with astonishing velocity along the dull wood paving of an immense empty street. When they had caught him up he had been haranguing under black trees, with an Oxford voice, an immobile policeman:

'You're the fellows!' he'd been exclaiming, 'who make old England what she is! You keep the peace in our homes! You save us from the vile excesses. . . .'

Tietjens himself he had always addressed with the voice and accent of a common seaman; with his coarsened surface voice!

He had the two personalities. Two or three times he had said:

'Why don't you kiss the girl? She's a *nice* girl, isn't she? You're a poor b——y Tommie, ain't cher? Well, the poor b——y Tommies ought to have all the nice girls they want! That's straight, isn't it? . . . '

And, even at that time they hadn't known what was going to happen. . . . There are certain cruelties. . . . They had got a four-wheel cab at last. The drunken boy had sat beside the driver; he had insisted. . . . Her little, pale, shrunken face had gazed straight before her. . . . It hadn't been possible to speak; the cab, rattling all over the road, had been pulled up with frightful jerks when the boy had grabbed the reins. . . . The old driver hadn't seemed to mind; but they had had to subscribe all the money in their pockets to pay him after they had carried the boy into the black house. . . .

Tietjens' mind said to him:

'Now when they came to her father's house so nimbly she slipped in, and said: "There is a fool without and there is a maid within. . . . " '

He answered dully:

'Perhaps that's what it really amounts to. . . .' He had stood at the hall door, she looking out at him with a pitiful face. Then from the sofa within the brother had begun to snore; enormous, grotesque sounds, like the laughter of unknown races from darkness. He had turned and walked down the path, she following him. He had exclaimed:

'It's perhaps too . . . untidy . . .'

She had said:

'Yes! Yes . . . Ugly . . . Too . . . oh . . . *private*!'

He said, he remembered:

'But . . . for ever . . .'

She said, in a great hurry:

'But when you come back . . . Permanently. And . . . oh, as if it were in public. . . . I don't know,' she had added. '*Ought* we? . . . I'd be ready. . . .' She added: 'I will be ready for anything you ask.'

He had said at some time: 'But obviously. . . . Not under *this* roof. . . .' And he had added: 'We're the sort that . . . *do not*!'

She had answered, quickly too:

'Yes—that's it. We're that sort!' And then she had asked: 'And Ethel's party? Was it a great success?' It hadn't, she knew, been an inconsequence. He had answered:

'Ah . . . *That's* permanent. . . . *That's public.* . . . There was Rugeley: The Duke . . . Sylvia brought him. She'll be a great friend! . . . And the President of the . . . Local Government Board, I think . . . And a Belgian . . . equivalent to Lord Chief Justice . . . and, of course, Claudine Sandbach. . . . Two hundred and seventy; all of the best, the modestly elated Guggumses said as I left! And Mr Ruggles . . . Yes! . . . They're established. . . . No place for me!'

'Nor for *me*!' she had answered. She added: 'But I'm glad!'

Patches of silence ran between them: they hadn't yet got out of the habit of thinking they had to hold up the drunken brother. That had seemed to last for a thousand painful months. . . . Long enough to acquire a habit. The brother seemed to roar: 'Haw-Haw—Kuryasch. . . .' And after two minutes: 'Haw—Haw—Kuryasch. . . .' Hungarian, no doubt!

He said:

'It was splendid to see Vincent standing beside the Duke. Showing him a first edition! Not of course *quite* the thing

for a, after all, wedding party! But how was Rugeley to
know that? . . . And Vincent not in the least servile! He
even corrected cousin Rugeley over the meaning of the
word *colophon*! The first time he ever corrected a superior!
Established, you see! . . . And *practically* cousin Rugeley.
. . . Dear Sylvia Tietjens' cousin, so the next to nearest
thing! Wife of Lady Macmaster's *oldest* friend. . . . Sylvia
going to them in their—quite modest!—little place in
Surrey. . . . As for us,' he had concluded, 'they also serve
who only stand and wait. . . .'

She said:

'I suppose the rooms looked lovely.'

He had answered:

'Lovely. . . . They'd got all the pictures by that beastly
fellow up from the rectory study in the dining-room on
dark oak panelling. . . . A fair blaze of bosoms and nipples
and lips and pomegranates. . . . The tallest silver candlesticks of course. . . . You remember, silver candlesticks and
dark oak. . . .'

She said:

'Oh, my dear . . . Don't . . . *Don't*!'

He had just touched the rim of his helmet with his
folded gloves.

'So we just wash out!' he had said.

She said:

'Would you take this bit of parchment. . . . I got a little
Jew girl to write on it in Hebrew: It's "God bless you and
keep you: God watch over you at your goings out and
at . . ." '

He tucked it into his breast pocket.

'The talismanic passage,' he said. 'Of course I'll wear
it. . . .'

She said:

'If we *could* wash out this afternoon. . . . It would make
it easier to bear. . . . Your poor mother, you know, she was
dying when we last . . .'

He said:

'You remember *that*... Even then you... And if I hadn't gone to Lobscheid. ...'

She said:

'From the first moment I set eyes on you. ...'

He said:

'And I... from the first moment... I'll tell you... If I looked out of a door... It was all like sand.... But to the half left a little bubbling up of water. That could be trusted. To keep on for ever.... You, perhaps, won't understand.'

She said:

'Yes! I know!'

They were seeing landscapes.... Sand dunes; close-cropped.... Some negligible shipping; a stump-masted brig from Archangel....

'From the first moment,' he repeated.

She said:

'If we *could* wash out...'

He said, and for the first moment felt grand, tender, protective:

'Yes, you *can*,' he said. 'You cut out from this afternoon, just before 4.58 it was when I said that to you and you consented... I heard the Horse Guards clock.... To now.... Cut it out; and join time up.... It *can* be done. ... You know they do it surgically; for some illness; cut out a great length of the bowel and join the tube up.... For colitis, I think....'

She said:

'But I *wouldn't* cut it out.... It was the first spoken sign.'

He said:

'No it wasn't.... From the very beginning... with every word....'

She exclaimed:

'You felt that.... Too!... We've been pushed, as in a carpenter's vice.... We couldn't have got away....'

He said: 'By God! That's it....'

He suddenly saw a weeping willow in St James's Park; 4.59! He had just said: 'Will you be my mistress to-night?' She had gone away, half left, her hands to her face. . . . A small fountain; half left. That could be trusted to keep on for ever. . . .

Along the lake side, sauntering, swinging his crooked stick, his incredibly shiny top-hat perched sideways, his claw-hammer coat tails, very long, flapping out behind, in dusty sunlight, his magpie pince-nez gleaming, had come, naturally, Mr Ruggles. He had looked at the girl; then down at Tietjens, sprawled on his bench. He had just touched the brim of his shiny hat. He said:

'Dining at the club to-night? . . .'

Tietjens said: 'No; I've resigned.'

With the aspect of a long-billed bird chewing a bit of putridity, Ruggles said:

'Oh, but we've had an emergency meeting of the committee . . . the committee was sitting . . . and sent you a letter asking you to reconsider. . . .'

Tietjens said:

'I know. . . . I shall withdraw my resignation to-night. . . . And resign again to-morrow morning.'

Ruggles' muscles had relaxed for a quick second, then they stiffened.

'Oh, I say!' he had said. 'Not that. . . . You couldn't do that . . . Not to the *club*! . . . It's never been done. . . . It's an insult. . . .'

'It's meant to be,' Tietjens said. 'Gentlemen shouldn't be expected to belong to a club that has certain members on its committee.'

Ruggles' deepish voice suddenly grew very high.

'Eh, I say, you know!' he squeaked.

Tietjens had said:

'I'm not vindictive. . . . But I *am* deadly tired: of all old women and their chatter.'

Ruggles had said:

'I don't . . .' His face had become suddenly dark brown,

scarlet and then brownish purple. He stood droopingly
looking at Tietjens' boots.

'Oh! Ah! Well!' he said at last. 'See you at Macmaster's to-night. . . . A great thing, his knighthood. First-
class man.'

That had been the first Tietjens had heard of Macmaster's knighthood; he had missed looking at the honours
list of that morning. Afterwards, dining alone with Sir
Vincent and Lady Macmaster, he had seen, pinned up, a
back view of the Sovereign doing something to Vincent; a
photo for next morning's papers. From Macmaster's embarrassed hushings of Edith Ethel's explanation that the
honour was for special services of a specific kind Tietjens
guessed both the nature of Macmaster's service and the
fact that the little man hadn't told Edith Ethel who,
originally, had done the work. And—just like his girl—
Tietjens had let it go at that. He didn't see why poor
Vincent shouldn't have that little bit of prestige at home—
under all the monuments! But he hadn't—though through
all the evening Macmaster, with the solicitude and affection of a cringing Italian greyhound, had hastened from
celebrity to celebrity to hang over Tietjens, and although
Tietjens knew that his friend was grieved and appalled,
like any woman, at his, Tietjens', going out again to France
—Tietjens hadn't been able to look Macmaster again in the
face. . . . He had felt ashamed. He had felt, for the first time
in his life, ashamed!

Even when he, Tietjens, had slipped away from the
party—to go to his good fortune!—Macmaster had
come panting down the stairs, running after him, through
guests coming up. He had said:

'Wait . . . You're not going. . . . I want to . . .' With a
miserable and appalled glance he had looked up the stairs;
Lady Macmaster might have come out too. With his black,
short beard quivering and his wretched eyes turned down,
he had said:

'I wanted to explain. . . . This miserable knighthood. . . .'

Tietjens patted him on the shoulder, Macmaster being on the stairs above him.

'It's all right, old man,' he had said—and with real affection: 'We've powlered up and down enough for a little thing like that not to . . . I'm very glad. . . .'

Macmaster had whispered:

'And Valentine. . . . She's not here to-night. . . .'

He had exclaimed:

'By God! . . . If I thought . . .' Tietjens had said: 'It's all right. It's all right. She's at another party. . . . I'm going on . . .'

Macmaster had looked at him doubtingly and with misery, leaning over and clutching the clammy banisters.

'Tell her . . .' he said. . . . 'Good God! You may be killed. . . . I beg you . . . I beg you to believe . . . I will . . . Like the apple of my eye. . . .' In the swift glance that Tietjens took of his face he could see that Macmaster's eyes were full of tears.

They both stood looking down at the stone stairs for a long time.

Then Macmaster had said: 'Well . . .'

Tietjens had said: 'Well . . .' But he hadn't been able to look at Macmaster's eyes, though he had felt his friend's eyes pitiably exploring his own face. . . . 'A backstairs way out of it,' he had thought; a queer thing that you couldn't look in the face of a man you were never going to see again!

'But by God,' he said to himself fiercely, when his mind came back again to the girl in front of him, 'this isn't going to be another backstairs exit. . . . I must tell her. . . . I'm damned if I don't make an effort. . . .'

She had her handkerchief to her face.

'I'm always crying,' she said. . . . 'A little bubbling spring that can be trusted to keep on. . . .'

He looked to the right and to the left. Ruggles or General Someone with false teeth that didn't fit *must* be coming along. The street with its sooty boskage was clean, empty and silent. She was looking at him. He didn't know how long he had been silent, he didn't know where he had been; intolerable waves urged him towards her.

After a long time he said:

'Well . . .'

She moved back. She said:

'I won't watch you out of sight . . . It is unlucky to watch anyone out of sight. . . . But I will never . . . I will never cut what you said then out of my memory . . .' She was gone; the door shut. He had wondered what she would never cut out of her memory. That he had asked her that afternoon to be his mistress? . . .

He had caught, outside the gates of his old office, a transport lorry that had given him a lift to Holborn. . . .